Jonathan Kellerman is one of the world's most popular authors. He has brought his expertise as a child psychologist to numerous bestselling tales of suspense (which have been translated into two dozen languages), including fourteen previous Alex Delaware novels; *The Butcher's Theatre*, a story of serial killing in Jerusalem; and *Billy Straight*, featuring Hollywood homicide detective Petra Connor. His most recent novel is *Doctor Death*. He is also the author of numerous essays, short stories, and scientific articles, two children's books, and three volumes of psychology, including *Savage Spawn: Reflections on Violent Children*. Kellerman has won the Samuel Goldwyn, Edgar Allan Poe and Anthony Boucher awards and has been nominated for a Shamus award. He and his wife, the novelist Faye Kellerman, have four children.

flesh and blood

jonathan kellerman

headline

First published in Great Britain in 2001
by HEADLINE BOOK PUBLISHING

First published in paperback in Great Britain in 2002
by HEADLINE BOOK PUBLISHING

A HEADLINE paperback

10 9 8 7 6 5 4 3 2 1

ISBN 0 7472 6500 3

Typeset in Plantin by
Letterpart Limited, Reigate, Surrey

Printed and bound in Great Britain by
Mackays of Chatham plc, Chatham, Kent

HEADLINE BOOK PUBLISHING
A division of Hodder Headline
338 Euston Road
London NW1 3BH

www.headline.co.uk
www.hodderheadline.com

To my children
Jesse, Rachel, Ilana and Aliza

one

Sad truth: Had she been just a patient, I probably wouldn't have remembered her.

All those years listening, so many faces. There was a time I recalled every one of them. Forgetting comes with experience. It doesn't bother me as much as it used to.

Her mother phoned my service on a Saturday morning soon after New Year's.

'A Mrs Jane Abbot,' said the operator. 'She says her daughter's an old patient. Lauren Teague.'

Jane Abbot's name meant nothing to me, but *Lauren Teague* sparked an uneasy nostalgia. It was an 818 number, somewhere in the Valley. When I'd known the family they'd lived in West L.A. I searched my old case files before returning the call.

Teague, Lauren Lee. Intake date, ten years ago, the tail end of my Wilshire Boulevard practice. Shortly after, I cashed in some real estate profits, tried to drop out, met a beautiful woman, became friends with a sad, brilliant detective, learned more than I wanted to know about bad things. Since then I'd avoided the commitment of long-term therapy cases, stuck to court consults and forensic work, the kinds of puzzles that removed me from the confines of my office.

Lauren had been fifteen at referral. Thin file: one history-taking meeting with the parents followed by two sessions with the girl. Then a missed appointment, no explanation. The next day the father left a message canceling any future treatment. Unpaid balance for the final session; I'd made a halfhearted effort to collect, then written it off.

When old patients get in touch it's usually because they're doing great and want to brag, or exactly the opposite. Either way they tend to be people with whom I've connected. Lauren Teague didn't qualify. Far from it. If anything, I was the last person she'd want to see. Why was her mother contacting me now?

Presenting problems: poor school achiev., noncompliance at home. Clin. impressions: fath. angry; moth. possib. deprssd. Tension bet moth and father – marital strss? Parents agree re: Lauren's behavior as the prim. prob. Uneventful birth hx, only child, no sig. health probs., contact pediatric M.D. to verify. School: per Mom: 'Lauren's always been smart.' 'Used to love to read, now hates it.' B– aver. till last year, then 'change of attitude,' new friends – 'bums' (fath), some truancy, C's and D's. Basic mood is 'sullen.' 'No communic.' Parents try to talk, get no resp. Suspect drug use.

As I leafed through the file, Jane and Lyle Teague's faces came into semifocus. She, thin, blond, edgy, a former flight attendant, now a 'full-time mom.' A heavy smoker – forty-five minutes without tobacco had been torture.

Lauren's father had been slit-eyed, blank-faced, reluctant to engage. His wife had talked fast . . . nervous hands, moist eyes. When she'd looked to him for support, he'd turned away.

They were both thirty-nine, but he looked older . . . He'd done something in the building trades . . . here it was, *elect. contractr*. A powerful-looking man, fighting the advent of middle age with long hair, sprayed in place, that fringed his shoulders. Black pelt of beard. Muscles made obvious by a too-tight polo shirt and pressed jeans. Crude but well-balanced features . . . gold chain circling a ruddy neck . . . gold ID bracelet – how did I remember *that*? Put him in buckskins and he could've been a grizzly hunter.

Lyle Teague had sat with his legs spread wide, consulted his watch every few minutes, fondled his beeper as if hoping for intrusion. Unable to maintain eye contact – lapsing into dreamy stares. That had made me wonder about attention deficit, something he might've passed on to Lauren. But when I raised the topic of academic testing, he didn't stir defensively, and his wife said Lauren had been examined two years before by a school psychologist and found to be 'normal and extremely bright.'

'Bright,' he said, putting no praise into the word. 'Nothing wrong with her brain that a little discipline won't cure.' Accusing glance at his wife.

Her mouth twisted, but she said, 'That's what we're here to learn.'

Lyle Teague smirked.

I said, 'Mr Teague, do you think anything else is going on, besides Lauren's being spoiled?'

'Nah, basic teenage garbage.' Another look at his wife, this time seeking confirmation.

She said, 'Lauren's a good girl.'

Lyle Teague laughed threateningly. 'Then why the hell are we here?'

'Honey—'

'Yeah, yeah, fine.'

He tried to tune out, but I stuck with him, finally got him talking about Lauren, how different she was from the 'cute little kid' he'd once taken to job sites in his truck. As he reminisced, his face darkened and his speech got choppy, and by the end of the speech he pronounced his daughter 'a real hassle. Hope to hell you can do something with her.'

Two days later Lauren showed up in my waiting room, alone, five minutes late. A tall, slender, conspicuously busted, brown-haired girl, treated kindly by puberty.

Fifteen, but she could've passed for twenty. She wore a white jersey tank top, skimpy, snug, blue-denim shorts, and ludicrously high-heeled white sandals. Smooth, tan arms and long, tan legs were showcased by the minimal clothing. Pink-polished toes glinted at the tips of her sandals. The strap of a small black patent leather purse striped a bare shoulder. If she'd been studying the hookers on Sunset for fashion tips, she'd learned well.

When young girls flaunt, the result is often a comic

loss of equilibrium. Lauren Teague seemed perfectly at ease advertising her body – like father, like daughter?

She favored her father in coloring, her mother in structure, but bore no striking resemblance to either. The brown hair was burnt umber sparked with rust, thick and straight, hanging halfway down her back, parted dead center and flipped into extravagant wings at the temples. High cheekbones, wide mouth glossed pink, dominant but perfectly proportioned cleft chin, heavily lined, azure-shadowed blue eyes – mocking eyes. A strong, straight, uptilted nose was dashed by freckles she'd tried to obliterate with makeup. Lots of makeup. It stuccoed her from brow to jaw, creating a too-beige mask.

As I introduced myself she breezed past me into the office, taking long, easy strides on the impossible heels. None of the usual teenage slump – she held her back straight, thrust out her chest. A strikingly good-looking girl, made less attractive by cosmetics and blatancy.

Selecting the chair closest to mine, she sat down as if she'd been there a hundred times before. 'Cool furniture.'

'Thank you.'

'Like one of those libraries in an old movie.' She batted her lashes, crossed and recrossed her legs, threw out her chest again, yawned, stretched, folded her arms across her torso, dropped them to her sides suddenly, a cartoon of vulnerability.

I asked why she thought she was there.

'My parents think I'm a loser.'

5

'A loser.'

'Yup.'

'What do you think of that?'

Derisive laugh, toss of hair. Her tongue tip skated across her lower lip. 'May-be.' Shrug. Yawn. 'So . . . time to talk about my head problems, huh?'

Jane and Lyle Teague had denied previous therapy, but Lauren's glibness made me wonder. I asked her about it.

'Nope, never. The school counselor tried to talk to me a couple of times.'

'About?'

'My grades.'

'Did it help?'

She laughed. 'Yeah, right. Okay, ready for my neurosis?'

'Neurosis,' I said.

'We have psych this year. Stupid class. Ready?'

'If you are.'

'Sure. I mean – that's the point, right? I'm supposed to spit out all my deep, dark secrets.'

'It's not a matter of supposed to—'

'I know, I know,' she said. 'That's what shrinks always say – no one's gonna force you to do anything.'

'You know about shrinks.'

'I know enough. Some of my friends have seen 'em. One of them had a shrink give her that shi— That stuff about never forcing her, then the next week he committed her to a mental ward.'

'Why?'

'She tried to kill herself.'

6

'Sounds like a good reason,' I said.

Shrug.

'How's your friend doing?'

'Fine – like you really care.' Her eyes rolled.

I said nothing.

'That, too,' she said. 'That's the other shrink thing – just sitting there and staring. Saying "Ah-ah" and "Uh-huh." Answering questions with questions. Right?'

'Uh-huh.'

'Very funny,' she said. 'At what you charge, I'm not coming here forever. And *he's* probably gonna call to make sure I showed up and did a good job so let's get going.'

'Dad's in a hurry?'

'Yeah. So give me a good grade, okay? Tell him I was good – I don't need any more hassles.'

'I'll tell him you cooperated—'

'Tell him whatever you want.'

'But I'm not going to get into details, because—'

'Confidentiality, yeah, yeah. It doesn't matter. Tell them anything.'

'No secrets from Mom and Dad?'

'What for?' She played with her hair, gave a world-weary smile. 'I've got no cool secrets anyway. Totally boring life. Too bad for you – try not to fall asleep.'

'So,' I said, 'your dad wants you to get this over with quickly.'

'Whatever.' She picked at her hair.

'What exactly did he tell you to accomplish here, Lauren?'

'Get my act together, be straight – be a *good* girl.' She laughed, arced one leg over the other, placed a hand on a calf and tickled.

'Be straight,' I said. 'As in drugs?'

'They're paranoid about that, along with everything else. Even though *they* smoke.'

'They smoke dope?'

'Dope, tobacco. Little after-dinner taste. Sometimes it's booze – *cocktails*. "We're mature enough to control it, Lauren." ' She laughed. '*Jane* used to be a *stewardess*, working all these fancy private charters. They've still got this collection of tiny little bottles. I like the green melon stuff – Midori. But I'm not allowed to touch pot till I'm eighteen.' She laughed. 'Like I'd *ever*.'

'Pot's not for you?' I said.

'Pot's boring – too slow. Like hey, man, let's pretend we're in the sixties, get all wasted and sit around staring at the sky and talking about God.' Another gust of laughter, painfully lacking in joy. 'Pot sure makes *them* boring. It's the only time she slows *down*. And *he* just sits and veges on the TV, munches nachos, whatever. I'm not supposed to be talking about their bad habits, I'm the one who needs to change.'

'Change how?'

'Clean my *room*,' she singsonged. 'Do my *chores*, get ready in the *morning* without calling my mom a *bitch*, stop saying "fuck" and "shit" and "cunt." Go to class and pay attention, build up my *grades*, stop breaking *curfew*, hang out with *decent* friends, not low-life.' She rotated one hand, as if spooling thread.

'And I'm supposed to get you to do all that.'

'Lyle says no way, you never will.'

'Lyle.'

Her eyes got merry. 'That's something else I'm supposed to not do. Call him by his name. He hates it, it drives him crazy.'

'So no way you'll stop.'

She played with her hair. 'Who knows what I'll do?'

'How does he react when you do things that irritate him?'

'Ignores me. Walks away and gets involved in something else.'

'He has hobbies?'

'Him? Only thing he does is work, eat, smoke dope, stuff his face, watch TV. He has no faith in me. In you, either.' Conspiratorial smile. 'He says shrinks are just a bunch of overpaid clowns who can't screw in a lightbulb by themselves and I'm gonna just end up conning you like I con everybody. He's only paying for this because Jane's really getting on his nerves with all her nagging.'

'Mom has more faith in shrinks?'

'Mom's totally *worried*,' she said. 'Mom likes to *suffer*. They're— *Here's* a juicy one for you: They only got married 'cause they *had* to. One day I was looking for a bra in Jane's drawer and I found their wedding license. Two months *before* my birthday. I was conceived in sin. What do you think of that?'

'Is it a big deal to you?'

'I just think it's funny.'

'How so?'

'Here they are being all moral and . . . whatever.' Lifting the tiny black purse, she undid the clasp, peered inside, snapped it shut.

'Mom likes to suffer,' I said.

'Yeah, she hates her life. She used to work private charters, fly all around the world with superrich people. She regrets ever coming down to earth.' She shifted to the edge of the chair. 'How much longer do I have to be here?'

Rather than pick apart the fine points of free choice, I said, 'Half an hour.'

Opening the purse again, she pulled out a compact, checked her reflection, plucked an eyelash and flicked it away.

'Half an hour,' she said. 'No way do I have half an hour of problems – want to hear all of them?'

'Sure.'

She launched into a long, droning speech about stupid girlfriends getting on her case, stupid ex-boyfriends foolish enough to think they were still in her good graces, stupid teachers who didn't know anything more than the students, stupid parties, a stupid world.

Talking nonstop in the flat tones of a rehearsed witness, looking everywhere but at me.

When she was through I said, 'So everyone's getting on your nerves.'

'You've got that right . . . How much longer *now*?'

'Twenty-five minutes.'

'Shit. That much? You should have a clock up there. So people can keep track.'

'Usually people don't want to.'

'Why not?'

'They don't want to be distracted.'

She favored me with a bitter smile, scooted forward on the chair. 'Well, *I* want to leave early. Okay? Just today. Please. I've got some people waiting for me, and I need to get home by five-thirty or Jane and Lyle're gonna freak out.'

'People waiting for what?'

'Fun.'

'Friends are picking you up.'

She nodded.

'Where?'

'I told them to meet me a block from here. So can I *go*?'

'Lauren, I'm not forcing you—'

'But if I split early you'll fink, right?'

'Look,' I said, 'it's a matter of twenty minutes. As long as you're here, why not make good use of the time?'

I expected protest, but she sat there, pouting. 'That's not fair. I told you everything. There's nothing wrong with me.'

'I'm not saying there is, Lauren.'

'So what's the point?'

'I'd like to learn more about you—'

'I'm not worth learning about, okay? My life's boring, I already told you that.' She ran her hands over her torso. 'This is it, all of me, nothing exciting.'

I let several seconds pass. 'Lauren, is everything really going as well as it could for you?'

She studied me from under grainy, black lashes, reached into the purse again, and extricated a pack of Virginia Slims.

When she produced a lighter, I shook my head.

'Oh, c'mon.'

'Sorry.'

'How can you do that? People coming here all stressed out. Don't they complain – wasn't *Jane* climbing the walls? She's a *chimney*.'

'Mostly I see kids and teens,' I said. 'People manage.'

'Kids and *teens*.' She gave a short, cold laugh. 'Every teen *I* know smokes. Are you allergic or something?'

'Some of my patients are.'

'So why does everyone have to suffer because of a few? That's not democracy.'

'It's consideration,' I said.

'*Fine*.' She jammed the pack back into the purse. 'How much time left *now*?'

two

The second time she was twenty minutes late, hurried into the office muttering what might have been an apology.

Same getup, different color scheme: black tank top, sunburn pink shorts, lips coarsened by bright red paste.

Same precarious sandals and cheap little purse. She reeked of tobacco and a rose-heavy perfume. Her cheeks were flushed, and her hair was mussed.

She took a long time settling in the chair, finally said, 'Got hung up.'

'You and your friends?'

'Yeah.' Hair flip. 'Sorry.'

'Hung up where?'

'Around . . . the pier.'

'Santa Monica?' I said.

'We like the beach.' She massaged one bare, bronze shoulder.

'Nice sunny day,' I said, smiling. 'Classes must have let out early.'

Sudden, bright laughter tumbled from between the crimson lips. 'Right.'

'School's a drag, huh?'

'School would have to be on *uppers* to be a drag.' She produced the cigarette pack, bounced it on a shiny knee. 'When I was little they tested my IQ. I'm supposed to be supersmart. *They* say I should be studying more. *I* say I'm smart enough to know it's a waste of time.'

'No interest in any subject?' I said.

'Nutrition – love that garlic bread. Is today when we talk about sex?'

That caught me off guard. 'I don't recall our scheduling that.'

'*They* scheduled it. I've been *instructed* to talk to you about it.'

'By your parents.'

'Yeah.'

'Why?'

'It's mostly Lyle's idea. He's positive I'm doing the dirty, gonna get pregnant, stick him with a "little nigger grandkid." Like if I *was*, talking to you about it would *help*. Like just because I don't talk to *them*, I'm going to throw up my insides to some outsider.'

'Sometimes talking to an outsider can be safer.'

'Maybe for some people,' she said. 'But explain me this: When you're young everyone's always knocking into your head never talk to *strangers*, beware of *strangers*, watch out for *strangers*. So now they're *paying* for me to tell my *secrets* to a stranger?'

She ran a fingernail under the seal of the pack, slit it

open, played with the foil flap. 'What bullshit.'

'Maybe they're hoping eventually you won't consider me a stranger.'

'They can hope all they want.' Low, tight laugh. 'Hey, I'm not trying to be rude, it's just coming out that way— Sorry, you seem like a nice guy. It's just that I shouldn't have to *be* here, *okay*? Face it: They're just using you to punish me – like grounding me or threatening not to let me get my license next year. None of *that* worked, and *this* won't either. You have to *care* to be controlled, and I *don't* do caring.'

'What are they punishing you for, Lauren?'

'They say it's my attitude,' she said, 'but you know what I think? I think they're jealous.'

'Of what?'

'My happiness.'

'You're happy and they're not.'

'They're making themselves out to be all . . . in control. Especially *him*.' She lowered her voice to a hostile baritone parody: ' "Lauren, you're screwing up your *life*. This therapy crap is goddamn *expensive*. I want you to go in there and spill your *guts*." '

Last week she'd talked about spitting out secrets. The emetic approach to insight.

'So,' I said, 'your parents aren't happy, they're taking it out on you, and I'm the weapon.'

'They're stuck where they are and I'm cool, free, enjoying my life, and that bugs them. Soon as I get my own money, I'm out of there, bye-bye, Lyle and Jane.'

'Do you have a plan to get money?'

She shrugged. 'I'll figure something out – I'm not talking right now. I'm not impractical. I know even McDonald's won't hire me without *their* permission. But someday.'

'Did you try to work at McDonald's?'

Nod. 'I wanted my own money. But *they* said no. "No outside work until your grades come up." Which they won't, so forget *that*.'

'Why won't your grades come up?' I said.

''Cause I don't want them to.'

'So it's a few more years of this.'

Her eyes shifted. 'I'll figure something out— Listen, forget sex. I don't want to talk to you about it. Or anything else. No offense, but I just don't want to spill my guts.'

'Okay.'

'Okay, great.' She shot to her feet. 'See you next week.'

Ten minutes to go. I said, 'No way you can stick it out?'

'Are you going to tell them I split early?'

'No, but—'

'Thanks,' she said. 'No, I really *can't* stick it out, this is hurting my head— Tell you what, next week I'll come on time and stay the whole time, okay? Promise.'

'It's only ten minutes.'

'Ten minutes too long.'

'Give it a chance, Lauren. We don't have to talk about your problems.'

'What, then?'

'Tell me about your interests.'

'I'm interested in the beach,' she said. 'Okay? I'm interested in freedom – which is exactly what I need right now. Next week I'll be good – I mean it.'

Next week. Conning me or did she really intend to return?

'I've gotta get out of here.'

'Sure,' I said. 'Take care.'

Big smile. Hair flip. 'You're a doll.' Swinging the purse like a slingshot, she hurried out. I caught up with her in the waiting room, just as she whipped out her lighter.

Jamming the cigarette in her mouth, she shoved at the door. I watched her trot down the hall, a girl in a hurry, haloed by a cloud of smoke.

I thought about her a few times – the image of self-destructive escape. Then that faded too.

Six years later I was invited to a bachelor party the weekend before Halloween.

A forty-five-year-old radiation oncologist at Western Pediatrics was getting married to an O.R. nurse, and a consortium of hospital physicians and administrators had rented the presidential suite of the Beverly Monarch hotel for the send-off.

Steaks, ribs, buffalo wings, assorted fried and grilled stuff on the buffet. Iced tubs of beer, serve-yourself bar, Cuban cigars, gooey desserts. My contact with the honoree – a mumbling loner lacking in social skills – had been a few stiff, unproductive discussions about patient care, and I wondered why I'd been included in the festivities. Perhaps every face helped.

There was no shortage of faces when I arrived late. The suite was vast, a string of mood-lit, black-carpeted rooms packed with sweaty men. Penthouse level – no doubt a great view – but the drapes were drawn and the air felt heavy. Suit jackets and neckties were heaped on a sofa near the door under a hand-lettered sign that said, GET CASUAL! I made my way through testosterone guffaws, random backslapping, blue cigar fog, the strained glee of boozy toasts.

A crowd swarmed the food. I finally got close enough to redeem a skewer of teriyaki beef and a Grolsch. Belched cheers and scattered applause from the next room drew me to a larger throng. I drifted over, found scores of eyes trained forward on the hundred-inch projection TV the hotel provided for presidents.

Skin flicks flashing larger than life. Bodies squishing and squirming and slapping in time to an asthmatic sax score. The men around me gaped and pretended to be casual. I wandered away, got more food, stood to the side, chewing and wondering what the hell I was doing there, why I just didn't wipe my mouth and leave.

A pathologist I knew sauntered by with a whiskey in his hand. 'Hey,' he said, eyeing the screen. 'Aren't you the guy who's supposed to explain why we do this?'

'You've obviously mistaken me for an anthropologist.'

He chuckled. 'More like paleontologist. I'll bet cavemen painted dirty pictures. How about we videotape this and show it at Grand Rounds?'

'Better yet,' I said, 'at the next gala fund-raiser.'

'Right. Ten-inch cocks and wet pussies – better have

oxygen ready for Mrs Prince and all the other biddies.'

A roar from the wide-screen crowd made both our heads swivel. Then a sharp peal – flatware on glass, shouts for quiet, and the vocal buzz faded out, isolating the *thump-thump* of the porn soundtrack. Moans continued to thunder in stereo. A woman's voice urged, '*Fuck it – fuck me,*' and nervous laughter rose from the audience. Then a tight, abrasive silence.

A thickset, ruddy man holding a nearly full beer mug – a financial officer named Beckwith – stepped into the space between the two front rooms. His eyeglasses had slid down his meaty nose, and when he righted them beer splashed and foamed on the carpet.

'Go, Jim!' someone shouted.

'Get a neuro workup, Jim!'

'That's why pencil pushers can't be surgeons!'

Beckwith staggered a bit and grinned. 'Here, here, gentlemen – and I *do* use the term loosely— Look at what we've wrought – is this a goddamn *blast* or *what!*'

Cheers, hoots, nudges, bottoms up.

'*You're* sure *blasted,* Jim!'

Beckwith rubbed his eyes and his nose, gave a one-armed salute, splashed more beer. 'Since all of us are such serious, no-*nonsense* citizens – since we'd never dream of abandoning God and spouses and country and moral obligation except for the *direst* emergency' – raucous laughter – 'thank *God* we've got ourselves one *hell* of an emergency, brethren! Namely the impending sentencing – uh, *matrimony* of our esteemed – steamed-*up* – buddy, the eternal, infernal, *nocturnal* Dr

19

Phil Harnsberger, wielder of the radioactive cancer-killer beam, better known to all of us as El Termina*dor*, aka *He Who Lurks Behind the Lead Door*! Come on out, *Phil* – where *are* you, *boy*?'

No sign of the groom.

Beckwith cupped his hands into a megaphone. 'Paging Dr Deathray! Dr Deathray to center stage, *stat*. Come on, Phil, *show* yourself, boy!'

Chants of '*Phil, Phil, Phil, Phil . . .*'

Then: '*Here he is!*'

Thunderous ovation as the crowd rippled and Phil Harnsberger, clutching a martini glass, was expelled from its midst and shoved next to Beckwith.

Balding and normally pallid, with a pink-red mustache demeaning his upper lip, the radiotherapist was flushed incandescent. His smile was a paranoid smear, and he seemed on the verge of tipping over. He had on a black T-shirt so grossly oversized that it skirted past the knees of his slacks. A yellow cartoon silk-screened across the front portrayed a hefty, leering bride gripping a leash that tethered a pint-sized groom prostrate before a hanging judge and looming scaffold. A bold legend protested: **I Dint Kill No One, Yer Honor, So Why the Life Sentence?**

Beckwith slapped Harnsberger on the back. Harnsberger flinched and tried to down some martini. Most of the liquid ended up on his chin, and he wiped himself with his sleeve.

'Sterile procedure!' someone shouted. 'Call the fucking JCAH!'

'Fucking germ culture – stat!'

Beckwith slapped Harnsberger again. Harnsberger labored at smiling.

'Hey, Phil, hey, old guy – and I *do* mean old – speaking of which, it's about *time* you lost your cherry!' Stooping, Beckwith pretended to search for something on the floor, examined Harnsberger's cuffs, finally straightened and picked the olive out of Harnsberger's martini. 'Ah, *here*, it is! Turned green from disuse!'

Whoops from the crowd. Harnsberger smiled but hung his head.

'Phil,' said Beckwith, 'you may be pathetic, but *know* we love you, big guy.'

Silence.

'Termina*dor*?' said Beckwith. 'Do you know it?'

Harnsberger muttered, 'Sure, Jim—'

'You know what?' said Beckwith.

'You love me.'

Beckwith backed away. 'Not so fast, Lone Ranger!' To the crowd: 'Don't ask, don't tell is okay for those fruits in the Navy, but maybe someone should inform the *bride*!'

Harnsberger flushed. Wild laughter. Beckwith closed back in on his target, going nose to nose. 'Seriously, Phil, you're *sure* you're having a good time?'

'Oh, yes, absolutely—'

Beckwith reached around and delivered yet another backslap, hard enough to cause Harnsberger to drop the martini glass. Beckwith crushed the glass underfoot, ground the shards into the carpet. 'Like the Jews say, moozel tav – happy batch-day, Phil. Sure hope you're

21

enjoying your last meal – er, last rites. Grub to your satisfaction?'

Harnsberger nodded.

'Get enough to drink?'

'Yes—'

''Cause none of us want you pissed off and beaming that *death* ray of yours down at us, Philly.'

Shouts of agreement. Harnsberger simpered.

Beckwith said, 'That's also why none of us want to be around when you get the *bill*!'

Momentary panic in Harnsberger's eyes. Beckwith slapped him again. 'Scared you there, huh, boy? Nah, don't get your co-*jone*-jones in an uproar, it's all taken care of – lifted it out of *patient* funds.' Beckwith rubbed an index finger against a thumb and winked. 'Sorry. No *kidney* transplants for Medi-Cal patients this month!'

Peals of merriment.

Beckwith took hold of Harnsberger's arm. 'And now, for the pièce de résistance, Phil. Pieces. So to speak— Sure you've eaten enough?'

'I'm sure, Jim.'

'Well . . .' Beckwith grinned. 'Maybe not.' He flourished an arm. Nothing happened for a moment; then the lights dimmed and music surged from behind the giant TV. Warp-speed disco beat, louder than the porn score.

The crowd parted, and two women in long black trench coats pranced into the clearing. As Beckwith slipped from view they positioned themselves on either side of Harnsberger.

Young women – tall, shapely, coltish, stepping high on

spiked heels. Wide-smiling – tossing the smiles as if dispensing candy – they rotated their hips, thrust their pelvises, made the exaggerated moves of trained dancers. Long mass of coal black hair on one girl. Her partner's coif was white-blond, boy-short, gel-spiked.

Synchronized butt shakes as they flanked Harnsberger, rubbed his neck, kissed his cheek, bumped his hips. A pair of tongues flicked the radiotherapist's ears, now crimson. His face was polluted with arousal and fear.

The girls stomped and shouted, stroked their crotches, pretended to go for Harnsberger's fly, threw back their heads and pantomimed openmouthed laughter, began shoving him gently between them – back and forth, the way baby jackals play with a rabbit.

The music took on even more speed. Off came the trench coats; the girls wore identical black leather bustiers, black thongs, garter belts, and fishnet stockings.

Several beats of bump and grind. I stared along with everyone else, caught a side view of busty profiles, heard the girls whoop and laugh as they continued to tease Harnsberger. The black-haired girl tickled his chin, veneered herself against him, ran her hands over his head, messed his hair. The blonde took hold of his face, kissed him long and hard on the mouth as he tried to wriggle away, hands flying wildly. Suddenly he succumbed to the kiss, getting into it. He was reaching for the blonde's rear when she shoved him away, did an athletic squat, danced back up to him, shook her head from side to side, peeled back a bustier cup and flashed a nipple, let the leather flip back up.

The black-haired girl joined her for more crotch rubbing and prancing. Both bras teased down on cue, now shed and tossed to the crowd.

Full, young breasts bobbled and rotated. The girls pinched their nipples hard, bent low, dropped to perfect splits, bounced up, danced wildly, played with their G-strings.

Pointing at Harnsberger and moving in on him, but this time they guided him offstage and returned, just the two of them, holding hands. The G-strings popped, snapped back on firm, flat pubises.

A bit more genital hide-and-seek, then the black-haired girl got down on all fours, rotated her buttocks, pulled at the blonde's ankle. The blonde stood there, shaking her head no, pouting, feigning resistance. Hoarse screams of encouragement from the choir. Everyone *paying attention*.

In a flash both girls were naked but for garter belts and fishnets. The music slowed to languid sludge in a too-sweet key, and they began caressing each other, vamping, stroking, kissing, tongues lizarding.

The black-haired girl sank to the carpet, lay on her back, arched her pelvis. The blonde shimmied between her partner's legs, lowered to her knees, bowed her head prayerfully, grazed the dark girl's abdomen with platinum spikes.

Tonguing the dark girl's navel. The dark girl writhed.

The blond girl looked up, placed a finger on her lip, as if contemplating what to do next. A big-eyed travesty of innocence, holding out her hands as if seeking counsel from the crowd.

The crowd cheered her on.

She tilted her head back to the dark girl's crotch, began to dip again, raised her face. Kneeling in place but not moving as the dark-haired girl, still bucking, took hold of her arm and urged her down.

The blond girl studied the audience. Took in the entire room.

Turning my way, giving me a full view of her face.

Long, oval face beneath the silvery spikes. Pale eyes under plucked brows, dominant but perfectly proportioned cleft chin.

Recognition was a splinter in my chest.

Hers too. The slyness dropped off her face, replaced by . . . a queasy smile.

She stared at me, and her head froze above the black-haired girl's writhing hips. I thought I saw her give the faintest headshake – denying something?

The music oozed on. The black-haired girl kept gyrating, started to realize something was off. Made a grab for Lauren's head.

Lauren didn't budge.

Then she did.

As she allowed herself to be dragged down, I escaped.

three

I drove home nearly blind with shame, cutting through dark, cold streets as if nothing mattered.

The closest I've come to having children are the people who've depended on me. Encountering Lauren had given me a glimpse of what the parents of whores and felons go through.

The look in her eyes when she'd recognized me – stripper's flaunt degrading to . . . imbalance. The uncertainty she'd never shown as a teenager.

Now she was twenty-one. Legal. That made me laugh out loud.

Why the hell had I gone to Harnsberger's party in the first place? Why hadn't I left when the tone of the evening became clear?

Because, as in most men, something in me craved fresh erotic imagery.

Robin was waiting up for me, but that night I was very poor company.

I slept terribly, woke the next morning wondering what,

if anything, I should do about the encounter. At eight o'clock I called my service, and the operator informed me Lauren had phoned at midnight and asked for an appointment.

'She sounded urgent,' said the operator. 'I knew about that cancellation at two, so I gave it to her. Hope that was okay, Dr Delaware.'

'Sure,' I said, sick with dread. 'Thanks.'

'We're here to serve, Doctor.'

At two P.M. precisely the bell on the side door rang and my heart jumped.

Patients who've never been to my house usually remain down at the gate. The bell ring meant Lauren had unlatched the gate, mastered the route across the front drive and through the garden. No warning dog bark; Robin had gone up to Carpinteria on a wood-buying trip, left at daybreak, taking Spike with her.

I put down the coffee I hadn't touched, hurried through the house, opened the door.

New face on the other side.

Fresh, scrubbed, expressionless, clipped snowy hair stripped of product, brushed forward, falling in a soft Caesar cut.

No makeup at all. The same blue eyes – tougher, tempered. An untested face, *except* for the eyes.

At twenty-one Lauren looked younger than she had at fifteen.

A bleached-denim shirt and easy-fit jeans covered her from neck to ankle. The shirt was buttoned to the top and cinched with a turquoise clasp. The jeans managed to hug her frame, advertise the tight waist, soft hips. On her feet were white canvas flats with straw soles. A big calfskin bag hung over one shoulder – rich, burnished roan, gold-clasped, conspicuously expensive.

'Hello, Lauren.'

Gazing past me she offered her hand. Her palm was cold and dry. I didn't feel like smiling, but when her eyes finally met mine, I managed.

She didn't. 'You work at home now. Cute place.'

'Thanks. Come on in.'

I stayed just ahead of her during the walk to my office. She moved fast – as eager to enter as she'd once been to leave.

'Very nice,' she said when we got there. 'Still seeing kids and teens?'

'I don't do much therapy anymore.'

She froze in the doorway. 'Your answering service didn't say that.'

'I'm still in practice, but most of my work is consultation,' I said. 'Court cases, some police work. I'm always available to former patients.'

'Police work,' she said. 'Yes. I saw your name in the paper. That school-yard shooting. So now you're a public hero.'

Still looking past me. Through me.

'Come on in,' I said.

'That's the same,' she said, eyeing my old leather couch.

'Kind of an antique,' I said.

29

'You're not – you really haven't changed that much.'

I moved behind the desk.

'*I've* changed,' she said.

'You've grown up,' I said.

'Have I?' She sat stiffly, made a move for the calfskin bag, stopped herself, started to smile, quashed that too. 'Still no smoking?'

'Sorry, no.'

'Filthy habit,' she said. 'Inherited it from Mom. She had a scare a few years back – spot on her X-ray, but it turned out to be a shadow – stupid doctor. So she finally stopped. You'd think it would teach me. People are weak. You know that. You make a living off that.'

'People are fallible,' I said.

One of her legs began to bounce. 'Back when I came to you, I gave you a real hard time, didn't I?'

I smiled. 'Nothing I hadn't seen before.'

'It probably didn't seem like it, but I was actually getting into the idea of therapy. I'd psyched myself up for it. Then they killed it.'

'Your parents?'

The surprise in my voice made her flush. 'They *didn't* tell you.' Her smile was cold. 'They claimed they did, but I always wondered.'

'All I got was a cancellation call,' I said. 'No explanation. I phoned your house several times, but no one answered.'

'Bastard,' she said with sudden savagery. 'Asshole.'

'Your father?'

'Lying asshole. He promised he'd explain everything

to you. It was *his* decision— He never stopped complaining about the money. The day I was supposed to see you, he picked me up from school. I thought he was making sure I showed up on time – I thought you'd lied to me and finked to him about my coming late. I was furious at you. But instead of heading to your office, he drove the other way – into the Valley. Over to this miniature golf course – this Family Fun Center. Arcades, batting cages, all that junk. He parks, turns off the engine, says to me: "You need quality time with your dad, not hundred-buck-an-hour baby-sitting with some quack." '

She bit her lip. 'Doesn't that sound a little . . . like he was jealous of you?'

As I mulled my answer she said, 'Seductive, don't you think?'

I continued to deliberate. Took the leap. 'Lauren, was there ever any—'

'No,' she said. 'Never, nothing like that, he never laid a finger on me. Not for anything creepy *or* for normal affection. The fact is, I can't remember him *ever* touching me. He's a cold fish. And guess what: He and Mom finally got divorced. He got himself a bimbo, some slut he met on the job— So they never told you they canceled, that it wasn't my idea. Figures. They brought me up with lies.'

'What kind of lies?'

The blue eyes met mine. Got hard. 'Doesn't matter.'

'That day at the golf course,' I said. 'What happened?'

'What happened? Nothing happened. We played a few holes, finally I said I was bored, started nagging and

31

whining to be taken home. He tried to convince me. I sat down on the green and wouldn't budge. He got mad – got all red-faced like he does, finally drove me home, steaming. Mom was in her room— It was obvious she'd been crying. I thought it had to do with me. I thought *everything* had to do with me – thought it all the time, and it just sat there in my head like a tumor. Now I know better; they were totally messed up all along.'

She crossed her legs. 'A few weeks later he walked out. Filed for divorce without telling her. She tried to get child support out of him, he claimed business was lousy, never gave us a penny. I told her to sue his ass, but she didn't. Not a fighter – she never has been.'

'So you lived with her.'

'For a little while. If you call it living. We lost the house, moved into an apartment in Panorama City, real dive – gunshots at night, the whole bit. Things sucked, we were broke, she was always crying. But I was having a great time 'cause she wasn't even trying to discipline me and finally I could do what I wanted. She wouldn't fight with *me* either.'

She took a tissue from the box I position strategically, crumpled it into a ball, picked it open.

'Men suck,' she said, staring at me. 'Now let's talk about last night.'

'Last night was unfortunate.'

Her eyes sparked. '*Unfortunate?* That's the best you can do? You know the problem with this goddamn world? No one ever says they're sorry.'

'Lauren—'

32

'Forget it.' She waved the tissue dismissively. 'I don't know why I even bothered.' She began rummaging through the leather bag. 'End of session. How much do you charge now? Probably more, now that your name gets in the papers.'

'Please, Lauren—'

'No,' she said, shooting to her feet. 'The time's mine, so don't tell me how to spend it. No one tells me what to do anymore. That's what I like about my job.'

'Being in control.'

Her hands slapped onto her hips, and she glared down at me. 'I know you're dishing me shrink talk but in this case you happen to be right. Last night you were probably too turned on to notice, but I was in charge – Michelle and me. All you guys with your mouths hanging open and your dicks stiff, and we were calling the shots. So don't judge me as if I'm some brainless slut.'

'No judgments.'

Her hands fisted and she stepped closer. 'Why'd you have to leave like that? Why were you ashamed of me?'

As I considered my answer, she gave a knowing smile. 'I turned you on and that freaked you out.'

I said, 'If you were a stranger, I probably would've stuck around. I left because I was ashamed of myself.'

She smirked. '*Probably* would've stuck around?'

I didn't answer.

'But we *are* strangers,' she said. 'How can you say we're not?'

'The fact that you're here—'

'So what?'

'Lauren, once you came to me for help, I had a duty to be there for you. Like a surrogate parent. I felt my presence caused you shame too, but it was my own embarrassment that got me out of there.'

'How noble,' she said. 'Man, you're confused. Like all guys are— Okay, I got what I came for. Now I'm going to pay you.'

'There's nothing to pay for.'

She wagged a finger. 'Oh no, you don't. You've got the title and respectability, and in your eyes I'm just some stripper-slut. But once I pay you, the balance of power equalizes.'

'I am not judging you, Lauren.'

'You *say*.' She whipped a wad of cash out of her jeans pocket. 'What's the tab, Doc?'

'Let's talk about—'

'How much?' she demanded. 'What's your hourly fee?'

I told her. She whistled. 'Not too shabby.' She peeled off bills, handed them to me. 'Okay, here you go, and you don't even have to declare it to the IRS. I'll find my own way out.'

I followed her anyway. When we reached the door, she said, 'My roll – that stash I paid you from? Did you see the size of it? That's my tip money, honey. I do *great* with tips.'

four

Now, four years later, I had to talk to her mother.
Mrs Jane Abbot.

So she'd remarried. Was life treating her more kindly? Had the spot on her lung recurred? I was curious but could've lived without finding out.

Life would be so much easier if I was one of those flakes who felt no obligation to return calls.

My pompous little speech to Lauren about surrogate parenthood rang in my ears. I put off the call anyway. Revved up the coffee machine, tidied up an already clean kitchen, checked the stores in the pantry. When I returned to the kitchen I discovered I'd forgotten to put coffee in the filter and started from scratch. Listening to the machine bubble offered another few minutes of respite, and when I finally sat down to drink I dropped a little brandy in the mug, took my time sipping, scanned a newspaper I'd already covered from front to back.

Finally, the inevitable. Staring at the big pine that nearly blocks the kitchen window, I punched numbers.

Two rings. 'Hello?'

'Mrs Abbot?'

'Yes, who's this?'

'Dr Delaware.'

Two beats of silence. 'I didn't know if you'd phone— Do you remember me?'

'Lauren's mom.'

'Lauren's mom,' she said. 'My claim to fame.' Her voice broke. 'It's Lauren I'm calling about, Dr Delaware. She's missing. For a week. I know you work with the police. I've seen your name in the papers. Lauren saw it too. That impressed her. She always liked you, you know. It was my husband – my ex-husband – who stopped her from seeing you. He was a very mean man – *is* a mean man. Lauren hasn't had contact with him in years. But that's neither here nor there— The problem I've got now is I can't find her. She's been living on her own for a while, but this – it just feels wrong. By the third day I called the police, but they say she's an adult and unless there's evidence of a crime there's nothing they can do other than have me come in and file a report. I could tell they weren't taking me seriously. But I know Lauren just wouldn't take off like that. Not without telling me.'

'Does she ever travel?'

'Occasionally, but not for this long.'

'So you're in regular communication with her,' I said, wondering if Lauren was still stripping, and did her mother know.

Pause. 'Yes. Of course. I call her, she calls me. We manage to stay in touch, Dr Delaware.' Adding, 'I live in the Valley now,' as if that explained the lack of face-to-face contact.

'Where does Lauren live?' I said.

'In the city. Near the Miracle Mile. She wouldn't just walk out without telling me, Doctor. She didn't tell her roommate anything either. And it doesn't look as if she packed a suitcase. Don't you think that's frightening?'

'There could be an explanation.'

'Please, Dr Delaware, I know how things work. It's who you know. You've worked with the police— With your contacts, they'll listen to you. You must know someone who can help.'

'What's Lauren's address?'

She recited some numbers on Hauser. 'Near Sixth Street. Not far from the museum complex – the La Brea Tar Pits. I used to take her to the tar pits when she was little— Please, Dr Delaware, call your contacts and ask them to take me seriously.'

My contact was Milo. His turf was West L.A. Division, and Hauser near Sixth was Wilshire. Petra Connor, my only other LAPD acquaintance, worked Hollywood Homicide.

A pair of homicide detectives. Jane Abbot didn't want to hear that.

I said, 'I'll make a call.'

'Thank you, so much, Doctor.'

'How's Lauren been doing?'

'You'd be superproud of her – I am. She— We had a few rough years after her father walked out on us. She dropped out of high school without graduating – it was kind of . . . But then she pulled herself together, got her GED, attended JC, got her associate's degree with honors, and transferred to the U this past fall. She just finished her first quarter, got all As. She's majoring in psychology, wants to be a therapist. I know that's your influence. She admires you, Doctor. She always said what a caring person you were.'

'Thank you,' I said, feeling surreal. 'It's midquarter break at the U, for another few weeks. Sometimes students travel.'

'No,' she said. 'Lauren wouldn't have gone anywhere without telling me. And not without luggage.'

'I'll do what I can.'

'You're a good man, I always sensed that. You were a great influence on her, Doctor. You only saw her that couple of times, but it had an impact. She once told me she wished you were her father instead of Lyle.'

I tried Milo at home first, got no answer, just the tape with Rick Silverman's voice on it. I tried the West L.A. detectives' room.

'Sturgis.'

'Morning, this is your wake-up call.'

'Got sunrise for that, boyo.'

'Putting in weekend overtime?'

'What's a weekend?'

'Thought the murder rate was down,' I said.

'Exactly,' he said. 'So now we're all ball-and-chained to subarctic cold cases. What's up?'

'I need a favor.' I told him about Lauren, letting him

know she'd been a patient, knowing he'd understand what I could and couldn't say.

'She's how old?' he said.

'Twenty-five. Missing Persons told her mother the only option was filing a report.'

'Did she file?'

'I didn't ask her,' I said.

'So she wants some strings pulled . . . Problem is, Missing Persons is right. An adult case, without some evidence of disability or blood and guts or a stalking boyfriend – it comes down to routine for the first few weeks.'

'What if it were the mayor's daughter?'

Long sigh. 'What if I went down in a light plane off the coast of Cape Cod? I'd be lucky to get two drunks in a rowboat as a search party, let alone a Navy destroyer and a fleet of choppers. Okay, I'll put in a call to MP. Anything else I should know about this girl?'

'She's enrolled at the U, but it's possible she got involved in something less than wholesome.'

'Oh.'

'Four years ago she was working as a stripper,' I said. 'Private parties. She may still be stripping.'

'The mother told you this?'

'No, I learned it myself. Don't ask how.'

Silence. 'Okay. Spell her full name.'

I did and he said, 'So we're talking bad girl here?'

'I don't know about that,' I snapped. 'Just that she danced.'

He didn't react to my anger. 'Four years ago. What else?'

'She's done one quarter at the U. Straight As, according to her mother.'

'Mama knows best?'

'Some mamas do.'

'What about this one?'

'Don't know. Like I said, it's been a long time, Milo.'

'Your own cold case.'

'Something like that.'

He promised to get back as soon as possible. I thanked him and hung up, took a longer than usual run, returned home sweat-drenched and faded, showered off, got dressed, went down to the pond and fed the koi without bothering to enjoy their colors. Returning to my office, I started to clear some custody reports.

I ended up thinking about Lauren.

From stripping to straight As at the U . . . I decided to call Jane Abbot, let her know I'd followed through. Maybe that would be the end of it.

This time a machine answered. A man's voice, robotic, one of those canned recordings women use as a security device. I delivered my message, worked for a few more hours on the reports. Shortly after noon I drove into south Westwood, bought a take-out Italian sandwich and a beer at Wally's, returned to Holmby Park, where I ate on a bench, trying not to look ominous among the nannies and the rich kids and the old people enjoying green grass as cars whizzed by. When I got back the message light on my answering machine was a blinking red reproach.

One call. Milo sounding even more tired: 'Hey, Alex, getting back to you on Lauren Teague. Call whenever you've got a chance.'

I jabbed the phone. Another detective answered, and it took a few moments for Milo to come on the line.

'The mother did file a report. Yesterday. MP ran a background on Lauren.' He coughed. 'She's got a record, Alex. They haven't informed the mother yet. Maybe they shouldn't.'

'What kind of record?' I said.

'Prostitution.'

I kept silent.

He said, 'That's all, so far.'

'Does that alter the chance that someone will actually look for her?'

'The thing is, Alex, there's nothing to go on. They asked the mother for any known associates, and she came up with zilch. MP detective's feeling is that Mama is not in the loop when it comes to Lauren's private life. And maybe Lauren traveling isn't exactly an aberration. Her arrests weren't only here. Nevada too.'

'Vegas?'

'Reno. Lots of girls work that route, hopping on cattle-car flights, doing one-, two-day turnarounds for fast cash. So maybe her picking up without explanation is just part of her lifestyle. Student, or not.'

'She's been gone for a week,' I said. 'Not exactly a turnaround.'

41

'So she stayed to play the tables. Or got herself a lucrative gig she wants to milk for a while. The point is, we're not talking Suzy Creamcheese wandering away from the church bus.'

'When was her most recent arrest?' I said.

'Four years ago.'

'Here or Nevada?'

'Good old Beverly Hills. She was one of Gretchen Stengel's girls, got nabbed at the Beverly Monarch Hotel.'

Site of Phil Harnsberger's bachelor bash. The hotel's vanilla rococo façade flashed in my head.

Tip money. *I do great with tips.*

'What month four years ago?' I said.

'What's the difference?'

'Last time I saw her was four years ago. November.'

'Hold on, let me check . . . December nineteenth.'

'Gretchen Stengel,' I said.

'The Westside Madam herself. At least she wasn't working the street for crack vials.'

I gripped the phone so hard my fingers ached. 'Is there any record of a drug history?'

'No, just the solicitation bust. But Gretchen's girls did tend to party hard— Look, Alex, you know passing judgment on people's sex lives isn't my thing, and I don't even think much about dope unless it leads to someone being made dead. But the fact that Lauren's a working girl does have to be taken into account here. Most likely she split for a gig and the roommate's covering for her with Mom. I can't see any reason to panic.'

'You're probably right,' I said. 'Mom may be out of the loop. Though she's not totally unaware – told me Lauren went through some rough times, and her voice tightened up when she said it. And with the last arrest four years ago, maybe Lauren did turn herself around. She did enroll at the U.'

'That could be.'

'I know, I know – cockeyed optimism.'

'Hey, it gives you that boyish charm . . . So you treated her four years ago?'

'Ten. I saw her once four years ago. Follow-up.'

'Ah,' he said. 'Ten years is a long time.'

'It's a damned eon.'

Long pause. 'You still sound . . . protective of her.'

'Just doing my job.' Surprised at the anger in my voice. I avoided further discussion by thanking him for his time.

He said, 'The MP guy did agree to make some calls to hospitals.'

'Morgues too?' I said.

'That too. Alex, I know you didn't want to hear about the girl's sheet, but in this case maybe it puts things in a more positive light – she's got a rationale for cutting out without explanation. Best thing to tell the mom is just wait. Nine times out of ten, the person shows up.'

'And when they don't, it's too late to do anything about it anyway.'

He didn't answer.

'Sorry,' I said. 'You've done more than you had to.'

He laughed softly. 'No, I had to.'

43

'Up for lunch sometime?' I said.

'Sure, after I chip away at some of this ice.'

'Subarctic, huh?'

'I wake up middle of the night with penguins pecking my ass.'

'What kinds of cases?'

'Potpourri. Ten-year-old child murder, parents probably did it but no physical evidence. Twelve-year-old convenience store robbery-gone-bad, no witnesses, not even decent ballistics, 'cause the bad guys used a shotgun; drunk snuffed out in an alley eight years; and *my* personal favorite: old lady smothered in her bed back when Nixon was president. Should've gotten my degree in ancient history.'

'English lit's not a bad fit either.'

'How so?'

'Everyone's got a story,' I said.

'Yeah, but once I'm listening to them, you can forget happy endings.'

five

The roommate's covering for her . . .

A roommate who lived the same life as Lauren? If so, no reason for her to talk to Jane. Or the police. Or anyone else.

Jane Abbot claimed Lauren admired me. I found that hard to believe, but perhaps Lauren had mentioned me to the roommate and I could learn something.

I called the 323 number Jane had given me for Lauren, got another male robot on the machine, hung up without leaving a message.

I thought some more the path Lauren's life had taken. Given the little I knew about her family life, I supposed there was no reason to be surprised. But I found myself succumbing to letdown anyway.

Ten years ago. Two sessions.

When her father had terminated, had I let it go too easily? I really didn't think so. Lyle Teague had never accepted the idea of therapy. Even if I'd managed to reach him by phone, there was no reason to believe he'd have changed his mind.

No reason at all for me to feel I'd failed, and I told myself I felt comfortable with that. But as the afternoon grayed Lauren's disappearance continued to chew at me. Just after two P.M., I left the house, gunned the Seville down the glen to Sunset, and headed east, through Beverly Hills and the Strip, to the roller-coaster ramp that was the crest of La Cienega.

Catching Third just past the Beverly Center, I picked up Sixth at Crescent Heights and cruised past the tar pits. Plaster mastodons reared, and groups of schoolkids gawked. They pull bones out of the pits daily. One of L.A.'s premier tourist spots is an infinite graveyard.

Lauren's apartment on Hauser sat midway between Sixth and Wilshire, a putty-colored six-unit box old enough for fire escapes. I made my way up a chunky cement path to a glass door fronted by wrought-iron fettuccine. Through the glass: dim hallway and dark carpeting. A column of name slots and call buttons listed TEAGUE/SALANDER in apartment 4.

I pressed the button, was surprised to be buzzed in immediately. The hallway smelled of beef stew and laundry detergent. The carpeting was an ancient wool – flamingo-colored leaf forms over mud brown, once pricey, now heeled and toed to the burlap. Mahogany doors had been restained streaky and lacquered too thickly. No music or conversation leaked from behind any of them. A flight of chipped terracotta steps at the rear of the building took me upstairs.

Unit 4 faced the street. I knocked, and the door opened before my fist lowered. A young man holding a white washcloth stared out at me.

Five-six, one-thirty, fair-haired and frail-looking, wearing a sleeveless white undershirt, very blue jeans cinched by a black leather belt, black lace-up boots. A heavy silver chain looped a front jeans pocket.

'Oh. I thought you were . . .' Breathy-voiced, pitched high.

'Someone else,' I said. 'Sorry if I'm interrupting. My name's Alex Delaware.'

No recognition in the wide, hazel eyes, just residual surprise. The fair hair was dun tipped with yellow, clipped nearly to the skull. Zero body fat but what was left was string, not bulk. Tiny gold ring in his right earlobe. A tattoo – 'Don't Panic' in elaborate blue-black script – capped his left shoulder. A band of thorns in the same hue circled his right biceps. He looked to be around Lauren's age, had the round, unlined face, pink cheeks, and arched brows of an indulged child. As he looked me up and down, surprise began to give way to suspicion. He clenched the washcloth, and his head drew back.

'I'm an old acquaintance of Lauren's,' I said. 'One of her doctors, actually. Her mother called me, concerned because she hasn't heard from Lauren for a week—'

'One of her doctors? Oh . . . the *psychologist* – yes, she told me about you. I remember your name was one of the states – are you Native American?'

'Kind of a mongrel.'

He smiled, pulled at the silver chain, produced a saucer-sized pocket watch. 'My God, it's *two*-forty!'

Another eye rub. 'I was catching a nap, heard the bell, thought it was *three*-forty, and *jolted* up.'

'Sorry for waking you.'

He let the washcloth unfurl, waved it in a tight little arc. 'Oh, don't apologize, you did me a favor. I have . . . an old friend dropping by, need the time to pull myself together.' A hip cocked. 'Now why are we having this conversation out in the *hall*?' A bony arm shot forward. His grip was iron. 'Andrew Sa*lan*der – I'm Lauren's roomie.'

He swung the door wide open, stepped aside, and let me into a large parlor with a high, cross-beamed ceiling. Heavy ruby-and-gold brocade drapes sealed the windows and plunged the space into gloom. New smells blew toward me: cologne, incense, the suggestion of fried eggs.

'Let there be light,' said Andrew Salander as he rushed over and yanked the curtains open. A cigar of downtown smog hovered above the rooftops of the buildings across the street. Exposed, the living room walls were lemon yellow topped by gilded moldings. The cross-beams were gilded as well; someone had taken the time to hand-leaf. French cigarette prints, insipid old seascapes in decaying frames, and frayed samplers coexisted in improbable alliance on the walls. Deco and Victorian and tubular-legged modern furniture formed a cluttered liaison. A close look suggested thrift-shop treasures. A keen eye had made it all work.

Salander said, 'So Mrs A called you. Me, too. Three times in as many days. At first I thought she was being

48

menopausal, but it has been six-plus days, and now *I'm* starting to get concerned about Lo myself.'

He pulled a tattered silk throw off a sagging olive velvet divan and said, 'Please. Sit. Excuse the squalor. Can I get you something to drink?'

'No thanks. It's far from squalid.'

'Oh, please.' A hand waved. 'Work in progress and very little progress at work – Lo and I have been going at this since I moved in. Sundays at the Rose Bowl Swap Meet, Western Avenue, once in a while you can still find something reasonable on La Brea. The *problem* is neither of us has time to really give it our all. But at least it's habitable. When Lo lived here by herself, it was utterly bare – I thought she was one of those people with no eye, no artistic sense. Turns out she has fabulous taste – it just needed to be brought out.'

'How long have you been rooming together?'

'Six months,' he said. 'I was in the building already – downstairs in Number Two.' He frowned, sat on a mock-leopard-skin ottoman, crossed his legs. 'Month to month, I was supposed to move out to . . . Then things changed, as they so often do, and the landlord leased my space to someone else and suddenly I found myself without hearth or home. Lo and I had always had a good rapport – we used to chat at the laundromat, she's easy to talk to. When she found out I was stuck, she invited me to move in. At first, I refused – charity's one of many things I *don't* do. But she finally convinced me two bedrooms were too much for her and I could share the rent.'

A fingertip grazed a plucked eyebrow. 'To be honest, I *wanted* to be convinced. Being alone's so . . . dark. I hadn't . . . And Lo's a wonderful person – and now she's flown off somewhere. Dr Delaware, *do* we need to worry? I really don't *want* to worry, but I must admit, I *am* bothered.'

'Lauren didn't give a clue where she was going?'

'No, and she didn't take her car – it's parked in her space out back. So maybe she *did* fly off – literally. It's not as if she's a Greyhound girl. Nothing slow suits her, she works like a demon – studying, doing research.'

'Research at the U?'

'Uh-huh.'

'On what?'

'She never told me, just said that between her classes and research job she had a full plate. You think that's what might've taken her somewhere – the job?'

'Maybe,' I said. 'No idea who she worked for?'

Salander shook his head. 'We're chums and all that, but Lo goes her way and I go mine. Different biorhythms. She's a morning lark, I'm a night owl. Perfect arrangement – she's bright and chirpy for classes and I'm coherent when the time rolls around for *my* work. By the time I wake up, she's usually gone. That's why it took a couple of days to realize her bed hadn't been slept in.' He shifted uncomfortably. 'Our bedrooms are our private space, but Mrs A sounded so anxious that I did agree to peek in.'

'The right thing to do,' I said.

'I hope.'

'What kind of work do you do, Mr Salander?'

'*Andrew*. Advanced mixology.' He smiled. 'I tend bar at The Cloisters. It's a saloon in West Hollywood.'

Milo and Rick sometimes drank at The Cloisters. 'I know the place.'

His brows climbed higher. 'Do you. So why haven't I seen you before?'

'I've driven by.'

'Ah,' he said. 'Well my Bombay martinis are works of art, so feel free to breeze in.' His face grew grim. 'Listen to me, Lauren's gone and I'm sitting here prattling— No, Doctor, she never gave me a clue as to where she was headed. But till Mrs A called I can't say I was ready to panic. Lauren did go away from time to time.'

'For a week?'

He frowned. 'No, one or two nights. Weekends.'

'How often?'

'Maybe every two months, every six weeks – I can't really recall.'

'Where'd she go?'

'One time she told me she spent some time at the beach. Malibu.'

'By herself?'

He nodded. 'She said she rented a motel room, needed some time to decompress, and the sound of the ocean was peaceful. As for the other times, I don't know.'

'Those weekends, did she usually take her car?'

'Yes, always . . . So this *is* different, isn't it?' He rubbed his armband tattoo, wincing as if the art were

51

new, the pain fresh. 'Do you really think something's wrong?'

'I don't know enough to think anything. But Mrs Abbot seems to be worrying.'

'Maybe Mrs A's getting us all overwrought. The way mothers do.'

'Have you met her?'

'Only once, a while back – two, three months ago. She came to take Lo out to lunch and we chatted briefly while Lo got ready. I thought she was nice enough but rather *Pasadena*, if you know what I mean. Coordinated ensemble, several cracks past brittle. I saw her as a perfect *fifties* person – someone who'd drive a Chrysler Imperial with all the trimmings and pile the backseat full of Bullocks Wilshire shopping bags.'

'Conservative,' I said.

'Staid,' he said. 'Theatrically sad. One of those women fighting the future with mascara and matching shoes and tiny sandwiches with the crust trimmed.'

'Doesn't sound like Lauren.'

'Hardly. Lauren is *très naturelle*. Unaffected.' The washcloth was wadded once more. 'I'm sure she's fine. She *has* to be fine.' He sighed, massaged the tattoo some more.

I said, 'So the time you met Mrs Abbot, she and Lauren went out to lunch.'

'Long lunch – must've been three hours. Lo came back alone, and she didn't look as if she'd had fun.'

'Upset?'

'Upset and distracted – as if she'd been hit on the

head. I suspected something emotional had gone on, so I fixed her a gimlet the way she likes it and asked if she wanted to talk about it. She kissed me here' – he touched a rosy cheek – 'said it wasn't important. But then she drank every drop of that gimlet and I just sat there emitting that I'm-ready-to-listen vibe – it's what I *do*, after all – and she—' He stopped. 'Should I be telling you this?'

'I'm beyond discreet,' I said. 'Because of what *I* do.'

'I suppose. And Lauren did say she liked you . . . All right, it's nothing sordid, anyway. She simply told me she'd spent her childhood fighting not to be controlled, had made her own way in the world, and now her mother was trying to do the same old thing, again.'

'Control her.'

He nodded.

'Did she say how?'

'No – I'm sorry, Doctor, I'm just not comfortable flapping my trap. There's nothing more to say, anyway. That's the entire kit and caboodle.'

I smiled at him. Didn't budge.

He said, 'Really, I've told you everything – and only because I know Lo liked you. She came across your name in the paper, some kind of police case, said, "Hey, Andrew, I knew this guy. He tried to straighten me out." I made some remark – how it obviously hadn't taken. She thought that was funny, said maybe it was patients like her who'd driven you to quit doing therapy and work with the cops. I' – his cheeks flamed – 'I made some crack about shrinks being more screwed up than their patients, asked if you were . . . like that. She said no, you seemed pretty . . . I think *conventional* was the word she used. I said, how boring, and she said no, sometimes conventional was exactly what you needed. That she'd screwed up, not making good use of her therapy, but looking back it had all been a setup anyway.'

'What do you mean?' I said.

'She realized that her parents had set her up to rebel. Tried to use you as a weapon against her, but you hadn't gotten sucked into their game, you had integrity— You're sure I can't get you a drink?'

My throat had gone dry. 'A Coke would be fine.'

He laughed. 'The soft stuff? Recovering juice fiend?'

'No, it's just a bit early for me.'

'Trust me, it's never too early. But all right, one cola-bean juice, coming up pronto. Lemon or iime?'

'Lime.'

He hurried into the kitchen, returned with a tall drink on ice and a glass of white wine for himself. Settling back down, he rested one elbow on a knee, placed his chin in a cupped palm, stared into my eyes.

I said, 'So Lauren felt her mother was trying to control her but she didn't say how.'

'And the next day she was going about her business with nary a mention of ma*ma*. Truth is, I don't think Mrs A looms large in her life. She's been on her own for years. And that's absolutely all I can tell you about her family dynamics, so drink up.' He drew out the pocket watch.

'Your friend,' I said.

He flinched. 'Yes.'

'Does Lauren have any friends I could talk to?'

'No.'

'No one at all?'

'Not a one. She doesn't date, nor does she chum around with the girls. We're both social isolates, Doctor. Yet another tie that binds.'

'The night owl and the morning lark,' I said.

'Makes for a cozy little aviary – this is absolutely the best living arrangement I've ever had. Lauren's a living doll and I simply *insist* that she be okay. Now, if you'd like, I can pour that drink into styrofoam and you can take it to go—'

As charming a dismissal as I'd encountered. Placing the drink on a side table, I stood. 'Just a few more questions. Mrs A said Lauren didn't pack a suitcase.'

'*I* told her that,' he said. 'I know every item in Lauren's wardrobe— She has luscious things. After I moved in I organized her closet. She owns two pieces of luggage – a pair of vintage Samsonites we picked up for a prayer at the Santa Monica flea market, and they're both here. So is her backpack from school. And her books. So she must be planning to return.'

He began to sip wine, stopped himself. 'That isn't good, is it? Running off without luggage.'

'Not unless Lauren's the impulsive type.'

'Impulsive as in meet someone hot and fly off to Cuernavaca? That *would* be nice.' He sounded doubtful.

'But unlikely.'

'Well,' said Salander. 'I just don't think that's Lo— If she'd fallen in love, I'd have known. She was a creature of routine: got up, jogged, went to class, studied, went to sleep, got up and did the same thing all over again. To tell the truth, she was a bit of a grind.'

'Strict routine except for occasional weekends away.'

'Except for.'

'She's in between quarters at school,' I said. 'What's she been doing with her vacation?'

'Going to work.'

'The research job.'

'A grind,' he said. 'She'd spend every spare moment studying if I didn't drag her out to do some antiquing.'

'Must have paid off,' I said. 'Mrs A said she got straight As.'

'Lo was so proud of that. Showed me her transcript. I thought it was adorable.'

'What was?'

'A grown woman, all excited like a little kid— She's studying psychology, wants to be a therapist herself. You must have been a good influence.' Staring at me again. 'You haven't touched your drink, is it okay?'

I picked up the Coke and drank. 'Terrific.'

'That's Mexican lime, not Bearss lime. More bite.'

More cola flowed down my gullet. 'Does the research job pay the bills?'

'Maybe some of it, but Lo also has investments.'

'Investments?'

'Some kind of nest egg she put away from when she worked full-time. She told me she can coast for a few more years before she has to hit the boards again. I give her a lot of credit, giving up something so lucrative for the sake of her studies.'

'The boards?'

'The runway – modeling,' he said. 'Nothing *Vogue*-coverish or anything like that. She worked the Fashion Mart scene since she was eighteen. Made good money but said she detested being a brainless face and body— Now, Doctor, I'm sorry to be ill-mannered, but my appointment – it's someone who . . . hurt me. I've been building my courage and finally I'm ready to face him and move on. Please.'

He indicated the door and led me out.

I said, 'Thanks very much for your time. If you don't mind, I'm going to have to look at Lauren's car out back. What kind is it?'

'Gray Mazda Miata. Don't steal it.' Nervous laugh.

I crossed my heart. 'No joyrides today.'

Louder laughter. We shook hands again.

'I'm not going to worry,' he said. 'There's no reason to worry.'

'I'm sure there isn't.'

'Watch,' he said. 'I'll be sitting here, worrying myself sick, and Lo will come waltzing through this door and I'll scold her for putting all of us through this.'

He walked me out into the hall, looked toward the staircase. Chewed his lip. 'You're a good listener— Any time you want a career switch, I can get you a job at The Cloisters.'

I grinned. 'I'll keep that in mind.'

He laughed. 'No, you won't. For a whole list of reasons.'

Out in back was a carport that fronted the alley. The Miata was the only car parked there, several years old, lots of nicks and dents, coated with several days of dust, locked, its oatmeal-colored canvas top set snugly. Campus parking sticker on the rear bumper, Thomas Guide map book in the driver's door pocket, pair of sunglasses on the center console, just below the gearshift. Nothing else.

I returned to the Seville, trying to organize what I'd learned from Salander.

No friends, no dates. A grind.

Rooming with a gay man said Lauren prized companionship, wasn't looking for sex.

Because she was still getting paid for it?

Working the Fashion Mart runway since eighteen. Maybe she really had done some modeling, or perhaps it was just a cover for selling her body in another way.

Weekends by herself. One in Malibu, other times unspecified. Keeping it vague to cover her trail as she met up with clients?

The night owl and the morning lark. If she wanted privacy, Salander was a perfect roommate. Still, the guy was perceptive. If Lauren had been working at her old profession, wouldn't he have caught on?

Maybe he had and chose not to tell me. My gut told me he'd been forthcoming, but you never knew . . .

I thought of what he'd told me about Lauren's

income. *Investments.* From her working days. Enough to coast for a few years.

I do great with tips.

Good clothes but otherwise living frugally. Before Salander had moved in, she'd had virtually no furniture. That and the old car said she knew how to make do.

Budgeting but spending on *luscious things* in her closet. Dressing for the job?

I wondered about the lunch with her mother, Lauren returning dazed and upset, complaining about Jane trying to control her. But that had been two or three months ago – no reason it would lead her to vanish now.

Vanish. Despite my reassurances to Salander, I was thinking worst-case scenario.

Seven days, no luggage, no car, no explanation.

Maybe Lauren *would* waltz in any minute. Straight-A student returned from a research trip – some professor asking her to attend an out-of-town meeting or convention, deliver a paper. She'd flown somewhere – that would explain no car. But it didn't solve the problem of wardrobe, and why hadn't she let anyone know?

Unless Salander wasn't as familiar with her wardrobe as he claimed and she *had* packed something. Tossed casual clothes into a bag.

Research . . . A project at my alma mater, a psych major, so probably a psych job. At the very department from which I'd obtained my union card.

I headed west on Wilshire, caught snail traffic at Crescent Heights – an orange-vested Caltrans crew, stupidest agency in the state, taking petty-fascist satisfaction in blocking off two lanes. I sat, idling along with the Seville, rolled a foot or two, sat some more, finally got past La Cienega. Unmindful of the noise and the dirt. New focus: yearning to feel useful.

six

I reached the city-sized campus of the U just after four-thirty. More people were leaving than arriving, and the first two parking lots I tried were being retrofitted for something. University officials gripe about budget constraints, but the jackhammers are always working overtime. It's a boom time for L.A., might endure till the next time the earth shrugs.

It was nearly five P.M. when I hurried up the stairs to the psych building, hoping someone would be around. The cement-and-stucco waffle had been repainted: from off white to a golden beige with chartreuse overtones. Uncommonly bright for a place devoted to the joys of artificial intelligence and compelling brain-lesioned rats to race through ever more Machiavellian mazes. Maybe boom times hadn't loosened up grant money and the new hue was an attempt to connote warmth and avail-ability. If so, eight stories of Skinner-box architecture said forget it.

By the time I entered the main office, half the lights

were out and only one secretary remained, locking up. But the right secretary – a plump, ginger-haired young woman named Mary Lou Whiteacre, whose five-year-old son I'd treated last year.

Brandon Whiteacre was a nice little boy, soft and artistic, with his mother's coloring and scared-bunny eyes. A freeway pileup had shattered his grandmother's hip and sent him to the hospital for observation. Brandon had escaped with nothing broken other than his confidence, and soon he began wetting his bed and waking up screaming. Mary Lou got my name from the alumni referral list, but the department wasn't picking up the tab. She was reeling from the crash and still chafing under the financial hardships imposed by a three-year-old divorce. Her HMO offered the usual cruelty. I treated Brandon for free.

My footsteps made her look up, and though she smiled she seemed momentarily frightened, as if I'd come to revoke her son's recovery.

'Dr Delaware.'

'Hi, Mary Lou. How's everything?'

The red hair was a flyaway frizz that she patted down. 'Brandon's doing great – I probably should have called you to tell you.' She approached the counter. 'Thanks so much for your help, Dr Delaware.'

'My pleasure. How's your mom?'

She frowned. 'Her hip's taking a long time to heal, and the other driver's being a butt – denying responsibility. We finally got ourselves a lawyer, but everything just drags out. So what brings you here?'

'I'm trying to locate a student who was involved in research.'

'A grad student?'

'Undergrad. I assume you have a record of ongoing projects.'

'Well,' she said, 'that's generally not public information, but I'm sure you've got a good reason . . .'

'This girl's gone missing for a week, Mary Lou. The police can't do much, and her mother's frantic.'

'Oh, no – but it's midquarter break. Students take off.'

'She didn't tell her mother or her roommate, though she did say she'd continued to come here even during the break, to do research. So maybe the job took her out of town. A conference, or some kind of fieldwork.'

'She didn't tell her mom anything?'

'Not a word.'

She crossed the room to a wall of file cabinets. Same golden beige. The outcome of someone's experiment on color perception? Out came a two-inch-thick computer printout that she laid on a desk and flipped through. 'What's her name?'

'Lauren Teague.'

She searched, shook her head. 'No one by that name registered with personnel on any federal or state grants – let's see about private foundations.' Another flip. She looked up, with the same worried expression I'd seen on her first visit to my office. Psychology's code of ethics forbids bartering with a patient. I'd traded something with her, wondered if I'd stepped over the line.

'Nothing.'

'Maybe there's a misunderstanding,' I said. 'Thanks.'

She crossed her mouth with an index finger. 'Wait a second – when it's part-time work, sometimes the professors hire out through one of those employee management firms. It avoids having to pay benefits.'

Another cabinet, another printout. 'Nope, no Lauren Teague. Doesn't look as if she's working here, Dr Delaware. You're sure the study was in psychology? Some of the other departments have behavioral science grants – sociology, biology?'

'I assumed psychology, but you could be right,' I said.

'Let me call over to the administration building, see what the central employee files turn up.' Glance at the wall clock. 'Maybe I can catch someone.'

'I really appreciate this, Mary Lou.'

'Don't even think about it,' she said, as she dialed. 'I'm a mom.'

No job listing anywhere on campus. Mary Lou looked embarrassed – an honest person confronting a lie.

'But,' she said, 'they do have her enrolled. Junior psych major, transferred from Santa Monica College. Tell you what – I'll pull our copy of her transcript. I can't give you her grades, but I will tell you which professors she took classes from. Maybe they know something.'

'I appreciate it.'

'Hey,' she said, 'we're not even close to even in the thank-you department . . . Okay, here we go: This past quarter she took a full load – four psych courses: Introductory Learning Theory with Professor Hall,

Perception with Professor de Maartens, Developmental with Ronninger, Intro Social Psych with Dalby.'

'Gene Dalby?'

'Uh-huh.'

'We were classmates,' I said. 'Didn't know he switched from clinical practice to teaching Social.'

'He came on full-time a couple of years ago. Good guy, one of the less pompous ones. Even though he drives a Jag.' Her eyes rounded and she pretended to slap her wrist. 'Forget I said that.' She began to return the transcript to the drawer.

'Lauren told her mother she got straight As.'

'Like I said, Dr Delaware, grades are confidential.' Her eyes dropped to the paper. Tiny smile. 'But if I was her mother I'd be proud. Smart girl like that, I'm sure there's an explanation. Here, let me write those professors' names down for you. Ronninger's on sabbatical, but the others are teaching all year. By this time I doubt they're in, but good luck.'

'Thanks. You'd make a good detective.'

'Me?' she said. 'Never. I don't like surprises.'

She locked up, and I walked her through the lobby, both our footsteps echoing on black terrazzo. When she was gone I strode back to the elevators and read the directory. Simon de Maartens's office was on the fifth floor, Stephen Z. Hall's and Gene R. Dalby's on the sixth.

I pushed the button and waited and thought about Lauren's lie to Andrew Salander. No research job. Probably covering for her real employment. Stripping, hooking, both. Resuming her old ways. Or she'd never stopped.

Runway modeling. Another lie? Or maybe gigs at the Fashion Mart were just another way to cash in on her looks.

Smart kid, but enrollment in college and good grades weren't contradictory to plying the flesh trade. Back when Lauren had worked for Gretchen Stengel, the Westside Madam had employed several college girls. Beautiful young women making easy money – big money. Someone able to compartmentalize and rationalize would find the logic unassailable: Why give up five-hundred-dollar tricks for a six-buck-an-hour part-time bottle-washing gig without benefits?

Salander had said Lauren was living off investments, and I wondered if her body was the principal. If so, her disappearance could be nothing more than a quarter-break freelance to accrue spare cash.

No car, because she was flying – jetting off somewhere with a sheik or a tycoon or a software emperor, any man sufficiently rich and deluded to fall for the ego sop of purchased pleasure.

Lauren serving as amusement for a few days, returning home nicely *invested.*

But if that was the case, why had she raised her mother's anxiety by not providing a cover story? And why hadn't she packed clothing?

Because this particular job required a new wardrobe? Or no clothing at all beyond the threads on her back?

She *had* taken her purse, meaning she had her credit

cards. What did a party girl require other than willingness and magic plastic?

Maybe she was punishing Jane by slipping away without explanation – letting Jane know she wouldn't be controlled.

Or perhaps the answer was painfully simple: rest and recreation after grinding away for grades. Cooling out in one of the places she'd used before – nice quiet Malibu motel – if *that* was true.

Maybe Lauren had done the L.A. to Reno shuttle, found her old stomping grounds lucrative, decided to stay for a while . . . The elevator doors wheezed open, and I rode up to Five. Professor Simon de Maartens's door was decorated with Far Side cartoons and a newspaper clipping about moose deaths from acid rain. Closed. I knocked. No answer. The handle didn't turn.

I had no more success at Stephen Hall's unadorned slab of chartreuse wood, but Gene Dalby's door was open and Gene was sitting at his desk, wearing a rumpled white shirt and khakis, bare feet propped, gray laptop resting on a skinny stalk of thigh. He typed, hummed tonelessly, wiggled his toes. A pair of huarache sandals sat near the legs of his chair. Coffee bubbled in an old white machine. A single window to his left framed rooftops and the northern edge of the campus botanical gardens. From a boom box on the ledge came supernatural guitar licks and a bruised voice. Stevie Ray Vaughan's 'Crossfire.'

I said, 'Uh, hi, Professor Dalby. Could we talk about my grades?'

Gene's head turned. Same bony pencil face and jug ears and rebellious ginger hair. His temples had silvered. Black-framed, half-lens reading glasses rode the center of a swooping askew hook of a nose. He grinned, placed the specs on the desk, did the same with the laptop. 'No way. You flunk.'

Jumping up to his full, ostrich-necked six-four, all loose limbs and oversized hands and bobbing head, he clasped my shoulders and shook his head in wonderment, as if my arrival heralded the second coming of something.

Gene is one of the most outgoing people I know, a paragon of unadorned friendliness, hyperactive maestro of the thunderous greeting. His good cheer is nearly constant, and he avoids complexity. Unusual traits in a psychologist. So many of us were introspective, overly imaginative kids who got into the field trying to figure out why our mothers were depressed no matter what we did. In grad school a lot of people found him too good to be true and distrusted him. He and I always got along, though it rarely went beyond off-color jokes and casual lunches.

'So,' he said. 'Alex. How long has it been?'

'A while.'

'Light-years, man. Here, sit— Coffee?'

I took a side chair, accepted a mug of something strong and bitter and vaguely coffeelike. He kicked the sandals under the desk. The office was tiny, and his size didn't help. He hunched like a pet confined by a cruel owner.

'Working during the break?' I said.

'Best time, less distraction. Besides, back when I was in practice I used to see fifty, sixty patients a week. That was *real* work. This academic racket is legalized theft. Nine months a year, make your own hours.' He laughed. 'These guys love to complain, but it's a paid vacation.'

'When did you make the switch?' I said.

'Three years ago. Sold the practice to my associates and presented the department with an offer they couldn't refuse: They take me on part-time, no job security, no benefits, and I carry a heavy teaching load, in exchange for a clinical full professorship and no assignment to committees.'

'No publishing treadmill.'

'Exactly, but the funny thing is even though I didn't plan to, I'm doing research anyway. First time in years. Asking questions that really interest me rather than churning out garbage in tribute to the tenure gods. And I *love* the teaching, man. The kids are great. Despite what the idiot pundits say, students *are* getting smarter.'

'What kind of research are you doing?' I said.

'Political attitudes in little kids. We go out to grade schools, try to gauge their perceptions of candidates. You'd be surprised how much little kids know about the scumbags who run for office. I feel like I'm home – social psych was always my first love. I went into clinical because I also liked clinical and I thought it would be nice to help people and all that. But, mainly, because I needed to make a buck. Married with kids – unlike you, I never went through the swinging bachelor stage.'

'You've got the wrong guy there, Gene.'

'I don't think so, man. I distinctly recall you being a departmental love object. Even the girls who *didn't* shave their legs looked at you *that* way.'

'I must have missed it,' I said.

He grinned. 'Listen to him, that coyness – all part of the charm. Anyway . . . you look great, Alex.'

'You too.'

'I look like I always did – Ichabod Crane on meth-amphetamine. But yeah, I'm doing what I can to stay in shape, got into long-distance hiking. Jan and I did the John Muir Trail last summer, Alaska before that.' He turned the volume down on Stevie Ray.

I named the song.

He said, 'S.R.V. He was the man. Sad, huh? Struggles his whole life with dope and booze, plays bars for chump change, finally gets sober, makes it big, and the damn plane goes down. Talk about an object lesson.'

'Live life to the fullest,' I said.

'Live life and don't *worry*. Be happy – like that other song. Been telling that to patients for years, now I'm following my own advice. Not that it took courage or some big-time follow-your-bliss thing to motivate me. I got lucky – bought in at ground level with a start-up software company, turned a penny stock into dollars. Ten years of bad stock tips from my brother-in-law, finally one pays off. We're not talking private jet here, but now if I don't like the taste of something I don't have to eat it. The kids are in college and Jan's law practice is doing fine. Life is shockingly good, thanks to dot-com madness. The company's going to shit, but I've already sold.'

'Congratulations.'

'Yeah,' he said. 'Even traded the Honda for a Jag— Don't hate me 'cause I'm beautiful.' He shifted in his chair, cracked his knuckles. 'So what brings you here? Doing some teaching yourself?'

'No, I'm trying to locate a student named Lauren Teague.'

'Locate as in . . . ?'

I told him about the seven-day absence, implied without spelling it out that Lauren had once been a patient, emphasized Jane Abbot's anxiety.

'Poor lady,' he said. 'So you were here and just dropped in?'

'No, I thought you might be able to help me. Lauren told her roommate she had a research job here, but that doesn't seem to be true. She was in four classes last quarter, one of them your Intro Social section. I'm checking with all the profs, see if anyone remembers her.'

'Lauren Teague,' he said. 'I sure don't. Had five hundred plus kids in that class. What others did she take?'

I named the courses.

'Let's see,' he said. 'Herb Ronninger is out in the Indian Ocean somewhere studying violent preschoolers – his class pulls over *six* hundred, so even if he were here I doubt he could help you. De Maartens and Hall are young-buck new-hires, and Learning and Perception tend to be a bit smaller. Let me call them for you.'

'I already tried their offices. Do you have home numbers?'

'Sure.' He found and copied the listings, handed them to me.

'Thanks.'

'Lauren Teague,' he said, putting his glasses back on. He opened a bottom desk drawer, rifled papers for a while, pulled out a list of names and grades. 'Yeah, she was enrolled all right . . . Did well, too. *Very* well – eighteenth out of 516 . . . Good, solid As on all her exams . . . B plus on her paper.' More scrounging produced another list: "Iconography in the Fashion Industry." Oh, *her.*'

'You remember her.'

'The model,' he said. 'I thought of her that way because she looked like one – all the basics: tall, blond, gorgeous. And when I read the paper, I figured she'd been writing from experience. She also stood out because she was quite a bit older than the average junior – pushing thirty, right?'

'She's twenty-five.'

'Oh,' he said. 'Well, she seemed older. Maybe because she dressed maturely – pantsuits, dresses, expensive-looking stuff. I remember thinking, This girl has money. Kind of aloof, too. She used to sit in the back by herself, take notes constantly. Never saw her with any other students . . . So why'd I give her a B plus on the paper? If the students want them, I hand them back, don't know if she picked hers up . . . but I do keep a comment card . . .' Bending low, he began tossing papers out of drawers, created a high pile on the desk. 'Okay, here goes.' He flourished a stack of rubber-banded blue index cards. 'My notes say, "High on anger, low on data." If I remember, it was a bit of a screed, Alex.'

'Anger at the fashion industry?' I said.

'From what I recall. Probably the usual feminist stuff – woman as meat, subservient roles coerced by unrealistic conceptions of femininity. I get at least two dozen every quarter. All valid points, but sometimes they substitute passion for data. I really can't remember this particular paper, but if I had to guess, that would be it. So she left without telling Mom. Is that an aberration?'

'According to Mom.'

He scratched his chin. 'Yeah, as a parent that would worry me.' Placing his feet on the floor and his hands on his knees, he looked at me over the rims of the half-glasses. 'It's funny – actually it's anything but funny – your coming around about a missing student. When you first told me, it gave me a start. Because something like this happened last year. Another girl – some kind of campus beauty queen. Shane something, or Shana . . . Shanna – I don't recall her exact name. Left her dorm room one night and never came back. Big stir on campus for a few days, then nothing. It affected me more than it might've because Jan and I had just sent our Lisa off to Oberlin. She was fine in the separation-anxiety department, but we weren't doing so well. I'd *just* started to settle down – had stopped phoning the poor kid twelve times a day – and this Shanna thing happens.'

'She was never found?'

He shook his head. 'Talk about the ultimate parents' nightmare. There's no word I despise more than *closure* – pop-psych crapolsky. But not knowing's got to be worse. I'm sure it has nothing to do with the Teague girl – it just reminded me.'

'Gene, in terms of the research job, is there something I might've missed? I checked federal, state, and private grants, including part-time positions.'

He thought awhile. 'What about something off-campus? Paid subject positions. You see ads in the *Daily Cub*. "Feeling low or moody? You may be clinically depressed and qualify for our cool little clinical trials." Pharmaceutical outcome studies, obviously the FDA or whoever's in charge doesn't see a problem using paid participants. The *Cub*'s out of circulation till next quarter, but maybe you can find something. Still, what would that tell you about where she is?'

'Probably nothing,' I said. 'Unless Lauren signed up for a study because she had a specific problem – as in depression. Depressed people drop out.'

'Her mother wouldn't know if she was that low?'

'Hard to say. Thanks for the tip, Gene – I'll look into it.'

I got up, placed the coffee on a table, and headed for the door.

'You're really extending yourself on this, Alex.'

'Don't ask.'

He stared at me but said nothing.

No longer a clinician, but he knew enough not to press it.

seven

The story was easy to find.

Shawna Yeager.

Beautiful face, heart-shaped, unlined, crowned by a tower of pale ringlets. Almond eyes, shockingly dark. Pixie chin, perfect teeth, beauty undiminished by grainy black-and-white miniaturization, the cold, metal frame of the microfiche machine, the stale air of the research library microfilm vault.

I stared at lovely glowing shoulders exposed by a strapless gown, sparkly things dotting the bodice. The gown Shawna Yeager had worn at her coronation as Miss Olive Festival. Silly little rhinestone crown pinned to the luxuriant curls, happiest-girl-in-the-world grin.

The contest had taken place two years ago in her hometown, an aggie community east of Fallbrook named Santo Leon. Shawna Yeager held a scepter in one hand, a giant plastic olive in the other.

The *Daily Cub* article said she'd graduated fifth in her class at Santo Leon High. A single paragraph summed up her precollege history: small-town beauty queen/

honor student travels to the city to attend the U. Shawna had surprised her friends by not pledging a sorority, choosing instead to live in one of the high-rise dorms. Turning into a 'study grind.'

She'd majored in psychobiology, talked about premed, used her beauty contest winnings and income from a summer teacher's aide job to pay her bills.

She'd been enrolled for only a month and a half when she left the dorm on a late October night, informing her roommate that she was heading to the library to study. At midnight the roommate, a girl named Mindy Jacobus, fell asleep. At eight A.M. Mindy woke, found Shawna's bed empty, worried a bit, went to class. When Shawna still hadn't returned by two P.M., Mindy contacted the campus police.

The unicops engaged in a comprehensive search of the U's vast terrain, notified LAPD's West L.A. and Pacific Divisions, Beverly Hills and Santa Monica Police, and West Hollywood sheriffs of the girl's disappearance.

No leads. The campus paper carried the story for a week. No sightings of Shawna, not even a false report. Her mother, Agnes Yeager, a widowed waitress, was driven to L.A. from Santo Leon by a representative of the chancellor's office and provided living quarters in a graduate student dorm for the duration of the search.

A *Cub* follow-up – still no news – said the search had lasted three weeks.

After that, nothing.

I returned to the microfilm librarian, filled out cards, obtained spools from the *Times* and the *Daily News* for the corresponding dates. Shawna's disappearance merited two days of page 20 media attention, then a senator's drunken son crashed his Porsche on the I-5, killing himself and two passengers, and that story took over.

I returned to the *Cub* spool, wrote down the reporter's name – Adam Green – and studied Shawna Yeager's beauty contest photo some more, searched for a resemblance to Lauren.

She and Lauren did share a sculpted, blond loveliness but nothing striking. Both A students. Psychology major, psycho*biology* major.

Both were self-supporting too, one banking on pageant money, the other, 'investments.' Had each been on the lookout for extra income? Consulted the campus classifieds and gotten involved in one of the research studies Gene Dalby had described?

I searched for more parallels, found none. All in all, nothing dramatic. And plenty of differences:

At nineteen Shawna had been considerably younger than Lauren when she disappeared. Small-town olive queen, big-city call girl. Divorced mother, widowed mother. And Shawna had vanished during the second month of the quarter, Lauren during the break.

I scrolled to the *Cub*'s want ads, worked backward until I came upon a boldface entry in the middle of the *JOBS!!* section, posted two weeks before Shawna vanished.

Tired? Listless? Inexplicably sad?

These may be normal mood changes, or they may be signs of depression.

We are conducting clinical trials on depression and are looking for \$\$ PAID \$\$ volunteers.

You will be offered free evaluation and, if you qualify, may receive experimental treatment as well as a handsome stipend.

No address, just a phone number with a 310 area code. I copied the information, kept scrolling, found two similar ads for the entire month, one researching phobias and featuring a different 310 listing, the other a study of 'human intimacy' that provided a 714 callback.

'Human intimacy' had a sexual flavor to it. Racy research in Orange County? Sex was commerce to Lauren. Might something like that have caught her eye?

I obtained microfiche for the last quarter, checked classified after classified. No repeat of the intimacy ad, nothing even vaguely similar, and the only paid-research solicitation was for a study on 'nutrition and digestion,' with a campus phone extension that meant the med school. I wrote it down anyway, left the library, headed for the Seville.

Two girls gone missing, a year apart, very little in common.

Shawna had never been found. I could only hope that Lauren's disappearance would amount to nothing at all.

80

I drove home trying to convince myself she'd show up tomorrow, a little richer and a lot tanner, laughing off everyone's worries.

Gene Dalby had pegged her at thirty, and maybe he was right about her maturity. She'd been living on her own for years, had street smarts. So no shock if the last week came down to a quick jaunt to Vegas, Puerto Vallarta, even Europe – money shrinks the world.

I drove up the bridle path that leads to my house imagining Lauren partying with a potentate. Then seeing the dark side of the fantasy: Those kinds of adventures can go very bad quickly.

Lauren getting herself into something she hadn't counted on.

Silly to let my mind run. I barely knew the girl.

The *girl*. She was well past childhood. No sense obsessing.

I'd bother Milo one more time, tell him about Shawna Yeager, receive the expected response – the *logical* detective's response—

Interesting, Alex, but . . .

I pulled up in front of the carport, pleased to see Robin's Ford pickup there, ready to stop wondering about a near stranger and be with someone I cared about.

But as I parked and climbed the stairs to the front door, I wondered: What would I tell Jane Abbot?

I knew I'd say little, if anything, to Robin about my day.

Confidentiality protects patients. What it does to

therapists' personal relationships can be interesting. Private by nature, Robin's never had a problem with my not discussing work in detail. Like most artists, she lives in her head, can do without people for long stretches of time, hates gossip.

We've had perfectly romantic dinners where neither of us uttered a word. Part of that's her, but I tend to drift off and ruminate. Sometimes I feel she's not with me, and I know there are instances when she views me as inhabiting another planet.

Mostly, we connect.

I called out a 'Looocey, I'm home, babaloo!' and she shouted back, 'Ricky!'

She was in jeans and a black tank top, everything filling nicely as she squatted to fill Spike's feed bowl and sang along with the radio. Country station, Alison Krauss and Keith Whitley doing 'When You Say Nothing At All.' Whitley's rich baritone exhumed from the grave. Technology could resurrect sound waves, but it couldn't dampen a mother's grief.

Robin finished pouring kibble, stood, and stretched to her full, barefoot five-three. No bra beneath the tank top, and when I pressed her to me her breasts spread across my shirtfront. When I kissed her, her tongue tasted of coffee. Her auburn curls were loose and longer than usual – six inches past the middle of her back. When she gets her hair done, it's a half-day, three-figure affair at a place in Beverly Hills that reeks of nail polish and people trying too hard. I couldn't remember the last time she'd spent the time and money. Busy with a seemingly endless flow of guitar construction and repairs. 'Better than the alternative' was her comment when I remarked on her long days. A few weeks ago she'd recorded a new phone message:

'Hi, this is Robin Castagna. I'm out in the studio carving and gluing, would love to talk to you, however, it's going to be a while before I can be polite. If you have an urgent message, please leave it in detail, but . . .'

We kissed some more, and Spike yelped in protest. He's a French bulldog, twenty-five pounds of black brindle barrel, bat ears perked, and deceptively soft brown eyes. I'm the one who rescued him on a hot, arid summer day, but forget gratitude; the moment Robin smiled at him, I came to be viewed as an annoyance.

Keeping one hand on Robin's bottom, I set my briefcase on the table. Spike nudged her shin. She said, 'Hold on, handsome.'

'Sure,' I said. 'Keep feeding his ego.'

She laughed. 'You ain't chopped liver either.'

Spike's flat face pivoted, and he glared at me – I can swear he understands English. His attenuated larynx let out a strangled growl, and he pawed the floor.

'Tom Flews deigns to speak,' I said.

Grumble, grumble.

'Don't feud, boys,' said Robin, bending to pet him. 'Long day, sweetie?'

'Me or him?'

'You.'

I'd thought the cheer in my voice sounded authentic,

wondered why she'd asked. 'Long enough, but over.'

Spike sputtered. A twenty-one-inch neck quivered. Drool sprayed.

'I'm staying for the evening, pal. Deal with it.'

His eyes pinched at the corners as he let out a belly grunt. I kissed the back of Robin's neck, as much out of spite as anything. Spike began bouncing higher than stumpy legs had any right to take him, and Robin added something from the fridge to his dinner and toted it to the service porch. His nose was buried before the dish hit the floor.

'Is that last night's Stroganoff?' I said.

'I figured we're finished with it.'

'We are now.'

She laughed, bent, picked up a stray bit of meat, hand-fed it to him. Breathing hard, he plunged his neck back into the bowl. 'Bon appétit, monsieur.'

'He'd prefer foie gras and a fine burgundy,' I said, 'but he'll condescend.'

She laced her arms around my neck. 'So, what's up?'

'What shall *our* dinner be?'

'Haven't thought about it,' she said. 'Any ideas?'

'How about his leftovers?'

'Now you're being cranky.' She started to leave, but I held her back, stroked her neck, her shoulder blades, slipped my hands under the tank top and kneaded the knobs of her spine, cupped a breast—

'Food, first,' she said. 'Then, maybe.'

'Maybe what?'

'Fun. If you behave yourself.'

'Define your terms.'

'I'll define them as we go along. So what went wrong today?'

'Who says anything went wrong?'

'Your face. You're all stressed around the edges.'

'Wrinkles,' I said. 'The aging process.'

'Don't think so.' Her small, fine-boned hand topped my knuckles.

'Look,' I said, stretching my lips with my thumbs and letting go. 'Mr Happy.'

She said nothing. I sat there and enjoyed her face. Another heart-shaped face. Olive-tinted, set upon a long, smooth stalk, framed by the mass of curls. Straight, assertive nose, full lips swelled by a hint of overbite, the faintest beginnings of crow's-feet and laugh lines around almond eyes the color of bittersweet chocolate.

'I'm fine,' I said.

'Okay.' She played with her hair.

'How was *your* day?'

'No one bugged me, so I got more done than I'd planned.' Her hand finger-walked over to mine, and she began playing with my thumb. 'Just tell me this, Alex: Is it one of your own cases or something Milo's gotten you into?'

'The former,' I said.

'Got it,' she said, zipping a finger across her lips. 'So nothing dangerous. Not that I'm harping.'

'Not remotely dangerous,' I said. Remembering the talk we'd had last year. After I'd role-played with a group of eugenic psychopaths and ended up too close to dead.

The pledge I'd given her . . .

'Good,' she said. "Cause when I see you . . . burdened, I start to wonder if maybe you're feeling constrained.'

'It's just a case from the past that I might've handled better. I need to make a few phone calls, and then we can figure out dinner, okay?'

'Sure,' she said.

And that's where we left it.

I went into my office, poured the contents of my briefcase onto the desk, found the numbers Gene Dalby had given me for Professors Hall and de Maartens, and dialed. Two answering machines. I left messages. Next: Adam Green, the student journalist. Information had four Adam Greens listed in the 310 area code. No sense, at this stage of the game, trying to figure out which, if any, was the kid who'd covered the Shawna Yeager story. He'd spent three weeks of his life on the story a year ago. What could he possibly have to offer?

Arranging the photocopies I'd made of the *Daily Cub* microfiches, I retrieved the three phone numbers accompanying the want ads. The depression and phobia study listings were out of service, and the Orange County intimacy project – I'd saved the best for last – connected to a Newport Beach pizza parlor. In L.A. it's not just the tectonic plates that shift.

Finally, I looked up hotels and motels in Malibu and made a dozen calls. If Lauren had checked into any of the establishments, she hadn't used her real name.

One last call: Jane Abbot. That would wait till tomorrow.

No, it wouldn't. I dialed the Valley number, planning to be vague but supportive, careful not to leech her hope. The phone rang four times, and I rehearsed the little speech I'd deliver to her robot guardian – ah, here he was: '*No one can take your call but if you care to . . .*'

Beep.

'Mrs Abbot, this is Dr Delaware. I've talked to a police detective about Lauren. Nothing really to report, but he's been made aware of the details. I'll stay on it, get back to you the moment I learn—'

A real man's voice broke in, very soft, halting. 'Yes?'

I identified myself.

Long silence.

I said, 'Hello?'

'This is *Mr* Abbot.' More of an announcement than an exchange.

'Mr Abbot, your wife spoke to me recently—'

'*Mrs* Abbot,' he said.

'Yes, sir. She and I—'

'This is *Mr* Abbot. *Mrs* Abbot isn't *here*.'

'When will she be back, sir?'

Several seconds of dead air. 'The house is empty . . .'

'Your wife called me about Lauren, and I was getting back to her.'

More silence.

'Her daughter, Lauren,' I said. 'Lauren Teague.'

Still nothing.

'Mr Abbot?'

'My wife's not here,' said the frail voice plaintively. 'She goes out, comes back, goes out, comes back.'

'Are you all right, sir?'

'I'm upstairs, trying to read. Robert Benchley – ever read Benchley? Funny as hell, but the words get small . . .'

'I'll call back later, Mr Abbot.'

No reply.

'Sir?'

Click.

eight

I hung up, tried to figure out what had just happened.

Robin knocked on the doorjamb and said, 'Ready.' She'd put on a tiny little charcoal sweater over a long, gray tweed skirt and glossed her lips. Her smile made putting the call aside a little easier.

We ended up at a Japanese place on Sawtelle, south of Olympic, the only business open at night in an obscure little strip mall. We were the only non-Asians in the room, but no heads turned. A gaunt chef chopped something eelish behind the sushi bar. A tiny woman showed us to a corner booth, where we drank sake, laced fingers, and talked very little, then not at all. The service was formal but perfect as another diminutive woman brought us boxes of warm sake and pinches of exquisite food. The quiet and the dimness took hold, and when we stepped out into the night ninety minutes later, my lungs and brain were clear.

When we got back, Spike was baying miserably, and we took him for a short walk up the glen. Then Robin ran a bath and I stood around doing nothing. Finally, I gave in and checked my messages, thinking again about Jane Abbot's husband.

Callbacks from Professors Hall and de Maartens. In Hall's case by proxy – a young man identifying himself as 'Craig, the Halls' house sitter,' informed me cheerfully that 'Stephen and Beverly are in the Loire Valley with their children and won't be back for another week. I'll pass the message along.'

De Maartens spoke for himself, in a mellow, accented, puzzled voice. 'This is Simon de Maartens. I have checked my records, and Lauren Teague was indeed enrolled in my class. Unfortunately, I have no personal recollection of her. Sorry not to have been more helpful.'

Robin called out, 'Join me,' from the bathroom, and I was out of my clothes when the phone jangled. I let it ring and had a good soak, took my time washing her hair, then just lying back in the womb-warmth of the tub. Scrubbing and sponging led to caressing and nibbling, then giggling aquatic contortions that flooded the floor. We tripped to bed, made love till we were breathless, left the covers soaked and foaming with soap bubbles.

I was still gasping when Robin got up, wrapped herself in one of my ratty robes, danced into the kitchen, and returned with two glasses of orange juice. She poured juice down my gullet, spilled a good deal of the liquid, thought that was hilarious. My revenge was sloppy, and we changed the sheets. When she went to dry her hair, I put on a T-shirt and shorts, stepped onto the rear terrace, propped my elbows on the redwood railing, stared out at looming black shapes – the pines and cedars and blue gums that coat the hills behind our property.

Feeling like a California guy.

I was somewhere on the way to torpor when Robin's voice stirred me: 'Honey? Milo's on the phone. He says he called half an hour ago.'

The ring I'd ignored.

She said, 'You can take it in here. I'm going down to the pond – there's a spotlight out.'

I went inside, picked up the bedroom extension. 'What's up?'

'Your girl,' said Milo. 'The Teague girl. She's *my* business now.'

Nine P.M., Sepulveda Boulevard. The commercial strip south of Wilshire and north of Olympic. Discount outlets, animal emergency rooms, ironworks, furniture wholesalers. Except for the veterinarians, everything shut down for the night. A cat screeched.

West side of the street, Milo had said. *The alley.*

Not far from the restaurant where I'd stuffed my face three hours before. Now the thought of eating churned my stomach.

A patrol car blocked the alley, ruby-sapphire lights flashing, the crown jewels of trouble. The uniform with his foot propped on the front bumper was young and pumped up and distrustful, and his palm shot out reflexively as I edged the Seville near. I stuck my head out, called out my name. He wasn't hearing it, scowled

91

at the Seville's grille, ordered me to move it. I shouted louder, and he sauntered over, uni-browed angrily, hand on his holster. My face was hot, but I forced myself to talk slowly and politely. Finally, he made the call that cleared me, and when I got out he said, 'Over there,' as if imparting something profound.

Pointing south down the alley, but there was no need for direction. The knot of vehicles was a huge, chrome tumor under the sizzle of power lines. As I ran toward the crime scene, the stench of rotted upholstery and gasoline and putrefying vegetables nearly gagged me.

I spotted Milo next to the coroner's van, hunched and scrawling furiously. One of his legs was bent, and the roll of his belly protruded far beyond his lapels. He licked his pencil, then jockeyed for comfort the way big, heavy men often do.

The high-intensity spots the techs had set up turned his face white and powdery, as if dusted with flour, showcasing pouches and pits, the saggy smudges under his eyes. I continued toward him, feeling numb and sick and out of place.

When I was ten feet away, he looked up. Now his face was strangely diffuse, as if my eyes had suddenly lost acuity. Except for *his* eyes: They gleamed, sharp, too bright, jumpy as a coyote's, emerald green bleached by the spots to sea foam. He had on a flesh-colored, poly-wool sport coat, baggy brown cords, white wash-and-wear shirt with a skimpy, curling collar, and a skinny green tie that glistened like a strip of tooth gel. His hair needed cutting; the top, ink black, left longish, as usual, shot off in all directions, and the spiky forelock that shaded his brow arched over his high-bridged nose. His temples, clipped to bristle, were snow white from ear top to the bottom of Elvisoid sideburns. The contrast was unnatural; recently, he'd taken to calling himself El Skunko, was making more and more cracks about senility and mortality. He was less than a year older than I, seemed to have aged a lot during the last year or so. Robin told me I looked young when she thought I needed to hear that. I wondered what Rick told Milo.

He closed his notepad, rubbed his face, shook his head.

'Where is she?' I said.

'Already in the van,' he said, tilting his head toward the coroner's transport. The doors were closed. A driver sat behind the wheel.

I started toward the van. He held my arm. 'You don't want to see her.'

'I can handle it.'

'Don't put yourself through it. What's the point?'

I continued to the van, and he opened the door, slid out the gurney, unzipped the first two feet of the body bag. I caught a nose-full of rotten-meat stench and a glimpse of misshapen green-gray face, purplish, swollen eyes, protuberant tongue, long blond strands, before he resealed the bag and led me away.

As the van drove off he sighed, rubbed his face again, as if washing without water. 'She's been dead for a while, Alex. Four, five days, maybe more, at the bottom of one of the dumpsters, under a load of trash.' He pointed.

'That one, behind the patio furniture outlet. Someone wrapped her in heavy-duty plastic – industrial sheeting. Nights have been cool, but still . . .'

'Who found her?' I said.

'The outlet uses a private trash service. They pick up once a week, at night, showed up a couple of hours ago. When they latched the dumpster onto their truck and upended it, she fell out— Do you really want to hear this?'

'Go on.'

'Part of her rolled out. A leg. The driver heard her hit the ground, went over to check, and uncovered the rest of her. She was bound, hands and feet – hog-tied. Shot in the back of the head. Two shots, close range, both in the brain stem. Coroner says one bullet would've done the trick. Someone was being careful. Or angry. Or both. Or just liked to play with his firestick.'

'Large caliber?'

'Large enough to blacken her eyes and do that to her face. Alex, why are you—'

'Sounds like an execution,' I said. It came out calm and flat. My eyes filled with water, and I swiped at them.

He didn't answer.

'Four or five days or more,' I went on. 'So it happened soon after she disappeared.'

'Looks like it.'

'How'd you identify her?'

'Moment I saw her, I knew exactly who she was. When I spoke to Missing Persons for you, they sent me her sheet and I'd seen her booking photo.'

'Well,' I said. 'Now you've got a relief from your cold cases.'

'I'm sorry about this, Alex.'

'I just left a message for her mother. Told her I was still working on finding Lauren. Nothing like success, huh?' My eyes brimmed, and a hand-wipe didn't do the trick. As I reached for my handkerchief, Milo turned away.

I stood there and let the tears gush. What the hell was *this* all about? I was no stranger to tragedy, had trained myself to maintain distance.

Lauren was dead at twenty-five, but my memories were dominated by a fifteen-year-old face. Too much makeup, useless little black purse. Ridiculous shoes.

I've changed.

You've grown up.

Have I?

My gorge rose, and this time I didn't think I could hold back.

Milo's voice was far away, fuzzed and funneled by distance. 'You all right?'

I tried to mouth the word 'Fine.' Turned and sprinted up the alley, found a spot away from the crime scene, and vomited convulsively.

The burn of rice wine, the fishy aftertaste of a fine Japanese dinner.

I waited in Milo's unmarked as he did what he needed to do. My throat was raw, and my body was sheathed in clammy sweat. Yet I felt strangely serene. Milo'd left his cell phone on the front seat, and I called Robin.

She picked up right away – waiting.

'Sorry to ruin another evening,' I said.

'What happened?'

'Someone got killed. The case I mentioned today – what I couldn't talk about. A girl I once treated. You'll probably read about it in the paper tomorrow. They just found her body.'

'Oh, God – a *child*?'

'A young woman. She was a child when I met her. She'd gone missing, her mother asked me to help – I may end up going with Milo to notify her. I'm not sure when I'll be back.'

'Alex, I'm so sorry.'

A laugh slipped out from between my lips. Inappropriate. Inexplicable.

'Love you,' I said.

'I know you do.'

Milo got behind the wheel, and I told him about Shawna Yeager.

He said, 'I remember that one – the beauty queen. Guy named Leo Riley ended up with it, thank God.'

'Tough one?'

'Impossible from the get-go, not a shred of physical evidence and no witnesses. Leo used to gripe about it – his last case before retiring and he had to end it open. His hunch was some warpo got hold of the girl, did his thing, put her where she'll never be found.' He eyed the dumpster. 'Whoever did this didn't care about that.'

'True,' I said.

'Why'd you tell me about the Yeager girl?'

I repeated my conversation with Gene Dalby.

He said, 'Two students, blond, good-looking, a year apart. If I'm right about the Yeager girl being a sex thing, that's a long time between victims. Nothing you've said screams patterns.'

'Just thought I'd mention it.'

'I'll keep it in mind if nothing else turns up on Lauren. Meanwhile, I've got uniforms headed over to her apartment to secure the premises and keep an eye on the roommate. Got a name on her?'

'Him. Andrew Salander. Mid-twenties. Tends bar at The Cloisters.'

'The Cloisters,' he said, running a hand through his hair. 'Short, skinny, pale kid with tattoos?'

'That's him.'

'Andy.' His smile was uneasy. 'Claims to fix a mean martini.'

'He doesn't?'

'Hell if I know – I hate martinis.' He frowned. 'So she roomed with Andy. Any idea how long?'

'He told me about six months. Said he'd been living downstairs in the same building, couldn't make the rent and Lauren invited him to share.'

'Interesting.' Turning the green eyes on me. 'What do *you* think of that? Her living with him.'

'Maybe she considered him safe.'

'Maybe he was.'

'You know something about him that makes you doubt it?'

'No,' he said. 'A little too chatty for my taste, but he always seemed like a nice kid. Then again, his roomie got killed. We'll just have to see.' He shifted in the seat. 'Meanwhile, the fun part of the job: notifying Mom.'

'I'll go with you.'

'I know you will,' he said. 'I wasn't even thinking of talking you out of it.'

'Sherman Oaks,' he said from the passenger seat.

We'd swapped the unmarked for the Seville, and I was driving north on Sepulveda. I jumped onto the 405 north on-ramp, veered to the fast lane, pushed the car up to eighty-five.

Years ago the freeway would've been a clear sail at this hour. Tonight I had plenty of company, mostly big trucks lumbering and small cars rushing . . . The nerve to get in my way. I had big plans – Jane Abbot's life to ruin.

I wondered if she was home yet. Or would we find the addled husband, alone? From mean old Lyle to that. Marital luck didn't seem to be her specialty.

If she *was* home, what would I say – how would I *tell* her?

'Devana Terrace,' said Milo, reciting the address he'd gotten from Motor Vehicles. 'South of Ventura Boulevard.'

I knew the neighborhood. Nice. Whatever his mental state, Jane Abbot's second husband had provided well. Remembering his feeble voice, I wondered what she'd settled for.

'The Valley,' I said. 'Lauren's father took her to a miniature golf course in the Valley the day he terminated therapy.' I told him about Lyle Teague's deception.

'Nice man,' he said. 'You trying to tell me something about him?'

'No. Lauren denied abuse.'

'But you were concerned enough to ask her.'

'There was a seductive quality to his behavior. Lauren alluded to it herself – the time she came back to see me. She said it sounded as if he'd been jealous of her time with me. But she was very clear about there being no molestation.'

'Protesting too much?' he said.

'Who knows? I didn't have time to find out.'

He grunted, stretched his long legs. 'So after Daddy killed therapy, you saw her only that once?'

'I'm still not sure why she originally made the appointment, but she ended up unloading on me. Maybe that's all she wanted.'

He was quiet for a while. I put on more speed and he laughed nervously and I slowed to eighty. He said, 'From acting-out teenybopper to stripping and doing tricks. Lots of girls in the skin trade have abuse in their backgrounds.' Another laugh. 'Who the hell am I lecturing to?'

'If her father did abuse her, he's sure not going to admit it now.'

'Let's see how he reacts to all this – and sooner, rather than later. He may be a shmuck, but as her parent he also merits notification.'

'If you can find him.'

'Why wouldn't I?'

'He walked out on Lauren and her mother years ago, remarried. Sometimes men who run, run far.'

He whipped out the cell phone. 'Lyle Teague?'

'He'd be about fifty.'

He began punching numbers. The fast lane was clear for a mile or so, and I sped up once more. Milo said, 'Have mercy on my colon, Dr Daytona,' and again I eased up on the gas pedal.

A moment later he had Lyle Teague's address. 'Reseda. Looks like everyone's in the Valley.'

'Lauren lived in the city.'

'Yeah,' he said. 'Maybe no coincidence. Distancing herself from Mom and Dad.'

'Or she wanted to be closer to the U.'

'Then why didn't she live on the Westside?'

'More bang for her rental buck,' I said.

'Speaking of which,' he said, 'any idea how *she* made the rent?'

'She told Salander investments, never got specific.'

'A student with investments,' he said. 'Tell me everything you know about her, Alex. Right from the beginning. The long version.'

Death ends confidentiality. Freed from that hurdle, I spilled. Not much confidentiality to honor anyway. Therapy with Lauren had amounted to so little, and the retelling drove home how little I'd accomplished. When I got to Phil Harnsberger's party, my voice grew louder, faster. Milo kept his eyes on his pad, looked up only when the Ventura Freeway appeared and I forgot to veer to the right. Realizing my error, I asserted myself across three lanes as he sat up and gripped the armrest. Managing to bounce onto the eastbound off-ramp, I tortured my shock absorbers, drove for another couple of miles, exited at Van Nuys, found the south end of the Valley comfortably quiet.

He said, 'Well, that got my heart rate up. No need for the treadmill.'

'When's the last time *you* saw the inside of a gym?'

'Sometime in the Pleistocene era. Me and all the other Neanderthals, pumping chunks of granite.'

I stayed on Van Nuys, reached Valley Vista, turned left, found Devana Terrace, and cruised slowly, looking for Jane Abbot's address.

Dark street. Pretty street. I finished the account of Lauren's strip, the recognition that had passed between us like a virus.

Milo wanted nothing to do with the confessor role, waved his pen, said, 'Remember the other girl's name?'

'Michelle.'

'Michelle what?'

'Lauren never said.'

'Same age as Lauren?'

'Approximately. Around the same height, too. Dark-haired, maybe Latin.'

'Blonde and brunette,' he said, and I knew what he was thinking: Someone ordering a match pair for the evening?

101

After I'd left, how far had Lauren and Michelle taken things?

He said, 'Anyone mention the name of the company they worked for?'

'No. And even if you find the guys who organized the party, I doubt they'll admit to anything. We're talking medical school professors and financial types, and this was four years ago.'

'Four years ago would be right around the time Lauren was working for Gretchen Stengel. So maybe Gretchen had a party-rental sideline.'

'Where is Gretchen?'

'Don't know. She served a couple of years for money laundering and tax evasion, but your guess is as good as mine.' He closed his pad. 'Investments . . . So maybe Lauren stayed in the game. Be interesting if she and Michelle maintained a relationship.'

'Andrew Salander said Lauren didn't have any friends.'

'Maybe there were things Lauren didn't tell Andrew. Or he didn't tell you.'

'That could very well be,' I said. Thinking: Lauren lied about the research job, so she'd probably erected other barriers. Constructing her own confidentiality.

Now all her secrets were trash.

nine

The house was too easy to find.

Two-story white colonial at the end of the block, almost grand behind black stripes of iron fencing, so brightened by high-voltage spots that it seemed to inhabit its own private daylight. Mullioned windows, green shutters, semicircular driveway, two gates, one marked ENTRY. Milo tightened the knot of his tie as I parked. We got out and walked toward the entrance gate. The night seemed drained of life force, or maybe it was the task at hand.

Lights yellowed a couple of upstairs windows, and the fanlight above the front door flashed chandelier sparkle. A white Cadillac Fleetwood blocked the view of the front door. Shiny enough to be brand-new but of a size no longer hazarded by Detroit. Handicap license plate. A metallic blue Mustang coupe, also spotless, was parked behind the Caddy, trailing the big car like an obedient child.

Milo glanced at the call box, then at me. 'Either way.'

I pushed the button. A digital code sounded, then a ringing phone.

Jane Abbot said, 'Yes?' in a sleepy voice.

'Mrs Abbot, it's Dr Delaware.'

Her breath caught. 'Oh . . . what is it?'

'It's about Lauren. May I please come in?'

'Yes, yes, of course . . . Just one second, let me . . . Hold on.' Her voice climbed in pitch with each truncated phrase, and the last word was a tight screech. Moments later the door opened and Jane Abbot ran out wearing a quilted silk robe, hair pinned up. In her hand was a remote control that she aimed at the gate. Iron panels slid open. She was two feet away when we stepped through.

Ten years since I'd seen her. She was still trim and fine-boned, the blond hair now a salon ash barely darker than the platinum Lauren had sported. The decade had hollowed her face and loosened her skin and acid-etched fissures in all the typical places. As she ran toward us she breathed through her mouth. Fluffy slippers flapped on brick.

Milo had his badge out, but it wasn't necessary. He had that terrible sadness on his face, and Jane Abbot's curse was comprehension. She raised her hands to her head, jerked away from him, and stared at me. I had nothing better to offer, and she screamed and beat her breast, tripped and stumbled as her legs gave way. A slipper flew off. Pink slippers. The things you notice.

Milo and I caught her simultaneously. She struck at us, all bones and tendons, oddly slippery through the chenille of her robe. Her grief was raw and head-splitting, but no one else came to the door of the house.

No reactions from the neighbors either, and I had a sudden taste of the solitude she'd face.

I picked up the slipper, and we guided her across the driveway and back inside.

Except for the chandeliered entry and a front room lit by a ceramic table lamp shaped like a beehive, the house was dark. Milo flipped a switch and revealed an interior surprisingly modest in scale: low ceilings, white wall-to-wall carpeting, furniture that had been pricey during the fifties, grass-cloth walls painted pink-beige and crowded with what looked to be real Picassos and Braques and tiny Impressionist street scenes. A sliver of eastern wall held built-in white bookshelves filled with hardcover books and black-spined folders, interspersed with framed plaques and gilded trophies. A rear wall of glass looked out onto nothing. We sat Jane Abbot down on a stiff, ocean blue sofa, and I settled next to her, smelling her perfume and metallic sweat. Milo took a facing armchair much too small for him. His pad wasn't out yet. It would be soon.

Jane's hands shook, caught in the fabric of her robe, became sharp-knuckled, paralyzed talons. Her cries degraded to gasps, then snuffles, then tortured squeaks that caused her to twist and jerk.

Milo watched her without seeming to. Relaxed but not blasé. How many times had he done this? Suddenly she became still, and silence captured the house – a cold, rotten inertia.

Where was the husband?

'I'm sorry, ma'am,' said Milo.

'My God, my God – when did it happen?'

'Lauren was found a few hours ago.'

She nodded, as if that made sense, and Milo began giving her the basics, speaking slowly, clearly, in low, even tones. She kept nodding, began rocking in sync with his phrasing. Shifted her body away from me and toward him. The logical realignment. I welcomed it.

He finished, waited for her to respond, and, when she didn't, said, 'I know this is a hard time to be answering questions, but—'

'Ask anything.' She clutched her head again, and her face crumpled. 'My baby – my precious *baby*!'

More tears. A beeper went off. Milo reached for his and Jane Abbot pulled one out of her robe.

'My other baby,' she said wearily. She rose unsteadily, one foot still bare. I was holding the slipper, handed it to her. She took it, smiled terribly, shuffled to the next room, and turned on the light. The dining room. Mock Chippendale furniture, more pretty paintings.

She touched something near a side door, and the walls hummed and the door slid open. Home elevator. 'I'll be right back.' She stepped in, disappeared.

Milo exhaled, got up and walked around, stopped at the bookshelves, pointed to one of the trophies. 'Hmm.'

'What?'

'Couple of Emmys . . . from the fifties . . . early sixties. Writers Guild awards – and this one's from the Producers Guild . . . Melville Abbot. All for comedy. Here's a picture of Eddie Cantor . . . Sid Caesar . . .

"Dear Mel." Ever hear of the guy?'

'No,' I said.

'Me neither. TV writer. You never hear of them . . .'

He pulled out one of the black-spined volumes, muttered, 'Script,' just as the elevator door slid open and Jane Abbot came out pushing a man in a wheelchair. Her pink robe had been replaced by a long black-and-silver silk kimono. She still wore the fuzzy slippers.

The man wore perfectly ironed, pale blue pajamas with white-piped lapels. He looked to be eighty or more. A brown cashmere blanket draped a lap so shrunken it barely tented the fabric. His small, gray egg of a head was hairless but for puffs of white at the temples. His nose was a droopy, salmon-colored balloon, his mouth, pursed and lipless above an eroded chin. Small brown eyes – merry eyes – took us in, and he chuckled. Jane Abbot heard it and flinched. She stood behind him, hands squeezing the bar of the chair, her grimness a reproach.

He gave a thumb-up wave, called out in a jarringly hearty voice: 'Evening! *Les gendarmes? Bon soir!* Mel Abbot!' Decibels above the tentative phone voice of a few hours ago.

Jane moaned softly. Abbot grinned.

'Pleased to meet you, sir,' said Milo, approaching the wheelchair.

'*Les gendarmes*,' Abbot singsonged. '*Les gendarmes du Marseilles*, the constabulary, *de stiff awm o' de law*.' He craned, tried to look back at his wife. 'Alarm go off again, dearest?'

'No,' said Jane. 'It's not that . . . It's different, Mel. Something— Mel, something *terrible* has happened.'

'Now, now,' said Mel Abbot, winking at us. 'How terrible can it be? We're all alive.'

'Please, Mel—'

'Now, now, now,' Abbot insisted. 'Now, now, now *now*, cutie pie.' Raising a palsying hand, he reached back, groped without success. Finally, Jane took hold of his fingers, closed her eyes.

He winked at us again. 'Like when they asked Chevalier, How does it feel to turn eighty? And Chevalier says, How does it *feel*?' Studied pause. 'I'll *tell* you how it feels. Considering the *alternative*, it feels terrific!'

'Mel—'

'Now, now, dearest. What's another false alarm citation? *Así es la vida*, you plays, you pays, we can afford it, *denks Gott*.' Melville Abbot freed his hand and waved floppy fingers. His head lolled, but he managed another wink. 'The main thing is everyone's alive, like Chevalier said, when they asked him how does it feel to turn eighty.' Wink. 'And Chevalier says—'

'Mel!' Jane lurched forward and grabbed his hand.

'Dearest—'

'No *jokes*, Mel. Please. Not *now* – no more jokes.'

Abbot's eyes bugged. His crushed-crepe face bore the humiliation of a child caught masturbating.

'My wife,' he said to us. 'I'd say take her, but I wouldn't mean it. Can't live with 'em, can't live without— State trooper stops a fellow on the highway, fellow says, I wasn't speeding, Officer. Trooper says,

Didja notice a mile back your wife fell outta the car? Fellow says, Oh, good, I thought I was going deaf.'

Jane must have squeezed his fingers because he winced and said, 'Ouch!' She moved around to the front of the wheelchair and kneeled before him.

'Mel, *listen* to me. Something *bad* has happened – something terrible. To *me*.'

Abbot's eyes hazed. He looked to us for rescue. Our silence made his mouth drop open. Oversized dentures, too white, too perfectly aligned, emphasized the ruin that was the rest of him.

He pouted. Jane placed her hands on his narrow shoulders.

'What's wrong with a little levity, dearest? What's life without a little spice—'

'It's Lauren, Mel. She's—' Jane began weeping. The old man stared down at her, licked his lips. Touched her hair. She rested her head on his lap, and he stroked her cheek.

'Lauren,' he said, as if familiarizing himself with the name. His eyes closed. Movement behind the lids – flipping through a mental Rolodex? When they opened he was smiling again. 'The *pretty* one?'

Jane shot to her feet, and the chair rolled back several inches. Gritting her teeth, she inhaled, spoke very slowly. 'Lauren, my *daughter*, Mel. My child, my baby – like your Bobby.'

Abbot considered that. Turned away. Pouted again. 'Bobby never comes to see me.'

Jane shouted, 'That's because Bobby—' She stopped

herself, murmured, 'Lord, Lord.' Kissed the top of the old man's head – hard, more of a blow than a gesture of affection – and covered her face with her hand.

Abbot said, 'Bobby's a doctor. Big-shot plastic surgeon – Michelangelo with a knife, big industry practice, knows where all the wrinkles are buried.' He brightened, turned to his wife. 'What do you say we go out for breakfast? All of us? We'll pile into the Caddy, go over to Solly's and have some . . .' A second of confusion. '. . . whatever with onions . . . Omelette? Maybe with lox?' To us: 'That means you, gents. Breakfast is on me, long as you don't give us a ticket for the false alarm.'

Jane Abbot lied to him as she wheeled him back to the elevator. Making breakfast plans, telling him they'd have lox and onions, maybe pancakes – she needed some time to straighten up, he should think about what he wanted to wear, she'd come back in a few minutes.

The lift arrived, and she pushed him in.

'I'll wear a cardigan,' he said as the door closed behind them. 'One of the good ones, from Sy Devore.'

Milo said, 'My, my,' when we were alone again. He made another trip to the bookshelves. 'Look at this: Groucho, Milton Berle – the guy knew everyone. Here's a photo from a Friars Club Roast they did for him twenty years ago . . . The fires sure dim, don't they. Gives me hope for the future.'

I inspected the signatures on the artwork. Picasso, Childe Hassam, Louis Rittman, Max Ernst. A tiny Renoir drawing.

The elevator vibrated the walls, the door groaned open, and Jane Abbot ran out, as if escaping suffocation. Her eyes were sunken and inflamed. She looked old, and I tried to think of her as a young flight attendant, smiling easily. 'I'm sorry, he's just – it's been getting worse. Oh, God!'

She collapsed on the sofa, cried softly. Stopped and talked to her lap. 'Bobby – his son – died ten years ago. Skiing accident. He was Mel's only child. Mel's wife – Doris – had been ill for a while. Bad arthritis, she bound up to the point where she couldn't move. Bobby's death made her worse, and eventually she needed round-the-clock care. After my divorce I went to nursing school, got my LVN, hired out for private duty. I took care of Doris until she died. Terrific lady, never lost her spirit. For five years I cared for her, sometimes I did two shifts a day. Basically, I moved in here. Mel was older than her, but back then he was in great shape. We all got along great. He had the best sense of humor – they both did.'

She clawed a cheek. 'The man used to be pure sunshine. And brilliant. He had a repertoire of thousands of jokes, could rattle them off by category – you name it, he'd know twenty gags. After Doris's funeral I moved out and got a job at a rest home. Two months later, Mel called me. When he asked me out, I thought it was for old times' sake – to thank me. When he showed up at my apartment all spiffed up with a corsage, I was taken aback – shocked, really. I had no idea. But I didn't want to hurt his feelings, so I went along with it. He took

111

me to The Palm, we ate steak, drank great wine, and I ended up having the best time of my life. He was . . . We dated for a long time. I finally agreed to marry him two years ago. I quit smoking for his health. I know the age difference is . . . but it's not what it seems.'

'No need to explain, ma'am.'

'Sure there is,' she said. 'Sure there is – there's always a need to explain. I know you're thinking this is another May–December gold-digger routine. But it isn't. Mel's well-heeled, his art alone . . . But we have a prenuptial, and I don't know the details of his finances – don't want to know. I get an allowance. I've never asked him to amend his will. He's the nicest man in the world. Until recently we—'

'Ma'am—'

'—just had the greatest time. Traveling, taking cruises, living life. Lauren only met him a few times but she liked him – he made a point of telling her how gorgeous she was, "a regular Marilyn." She never got that from her father. Lauren's never gotten anything from her father, and maybe that was my fault.'

She sobbed. I sat down next to her.

'So Lauren didn't come by often,' said Milo.

'She was always busy. With school and all that – the times she was here, she loved Mel's jokes.' Her eyes hardened. 'Lyle never told her jokes. Lyle wouldn't know a joke if it— There wasn't much to laugh about in our family. I'm sure you remember that, Dr Delaware.'

I nodded.

'What a *grim* life we had. Mel taught me what real

living was all about. Then, a year ago, he had the first stroke. Then another. And another. His legs went first, then his mind. Sometimes he's clear as a bell, but mostly he's like what you just saw. My other baby. Thank God the elevator was already in place for Doris or I don't know what we'd do. So it's not that bad. He weighs next to nothing, getting him in the chair's no problem – my training. Bathing him's a bit of a— But no big deal, for the most part, things go smoothly.' Her face constricted, and tears gushed from her eyes. 'For the most part, they go very very *smoothly*.'

I took her hand. Her skin was dry and cold, thrummed by an unseen tremor.

'He'll be beeping me soon,' she said. 'He misses me when I'm not there.'

'Do what you need to do, ma'am,' said Milo. 'We'll work *with* you.'

'Thank you. You're sweet. Oh, this is . . . oh . . .' She threw up her hands, laughed horribly.

'A few questions, ma'am. If you feel you can handle it—'

'I can handle anything,' she said, without conviction.

'Some of these questions are going to seem stupid, but they need to be asked.'

'Go ahead.'

'Can you think of anyone who'd want to harm Lauren?'

'No,' she said quickly. 'Everyone loved her. She was sugar.'

'No ex-boyfriends? Anyone with a personal grudge?'

'She never had a boyfriend.'

'Never?' said Milo.

Silence.

Jane Abbot said, 'She was going places. With her work, her education. Didn't have the time for relationships.'

'Did she tell you that?'

'She told Mel that. When she'd come over, he'd say "You're so gorgeous, doll. Why no stud on your arm?" Or something like that. She'd laugh and say she didn't have time to waste on a man, and Mel would make cracks about if only he were two hundred years younger . . . When— *If* he figures out what happened, it'll crush him.'

Her nose began to run, and I handed her a tissue.

'Her work,' said Milo.

'Modeling – she freelanced, saved up quite a bit of money. It allowed her to go back to school.'

'No time for boyfriends,' he said. 'Not a single one.'

'No one that I ever met.' Her eyes shifted to the floor, and I knew she was holding back. Aware of Lauren's real profession?

'Busy with her studies,' said Milo.

'Yes. She loved her classes. Loved psychology, planned to go all the way – get a PhD.' To me: 'You inspired her. She thought you were great.'

Milo said, 'In addition to classes, did she do any psychological work?'

'You mean like volunteering? I don't think so.'

'Volunteering, research.'

'No,' said Jane. 'Nothing that she mentioned.'

'What about travel?'

'She took off from time to time. But only for a day or two. Not a week – that's how I knew something was wrong. Andy – her roommate – knew it too. I could tell when I spoke to him. He was worried. He knew this was wrong.'

'Andy,' said Milo. 'Lauren and he get along pretty well?'

'Famously, like two peas. He finally got Lauren to spruce that place up. He has a great eye – most of them do.'

'Them?'

'Gays. They're clever that way. It was a smart arrangement. I told Lauren that. No hanky-panky and he had a great eye for decorating.'

'What did she say to that?'

'She agreed.'

'So,' he said, 'you're not aware of any conflict between her and Andy?'

She stared at Milo. '*Andy?* You can't be— No, no, ridiculous. He'd have no reason— He's more of a girl than a boy. They were like two sorority sisters.'

'No reason for conflict because no sexual tension.'

She blanched. 'Well, yes – aren't so many things like this . . . physical – men hurting women because they're . . . twisted?'

'You think this might've been a sexual crime?'

'Well, no,' she said. 'I don't think anything – what do I know? Was there— *Did* someone abuse her?'

'Nothing points that way, ma'am, but we'll have to wait for the coroner.'

'The coroner.' Jane began crying again. I was ready with another tissue, and Milo wrote in his pad. I hadn't seen him take it out.

'When Lauren went off for a few days, where'd she go, Mrs Abbot?'

She looked up. 'I don't really know.' Another eye shift, and something new had come into her voice. Wariness. Milo had to have heard it, but he kept his eyes on the pad.

'So she never told you details, just that she was taking off,' he said.

'Lauren was twenty-five, Detective.' Long bout of crying. 'Sorry. I was just thinking: She'll never be twenty-six . . . Lauren was a private person, Detective. I knew I had to respect that if I wanted to . . . keep getting along. We had . . . a history. Dr Delaware can fill in the details. Lauren was a really rebellious teenager. Even as a small child, if I pushed, she'd pull. If I said black, she'd insist it was white. Then my ex walked out on us and we got poor overnight and Lauren didn't want to know about that. She ran away when she was sixteen, never lived with me again. For years, I barely heard from her. I tried . . .' She looked at me for support.

I mustered a nod.

'We reconnected,' she went on. 'All those years of barely hearing from her, and she wanted to reconnect. I was afraid if I bugged her, I'd lose her. So . . . I didn't. And now . . . maybe if I'd . . .'

'No reason to blame yourself,' I said.

'No? Do you mean that, or is that something you just say to all the . . . whatever I am?'

Her head dropped into her hands. The nape of her neck was moist with sweat. I thought about the lunch that had sent Lauren home upset. Complaining Jane was trying to control her. At odds with Jane's speech about restraint.

She sat up suddenly, flushed, cold-eyed. 'What I'm trying to say is I was trying to get to know her again. To know my daughter. And I thought I was doing pretty good. And now . . . I should be able to tell you more but I can't. 'Cause I don't know – it's come to this and I don't *know*!'

'You're doing fine, ma'am.'

She laughed. 'Sure I am. My baby's dead and the one upstairs will be beeping me soon. I'm doing fantastic, just fantastic.'

'I'll do everything I ca—'

'Find whoever did this, Detective. Take this seriously and find him – not the way the cops took it like a joke when Lauren went missing—'

'Of cour—'

'Find him! So I can look him right in the eye. Then, I'll slice his balls off.'

117

ten

Milo questioned her a bit longer, honing in on Lauren's finances, any jobs she might've worked between seventeen and twenty-five, any business acquaintances.

'Modeling,' said Jane. 'That's the only work I know about.'

'Fashion modeling.'

Nod.

'How'd she get into that, ma'am?'

'I guess she just . . . applied and got work. She's – was a beautiful girl.'

'Did she ever mention an agent? Someone who got her work?'

Jane shook her head. She looked miserable. I've seen the same thing happen to other surviving parents. The pain of ignorance, realizing they'd raised strangers. 'She paid her own way, Detective, and that's more than you can say for a lot of kids.'

She unlaced her hands, glanced toward the elevator. 'I don't like it when he gets too quiet. As is, I barely sleep –

always worried about something happening to him.' Sickly smile. 'This is a bad dream, right? I'll wake up and find out you were never here.'

She sprang up, ran to the elevator. We saw ourselves out, trudged back to the Seville. From somewhere in the hills, an owl hooted. Plenty of owls in L.A. They eat rats.

Milo looked back at the house. 'So she knows nothing. Think it's true?'

'Hard to say. When you asked her about Lauren's travel, her eyes got jumpy. Also, when she began talking about Lauren's modeling. So maybe she knows – or suspects – about how Lauren really paid the rent.'

'Something else,' he said. 'She was quick to tell us about her prenup with Mel. But even if she did marry him for the loot, I can't see what that has to do with Lauren. Still, I think I'll follow the money trail – Lauren's finances. This one *smells* like money.'

'Sex and money,' I said.

'Is there a difference?'

I got behind the wheel and turned the key. The dash clock said 1:14 A.M. 'Too late for Lyle in Reseda?'

He stretched the seat belt over his paunch. 'Nah, never too late for fun.'

I drove back to Van Nuys Boulevard, turned right and picked up the 101 west at Riverside. The freeway had nearly emptied, and the exits before the Reseda Boulevard off-ramp zipped by like snapshots.

As I got off Milo said, 'Daddy and Mommy live pretty close. Wonder if they had any contact.'

'Mommy says no.'

'So near and yet so far – nice metaphor for alienation, huh? Not that I'm in any mood for that kind of crap.'

Lyle Teague's street was a scruffy, treeless stretch, south of Roscoe, smelling of infertile dirt and auto paint. Apartments that looked as if they'd been put up over the weekend mingled uneasily with charmless single-family boxes. Old pickups and cars that had rolled off the assembly line without much self-esteem crowded curbs and front lawns. Crushed beer cans and discarded fast-food containers clumped atop storm gutters. My slow cruise brought forth a chorus of canine outrage. Dogs that sounded eager to bite.

The Teague residence squatted on a third-acre table of what looked to be swept dirt. Eight-foot chain link gave the property a prison-yard feeling. Something in common with his ex-wife: They both liked being boxed off.

But this house was dark, no outdoor lighting. Milo used his penlight to sweep the property. The narrow beam made it a lengthy exercise, alighting on windows and doors, lingering long enough to arouse suspicion, but neither that nor the continuing hound concerto brought anyone out to check.

The flashlight continued to roam, found a GUARD DOG ON DUTY sign, but no animal materialized to back up the warning. A chain heavy enough to moor a yacht tied the gate to the fence. A fist-sized padlock completed the welcome. The house was a basic box with a face as flat as Spike's but none of my pooch's personality. Pale stucco on top, dark wood siding below. A few feet away sat a prefab carport. A long-bed truck with grossly oversized tires and chromium pipes rested in front of the opening. Too tall to fit inside.

'No squawk box, no bell,' said Milo, scrutinizing the gate.

'Different tax bracket than Jane's.'

'Could make a fellow irritable.' He rattled the chain, called out, 'Hello?' got no response, pulled out his cell phone, dialed, waited. Five rings, then a voice on the other end barked loud. I couldn't make out the words, but the tone was clear.

'Mr Teague— Sir, please don't hang up— This is Detective Sturgis of the Los Angeles Police Force . . . Yes, sir, it's for real, it's about your daughter . . . Lauren . . . Yes, sir, I'm afraid I am . . . Sir, please don't hang up— This isn't a prank . . . Please come outside, we're right in front of your house . . . Yes, sir, at the gate— Please, sir. Thank you, sir.'

He pocketed the phone. 'Woke him up and he's not pleased.'

We waited. Two minutes, three, five. Milo muttered, 'Tobacco Road,' checked his watch.

Still no lights on in the little house. Finally, the door opened and I saw the outline of a figure standing in the opening.

Milo called out, 'Mr Teague? We're over here.'

No answer. Twenty seconds passed. Then: 'Yeah, I see you.' Gravel voice. Thicker than I remembered, but I didn't remember much about Lyle Teague. 'Whyn't you show some ID?'

Milo flashed the badge and waved it. The skimpy moon provided little help, and I wondered what Teague could see from this far.

'Do it again.'

Milo's black brows rose. 'Yes, sir.' Another wave.

'How do I know it's not a Tijuana special?'

'Department's not that hard up, sir,' said Milo, forcing himself to keep his voice light.

Teague took a few steps closer. Silent steps. Bare feet, I could see them now. Saw the barrel of his bare chest. Wearing nothing but shorts. One hand tented his eyes, the other remained pinioned to his side. 'I've got a shotgun, here, so if you're not who you claim to be, this is fair warning. If you are, don't lose your cool, I'm just protecting myself.'

Before the speech was complete, Milo had stepped in front of me. His hand was under his jacket, and his neck was taut. 'Put the shotgun down, sir. Go back inside your house, phone the West L.A. division at a number I'm going to give you, and check me out: Milo Sturgis, Detective Three, Homicide.' He recited his badge number, then the station's exchange.

Teague's shotgun arm flexed, but the weapon remained sheathed in darkness.

Milo said, 'Mr Teague, put the shotgun down, now. We don't want any accidents.'

'Homicide.' Teague sounded uncertain.

'That's right, sir.'

'You're saying . . . This is about Lauren? You're saying she . . . ?'

'I'm afraid so, Mr Teague.'

'Shit. What the hell *happened*?'

'We need to sit down and talk, sir. *Please* put down the shotgun.'

Teague's gun arm remained pressed to his side. He stumbled closer, catching just enough moonlight to limn his flesh. But the light didn't reach above his shoulders, and he turned into a headless man: white torso, arms, legs, making their way toward us unsteadily.

'Fuck,' whispered Milo, stepping back. 'Put the gun down, sir. Now.'

'Lauren . . .' Teague stopped, spit, kneeled. Placed the shotgun on the ground, straightened, shot both arms up at the sky. Laughed and spit again. Close enough so I could hear the *plink* of saliva hitting dirt.

'Lauren— Lord, Lord, this is *fucked*.'

He made his way over to the gate, head down, arms stiff and swinging. Reaching into a shorts pocket, he took a long time to produce a key, tried to spring the padlock, fumbled around the hole, cursed, began punching the chain link.

Milo said, 'Let me help you with that, sir.'

Teague ignored him and gave the lock another stab, with no more success. Breathing hard. I could smell his sweat, vinegary, overlaid with the rotted malt of too many beers. He pounded the fence again, cursed raggedly. Getting a closer look at him sprang a memory latch in my head. Same face, but his features had coarsened and his eyes had regressed to piggish slits. A clot of scar tissue weighed down on the right eye. Still bearded with a full head of long, wavy hair, but the strands were gray and drawn back in a ponytail that dangled over one beefy shoulder, and the once-barbered facial pelt was an unruly bramble.

As he attacked the fence his biceps bunched and his chest swelled. Big, slablike muscles but slackened – drained of bulk, like goatskins emptied of wine.

'Give that to me,' said Milo.

Teague ceased punching, stared at the lock, panted, tried once more to fit the key into the hole. His knuckles were bloody, and wild hairs, pale and brittle as tungsten filament, had come loose from the ponytail. The shotgun, lying in the dirt like a felled branch, might've made him feel younger, sharper.

Finally, he succeeded in springing the lock, ripped the chain free, and flung it behind him. It clattered in the dirt, and he yanked the gate open, holding his hands out defensively, letting us know he didn't want to be comforted.

'Inside,' he said, hooking a thumb at his house. 'Fuck if I'm going to let any of these bastards see it.' Squinting at me, he stared, and I prepared myself for recognition. But he turned his back on both of us and began marching toward his front door.

We walked along with him.

Milo said, 'By the bastards you mean the neighbors?'

Teague grunted.

'Neighbor troubles?' asked Milo.

'Why do you think I came out carrying? If the assholes

were human, they'd be neighbors. They're fucking animals. Couple of months ago they poisoned my Rottweiler. Tossed in meat laced with antifreeze, the damn dog got kidney failure and started shitting green. Since the summer we've had three drive-bys. *All* those shitty apartments crammed with low life. Fucking wetbacks, cholos, gangbangers— I'm not prejudiced, hired plenty of them in my day, for the most part they worked their asses off. But that scum, over there?' His lower jaw shot out and beard hairs bristled. 'I'm living in a war zone – this used to be a decent neighborhood.'

The shotgun was in reach. Milo got to it first, emptied the weapon, pocketed the shells.

Teague laughed. 'Don't worry, I'm not blowing anyone's head off. Yet.' He stared at me again, looked puzzled, turned away.

'Yet,' said Milo. 'That's not too comforting, sir.'

'It's not my goddamn job to comfort you.' Teague stopped, placed his hands on his hips, spit into the dirt, resumed walking. The shorts rode lower, and strands of white pubic hair curled above his waistline. I remembered the way he'd dressed to showcase his body. 'Your job is to find out the low-life motherfucker who killed my daughter and bust his fuckin' ass.'

'Agreed,' said Milo. 'Any suggestions in that regard?'

Teague halted again. 'What're you getting at?'

'Any specific low-life motherfucker in mind?'

'Nah,' said Teague. 'I'm just talking logic . . . How'd they— What did they do to her?'

'She was shot, sir.'

'Bastards . . . Nah, I can't tell you a damn thing. Lauren never told *me* a damn thing.' Wolfish grin. 'See, we didn't *relate*. She thought I was a piece of shit and told me so whenever she had the opportunity.'

We reached the house. The door was still open. Reaching in, Teague switched on a light. A bare bulb hung from the raw fir ceiling of a twelve-by-twelve living room paneled in rough knotty pine. Red linoleum floors, faded hooked rug, brown-and-black-plaid sofa, coffee table hosting a Budweiser six-pack and five empties. A green tweed La-Z-Boy faced a big-screen TV. Illegal cable converter on top. Very little space to walk. Two openings along the rear wall, one leading to a cramped kitchen, the other exposing a chunky corridor with two doors to the right. The smell of must and lager and salted nuts, but no clutter. The carpet was old but clean, the linoleum rubbed dull. Different tax bracket.

Teague said, 'You can sit if you want, I'm staying on my feet.' Standing next to the recliner, he folded his arms across his chest. The scar tissue over his eye was the color of cheap margarine. A hairline scar ran from the corner of the socket down to his jaw. The right eye was filmy. Not inert, but lazier than its mate.

Milo and I remained standing. Teague looked us over, tilting his head so his left eye caught a full view of my face. 'Do I *know* you?'

'Alex Delaware. Lauren was my patient—'

'The *shrink*?' His jaw shoveled. 'Oh, fuck – what are *you* doing here?'

Milo said, 'Dr Delaware's a police consultant. In the case of your—'

One of the hallway doors opened and a woman's voice called out, 'Lyle, everything okay?'

'Go back inside,' Teague barked. The door shut quietly. 'Consultant? What the hell does *that* mean? You're saying you know something about Lauren? She's been seeing you again?'

'No,' I said. 'Lauren went missing and your ex-wife called me because she'd heard I had police contacts—'

'Police contacts.' Teague grabbed the bottom of his beard, twisted, let go. To Milo: 'What *is* this bullshit?'

'Just what the doctor said. Now, I'd like to ask you—'

'Missing?' said Teague. 'For how long?'

'Several days.'

'From where?'

'Her apartment.'

'Where's that? She never told me where she was bunking down.'

'Hauser Street, in L.A.'

'She used to live all over,' said Teague. 'The streets. After she ran away. She got wild – which any idiot could see coming.'

'Where on the streets, sir?'

'Hell if I know. Jane used to call me up to go looking for her, I could never find her. Hauser . . . That where it happened?'

'She was found on the Westside,' said Milo. 'Back of a furniture store on Sepulveda. Someone shot her and left her body in an alley.'

Spitting out the details matter-of-fact, watching Teague's reaction.

Teague said, 'West L.A. We used to live there, over near Rancho Park.' He began to draw himself up. Gave up and slumped. 'This is shit. My life can't be this fucked up.'

The door opened again, and the hallway light went on. A woman stepped out wearing a long blue Dodgers T-shirt and nothing else. Seeing us, she threw a protective hand over her belly, ducked back inside, reappeared seconds later wearing acid-washed jeans under the same shirt.

'Lyle? Something the matter?'

'I said *go* inside.'

The woman stared at us. 'What's going on?' Bleary eyes, faint southern inflection. A good deal younger than Teague – maybe thirty, with long, limp, brown hair, grainy skin, wide hips, dimpled knees. Full face distorted by confusion. Well-proportioned but forgettable features. As a child she'd probably been adorable.

'*Lyle?*'

Teague swiveled fast and faced her. 'They're the goddamn *police*. Lauren got herself *murdered* tonight.'

The woman's hand slapped over her mouth. 'Oh my God— Omi*god*!'

'Go back to bed.'

'Omigod—'

Milo extended his hand. 'Detective Sturgis, ma'am.'

The woman blubbered, shivered, hugged herself. Took the hand. 'Tish. Tish Teague—'

'*Patricia*,' corrected her husband. 'Keep it down. Don't wake up the kids.'

'The kids,' said Tish Teague, dully. 'You don't need them, do you?'

'Oh, Jesus,' said Teague. 'Why the hell would he need *them*? Get back in and go to sleep. It doesn't concern you. You and Lauren had nothing, you can't do any good.'

The young woman's lips trembled. 'I'll be here if you need me, Lyle.'

'Yeah, yeah – go, git.'

'Nice to meet you,' said Tish Teague.

'Bye, ma'am,' said Milo.

Biting her lip, she fled.

'I left Lauren's mother for her,' said Teague, laughing. 'Met her on a construction job. She was this nineteen-year-old piece of ass, drove one of the roach coaches. Now we got two kids.'

'How old are your children?' said Milo.

'Six and four.'

'Girls, boys?'

'Two girls. When you called and said something happened to my daughter, I was thinking one of them. That's what confused me.' He shook his head. 'Lauren. Didn't see much of Lauren.'

'When's the last time you did see her?'

'Long time,' said Teague. 'Real long time. She held it against me.'

'Held what?'

'Everything. The divorce, bad luck – life. Anything

shitty was my fault. She told me so. Called me up a few years ago and told me I was a selfish motherfucker who didn't deserve to live.' Sick smile. 'Because I didn't want to stick around with that cold thing called Jane.' He hitched up his shorts. 'Our marriage was crap from day one.' To me: '*That* was the problem, *that's* what screwed Lauren up. *Us.* Jane and me. The whole thing – bringing Lauren to you – was a goddamn con. My wife's idea. 'Cause she doesn't like to face reality. Like Lauren was gonna straighten out, living in our shitty environment. She – Jane – wasn't gonna be honest with you, she was just conning you, pal. One big happy family. That's why I ended it. We were wasting *your* time and *my* money. Load of bullshit.'

Hands on hips again. His good eye bore into mine. My silence made his neck tendons fan.

'Why's he have to be here?' he demanded of Milo.

'I want to solve your daughter's murder. Dr Delaware's been helpful to us on a lot of cases. If it's a big deal, I can have him wait in the car. But I'd think you'd be interested in helping us get down to brass tacks.'

Teague's eyes brightened. 'My daughter. Every time you say that I flash to Brittany and Shayla.' To me: 'You haven't changed much, you know? Got that young face – smooth. I remember your hands, man – real smooth. Nice easy life, huh?' Back to Milo: 'Brass tacks, huh? Well, I can't give you any kind of tack at all. After the divorce, I didn't see Lauren for . . . must be what? Four, five years. Then she drops in one night, tells me I'm a piece of shit, Merry Christmas.'

131

'She visited on Christmas?'

'Deck the goddamn halls— Yeah, it was four years, Shayla'd been born a few months before – October. Lauren musta found out somehow, though I don't know how. 'Cause she came by, said she wanted to see the baby, she'd never seen Brittany and she was already two, she had a right to see her sisters. A *right*. She brought gifts for the girls. I guess cussing me out was her Christmas present to me.'

Phil Harnsberger's party had taken place four years ago in November. The next day Lauren had come to my office, talked about her father remarrying. No mention of her half sisters, but soon after she'd come to meet them.

Moving around to the front of the La-Z-Boy, Teague sat down on the edge. The chair rocked, and he stilled the movement by bracing his feet. 'Go ahead, sit, there's no fleas.'

We settled on the plaid couch.

'Four years ago,' said Milo. 'Did she visit again?'

'Not till a year ago,' said Teague. 'Christmas again, same damn thing. She just showed up with presents. We were in the middle of putting up the tree. Presents for the kids, not me and Patricia. She made that clear. Patricia never did a thing to her, so I don't know what she had against her, but she wouldn't give her the time of day, just blanked her out like she didn't exist. She brought armloads of shit – toys, candy, you name it. Walked right past me and Patricia and headed for the girls. I could've kicked her out, but what the hell, it was

Christmas. The girls didn't know who the hell she was, but they loved those toys and candy. Patricia offered her a piece of pie, she said no, thanks, I went to get a beer, and when I came back, she was gone.'

'Any other visits?'

'No – wait, yeah. Once more, a few months after – Easter. Same thing, toys, crapola for the kids. These huge chocolate bunnies and some kids' dresses from an expensive place in Beverly Hills – some French shit.'

'No contact since last Easter?'

'Nope.' Teague scowled. 'Both times she turned the kids hyper, it took days to settle them down.' Looking to me for confirmation.

I said, 'Overstimulation.'

His good eye winked. 'Hey, that's a good one.'

Milo said, 'During those three visits, did she talk to you at all, tell you what she was up to?'

'Nah, just a fuck-you look, where are the kids, walk right past me, dump the gifts, good-bye.'

'Nothing about her life? Not a single detail.'

'She bragged, some,' said Teague.

'About what?'

'College plans. Having money. She was dressed expensive, especially the last time – Easter. Fancy suit, fancy shoes. I had my theories about where she was getting money, but I kept my mouth shut. Why start up?'

'What kind of theories, sir?'

'You know.'

Milo shrugged, gave an innocent look.

Teague eyed him skeptically. 'You've gotta know – the wild life.'

'Illegal activities?'

'Whoring,' said Teague. 'She got in trouble for that a few years back. You don't know about it, huh?'

'The investigation has just begun.'

'Well, start by checking your own goddamn records. Lauren got busted for hooking when she was nineteen. Reno, Nevada. Got her ass thrown in jail with no money on her, called me to make her bail – no hide or hair of her for years, and she calls *me*. Then nothing for a couple of years till that Christmas, and all of a sudden she's a big shot and I'm shit.'

Making no mention of the arrest as one of Gretchen Stengel's girls. The Westside Madam's name had hit the news big time, but none of her call girls had been exposed. Nor had the clients.

Milo scrawled in his pad. 'So there was another contact before the Christmas visit.'

'I wasn't counting phone calls,' said Teague.

'Any other calls?'

'Nope.'

'Did you send her bail money?'

'No way. I said forget it, you made your own bed, now sleep in it. She cussed me out and hung up.'

Teague snorted. 'She tried to bullshit me, told me the whole thing had been a mistake, she'd been working at one of the casinos, escorting rich guys, nothing illegal, the cops had "overreacted." She said she just got caught with no cash on her, all she needed to do was get home to her credit cards, she'd fix it if I'd float her the dough. Credit cards – letting me know she was living the high life and here I was stuck, recuperating.'

'You were sick?' said Milo.

Teague touched the scar clump. 'I used to have my own electrical business, was doing a job out in Calabasas. Someone fucked up, I ended up duking it out with a mass of rebar. I was in a coma for a week, had double vision for months. I still get headaches.' Glancing at the beer cans. 'I sued, tied myself up for years, the lawyers took most of it. Then *she* tells me she's pregnant.' Cocking his head toward the bedroom. 'I was on painkillers, halfway groggy most of the time, and Lauren calling out of nowhere, whining about the police over*reacting*.'

Defiance spiked his voice. Even in death Lauren pushed his buttons.

'How'd she make her bail?' said Milo.

'How should I know?' Teague shook his head, picked something out of his beard. 'I could've thrown her out the first Christmas, but I wanted to be decent. She might not've considered herself my daughter. But I was too mature to let that get to me.'

'She said she didn't consider herself your daughter?'

Teague laughed. 'That's just one of the things she unloaded on me. Big truckload of shit, and I just sat there, being cool. That's the way I always was with her – when she was a kid. She'd open up a big mouth and I'd just shine her on.'

Long silence.

Teague said, 'Lauren and I, we never— She was always a handful. From day one she always tried to make me feel . . . like an idiot. Everything I said and did was insensitive. And stupid.' He placed his palm over his heart. 'Lauren was— Sometimes there're people you just can't get along with, no matter what the hell you do. I was hoping maybe one day she'd grow up, understand, maybe she'd start being . . . polite.'

He shook his head. Moisture in his eyes, for the first time. 'Least I got two others . . . They love me, those two. No shit outta their mouths— You really have no idea who did it?'

'Not yet,' said Milo. 'Why?'

'No why. I was just thinking it couldn't be any big mystery. Look for a low life, pal. 'Cause Lauren chose a low-life lifestyle. Fancy clothes and all. Last time she was here, bragging about enrolling in college, I had my doubts.'

'About what?'

'About her being a student. I figured it was another one of her cons.' To me: 'She lied since she got out of diapers – whether you saw it or not, that's the truth. When she was four, five years old she'd point to red, tell you it was blue, just about convince you. To me, she didn't look like a student, never seen a student dress like that, flash all that jewelry.'

'Expensive stuff,' said Milo.

'To my eye, but what the hell do I know – I don't shop on Rodeo. Her mother liked all that crap too, used to lean *hard* on my checkbook. I had a good business back then, but who wants to blow it on that crap?' He pitched forward. Smiled. 'She married an old guy. My ex. Senile old bag of shit. She's soaking him for his dough, waiting for him to croak— Did you tell her about Lauren yet?'

'Just came from her place, sir.'

Teague's smile died. Suspicion slitted his eyes. 'She probably told you I was an asshole.'

'We didn't discuss you,' said Milo. 'Only Lauren. And by the way, Lauren was enrolled at the U.'

'Yeah? Well, look where that got her.' Teague sat back in the recliner. The footrest shot out, and he stretched his legs. The soles of his feet were black and callused. He breathed in, let the air out. Beneath his rib cage his belly swelled. 'I know you think I'm an asshole. 'Cause I'm not faking out that everything was cool between me and Lauren. But at least I'm honest. Okay, so Lauren was in school. But that doesn't mean she wasn't still hanging around with low life. You won't hear that from my ex – she's living in a dreamworld, Lauren was some angel— How'd she take it?'

'Hard,' said Milo. 'Any contact between you and your ex?'

'Same as Lauren. Every so often, she used to call, throw it in my face.'

'When was the last time?'

Teague thought. 'Years ago.' His smile was reborn. 'It's not like *she's* gonna come visit the kids. That pisses her off – my having kids. She and I tried real hard to have a bunch and all we could squeeze out was Lauren. Clear to see it was her problem— Anyway, check out Lauren's lifestyle, that's my suggestion. She was living the life, riding high on the wave. But it wasn't for free.'

'Few things are,' said Milo.

'Wrong,' said Teague. '*Nothing* is.'

eleven

'**A** prince among men,' said Milo.

I was driving east on Ventura Boulevard. Blackened storefronts, bare sidewalks, a breeze had kicked up, and scraps of litter danced above the cement. Warm breeze. Unseasonal winter.

'He hated her, didn't he, Alex?'

'You consider him a suspect?' I said.

'Can't eliminate him. Am I the only one who picked up nuances of paranoia?'

'Unhappy man,' I said. 'Lots of anger. But he didn't try to soft-pedal. Doesn't that imply nothing to hide?'

'Or he's trying to be clever, pull some kind of stupid double bluff. What a family. The more I learn, the sorrier I feel for Lauren.'

I knew what was taking place: Lauren's corpse had begun as business as usual, inanimate as the mountain of forms he was forced to fill out on every case. Enlarging her humanity brought out his empathy. It's happened to him on most of the cases we've worked together.

I said, 'You didn't ask him where he was the night Lauren was killed.'

'I don't know when she was killed -- waiting till the coroner gives me an estimate. Also, there was no sense threatening him right off. If nothing else slam-dunks, he'll get a recontact. Maybe I can pay him a morning visit, see what he's like when he's not beered up.'

'And the shotgun's not within arm's reach.'

'Yeah, that was fun, wasn't it? Loose cannon like that having access to a double-barrel. Just what the Founding Fathers had in mind . . . Wifey number two seemed quite the sheep. Think he slaps her around?'

'He dominates her.'

'I wonder if Lyle and Jane had violent stuff going on when they were hitched – Jane kept saying he was mean. Maybe something else Lauren was exposed to. That never came out when you treated her?'

'She complained about them but never mentioned violence. But the treatment wasn't much.'

'Two sessions.' He rubbed his face. 'Twenty-five years old and what did she have to show for it besides a nifty wardrobe? . . . People and their garbage. Some jobs you and I've got.'

'Hey,' I said. 'Sure beats being rich and relaxed.'

He laughed. 'You won't catch me admitting this again, but your gig just might be tougher than mine.'

'Why's that?'

'I know what people are. You try to change 'em.'

As I turned onto Laurel Canyon, he phoned the officer

at Lauren's apartment, found out Andrew Salander hadn't returned.

I said, 'He works the night shift.'

'You up for The Cloisters?'

'Sure,' I said. 'One of my favorite spots.'

He laughed again. 'Yeah, I'll bet. Ever been to a gay bar?'

'You took me to one,' I said.

'I don't remember that. When?'

'Years ago,' I said. 'Tiny little place over in Studio City. Disco music, serious drinking, lots of guys who didn't look at all like you. Past University City – back of an auto body shop.'

'Oh yeah,' he said. 'The Fender. Closed down a long time ago – I actually took you there?'

'Right after our first case together – the Handler murder. The way I figured it, some friendship rapport was developing and you were still nervous.'

'About what?'

'Being gay. You'd already made the grand confession. I didn't get overtly repulsed, but you probably figured I needed more testing.'

'Oh, come on,' he said. 'Testing you for what?'

'Tolerance. Could I really handle it.'

'Why am I not remembering any of this?'

'Advanced middle age,' I said. 'I can describe the room precisely: aluminum ceiling, black walls, Donna Summer on tape loop, guys going off in pairs.'

'Whoa,' he said. Then nothing.

A few miles later he said, 'You weren't *overtly* repulsed. Meaning?'

'Meaning, sure, it threw me. I grew up with sissies getting beat up on the school yard and "fag" as acceptable speech. I never pounded on anyone, but I never stepped in to stop it either. When I started working, my practice emphasized traumatized kids, and homosexuality never came up much. You were the first gay person I'd ever known socially. You and Rick are still the only gay people I know in depth. And sometimes I'm not sure about you.'

He smiled. 'Aluminum ceilings . . . guys who didn't look like me, huh? So who'd they look like?'

'More like Andrew Salander.'

'There you go,' he said. 'I am the great individualist.'

The Cloisters was on Hacienda just north of Santa Monica, notched unobtrusively into the gray side wall of a two-story building. It was nearly three A.M., but unlike the postnuclear silence of the Valley, the streets here were alive, lit by a steady stream of headlights, sidewalk cafés still serving a garrulous clientele, the pavement crowded with pedestrians – mostly, but not exclusively, male. West Hollywood was one of the first L.A. neighborhoods to earn itself a nightlife. Now people emerge for after-dark strolls in Beverly Hills, Melrose, Westwood. One day, Los Angeles may grow up and become a real city.

I found a parking space half a block up, and we walked to the front door. No bouncer on duty and we stepped right in. I'd allowed myself the luxury of prediction and expected the place to be stone walls, refectory windows, gothic gloom. It turned out to be off-white plaster, recessed lighting dimmed to soft-and-easy, a mahogany-and-black-granite bar with a brass rail and beige suede stools, a few booths along the opposite wall. Light classical music eased from unseen speakers, and the conversation from the fifteen or so men inside was low and relaxed. Casually but well-dressed men in their thirties and forties. Shrimp and meatball bar snacks, toothpicks sporting colored cellophane frizz. But for the fact that there were only men, it could've been an upscale lounge in any slick suburb.

Andrew Salander was easy to spot, working alone behind the bar, wiping down the granite, refilling glasses, attending gregariously to half a dozen patrons. His dress duds were a pale blue button-down shirt under a white-and-blue-striped apron. We were right in his face when he noticed us – first me, then Milo, back to me, back to Milo. One of the drinkers saw the scared-animal heat in his eyes and turned toward us with hostile curiosity. Milo leaned on the bar and nodded at him, and the man returned to his Scotch.

'Mr Sturgis?' said Salander.

'Hi, Andy. Anyone to cover for you?'

'Uh . . . Tom's on break— Hold on, I'll get him.' Salander ran through a rear door and returned with a tall young man dressed in a similar shirt and apron, holding a cigarette. Tom stubbed out his light and put on a smile, and Salander came around through Dutch doors at the other end of the bar.

'Please tell me this isn't business,' he said to Milo. 'Please.'

Milo eased him toward the door. Waited to say 'Sorry,' until we were outside.

Salander wept. 'It can't be— I can't believe it, why would anyone *hurt* her?'

'I was hoping you might be able to help me with that, Andy.'

'I can't— Dr Delaware already knows that. I already told him everything I knew – didn't I, Doctor?'

I said, 'Is there anything else you might remember?'

'What? You think I was holding back?'

'Back when we thought Lauren was coming back, I can see your not wanting to violate her privacy. But now . . .'

'That's true, I was being discreet. But there's still nothing else I can tell you.'

'Lauren gave you no hint of where she was going?' said Milo.

'No. It wasn't that weird – her taking off. I already told the doctor she'd done it other times.'

'For a day or two.'

'Yes.'

'This was a week.'

'I know, but . . .' said Salander. 'I wish I could help.'

'Those short trips,' said Milo. 'Did you ever have any reason to think they were for anything other than rest and relaxation?'

'What do you mean?'

'Did Lauren ever mention another reason for traveling?'

'No. Why?'

'Okay, Andy, let's backtrack to the last time you saw her.'

'Last Sunday – a week ago,' said Salander. 'I didn't sleep well, got up around noon and Lo was in the kitchen.'

'How was she dressed?'

'Slacks, silk blouse – casual elegant, as always. She rarely wore jeans.'

'Did you guys talk?'

'Not much – just small talk. We had a light lunch before she left. Eggs and toast – I can eat breakfast any time of day. She left shortly after – I'd say one, one-thirty.'

'But she didn't say where.'

'I assumed the U.'

'Her research job.'

'That's what I figured.'

'On a Sunday?'

'She'd worked other Sundays, Detective Sturgis.'

'But this time she didn't take her car.'

'How would I know that unless I followed her down-stairs?'

'And you didn't.'

'No, of course not—'

'When did you notice she'd left the car?'

'When I went to get my own car.'

'Which was?' said Milo.

'Later that evening, when I left for work – around seven-thirty.'

'And what did you think when you saw Lauren's car?'

'I didn't – didn't think much, one way or the other.'

'Was that typical, Andy? Lauren not taking her car?'

'Not really. I just— It wasn't on my mind. I can't say I even consciously noticed it. When I got home she wasn't there, but that wasn't unusual either. She was often gone by morning. We were on different biorhythms – sometimes days would pass before we bumped into one another. I started to get a little concerned by Wednesday or so, but you know . . . She was an adult. I figured she had a reason for doing the things she did. Was I wrong?'

'About her having reasons?'

'About not doing something sooner. I mean, what could I have done?'

Milo didn't reply.

Salander said, 'I just wish— I feel sick— This is unbelievable.'

'Back to Sunday, Andy. What did you do after Lauren left?'

'Um, tried to go back to sleep, couldn't, got up and went shopping over at the Beverly Center. I thought I'd buy some shirts, but I didn't find anything, so I saw a movie – *Happy, Texas*. Hilarious. Have you seen it?'

Milo shook his head.

Salander said, 'You should see it. Really funny—'

'What'd you do after shopping?'

'Came back, had some dinner, got dressed for work, came here. The next day I slept late. Till three. Why are you asking me all this? You can't seriously think . . .'

'Routine questions,' said Milo.

'That's so TV,' said Salander. 'So Jack *Webb*.' Trying to smile, but his face had lost tone, as if someone had yanked out the bones.

'Okay, Andy,' said Milo. 'There are police officers at your apartment. It's going to be disruptive for a while. Legally, I don't need your permission to search, but I'd like to know that I have your cooperation.'

'Sure. Of course – you mean my room too?'

'If the search does carry over to your room, would you have a problem with that?'

Salander kicked one shoe with the other. 'I mean, I wouldn't want my stuff trashed, or anything.'

'I'll do it myself, Andy. Make sure everything gets put back in place.'

'Sure – but can I ask why, Mr Sturgis? What does my room have to do with anything?'

'I need to be thorough.'

Salander's narrow shoulders rose and fell. 'I guess. Why not, I have nothing to hide. Nothing's ever going to be the same, is it? Can I go back to work now?'

'When do you get off shift?'

'Four – then I clean up.'

'The officers may still be there when you arrive – you are planning to come home?'

'Where else would I go? At least for now.'

'For now?'

'I don't know if I can afford the place by myself . . . Oh, God, this is just so nauseating— Did she suffer?'

'I don't have the forensic details yet.'

'Who would do this?' said Salander. 'What kind of

twisted mind— Oh, Mr Sturgis, I feel as if everything's unraveling.'

Milo said, 'Yeah, it's rough.' He looked out at the traffic on Santa Monica, eyes unreadable. Then a glance at me.

I said, 'Andrew, that lunch Lauren had with her mother, when she said she didn't want to be controlled? Do you have any idea what she meant?'

'No. And when she was upset at Mrs A, she said she knew her mother loved her.'

'What about her father? Did he ever come up?'

'No, she never talked about him – refused to. Just clammed up the first time I brought him up, so I never did *that* again. It was pretty obvious she had no use for him.'

'But she never said why.'

Headshake. 'There are so many reasons, though, aren't there,' he said. 'So many men who screw up fatherhood.'

'So,' I said, 'you have no idea what the control issue was?'

'I just thought it was one of those family tension things, you know. I mean it's not as if she told me about any big festering Jerry Springer thing.'

Salander rubbed the back of his head against the wall. 'This is horrible, I hate this.'

'Hate what, Andy?'

'Talking about Lauren in the past tense – thinking about her suffering. Can I get back to work?'

'The show must go on?' said Milo.

Salander froze. 'That was unkind, Mr Sturgis. I *cared* about her, I really did. We cared for each other, loved to hang out together, but we didn't – *she* didn't confide in me. Can I help it if she didn't *confide*? What I told the doctor about that lunch is all that I remember. She came back and looked miffed, didn't want to talk about it, and I tried to get her to open up. But she really didn't.'

'What did she say – as closely as you can remember?' I said.

'Something to the effect that she'd come this far on her own and wouldn't be controlled – that's it. Come to think about it, she might not have even said controlled by Mrs A, specifically. I just assumed that's who she was talking about, because it was Mrs A she'd just had lunch with.' He sidestepped closer to The Cloisters' front door.

'Let's get back to that research job,' said Milo. 'What else do you know about it?'

'Something to do with psychology – or maybe I'm assuming that, too. I'm so shook up, I don't even know what I *know*.'

'When did the job start?'

Salander thought. 'Soon after the quarter started – so maybe two, three months ago. Or maybe even before the quarter – I can't swear to anything.'

'Was it a five-day-a-week job?' said Milo.

'No, it was irregular. Sometimes she'd work every day of the week, then she'd have days off. But I really wasn't paying attention to her schedule. Half the time she was up and around, I was sleeping.'

'What else did she tell you about the job?'

'Just that she enjoyed it.'

'Nothing else?'

'Nope.'

'Did she mention who she worked for? What the project was?'

'No, just that she enjoyed it. I'm sure you can find out at the U.'

'That's the problem, Andy,' said Milo. 'We can't seem to find any trace of her working at the U.'

Salander's mouth dropped open. 'How can that be? I'm sure it's some mistake – she definitely told me it was on campus. That I do remember.'

'Well,' said Milo.

'Why would she make up something like that?'

'Good question, Andy.'

'My . . . You think *the job* had something to do with . . .'

'I'm not saying anything, Andy. But when people don't tell the truth . . .'

'Oh, Lauren,' said Salander. He put his back to the wall of the building, cupped his hand over his eyes. 'Oh, my.'

'What is it?' said Milo.

'I'm all alone now.'

During the drive to Hauser and Sixth, Milo ran Salander's name through the files. One traffic ticket last year, no wants or warrants, no criminal record. Milo closed his eyes, and I realized how numb I felt – deadened and tired and marginal. We cruised the rest of the way in silence, gliding through city streets stripped of light and humanity.

Two squad cars and a crime-scene van were parked outside Lauren's building. A uniform guarded the entrance. Another was stationed upstairs. Someone had opened the door to apartment 4. Inside the living room a young black woman kneeled and dusted and scraped.

'Loretta,' said Milo.

'Morning, Milo.'

'Yeah, guess it is. Anything?'

'Lots of prints, as usual. So far, no blood, and the only semen's on the roommate's sheets. Nothing looks disturbed.'

'The roommate,' said Milo.

'Did both bedrooms,' said the tech. 'Was that okay?'

'Perfect.'

'Nothing's perfect,' said Loretta. 'Not even me.'

We entered Salander's room first. Midnight blue velvet walls and shabby-looking tapestry drapes turned the stingy space gloomy. A black iron queen-sized bed canopied by billows of what looked like cheesecloth took up most of the floor. A fake Persian rug left only a foot-wide border of scuffed board. Lining the ceiling were more of the gilded moldings I'd seen in the living room. A small TV and VCR perched atop a pale blue bureau decoupaged with pink cabbage roses. Replicas of Russian icons and filigreed crucifixes hung on the wall along with a white-framed photo of Salander and a stolid-looking couple in their fifties. At the bottom of the frame, someone had written in black marker: 'Mom and

Dad, Bloomington, Ind. "The Old Country".'

In the top drawer of the bureau, Milo found neatly folded clothing, tissues and eyedrops, a box of disposable contact lenses, six packets of condoms, and a passbook from Washington Mutual Bank.

'Four hundred bucks,' he said, flipping pages. 'Little Andy's highest balance for the year is fifteen hundred.' He ran through the book several times. 'Every two weeks he deposits nine hundred – gotta be his take home. On the fifteenth, he withdraws six hundred – the rent – spends around eight or so. Leaving a hundred or so in savings, but it looks like he eventually spends that too.'

'Tight budget,' I said. 'He will have trouble making the rent by himself.'

He frowned and replaced the bankbook. 'Giving him a legit reason to cut out.'

'You're worried about him? I noticed you did ask him about time and place.'

'No specific reason to worry,' he said. 'But no reason not to either. He's the last person to see her alive, and that's always interesting.'

Opening the closet door, he ran his hands over pressed jeans and khakis, two pairs of black slacks, several blue button-down shirts like the one Salander wore at the bar, a black leather jacket. Black oxfords, brown loafers, Nikes, and one pair of tan demiboots on the floor. Nothing on the top shelf. Plenty of empty space.

'Okay,' said Milo. 'On to the main event.'

Lauren's room was larger than Salander's by half. Bare

oak floors, walls painted the palest of yellows, and a low, narrow single bed with no headboard increased the feeling of space. Her dresser was a white, three-drawer affair. Flanking it on each side were low teak bookcases with the slightly askew stance of self-assembly. Hardback books filled every shelf.

Next to the bed was a matching teak desk with a built-in file drawer. Milo began there, and it didn't take long to find what he was looking for.

'Smith Barney brokerage account. Out of town – Seattle.'

'Wanting things private?' I said. Thinking: Lauren had thrived on secrets. Kept everything segmented.

He turned pages, ran his finger down columns. 'She kept some loose cash in a money market, the rest is in high-yield mutual funds . . . Well, well, well, look at this: quite a different league from little Andy. She's put away three hundred forty thousand dollars and some change in . . . a little over four years . . . First deposit is a hundred grand, four years ago, December . . . Then fifty a year for the next three – last one was three weeks ago. Nice and steady – wonder where it came from.'

I do great with tips.

He opened another drawer. 'Let's see if she keeps her tax returns here. Be interesting to know how she categorized her employment.'

He found a paper-clipped stack of Visa Gold receipts that he examined as I looked over his shoulder.

Six months' worth of records. Lauren had charged only a handful of purchases each month: supermarkets and gas stations, the campus bookstore at the U. And bills from Neiman-Marcus and several designer boutiques that amounted to 90 percent of her expenditures.

Dressing for the job . . .

No motel or hotel charges. That made sense if she'd paid cash to avoid leaving a trail. Or if someone else had paid for her time and lodgings.

The bottom dresser drawer yielded another stapled sheaf. 'Here we go,' he said, 'tucked in with the cashmere sweaters. Four years of short forms . . . Looks like she prepared them herself. Nothing before that – everything started when she was twenty-one.'

He scanned the IRS paper. 'She called herself a "self-employed photographic model and student," took deductions for car expenses, books, and clothing . . . That's about it . . . No student loans, no medical write-offs . . . no mention of any research gig either . . . Every year for the past four, she reported fifty thousand gross, deducted it down to thirty-four net.'

'Fifty thousand a year coming in,' I said, 'and she manages to invest every penny?'

'Yeah – cute, isn't it.' He moved to the closet, opened a door on a tightly stacked assortment of silk dresses and blouses, pantsuits in a wide array of colors, leather and suede jackets. Two fur coats, one short and silver, the other full-length and black. Thirty or so pairs of shoes.

'Versace,' he said, squinting at a label. 'Vestimenta, Dries Van Noten, Moschino – "arctic silver fox" from Neiman . . . and this black thing is . . .' He peeled back the long coat's lapel. 'Real mink. From Mouton on Beverly Drive – hand me back those Visa receipts . . . The average is a grand or so a month on threads – that's less than one of these suits, so she had to be spending more, had cash she didn't declare.'

He closed the closet door. 'Okay, add tax evasion to her hobby list . . . Over three hundred grand saved up by age twenty-five. Like Momma said, she took care of herself.'

'That first hundred plus the three fifty-thousand deposits is two fifty,' I said. 'Where'd the rest come from, stock appreciation?'

He returned to the brokerage papers, trailed his finger to a bottom line. 'Yup, ninety thou five hundred and two worth of "long-term capital appreciation." Looks like our girl played the skin game and rode the bull market.'

'That would explain the lie about having a job at the U,' I said, feeling a sad, insistent gnawing in my gut. 'When she was arrested in Reno at nineteen, she called her father for bail money, claimed she was broke. Two years later, she deposited a hundred thousand.'

'Working hard,' he said. 'The American way. She didn't call Mom because Mom was poor.'

'That and she might've cared enough about Jane to keep secrets.' I took the brokerage packet from him, stared at zeros. 'The first hundred was probably money she saved up. When she turned twenty-one, she decided to invest. I wonder if it came from multiple clients or just a few high rollers.'

'What makes you wonder?'

'A long-term client could be the reason she didn't take her own car on Sunday. Someone sent one for her.'

'Interesting,' Milo said. 'When the sun comes up, I'll check with taxi companies and livery services. Gonna also have to canvass the neighborhood, see if anyone saw her getting into a car. If she was hooking up with some pooh-bah who wanted it hush-hush, he wouldn't have had her wait right in front of her apartment. But maybe she didn't walk too far.' He whipped out his pad, scrawled furiously.

'Something else,' I said. 'Being in a cash business – wanting cash handy for expenditures – she could've been carrying a lot of money in her purse.'

He looked up. 'A high-stakes mugging?'

'It's possible, isn't it?'

'I suppose . . . In any event, the money stink has now grown putrid.' He placed the tax returns atop the desk. Nothing *but* papers on the desk. That made me wonder about something else.

'Where's her computer?' I said.

'Who said she had one?'

'She was a student. Every college kid has a computer, and Lauren was an A student.'

He gave the dresser drawers another shuffle, found a pocket calculator, grunted disgustedly. Returning to the closet, he searched the corners and the shelves. 'Nada. So maybe she was storing data someone wanted. As in trick book. As in a pooh-bah with a good reason to value his privacy.'

'Trick database,' I said. 'She was a modern girl.'

He frowned. 'I'll ask Salander if he ever saw a computer. And I just thought of something else that should be here but isn't. Birth control. No pills or diaphragm in her drawers.'

'No medical charges on her Visa either. So she either paid her doctor in cash or used the Student Health Service.'

'Call girls get checked up regularly,' he said. 'High-priced entertainment would have to be especially careful. She had to be using some kind of protection, Alex— Let me check the bathroom again. Why don't you take a look at her books meanwhile, see if anything pops out.'

Starting at the top of the left-hand case, I traced two and a half years of required reading.

Basic math, algebra, geometry, basic science, biology, chemistry.

Economics, political science, history, the type of fiction favored by English professors. Sections underlined in pink marker. *Used* stickers from the bookstore at Santa Monica College.

The neighboring case was all sociology and psychology – dog-eared textbooks and collections of journals stored in transparent plastic boxes. The volumes on the top shelf matched Lauren's classes last quarter. More pink underlining, *Used* stickers from the U bookstore – the charges I'd just seen on her Visa. Fifty grand a year but she watched her pennies.

Turning to the journals, I opened the first plastic box and found a collection of thirty-year-old issues of *Developmental Psychology*, each bearing the faded stamp of a Salvation Army thrift shop on Western Avenue and a ten-cent price tag. No receipt, no date of sale.

The rest of the magazines were of similar vintage and origin: American Cancer Society thrift, Hadassah, City of Hope. In a copy of Maslow's *Toward A Psychology of Being*, I found a Goodwill receipt dated six years ago. A few scraps from the same time span turned up in other volumes.

Six years ago.

Lauren had begun her self-education at nineteen, nearly four years before she'd enrolled in junior college.

Intellectually curious. Ambitious. Straight As. None of that had stopped her from selling her body for a living. Then again, why should it? Knowledge can be power in all kinds of ways.

I took a closer look at the material Lauren had acquired before she'd gone back to school. Most of it centered on human relations and personality theory. No underlined sections; back then, she'd approached her books with the awe of a novice.

I shook each volume, found no loose papers.

Back to the required texts on the top shelf. Nothing illuminating or profound in the pink passages, just another student hypothesizing about what might appear on the final exam.

I was just about to quit when something in the margin of her learning theory book caught my eye. A neatly printed legend that matched the lettering I'd seen on her school papers.

INTIM. PROJ. 714 555 3342

Dr D.

That flipped a switch: the 'human intimacy' study that had run in the *Cub* three weeks before Shawna Yeager's disappearance. Disconnected Orange County number – the Newport Beach pizza parlor. Same area code, but this number was different.

There was no evidence Shawna had even seen the ad, let alone checked it out, but she had been a psychobiology major . . . living off savings.

Intim. proj.

Right up Lauren's alley? What she considered a 'research job.'

But Lauren *hadn't* needed the money.

Maybe she'd been greedy. Or something else had attracted her to the ad.

Something personal, as Gene Dalby had suggested.

Intimacy. A beautiful young woman who *faked* intimacy for cash.

Dr D.

As in Dalby? No, Gene claimed to barely remember her, and I had no reason to doubt him. And his research was on politics, not intimacy.

Another of her teachers' names began with a *D* – de Maartens. The psychology of perception. Lots of Ds.

Who was I kidding – I knew whose initial she'd jotted.

You were a great influence on her, Doctor.

The last time I'd seen her, she'd paid for the privilege of unloading her anger – not unlike the pattern she'd adopted with her father.

Years later she'd thought of me, made the notation.

Intimacy . . .

Wanting something from me? Never building up the courage to ask?

I thought of that last, angry meeting, Lauren flashing the wad of bills, unleashing the acid of recrimination. I'd always felt she'd been after more than that.

But what *had* been her goal when she'd picked up the phone and dialed my service? *What had I not given her?*

twelve

Milo came back shaking his head. 'Nothing – maybe she kept her pills in her purse.'

I said, 'Here's something,' showed him the inscription, told him about the ad that had run before Shawna Yeager's disappearance.

'Ads probably run all the time.'

'Not really,' I said. 'From what I saw, they tend to come and go.'

'Did you find any ads before Lauren went missing?'

'No, but she could've seen it elsewhere.' It sounded feeble, and both of us knew it. He was enough of a friend not to dismiss me, but his silence was eloquent.

'I know,' I said. 'Two girls, a year apart, no striking links. But maybe there were other girls in between.'

'Blondes disappearing on the Westside? I'd know if there were. At this point I'm not eliminating anything, but I've got a full plate right now: get hold of Lauren's phone records, find out if she had a computer, look for possible witnesses to a pickup. Maybe find some known associates too. There's got to be someone other than

Salander and her mom who knew her. If all that dead-ends, I'll take a closer look at Shawna.' He returned the textbook to me. ' "*Dr D.*" You're sure that's you?'

'Theoretically it could be one of her professors – Gene Dalby or another one named de Maartens. Neither of them remembers her. Big lecture classes.'

'Well,' he said, 'I can't exactly interrogate them because of this – hell if it means anything at all. The main thing's still the money. Her job and the way she was killed – cold, professional, the body left out there, maybe as a warning – smacks to me of her getting in someone's way. That's why I'm not jumping on the Yeager girl's case – Leo Riley felt that one was sexual. If Lauren deposited fifty a year, who knows how much she was taking in. And that makes me wonder if some of her income came from supplemental sources. Like black-mail. Who better than a call girl to hoard nasty secrets and try to profit from them.'

'That would also be reason to make off with her computer.'

'Precisimoso. Big bucks at stake. College profs don't exactly fit the bill.'

'Some college profs are independently wealthy. Actually, Gene Dalby is.'

'You keep mentioning him. Something about him bug you?'

'Not at all,' I said. 'Old classmate, tried to be helpful.'

'Okay, then – onward.'

'So we just let the intimacy project lie? This might be a current number.'

He took the book back, produced his cell phone, muttered, 'Probably gonna get ear cancer,' and punched in the number. Nothing in his eyes told me he'd connected, but as he listened he groped in his pocket for his pad, wrote something down, hung up.

' "Motivational Associates of Newport Beach," ' he said. 'Friendly female voice: "Our hours are ten A.M. to blah blah blah." Sounds like one of those marketing outfits.'

'Intimacy and marketing,' I said.

'Why not? Intimacy sells product. Lauren sure would've known that. So this was a moonlight for her. She liked money, took another part-time gig. Make sense?'

'Perfect sense.'

'Look,' he said, 'feel free to follow up on it. Call the other professor too – de whatever-his-name-is. Something bugs you, let me know. Right now what bugs *me* is no computer. I need a ride back to the station to pick up my car, see if any messages came in, then I'm packing it in. You up for chauffeur duty, or should I lean on one of the boys in blue?'

'I'll drive you,' I said.

'What a guy,' he said airily as he strode out of the room.

As we left the apartment he said, 'I'm really sorry the way this turned out.'

Nine o'clock the next morning, I phoned Dr Simon de Maartens at home, and he picked up, sounding distracted. When I introduced myself his voice chilled.

'I already returned your call.'

'Thanks for that, but there are still a few questions—'

'Questions?' he said. 'I told you I don't remember the girl.'

'So you have no memory of her talking to you about doing some research.'

'Research? Of course not. She was an undergrad, only grad students are permitted into my lab. Now—'

'The perception course Lauren took from you,' I said. 'Did the class subdivide into smaller discussion groups?'

'Yes, yes – that's typical.'

'Would it be possible to get a list of the students in Lauren's section?'

'No,' he said. 'It would not be possible— You claim to be faculty and you are asking for something like that? That is appalling— What is your involvement in all this?'

'I knew Lauren. Her mother's going through hell, and she asked me to be involved.'

'Well . . . I'm sorry about that, but it's a confidentiality issue.'

'Being enrolled in a study section is confidential?' I said. 'Not the last time I checked the APA ethics code.'

'Everything about academic freedom is confidential, Dr Delaware.'

'Fine,' I said. 'Thanks for your time. The police will probably be getting in touch with you.'

'Then I will tell them exactly the same thing.'

Click.

Something bugs you, let me know.

I called Milo. No answers at home, in the car, or at his

desk. I told his voice mail: 'De Maartens was not helpful. He bears attention.'

A live woman answered at Motivational Associates of Newport Beach, informing me in a bored-to-death sing-song that the office was closed.

'Is this the answering service?'

'Yes, sir.'

'When does the office open?'

'They're in and out.'

'Is there another office?'

'Yes, sir.'

'Where?'

'L.A.'

'Do you have the number?'

'One moment, I have to take another call.'

She put me on hold long enough for me to wonder if the line had gone dead. Finally, she came back on with a 310 exchange. I called it and got her partner in ennui.

'The office is closed.'

'When will it be open?'

'I don't know, sir – this is the service.'

'What's the office's address, please?'

'One moment, I have to take another call.'

I hung up and looked it up in the phone book.

The twelve thousand block of Wilshire Boulevard put Motivational Associates' L.A. branch in Brentwood, just east of Santa Monica. A couple of miles from the U and even closer to the Sepulveda alley where Lauren's body had been found.

But no sense dropping by and confronting a bolted door. I booted up the computer and plugged in 'Motivational Associates.'

Three hits, the first a four-year-old article from the *Chicago Tribune* about a South Side shelter for battered women and the services it offered. Residential care, medical consultation, individual counseling, group therapy 'provided by **Motivational Associates**, a private consulting group that offers pro bono services, particularly in the area of human relations.' The gist of the article was human-interest coverage of several abused women who'd gained emotional strength, and the firm's participation earned no further mention.

The second reference was a shortened version of the *Trib* piece, picked up by the wire services and distributed nationally. Number three was an Eastern Psychological Association abstract of a paper presented two years ago at a regional convention in Cambridge.

'Buffington, Sandra, Lindquist, Monique, and Dugger, B.J. The Multidimensional Assessment of Intimacy: Factor Analysis of the Personal Space Grid Index (PSGI) and Self-Report Measures of Locus of Control, Trait Anxiety, Personal Attractiveness, Self-Concept and Extroversion.'

So much for racy research.

The authors' affiliations were University of Chicago for Buffington and Lindquist and **Motivational Associates, Inc.** for B.J. Dugger.

Dr D.

I pulled out my American Psychological Association

directory and looked up Dugger, betting on a woman. Barbara Jean, Barbara Jo—

Benjamin John. Not the day for me to play the ponies.

Dugger's birth date made him thirty-seven. He'd earned a BA in psychology from Clark University in Worcester, Massachusetts, at the age of twenty-one and a PhD, in social psychology, from the U of Chicago ten years later. Postdoctoral fellowship at UC, San Diego, then a two-year lapse until his first – and only – job: Director, Motivational Associates of Newport Beach, California. Areas of specialty: quantitative measurement of social distance and applied motivational research. The address he'd listed was on Balboa Boulevard, in Newport, and the number was the 714 I'd just called.

Not a clinician, so no need for a state license. That made checking with the Board of Psychology for disciplinary actions a waste of time. I called anyway. Zero.

I tried a pocketful of area codes for residential listings for Dr Benjamin J. Dugger. Nothing. Scanning his name on the Internet pulled up only the same abstract of the Cambridge paper, which I reread.

Jargon and numbers and high-powered statistics, the arcane nutrients of tenure. Nothing remotely sexy.

Still, it had been Dugger's number listed in Lauren's book, and as much as I disliked de Maartens, that made Dugger the prime candidate for 'Dr D.' And he'd been running his ad during the time Shawna Yeager disappeared. Milo was probably right about there being no link between the cases, but still . . .

I thought about it some more. Dugger's bio was about as provocative as the owner's manual for a plow.

Weaker than weak.

I reread the bio and something shot out at me.

Two time lapses: ten years between his bachelor's degree and his doctorate, another two between finishing school and taking his first job.

Nice first job. Most new PhDs enter the job market burdened by debt and are forced to accept temporary lectureships and entry-level slots. Benjamin J. Dugger had disappeared for two years, only to return in an executive position.

Offices in Newport Beach and Brentwood. A company sufficiently capitalized to offer free services. And what did personal-space research have to do with battered women?

It added up to money.

Some college profs are independently wealthy.

Simon de Maartens's hostility made me wonder about *his* financial situation. Time to learn more about both Dr Ds.

The Ovid files at the U's research library spit out forty-five publications for de Maartens, all on the psychophysics of vision in primates. He was thirty-three, and there were no lapses in his professional life: BA from Leiden University in the Netherlands, Oxford doctorate in experimental psychology at twenty-five, two-year postdoc at Harvard, where he served a three-year lectureship, then assistant professorship at the U and fast-track promotion two years later to associate. The usual society memberships and more than a handful of academic honors, including a grant and a service award from the Braille Institute – perhaps his chimp research offered human possibilities.

Benjamin J. Dugger had been less prolific: five articles, none more recent than two years ago, all in the same dry vein. The last three had been coauthored with Sandra Buffington and Monique Lindquist, the first two had been solos – summaries of Dugger's first-year graduate research study and dissertation: measuring personal space in hooded rats subjected to varying degrees of social deprivation. The dates allowed me to fix his graduate studies as beginning four years prior to receiving his PhD. That still left a six-year question mark between Clark University and Chicago.

Having nowhere else to go, I phoned both institutions and verified his degrees with the alumni associations. So far, nothing suspicious. Why should there be? I was groping.

Thinking about Lauren's body tumbling out of the dumpster, I called Chicago again and asked for Professor Buffington or Lindquist. The former was on sabbatical in Hawaii, but a woman answered Lindquist's extension with a high, bright, 'This is Monique.'

'Professor, this is Mr Lew Holmes from Western News Service. We've come across an article about some work you and your colleagues did on personal space and were wondering if one of you could talk to us about a piece we're putting together on dating in the nineties.'

'I don't think so,' she said, laughing. 'That research was pretty esoteric – lots of math, nothing about dating. Where'd you come across it?'

'It came up on our database,' I said. 'So you don't think you can help?'

'I think if you wrote about our research your readers would fall asleep.'

'Oh. Too bad. Sorry for bothering you, and I guess I won't follow up on Professor Dugger.'

'Professor— Oh, Ben. No, I doubt he could help you either.'

'Double too-bad,' I said. 'We're a California-based news service, and our clients are always looking for local sources to quote. With Professor Dugger being out here, it would've worked out great.'

'I don't want to speak for Ben, but I doubt he could illuminate you either.'

'Well, let me ask you this, Professor, are you doing any other research that might be of interest to our clients?'

'No, sorry. But I'm sure you'll have no trouble finding someone wanting the attention. Especially out in California. Bye—'

'What about Professor Dugger? Would he be doing anything else that might be interesting?'

'As in sex? Is that what you're getting at?'

'Well,' I said, 'you know how it is.'

'I sure do. In terms of Ben Dugger's recent work, I have no idea what he's been up to. It's been a while since we worked together.'

Matter-of-fact, no rancor.

'Maybe I'll give him a shot,' I said. 'I've got him in Newport Beach and Brentwood.' I read off the addresses. 'This firm he's got – Motivational Associates. What are they into, advertising?'

'Market research.' She laughed again.

'Something funny, Professor?'

'You're out for the sex angle – like every other reporter. If that's what you want from Ben Dugger, don't count on it.'

'Why's that, Professor?'

'That's . . . all I have to say. Bye, now.'

'Some kind of hang-up?' said Milo. 'Sounds more like he's a prude.'

'There's something there,' I said.

'She didn't imply anything nasty.'

'No,' I admitted. 'She was lighthearted. Like it was some kind of in-joke.'

'So maybe the guy's a Catholic priest or something.'

'That wasn't in his bio.'

He grunted over the phone. It was nearly noon. He'd taken two hours to return my call. Andrew Salander had verified that Lauren had owned a Toshiba laptop. After that Milo'd been tied up at the morgue, watching Lauren's autopsy. The coroner had found no evidence of sexual assault – of any recent intercourse. No illness, surgery, scarring, or drug use. The preliminary finding was that the first bullet fired into Lauren's brain stem – a 9 mm – had shut off her life functions nearly instantly. Until that second, a healthy girl.

171

'So she probably didn't suffer,' he said. 'I called her mom and told her she definitely didn't. Woman sounds as if she's been hollowed out and left to dry . . . So de Maartens is an uppity putz and Dugger doesn't like to talk about sex.'

'Dugger may also have money.' I gave him the logic on that.

'If I had to choose, I'd say press the Dutch guy 'cause he got hostile. If you're up to that, fine.'

'If I show up at his door, he'll slam it. I told him the police would probably be stopping by.'

'Promises, promises. I'll try to get to it eventually. So far, no record of any cab or limo making a pickup in the vicinity of Lauren's apartment. Her broker in Seattle knows her only as a voice over the phone. She cold-called him a few years ago, said she had money to invest. Which is a switch, usually it's the salesmen who call, so needless to say he didn't argue. He said Lauren did her homework about the market, knew what she wanted but was willing to listen to advice. Overall impression: smart. He was surprised to learn she was only twenty-five, figured her for a good ten years older.'

'What did he say she wanted?'

'Blue-chip funds, and she was patient enough to hold. He figured her for a high-income lawyer or some other executive type. I put two uniforms on the door-to-door, a couple of people think they remember her vaguely from the neighborhood – jogging, driving around in her convertible – but no one saw her getting picked up. Not the day she disappeared or any other time. I got hold of six months' worth of phone records. She actually used the horn very little. Talked to her mom every couple of weeks – the last call was two days before she disappeared. Nothing to Lyle – no surprise. The only things that did look interesting were five calls over the last two months to the same number in Malibu. Turns out to be a pay phone in Point Dume.'

'Lauren told Salander she went to Malibu for rest and recreation. Is the phone near a motel?'

'No. Shopping center at Kanan-Dume Road.'

'Have you found any cell phone account for her, or an answering service?'

'Not so far.'

'Don't you find that surprising, if she was making dates?'

Pause. 'A bit.'

'Unless,' I said, 'she didn't need a service because she wasn't casting her net. Had one client who paid all the bills. Maybe someone who lives in Malibu, doesn't want wifey-poo to hear Lauren's call, so he uses the pay phone.'

'Fifty grand plus from one john? One helluva habit.'

'Lots of passion,' I said. 'When those kinds of things go bad, they go very bad.'

'I'll drive there today, see what kinds of shops are nearby – maybe someone noticed something. Maybe I'll drop in on de Maartens on the way back. Where's he live?'

'Don't know, but his number's a 310.'

'I'll get it. Thanks for all the work, Alex.'

'However useless.'

'Hey,' he said, 'you can never tell what'll pan out.'

Lying through his teeth. What else are friends for?

Just after one P.M. I got in the Seville and drove to Motivational Associates' Brentwood office.

The building was one of a group of towers that had sprouted on Wilshire during one of the booms. Four stories for parking, eight for offices, zebra-striped walls of white aluminum and black glass. The packing carton a serious building came in.

I walked past an empty guard desk to the directory. No pattern to the tenant mix: computer consultants, insurance agents, lawyers, an occupational therapy brokerage, a few psychotherapists. Motivational Associates was Suite 717, a third of the way down a gray-walled, plum-carpeted hallway. Black doors with tiny chrome signage. Dugger's was set between E-WISDOM and THE LAW OFFICES OF NORMAN AND REBBIRQUE.

No mail at or under the door, and when I peeked through the slot I saw an unlit waiting room, still no pile of letters. Either someone had collected or the post went to another location. I didn't knock – the last thing I wanted was to have to explain myself.

I'd returned to the elevator, was waiting for it to ascend from the lobby when the door to 717 swung open and a man came out carrying a scuffed brown leather briefcase. Locking the dead bolt, he made his way in my direction, swinging his keys.

Thirty-five to forty, five-ten, one sixty. Dark hair

trimmed close to the sides, thinning on top, freckled bald spot at the crown. He wore a shapeless oatmeal herringbone sport coat with brown-leather elbow patches, an open-necked white button-down shirt with blue stripes, faded beige cords that would've suited Milo had they been five waist sizes larger, and brown loafers with toes worn to gray gristle. A wadded selection from the morning's *Times* was stuffed into a pocket of the jacket, weighing the garment down on one side and making him appear lopsided. Three black plastic pens were clipped to his handkerchief pocket. Tortoiseshell eyeglasses dangled from a chain around his neck.

He arrived at the lift just as the door opened, waited for me to step in, then followed and stood near the door. Placing the briefcase on the floor, he punched in P3, and said, 'How about you?' in a pleasant voice. Straight nose, straight mouth, smallish ears, firm chin. Nothing out of proportion, but something – a blurring of contours – kept it just shy of handsome. The lapel of his sport coat was fuzzed where it met his shirt. Two white threads had come loose from his shirt collar.

I said, 'Same, thanks.'

He turned, offering a view of his bald spot. I noticed a worn gold monogram above the clasp of the case. BJD. As we descended he began whistling, and his hands grew active – fingers drumming, tapping, stretching, curling. A shaving nick bottomed his right earlobe. Another cut flecked his jawline. He gave off the smell of soap and water.

He stopped whistling. Said, 'Sorry.'

'No problem.'

'They used to play Muzak. Someone must've complained.'

'People tend to do that.'

'They do, indeed.'

No further exchange until we reached P3 and I hung back as he stepped out into the parking area. As he headed briskly toward a nearby aisle, I was watching from behind a concrete pillar.

His car was a white Volvo sedan, plain-wrap model, several years old. No alarm click, and he'd left the door unlocked. Tossing the briefcase across the seat, he slid in, started up, backed out blowing chalky smoke. I ran up the three flights to the lobby, was heading for the Seville when I saw him pull onto Wilshire, going west.

Toward the beach? Malibu?

He was ten blocks ahead of me, and it took several traffic violations for me to catch up. I stayed two car lengths behind in the neighboring lane and tried to watch him. He kept both hands on the wheel; his lips were moving and his head was bobbing. Either a hands-off cell phone or singing to himself. My guess was the latter: he looked utterly at peace.

He drove to Long's Drugstore in Santa Monica, stayed inside for ten minutes, emerged with a big bag of something, got back on Wilshire and drove to Broadway and Seventh, where he pulled up in front of a narrow, white-clapboard Victorian, once a three-story house, now THE PACIFIC FAITH APOSTOLIC CHURCH. One of the few old ones that had survived the Northridge quake.

The white boards were freshly painted, and a crisp picket fence boxed off the church's yard. Sandboxes and swings and slides and monkey bars. Three dozen munchkins, mostly brown-skinned and dark-haired, scooted and jumped and shouted and squatted in the sand. Three young women wearing braided hair and long, pale dresses watched from the sidelines. A rainbow-lettered banner across the fence announced FAITH PRESCHOOL, SPRING REGISTRATION STILL OPEN.

Dr Benjamin Dugger parked at the curb, walked through the picket gate, and entered the church. If he was burdened with sin, the bounce in his stride didn't say so. He remained inside for fifteen minutes, emerged minus the bag from the drugstore.

Back to Wilshire. His next stop was a fish-and-chips place near Fourteenth Street, where he came out with another bag, smaller and grease-spotted. Lunch was enjoyed on a bench at Christine Reed Park, behind the tennis courts, where I watched from the Seville as he shoved french fries and something breaded into his mouth, drank from a can of Coke, and shared leftovers with the pigeons. A quarter of an hour later he was back on Wilshire, heading east this time, staying in one lane, sticking to the speed limit.

He entered Westwood Village, parked in a pay lot on Gayley, and entered a multiplex theater. Two comedies, a spy thriller, a historical romance. Showtimes said he'd chosen either one of the comedies or the romance.

What a sinister fellow.

I drove home.

★ ★ ★

At three, deciding I should stick to what I knew, I phoned the Abbot house. The robot voice answered and, feeling grateful when neither Jane's nor Mel's broke in, I hung up.

At 4:43, Milo called. 'The pay phone's in a gas station. Nearby are a gym, an insurance agency, and a café. No one remembers Lauren. The owner of the station doesn't recall any frequent callers. It's a busy place, lots of traffic, for him to notice someone they would've had to set up office in the booth. I also dropped in on a bunch of motels and showed Lauren's picture around. Zero. I'm back at my desk, figured I'd check out snippy Professor de Maartens. Who, as it turns out, lives in Venice. Want to tag along?'

I debated whether to tell him I'd followed Benjamin Dugger. By now, the tail seemed ludicrous. No reason to share.

'Sure,' I said. 'The charm of my company?'

'Just the opposite. You pissed him off once – maybe that can be harnessed.'

thirteen

Simon de Maartens lived on Third Street, north of Rose. The beach was a short walk west. Crossing Rose brought you into gang territory.

The block was filled with tiny houses, some divided. Intermittent bright spots – fresh paint, brand-new skylights, flower beds, staked saplings – said gentrification had arrived. De Maartens's abode was a brown-stucco, side-by-side duplex with a gray lawn, curling tar-paper roof, and flaking woodwork. The blue VW van in its driveway was patched and primered. Its rear bumper sagged, and so did the independent wealth hypothesis.

'Doesn't look as if he's been seduced by externals,' said Milo. 'Life of the mind and all that?'

'Could be.' I realized the same could be said of Benjamin Dugger: Newport and Brentwood offices but a frayed lapel.

Not exactly the high rollers I'd conjured when imagining Lauren spirited away to some casbah.

He switched off the engine. 'How about I do the talking, and work you in as needed?'

'Sounds good to me.'

We were halfway to de Maartens's front door when loud barking came from the brown house and a big, yellow face parted the curtains of the front window. Some kind of retriever. Steady barking but no enmity – announcing our presence without passing judgment. The door began opening before we got there, and a young, red-haired woman smiled out at us.

She was tall and solidly built, wore a black T-shirt and green drawstring pants, held a paintbrush in one hand. Wet, blue bristles. Her hair was the color of fresh rust, cut in a pageboy that hung to midneck, the bangs perfectly straight above inquisitive hazel eyes. The pants were baggy but the shirt was tight, accentuating a soft, friendly bosom and generous shoulders. Nice coating of flesh everywhere except for her hands, which were slim and white, with tendril fingers. The smell of turpentine blew through the doorway, along with classical music – something with woodwinds. No sign of the yellow dog. The woman had stopped smiling.

'Police, ma'am,' said Milo, flashing the badge. 'Are you Mrs de Maartens?'

'Anika.' Pronouncing her name as if it were required for border crossing. 'I thought you were UPS.' 'Thought' came out 'taut.' Her accent was thicker than her husband's, harder around the edges. Or maybe that was anxiety. Who likes the police on a sunny afternoon?

'Expecting a delivery?'

'I – I'm supposed to get art supplies. From back home. Was there a crime somewhere on the block?'

180

'No, everything's fine. Where's back home?'

'Holland . . . Why are you here?'

'Nothing to worry about, ma'am, we just wanted to talk to Professor de Maartens. Is he in?'

'You want to talk to Simon? About what?'

'A student of his.'

'A student?'

'It's better if we talk to the professor directly, Mrs de Maartens. Is he in?'

'Yes, yes, I go get him, hold on.'

She left the door open and headed toward the music. A big butter-colored form materialized. Heavy jowls, small bright eyes, short coat, droopy ears. Retriever mix, a splash of mastiff somewhere in the bloodline.

The dog regarded us for a second, then followed Anika de Maartens. Returned moments later with a man in tow. Man and beast walking in synchrony, the master's hand resting lightly on the animal's neck.

'I'm Simon. What is it?'

De Maartens was six feet tall and heavyset, with a whiskey-colored crew cut and a ruddy, bulb-nosed, thick-lipped face, as close to spherical as I'd seen on a human. Despite his clothing – gray sweatshirt, blue cutoffs, rubber beach sandals – he looked like a Rembrandt burgher, and I half expected him to whip out a clay pipe.

'Detective Sturgis,' said Milo, extending a hand.

Dr Maartens looked past it, kept coming toward us. 'Yes?' The sound of his voice made the dog's ears perk.

Milo began repeating his name.

'I heard you,' said de Maartens. 'I'm not deaf.' Smiling, as he and the dog stopped at the threshold. His head turned from side to side, and he stared blankly, settling on the space between Milo and me. That's when I saw his eyes: black crescents set in bluish sockets so deep they appeared to have been scooped out of his flesh. Immobile crescents, the merest sliver of black showing through dull black, no gleam of pupil.

A blind man.

The psychophysics of vision in primates. The Braille Institute Award.

He said, 'This is about the girl – Lauren.'

'Yes, sir.'

'Some of my students I do know,' said de Maartens. 'The ones who ask questions, visit during office hours. Voices that recur.' He touched his ear. The dog looked up at him adoringly. 'Lauren Teague was not one of them. She got an A in the class – a very high A, so perhaps she did not need to ask questions. I can produce her exams when I return to my office next week. But right now, I am on vacation and I do not see why I need to be bothered. What can you hope to learn from two exams?'

'So there's nothing you can tell us about Ms Teague?'

De Maartens's thick shoulders rose and fell. He canted his face toward me. Smiled. 'Is that you, Dr Delaware? Nice aftershave. After your second call when I grew cross, I called the department to see what records they have on her. Just her grade transcripts. All As. I should not have grown cross, but I was in the middle of something and I did not see the point. I still do not.'

He scratched behind the dog's ears, aimed his eye sockets back at Milo. 'Three times during the quarter, the class was divided into discussion groups of approximately twenty students each, supervised by teaching assistants. The groups were optional, nothing discussed was graded. It was an attempt by the department to be more personal.' Another smile. 'I checked with my department chairman, and he said it would be permissible to give you the names of the students in Lauren Teague's group. Her TA was Malvina Zorn. You may call the psychology department and obtain Malvina's number. She has been instructed to give you the names of the students in the group. The chairman and I have signed authorizations. That should be all you need.'

'Thank you, Professor.'

'You are welcome.' De Maartens rocked back and forth, then stopped. 'What exactly happened to Ms Teague?'

'Someone shot her,' said Milo. 'You can read it in the paper—' He flushed scarlet.

De Maartens laughed uproariously and ruffled the dog. 'Perhaps Vincent here can read it to me. No, I am sure my wife will give me every detail. She devours everything she can about crime and misfortune because this city frightens her.'

When we were back in the car I said, 'So much for that.'

Milo said, 'I don't see Lauren's academic life as the thing here, anyway. It's the people she *didn't* talk about that I'm interested in. I'll phone the psych department, though, get those students' names.'

He made the call, copied down a list of nine students that I inspected as we drove away. Three males, six females.

'Everyone out for the quarter,' he mumbled, as we drove away. 'Fun.'

'I'm your partner in futility.' I told him about following Benjamin Dugger. He was kind enough not to laugh.

'Old Volvo and delivering goodies to kids at the church, huh?'

'Yeah, yeah,' I said. 'Throw in the pro bono thing at the shelter in Chicago and he's Mother Teresa in tweed. You're right, guys like him aren't what got Lauren into trouble. She lived in a whole other world.'

'Speaking of which,' he said. 'I thought I'd drop in on Gretchen Stengel.'

'She's out of prison?'

'Paroled half a year ago. Found herself a new line of work.'

'What's that?'

'Similar to her old gig, but legal. Dressing the insecure.'

The boutique was on Robertson just south of Beverly, five doors north of a restaurant-of-the-moment where valets shuffled Ferraris and alfresco diners laughed too loudly as they sucked bottled water and smog.

Déjà View

Couture with a Past

Eight-foot-wide storefront, the window draped in black jersey and occupied by a single, bald, faceless, chromium mannequin in a billowing scarlet gown. A bell push was required for entry, but Milo's bulk didn't stop whoever was in charge from buzzing us in.

Inside, the shop's mirrored walls and black granite floor vibrated to David Bowie's 'Young Americans,' the bass tuned to migraine level. Nailed into the mirror were raw iron bolts from which garments dangled on chrome hangers. Velvet, crepe, leather, silk; wide color range, nothing above a size 8. A pair of orange Deco revival chairs designed by a sadist filled a tight oblong of center space. Copies of *Vogue, Talk*, and *Buzz* fanned across a trapezoid of glass posing as a table. No counter, no register. Seams in the rear wall were probably the dressing rooms. To the right was a door marked PRIVATE. The fermented-corn sweetness of gold marijuana tinctured the air.

A dangerously thin girl in her twenties wearing a baby blue bodysuit and a rosewood-tinted Peter Pan do stood behind one of the orange chairs, hips thrust forward, eyes guarded. White stiletto-heeled sandals put her at eye level with Milo. Pink eyes and dilated pupils. No ashtray or roach, so maybe she'd swallowed. The bodysuit was sheer, and the undertones of her flesh beneath the fabric turned the blue pearly. She seemed to have too many ribs, and I found myself counting.

'Yes?' Husky voice, almost mannish.

'I need something in a size four,' said Milo.

'For . . . ?'

185

'My thumb.' He stepped closer. The girl recoiled and crossed her arms over her chest. The music kept pounding, and I looked for the speakers, finally spotted them: small white discs tucked into the corners.

Out came Milo's badge. Rather than rattle the girl, it seemed to calm her. 'And the punch line is . . . ?' she said.

'Is Gretchen Stengel here?'

The girl gave a languid wave. 'Don't see her.'

Milo reached out toward the iron rack and fondled a black pantsuit. 'Couture with a past, huh?'

The girl didn't move or speak.

He examined the label. 'Lagerfeld . . . What kind of past does this one have?'

'It went to the Oscars two years ago.'

'Really. Did it win and make a speech thanking the little people?'

The girl snorted.

'So where's Gretchen?'

'If you leave your name I'll tell her you were here.'

'Gee, thanks. And you are . . .'

'Stanwyck.'

'Stanwyck what?'

'Just Stanwyck.'

'Ah,' said Milo. He dropped the sleeve, faced her, did one of those moves that makes him taller than you think possible. 'Don't they require two names for booking?'

The girl's lips tightened into a little pink bud. 'Is there anything else I can help you with?'

'Where's Gretchen?'

'At lunch.'

'Late lunch.'

'Guess so.'

'Where?'

Stanwyck hesitated.

'C'mon, Stan,' said Milo. 'Or I'll tell Ollie.'

Her eyes filmed with confusion. 'I don't run her appointment schedule.'

'But you do know where she is.'

'I get paid to be here, that's all.'

'Stan, Stan.' Milo sniffed the air conspicuously. 'Why make this complicated?'

'Gretchen doesn't like attention.'

'Well, I can sure understand that. But fame is like a dog with an unstable temperament. You feed it, think you've got it under control, but sometimes it bites you anyway. Now, where the hell is she?'

'Up the block.' She named the trendoid eatery.

He turned to leave.

Stanwyck said, 'Don't tell her I told you.'

'Promise,' said Milo.

'Yeah, right,' said the girl. 'And you've got a Porsche and a house on the beach and won't come in my mouth.'

We made our way past the valets, up brick stairs, and through a low picket gate to the front patio, turning the heads of the see-and-be-seen crowd. Lots of free-floating anxiety and ponytails on heads that didn't deserve them, big white plates decorated with small green food. Some high fashion, though quite a few people were dressed

187

worse than Milo. But at much higher cost, and everyone knew the difference. The maître d's were two white-jacketed, black-T-shirted sticks, both too busy to stop us. But one of them did notice us enter the inner dining room at the rear.

The room was low and dark and cheap-chic, noisy as a power plant. As we made our way among the tables, I heard a man in a five-hundred-dollar Hawaiian shirt urging a waiter, 'Speak to me of the crab cakes.'

Gretchen Stengel sat at a corner table opposite a sleek young woman with blue-black skin. A blue liter of esoteric water stood between them. The black woman picked at a salad, and Gretchen twirled a crayfish on a toothpick.

No problem recognizing the Westside Madam; three years ago she'd been evening news fodder for months, and, but for a few age lines, she hadn't changed much.

Sunken cheeks, lemon-sucking mouth, stringy brown hair, skinny upper body but broad-beamed below the waist. An ungainly waddle as her lawyers hustled her to and from court. Brown eyes that claimed injury when they weren't shielded by dark lenses. Today the glasses were in place – oversized black ovals that blocked expression.

It would have been easy to ascribe her pallor to the twenty-five months she'd spent behind bars for income tax evasion but she'd been pale before then. Floppy hats, kabuki-white makeup, and the omnipresent black glasses fed rumors that she hated the sun. Interesting choice, if it was one, for a girl growing up at the beach. Then again, most daughters of Pacific Palisades corporate lawyers don't grow up to be pimps.

Gretchen Stengel had been raised on two acres overlooking the ocean, attended the Peabody School and summer camps designed to pamper, vacationed at private villas in Venice and châteaus in southern France, flown the Concorde a dozen times before entering puberty.

Rocky puberty. Her arrest led to journalistic archaeology of the Stengel family and discovery of childhood learning problems, drug and DUI busts, and half a dozen abortions beginning when Gretchen was fourteen. At twenty she dropped out of Arizona State, having never declared a major. Unsubstantiated stories had her starring in a series of bottom-feeder porn loops featuring a variety of partners, not all of them two-legged.

Prior to her arrest none of her teenage problems had leaked out of sealed records, nor had she been disciplined by the system. Mildrew and Andrea Stengel were senior partners at Munchley, Zabella and Cater, a downtown firm with a wide reach. After leaving college, Gretchen moved back home to a guesthouse at their estate, attending openings of bad art and premieres of films that lost money, hanging out with the sweating throng of Eurotrash that filled Sunset Plaza cafés. Telling anyone who cared to listen that she was working on a screenplay, had a deal pending at one of the big independent production companies.

At some point she discovered long-hidden organizational skills and began mustering a small army of hookers: girls with great bodies and fresh faces and the ability to operate a credit-card machine. None was older than twenty-five, some had been Peabody School acquaintances, others she spotted on Sunset or the Colony. Many had never sold sex before. All were terrific at faking innocence.

The nerve center of the operation was Gretchen's free digs behind the parental swimming pool. She called her employees 'agents' and put them to work in the lounges and bars of hotels with 'Beverly' in their names. Clients paid for the room and the flesh, the girls divvied up for clothing and cosmetics and birth control, and Gretchen financed quarterly medical checkups. Other than doctor bills, phone and credit company charges, her overhead was nil. By the time *she* was twenty-five, Gretchen was pulling in seven figures a year and lopping off a zero when she filed with the IRS.

What tripped her up was never made clear. The rumor mill spat out the names of famous clients: movie stars, assorted film industry lampreys, politicians, developers. Supposedly, Gretchen had run afoul of the LAPD. But no john list ever materialized, and Gretchen sat mute during her indictment.

Her trial was slated to be the Next Big Media Event. Then Gretchen's lawyer pled her to a single evasion charge and a money-laundering misdemeanor, and bargained her sentence to thirty-two months in federal lockup, plus restitution and penalties. Gretchen served solid but truncated time: no interviews, no wheedling, seven months lopped off for good behavior.

Now she was selling used clothes in a high-rent closet that reeked of weed and hiring ex-employees to stroke the customers.

It suggested an inability to learn from experience, but maybe Gretchen had learned something other than crime doesn't pay.

Blaming her parents was easy but, like most pat solutions, that was just an excuse not to puzzle. Gretchen's older brother had achieved honors as a flight surgeon for the Navy, and a younger sister ran a music school in Harlem. Following Gretchen's arrest someone had suggested middle-child syndrome. They might as well have indicted the lunar cycle. Mildrew and Andrea Stengel were high-powered lawyers but by all accounts attentive parents. The week after Gretchen's conviction they resigned their partnerships and moved to Galisteo, New Mexico, purportedly to live 'the simple life.'

Milo and I walked up to the table. Gretchen had to have seen us, but she ignored us and tweaked the tail of the crayfish. Edging the creature toward her mouth, she changed her mind, drew back her arm, flicked the crustacean's tail as if daring it to resuscitate. Then back to her lips. Licking but not biting. Some weight-loss behavior-mod trick? Play with your calories but never ingest them?

Nearby diners had begun to stare. Gretchen didn't react. Her companion lacked Gretchen's composure and started fidgeting with her salad. Scallops on something saw-toothed and weedlike. She was young like Gretchen, with cropped hair, felonious cheekbones, and slanted eyes, wore a sleeveless yellow sundress, pink coral necklace and earrings, long, curving nails painted a lighter shade of coral. All that color achingly dramatic against flawless black skin.

Gretchen's cuticles were a wreck. She had on a shapeless black sweatshirt and black leggings. Her hair looked as if it hadn't been washed in a week. The black lenses did their trick, putting her somewhere else.

Milo moved so he could smile down at the black woman. 'Nice dress. Does it have a past?'

Painful smile in response.

'Have a bug,' said Gretchen, waving the crayfish. 'That's what they are. Bugs.' Her voice was nasal and scratchy. The black woman grimaced.

Milo said, 'Thanks for the biology lesson, Ms Stengel.'

Gretchen said, 'Actually, they're more like spiders.' To the black woman: 'Think spiders taste any good?' Her lips barely moved when she spoke. The black woman put her fork down and picked up her napkin.

'What about flies and caterpillars?' said Gretchen. 'Or slugs.'

Milo said, 'Lauren Teague.'

The black woman wiped her mouth. Gretchen Stengel didn't budge.

Milo said, 'Lauren—'

'It's a name,' said Gretchen.

The black woman said, 'If you'll excuse me, please,' and started to rise.

'Please stay,' said Milo.

'I have to go to the little girls' room.' She reached down for her purse. Milo had placed his foot over the strap.

'*Please*,' she said.

Conversation at neighboring tables had died. A waiter came over. A glance from Milo made him retreat, but seconds later one of the white-jacketed maître d's arrived.

'Officer,' he said, sidling up to Milo and managing to spit out the word while smiling wider than his lips had been built for. 'You *are* a police officer?'

'And here I thought I was being subtle.'

'Please, sir, this isn't the place and time.'

Gretchen twirled the crayfish. The black woman hung her head.

'For what?' said Milo.

'Sir,' said White Jacket. 'People are trying to enjoy their food. This is a distraction.'

Milo spied a free chair at a neighboring table, pulled it over, sat down. 'How's this for blending in?'

'Really, Officer.'

'Fuck it, Damien,' said Gretchen. 'Leave him alone, I know him.'

Damien stared at her. 'You're sure, Gretch?'

'Yeah, yeah.' She waved the crayfish. 'Tell Joel to make it spicier next time.'

'Oh.' Damien's acrobatic lips fluttered. 'It's too bland?'

'If you've got taste buds.'

'Oh, no— I'll bring you some extra sauce, Gretch—'

'No,' said Gretchen. 'That won't help, too late. It has to be cooked into the meat.'

'Really, Gretch—'

'No, Damien.'

Damien simpered. 'I am *so* sorry. I'll have a fresh batch prepared right now—'

'Don't bother. Not hungry.'

'I feel terrible,' said Damien.

'Don't,' said Gretchen, flicking the crayfish's tail. 'Just do better next time.'

'Sure. Of course. Certainly.' To the black woman: 'Is yours okay?'

'Perfect.' Glum tone. 'I'm going to the little girls' room.' She stood. Six feet tall in flats, sleek as a panther. Looking down at her purse, she left it there, edged past me, disappeared.

Damien said, 'Really, Gretch, I can get you another plate in no time.'

'I'm fine,' said Gretchen, blowing a kiss at him. 'Go away.'

When he departed she looked at me. 'Sit. Take Ingrid's chair, she'll be gone awhile. Bladder infection. I tell her to drink cranberry juice, but she hates it.'

'Old friend?' said Milo.

'New friend.'

'Let's talk about Lauren Teague. Someone shot her and dumped her in an alley.'

Gretchen's flat expression maintained. She put the crayfish down. 'How terrible. I thought she was too smart for that.'

'Too smart for what?'

'Going into business without me.'

'You think that's what killed her?'

Off came the sunglasses. The brown eyes were piercing and focused; childhood learning difficulties seemed remote, and I wondered how many of the rumors about her were true.

'So do you,' she said. 'That's why you're here.'

'Were you and she in touch?'

Gretchen shook her head. 'After I retired, I cut all ties to the staff.'

'How long has it been since you saw Lauren?'

Gretchen tried to pick something from between her teeth. Stubby nails weren't up to the task. She removed the toothpick from a crayfish and began probing. 'She resigned before I retired.'

'How long before?'

'Maybe a year.'

'Why?' said Milo.

'She never said.'

'You didn't ask?'

'Why should I?' said Gretchen. 'It wasn't as if there was a personnel shortage.'

'Any idea why she quit?'

'It could've been anything.'

'You never discussed it.'

'Nope. She e-mailed me, I e-mailed back.'

'She was into computers,' said Milo.

Gretchen laughed.

Milo said, 'What's funny?'

'That's like asking if she was into refrigerators.' She reskewered the crayfish.

'Any theories?' said Milo. 'About why she quit?'

'Nope.'

'What else do you remember about Lauren?'

'Great body, knew how to do makeup, no need for surgery. Some clients don't like bionics.'

'Think she might've picked up a steady?' said Milo.

'Anything's possible.'

'Did you know she'd gone back to school?'

'Really,' said Gretchen. 'How self-improving.' She folded her hands in her lap.

'When she was working for you, did she complain of problematic clients?'

'Nope.'

'No problems at all?'

'She was good with people. I was sorry to see her go.'

'Did she have any particular specialties?'

'Other than being gorgeous and smart and polite?'

'No kinks?'

Gretchen smiled. 'Kinks?'

'Anything out of the ordinary.'

Gretchen laughed. 'How could I even begin to answer that.'

'How about yes or no, and if it's yes, some details?'

Gretchen sat back and crossed her legs. Her back was against the wall, and she seemed to enjoy the support. 'The truth is, people are depressingly ordinary.'

'Guys were willing to pay big-time for ordinary?'

'Guys were willing to pay to have it on their terms.'

'So Lauren had no specialties?'

Shrug.

'What about special clients? Guys who requested her specifically?'

Gretchen shook her head. Picked up a crayfish and stared at the crustacean. 'Look at those eyes. It's as if he knows.'

'Knows what?'

'That he's dead.'

Milo said, 'Who requested Lauren?'

'Nothing comes to mind.'

Milo edged his chair closer to her. From the way he talked into her ear and her sudden, warm smile, they might've been lovers.

'Help me out here,' he said. 'We're talking murder.'

'I can help if you want to buy a dress.' She drew her head back and looked him up and down. 'I don't think you'd like our styles.'

Milo stayed close to her. 'Someone tied Lauren up and shot her in the back of the head and left her like garbage in a dumpster. Give me a name. Anyone who had a thing for Lauren.'

Gretchen touched his tie, lifted it, and kissed the tip. 'Nice syntho. Chez Sears? Tar-*zhay*?'

'What about girls she worked with? Friends on the staff?'

'Far as I recall, she went it alone.'

'What about Michelle?'

'Michelle,' said Gretchen. 'As in . . . ?'

'A brunette Lauren stripped with – they both did the

197

party scene. Back when you were in business. Was that one of your subsidiaries?'

'Uh-uh. I specialized.'

'In what?'

'Networking. The tools of commerce.'

'Nuts into bolts,' said Milo. 'So Lauren and Michelle were freelancing on the side?'

Gretchen smiled again. 'You're cute.'

'Did you have a Michelle on staff?'

'It's a common name.'

'How about a last name?'

Gretchen placed her lips next to Milo's ears. Flicked his lobe with her tongue. Gave a soft, dry laugh. 'I have nothing to offer because I'm nothing. A speck of lint in the navel of the least important creature in the universe. And that makes me free.'

'You're anything but nothing,' said Milo. 'I'd say you're a *presence*.'

'You are *so* sweet,' said Gretchen. 'I'll bet you treat the girls gently.'

Milo's turn to smile. 'So how about tossing me a bone? Off the record. Michelle what?'

'Michelle, *ma belle. Sont les* whatever.' Gretchen began toying with the crayfish. 'Those *eyes*. He's like, Let me sit on this plate dead and get all shriveled up but leave me intact, I just don't want to be chewed up.'

'Lauren didn't end up intact.'

Gretchen sighed. 'They really should remove the eyes.'

Milo said, 'So that's it? Nothing?'

'Have a nice day,' said Gretchen.

★ ★ ★

On the way out we met Ingrid returning.

Milo blocked her way. 'Lauren Teague was murdered.'

Lavender lips parted. 'Oh.' Then: 'Who's Lauren?'

'An old friend of Gretchen's.'

'I'm a new friend.'

'I don't think so, dear,' said Milo. 'I think you and ol' Gretch go way back— Ten to one I can get hold of your sheet like that.' Snapping fingers in front of her face. 'Seen Michelle recently?'

'Michelle who?'

'My, my, the same old song – Michelle the tall brunette who used to dance with Lauren.'

Ingrid shook her head. Milo's hand closed around her arm. 'We can discuss this in my office or you can continue your meal.'

Ingrid's eyes burned fiercely. She craned to get a look at Gretchen's table.

'Don't worry,' said Milo. 'I won't let her know you told me.'

'Told you what?'

'Michelle's last name.'

'I don't know any Michelle. I've heard *mention* of Michelle Salazar— Did Gretchen eat anything?'

'Not much.'

'Damn! She needs to *eat*. Please don't bother her at lunch again.'

fourteen

Milo punched the MDT's keypad, ran a search on Salazar, Michelle.

The screen lit up. Three hits: Michelle Angela, 47, with a record for larceny, Michelle Sandra, 22, imprisoned in Arizona for manslaughter, and Michelle Leticia, 26, arrested two years ago for prostitution, a year after that for possession of narcotics.

'There you go,' I said. 'The age is perfect.'

'Echo Park. Let's go— Would you recognize her?'

'No, it was dark,' I said. 'Maybe.'

Michelle Salazar lived in a two-story, peach-colored sixplex on a twisting street one block east of Michel-torena and two blocks north of Sunset. A brown sky hung low over the potholes, boxy hieroglyphics sang gang sagas, small children played in the dust. Two doors up a cluster of shaved-head young men in white tank tops and baggy pants crowded an old white van, sharing cigarettes and beer and lean looks.

As we got out of the unmarked, some of the beer

drinkers watched us. Milo's gun hand was relaxed but in the right place as he threw them a salute. Big group effort not to respond. We were in Ramparts Division, where a police scandal had broken a couple of years ago – CRASH officers forming their own criminal gang. LAPD claimed the bad cops had been weeded out. LAPD had denied the existence of bad cops for too long to have any credibility.

The lock on the building's front door was missing. Inside, a dark central hall was ripe with the gamy perfume of too-old *menudo*. Mailboxes set into the right-hand wall were padlocked and unmarked. Milo knocked on the first door, got no answer, tried the next unit and received a shouted '*Sí?*' in response.

'*Policía.*' Reciting the word quietly, but there was no way to make it inviting.

Long pause, then a woman said, 'Eh?'

'*Policía.*'

'*Policía por qué?*'

'*Señora, donde está Michelle Salazar, por favor?*'

Nothing.

'*Señora?*'

'*Número seis.*' A radio was turned up loud enough to block out further discourse. We made our way to the stairs.

Different smells up on the second floor: sour laundry, urine, orange soda.

Milo rapped on number 6. Another female voice said, 'Yeah?' and the door opened six inches before he could respond. Held in place by a loose chain, bisecting a woman's face. One watery brown eye, half a parched lip, sallow skin.

'Michelle Salazar? Detective Sturgis—' The door began to close, and he blocked it with his foot, reached around, undid the chain.

I didn't recognize her, but somehow I *knew* it was her. Last time I'd seen her, she'd had two arms.

She wore a green nylon robe with moth holes on the lapels. Thirty pounds heavier than when I'd watched her dance with Lauren. A once-pretty face had puffed in all the wrong places, and sprays of pimples crusted her forehead and chin. The same luxuriant mop of jet-black hair. One hand held a cigarette with a gravity-defying ash. Her left sleeve was tied back at elbow length. Empty space from the shoulder down.

'Oh, shit,' she said. 'I didn't do anything – please leave me alone.'

'I'm not here to hassle you, Michelle.'

'Yeah, right.' The room behind her was squalid with dirty clothes and old food and clumps of what looked like dog waste on gray linoleum. As if confirming that, a small, hairless thing with a white-fringed head pranced across my field of vision. Seconds later a high-pitched yelp sounded.

'It's okay, baby,' said Michelle. The dog mewed a few more times before withdrawing to tremulous silence.

'What is that, a Mexican hairless?' said Milo.

'Like you give a shit. Peruvian Inca Orchid.' Her voice

slurred, and her breath was sharp with alcohol. A blue bruise smeared the left side of her neck.

Milo pointed to the mark. 'Someone get rough with you?'

'Nah,' she said. 'Just playing around. I'm tired, man – go hassle someone else. Every time you guys got free time, it's always here.'

'Police harassment, huh.'

'Nazi tactics.'

'How foolish to waste time here,' said Milo. 'Place like this, a veritable church.'

Michelle rubbed her single arm against the front of her robe. 'Just leave me alone.'

'Ramparts guys visit a lot, huh?'

'Like you don't know.'

'I don't. I'm West L.A.'

'Then you got lost.'

'This isn't about you, Michelle. It's about Lauren Teague.'

Two rapid blinks. 'What?'

'West L.A. Homicide.' He showed her his card. 'Lauren Teague got killed.' Yet another recitation of the details. I hadn't gotten used to it, and my gut clenched.

Michelle began to shake. 'Oh, God, oh, Jesus – you're not lying?'

'Wish I was, Michelle. Can we come in?'

'It's a shitpile—'

'I don't care about interior decorating. I want to talk about Lauren.'

'Yeah, but—'

'Couldn't care less about your medicine cabinet, Michelle. This is about someone making Lauren dead—'

The tremors continued. She reached around with her right hand, took hold of the empty left sleeve, and squeezed. 'It's not that – it's . . . There's someone in there.'

'Someone you don't want listening in?'

'No, it's—' She glanced back. 'He didn't know Lauren.'

'Long as he doesn't come out shooting, he's no problem for me.'

'Hold on,' she said. 'Let me just go explain.'

'You wouldn't be trying to rabbit, Michelle?'

'Sure, I'm gonna jump out of a two-story window – one of you wants to wait down below to catch me, fine.'

'How about this,' said Milo. 'Have lover boy show himself, then go back to sleep or whatever he's doing.'

'Whatever,' she said, backing away, then stopping. 'Lauren's really dead?'

'As dead as they come, Michelle.'

'Shit. Damn.' The brown eyes misted. 'Hold on.'

We waited in the doorway, and a few moments later a man wearing nothing but red running shorts appeared from the left, rubbing his gums. Thirty-five or so, with unruly dishwater hair, a goatish chin beard, and sleepy, close-set eyes, shoulders brocaded by tattoos, chest acne, and fibroid scars up and down his arms. He held his hands up, accustomed to surrender, prepared to be rousted. Michelle materialized behind him, saying,

'They're cool, Lance – go back to sleep.'

Lance looked to Milo for confirmation.

'Pleasant dreams, Lance.'

The man returned to the bedroom, and Milo entered the apartment, maneuvering around the dog dirt, taking in everything. I followed his footsteps, struggled to keep my shoes clean.

The hairless dog perched on a folding chair, eyes bugging. The kitchen was an arbitrary clearing, with a hot plate and a mini fridge and a single plywood cabinet hanging crookedly. Cracked tile counters were piled high with empty soda cans and take-out cartons. An ant stream originated under the plate and continued up the wall. Two small windows were browned by dirty shades, and Latin music – maybe the din from the unit downstairs – percussed the floor.

Besides the dog's chair the only furnishings were a frayed brown sofa strewn with more empties, crushed cigarette packs, matchbooks, yet more dog droppings, and a redwood coffee table intended for outdoor use, similarly decorated.

Michelle stood watching us, playing with the sash of her robe. 'You can sit.'

'Been sitting all day, thanks. Tell me about Lauren.'

Michelle sat down and placed the dog in her lap. It stayed in place, silent but edgy as she plucked at its ear. Michelle stretched out her index finger, and the dog licked it. 'You just made me depressed beyond belief.'

'Sorry,' said Milo.

'Sure you are.' She reached around the dog and flicked

her empty sleeve. 'I'm like a pirate, see? Captain Hook. Only I've got no hook.'

She stroked the dog for a long time. 'Infection – not AIDS. For the record.'

'Recently?' I said. Reflexively. For a second I'd felt I was facing a patient. If my breaking in bothered Milo, he didn't show it.

Michelle said, 'Couple of years ago. One of those flesh-eating bacteria things. They said I could've died.' Tiny smile. 'Maybe I should've. The guy I was living with then didn't want to take me to the hospital, kept saying it was just a mosquito bite or something. Even when it started spreading up my arm. Then half my body swelled up like a balloon, then everything just started rotting and he split, left me alone. By the time they got to me – man, I felt I was disappearing. And it *hurt*.'

'I'm sorry,' said Milo. 'Really.'

'Yeah, sure – now you telling me this about Lauren . . . I can't believe it.'

'When's the last time you saw her, Michelle?'

Her eyes rose to the ceiling. 'A year ago – no, after that. Later – six months? Could've been five, yeah I think it was five months. She came by and gave me money.'

'Was that a regular thing?'

'Not regular, but she used to do it once in a while. Bring me food, bring me stuff. Especially after I got out of the hospital. When I was *in* the hospital, she was the only one who visited. And now she's dead— Why the fuck did God bother creating this fucked-up world?

What is He, some kind of fucking sadist?'

Her head drooped, and she ran her hand through her hair, pulling at black strands, muttering, 'Split ends, cheap shitty shampoo.'

'Five months ago,' said Milo. 'How was Lauren doing?'

She looked up. '*Her?* She was doing great.'

'How much money did she give you?'

'Seven hundred bucks.'

'Generous.'

'Her and me go way back – went way back.' Her eyes flashed, and she stroked the dog faster. 'In the beginning, *I* used to help *her* – taught her how to dance. In the beginning she used to dance like a white girl. I taught her all kinds of stuff.'

'Like what?'

'How to deal with reality. Developing your attitude. Technique.' Smiling, she ran her finger around the contours of her lips. 'She was smart, she learned fast. Smart about money too. Always saved whatever she could. Me, I have money, it just slips away, I'm extremely fucked up – and you won't hear me blaming the bacteria, even though that really did fuck me up, because even before the bacteria I was pretty fucked up. Personally.'

She lifted the sleeve, let it fall. 'Becoming a freak didn't help my self-image, but I get by. You can always find some guy who digs . . . Like I'm talking to someone who cares.'

Reaching into a pocket of the robe, she pulled out a

cigarette. No pack, just a loose cigarette; easier access with one arm. Milo was quick to light it for her.

'A gentleman.' She sucked smoke. 'So who offed Lauren?'

'That's the big question, Michelle.'

The brown eyes narrowed. 'You really don't know?'

'That's why we're here.'

'Aw,' she said. 'And here I was thinking it was my technique brought you over. Well, I sure can't tell you. Lauren and I – we went different ways. I thought she was getting it together. Back when we were dancing and working together, I always thought she had a better chance of getting it together.'

'Why's that?'

'First, like I said, she was smart. Second, she never got into dope in any big way. Had no jones for men either. She never got attached to anyone, let them get their hooks into her. Tell the truth, she was really kind of a nun – know what I mean?'

'Not a party girl,' said Milo.

'Not a party girl,' Michelle repeated. 'Even when she was partying, her real head was somewhere else, you know? It's like no matter what we did, and we did some shit, believe me, she was like . . . doing something but really not doing it, you know?'

'Detached,' I said.

'Yeah. At first it used to bug me. I used to worry some customer would pick up on it and that would screw the whole deal – kill the fantasy, you know? 'Cause all they want – customers – is to be God for five minutes. And I knew Lauren – no matter what she was doing – thought the customers were pieces of shit. At first I thought she was this snotty bitch with a I'm-too-good-for-it vibe, you know? Then I realized it was just her way of getting through the night, and I came to respect her for that. And I tried it myself.'

She tossed her hair. 'Being detached. I could never pull it off. Not without chemical help. That made me admire Lauren – like she had some special talent. Like she was going places. Now, look.'

She studied me. 'You're not a cop.'

I glanced at Milo. He nodded.

'I'm a psychologist. I knew Lauren years ago.'

'Oh,' she said. 'You're the one – what's your name – Del-something?'

'Delaware.'

'Yeah, she talked about you, said you tried to help her when she was a kid, she was too messed up to work with you. Did she come see you again? She said she was thinking of it.'

'When was this?' I said.

'Last time I saw her – five months ago.'

'No, she didn't. Her mother called me when she went missing.'

'Missing?'

'She was gone for a week before we found her,' said Milo. 'Left her car in the garage, took no luggage, didn't tell anyone. Looks like she had an appointment with someone who got mean. Any idea who?'

'I thought she got out of the job.'

'She told you that?'

'Yeah, said she was back in school, wanted to be a shrink. I said, "Girl, you look like nothing but a yuppie bitch right now, so why bother?" and she laughed. Then I told her to keep studying, and when she figured out why men are so fucked up, let me know.'

'You and she must've met some real sweethearts,' said Milo. 'Back when you were working.'

'You forget 'em,' said Michelle. 'Faces and dicks – one big picture that you rip up and throw out. I saw enough fat asses and melon bellies to last me halfway through hell.'

'What was working for Gretchen like?'

'Gretchen.' Her face hardened. 'Gretchen's got no heart. She fired me – I'm not going to have anything good to say about her.'

'What about dangerous types, Michelle? Customers you wouldn't see a second time?'

'Anyone's dangerous, given the right situation.'

'Did you and Lauren ever have any close calls?'

'Us? Nah. It was boring: bring your knee pads and fake out that you love to swallow, same old same old. Guys thinking they're in charge – meanwhile we knew they were pathetic.'

'Why'd Gretchen fire you?' said Milo.

'She *claimed* I wasn't reliable. So I was late a few times, so what – we're not talking brain surgery. What does it matter if you show up five minutes late?'

'What about Lauren? How'd she and Gretchen get along?'

She inhaled and smiled around a cloud of smoke. 'Lauren handled Gretchen – kissed up to her and did her job and was *reliable*. Then *she* quit on Gretchen. That was a switch.'

'When'd she quit?'

'Must've been . . . three, four years ago.'

'How'd Gretchen react to that?'

'I never heard one way or the other.'

'That the kind of thing make Gretchen mad?'

'Nah, Gretchen never got mad – never showed any feeling. Like I said, no heart. Cut her up and you'll find one of those computer thingies – slickon chip, whatever.'

'Lauren ever have any steady clients? Someone who really liked her and was willing to pay for it? Someone she was seeing recently?'

'Nope. Lauren hated every one of them. Basically, I think she hated men.'

'Did she like women?'

Michelle laughed. 'As in, Eat-me, girlfriend? Nah. We did doubles, playacted all the time, but basically Lauren wasn't *into* it. Switched off – what you said: detached.'

'Why'd she quit Gretchen?' said Milo.

'She told me she saved up enough money, and I believed her. When she came by to tell me, she looked great, was carrying this little computer—'

'Laptop?'

'Yeah, she said it was for school. And she had real great clothes on – better than usual. I mean, Lauren was always into clothes. Gretchen made us buy our own shit, and Lauren always knew where to get the good stuff cheap – she used to do some modeling down at the Fashion Mart, knew all the bargains. But this time she was wearing the real thing – Thierry Mugler pantsuit, black, like poured over her. And a pair of Jimmy Choo pumps. Back then I was living in a *real* dump, over in Highland Park, told her, Girl, you are taking your life in your hands coming around like that, dressed like that. She said she could handle herself, showed me . . .'

She trailed off, smoked some more.

'Showed you what?' said Milo.

'Protection.'

'She was carrying?' said Milo.

'Yeah, this little shooter – silver thing, kind of pretty, that fit in her purse along with the spray. I said, Whoa, what's that – school supplies? She said, A girl can't be too careful.'

'Did she seem afraid of anything?'

'Nah, she was real casual about it. Not that that means much. Lauren was never much of a talker – you just didn't push it with her.'

'So she came by to tell you she'd quit.'

'That and she gave me some money. That was the first time she brought me money—'

'Seven hundred?'

'Something like that – maybe five. It was usually between five and seven.'

'How often did she help you out?'

'Every few months. Sometimes she'd just slip it under the door and I'd find it when I woke up. She never made me feel like scum for taking it. She had a way of— She had class, should've been born rich.'

'Did Lauren ever say anything else that could help us find her killer?' said Milo. 'Anyone who might've had it in for her?'

'Nah, it was all school with her. School this, school that. She was jazzed because she was meeting a different class of people, professors, whatever.' Two eye blinks. 'She was real high on that – intellectuals, professors. Really got off on hanging around with smart people.'

'She ever mention any names of professors?'

'No.'

'She ever talk about doing any work with professors?'

She gazed at the floor. Rolled the dog over and scratched its abdomen. 'I'm thinking— Nah, I don't think so – why?'

'She told people she had a research job.'

'Oh.' Another eye blink. 'Well, she never told me.'

'Nothing like that, at all?'

'Uh-uh.' Dropping the cigarette on the floor, she ground it out, created a smoldering black wound on the linoleum, held out her hand. 'I been putting out for you, how about returning the favor, stud?'

Milo pulled out his wallet and gave her two twenties.

She rubbed the bills between her fingers. 'I used to do a whole lot less to get a whole lot more, but this doesn't suck – you're a sport.'

'Nothing about her job, huh?'

'Nothing . . . I'm getting tired.'

Milo handed her another twenty. She brushed the edge of the bill against the dog's groin.

He said, 'The money Lauren saved up. Was that all from working with Gretchen?'

'Probably. Like I said, she saved. The rest of us, the minute we had a dollar, it was gone, but Lauren was this little Scroogie thing, counting every buck.'

Milo turned to me.

I said, 'Did Lauren talk about her family?'

'She used to in the beginning, but then she stopped. She hated her father, wouldn't say a word about him. Called her mom weak but okay. Said she'd married some old guy, was living in a nice house. Lauren was happy for her, said she'd screwed up plenty but was finally getting it together.'

'Screwed up how?' I said.

'Life, I guess. Screwing up. Like everyone does.'

'Did she ever talk about her mother trying to control her?'

She produced another cigarette. Waited for Milo to light it.

'Not that I remember – from what she said her mom sounded like a wimp, not a bitch.' She put the cigarette to her lips, inhaled, held her breath. When she opened her mouth again, no smoke emerged.

'So she hated her father,' I said.

'He walked out on them, married some stupid cow, had a couple more kids. Little kids. She said they were cute but she didn't know if she'd ever connect with them, because her dad was an asshole and the cow was stupid and she didn't know if she wanted to invest any time in it. She was always talking like that. Everything was an investment – your face, your body, your brain. You had to think of it like money in the bank, not give anything away for free.'

Another deep inhalation. She coughed. Smoked rapidly, burning the cigarette nearly down to the filter. 'She was smart, Lauren was. She shouldn't be dead. Everyone else should be, but not her.'

'Everyone else?' I said.

'The world. Whoever killed her should fry in hell and then get eaten by rats.' Crooked smile. 'Maybe I'll be down there by then and I can train the rats.'

'A gun and a computer,' I said as we left the building. The angry young men two doors up hadn't gotten any more lighthearted, and this time Milo stared at them until their heads turned. 'Like Michelle said, not exactly school supplies.'

'Lauren told Michelle she was out of the game, but she'd stayed in it,' he said. 'No one talks about her being jumpy or afraid. Not Andy or Michelle or her mother. So maybe the gun was to protect what was in the computer.'

'Data,' I said. 'Secrets. And something else: Despite the gun and Lauren's street smarts, someone managed to hog-tie her and shoot her in the head. Maybe she got caught off guard because the killer was someone she never imagined would hurt her. Someone she knew and trusted. As in big-bucks steady customer who'd been generous for years. Not blackmail – fee for service. But then the customer decided to end the relationship, realized the potential for blackmail existed, and took preventative measures.'

We got in the car. He sat behind the wheel, staring at the dash.

'For all we know,' I said, 'Lauren was killed with her own gun. Michelle said a little silver shooter. Plenty of small nine-millimeters around. Someone she trusted and allowed to get close to her purse.'

Still no answer.

'Maybe I'm making too much out of it,' I said, 'but you know how we always talk about the eyes giving it away – how people shift their gaze when they're lying or holding back. Michelle started blinking and fidgeting when the subject of professors came up.'

'Yeah, I noticed that. When she talked about Lauren enjoying hanging out with "intellectuals." So maybe Lauren did tell her about some big-time john with a PhD . . . So why wouldn't Michelle say so?'

'Maybe she thinks there's a chance to profit from it.'

'Blackmail a killer?' he said. 'Not too bright.'

'Michelle's no paragon of judgment. And Lauren's death means no more money under the door.'

He looked up at the peach building. 'Or maybe she's just used to holding back. Whores live by that creed . . . I'll try her again in a couple of days, see if I can pry out the name of some rich intellectual.'

'Ben Dugger's résumé – the easy way he slid into owning his own company, offices in Newport Beach and Brentwood – says money. And those lapses in his education are interesting.'

'Volvo and a frayed shirt says big spender?'

'Maybe he's selective about what he spends on. Lauren did write down his number. And Monique Lindquist's comment about his not talking about sex still has me wondering. During the ride down the elevator in his building, he was in fine spirits. Humming. Literally. Walking with a bounce and enjoying lunch in the park. So either he doesn't know Lauren's dead, or he does and he doesn't care. Maybe it's not high priority, but somewhere along the line I'd take a closer look at him.'

'High priority,' he said. 'Right now, I've got nothing else going.' He tapped the MDT. 'Let's see what *our* computers say about this *intellectual*.'

fifteen

The crime files had nothing to say about Benjamin Dugger. DMV spit out his address.

The beach. An icy, white high-rise on Ocean Avenue in Santa Monica, one of those no-nonsense things knocked into place in the fifties and filled with moderate-income retirees until someone figured out that heart-stopping views of the Pacific and sweet air weren't bad things after all. Now units started at a half million.

The nineties upgrade included new paint and windows, palm trees transplanted from the desert, and locked-door security. We stood out in front. Milo had punched the buzzer three times so far.

He peered through. 'Doorman's right there, yapping with some woman, pretending he doesn't see or hear.' He cursed. 'Give me hookers over petty bureaucrats any day.'

Echo Park to Santa Monica had been a rush-hour crawl across the city, and it was nearly five P.M. Ocean Avenue teemed with tourists, and restaurants ranging from quick grease to wait-at-the-bar haute were jammed.

Across the street salt-cured planks and a cheery white arch marked the entry to the Santa Monica Pier, newly rehabbed. The Ferris wheel was still dormant. Evening lights started to switch on. Old Asian men carrying rods and reels exited the wharf, and kids holding hands entered. The ocean at dusk was polished silver.

Just a short ride up the coast was Malibu, where Lauren had supposedly escaped for rest and recreation. Where she'd called a pay phone at Kanan-Dume.

'Come *on*,' said Milo. He buzzed again, tapped his foot, clenched his hands. 'Bastard actually turned his back.' He toed the doorframe. Pounded on the glass. 'Finally.'

The door opened. The doorman wore a bright green uniform and matching hat. Around sixty and a head shorter than me, with a squat, waxy face scored with frown lines and the squint of someone weaned on No.

He inspected the glass in the door, wagged a finger. 'Now look here, you coulda broke—'

Milo advanced on him so quickly that for a moment I thought he'd bowl the little man down.

Green Suit stumbled backwards. His uniform was pressed to a shine, festooned with gold braids and tarnished brass buttons. A gold plastic badge said GERALD.

'Police business.' The badge flashed an inch from Gerald's eyes.

'Now what kind of business are we talking about here?'

'Our business.' Milo moved around him, swung the

door out of his grasp, and stepped in. Gerald hurried in after Milo. I caught the door and brought up the rear.

The lobby was a chilly vault filled with a clean, salty smell and the giddy glissando of Hawaiian guitar music. Dim, despite mirrored walls. Plush carpeting blunted our footsteps. A grouping of aqua leather chairs blocked our way to the doorman's station. We stepped around, headed for the elevators. Gerald the doorman huffed to keep up.

'Wait a minute.'

'We waited enough.'

'I was on the *phone*, sir.'

We continued to the directory. B. Dugger: 1053. Top floor. The penthouse. The money trail . . .

Gerald said, 'We're a high-security—'

'Is Dr Dugger in?'

'I must call up first.'

'Is he in?'

'Until I call, I couldn't say—'

'Don't call. Just tell me. Now.' A big finger wagged in Gerald's face.

'But—'

'*Don't argue.*'

'He's in.'

As we boarded the lift the doors closed on the doorman's frog-eyed outrage.

'Yeah, I know,' said Milo. 'Just doing his job. Well tough shit – he's the one chosen by God as today's scapegoat.'

Three apartments on the penthouse level, all with high, gray double doors. Dugger's was one of the pair that faced the beach. Dugger answered Milo's knock within seconds, a rolled magazine in his hand, reading glasses hanging from a chain around his neck.

His clothes were a variant of yesterday's rumpled casual: white shirt, sleeves rolled to the elbow, beige Dockers, crepe-soled brown loafers. The magazine was *U.S. News.*

'Dr Dugger?' said Milo, flashing the badge.

'Yes – what's going on?'

I was standing behind Milo, and Dugger hadn't looked at me closely.

'I'd like to ask a few questions.'

'The police? Of me?'

'Yes, sir. May we come in?'

Dugger stood there, perplexed. Through the doors I caught an eyeful of floor-to-ceiling glass, black-granite flooring, endless ocean. What I could see of the furniture looked medium-priced and insipid.

'I'm sorry, I don't understand,' he said.

'It's about Lauren Teague.'

'Lauren? What about her?'

Milo told him.

Dugger went ghostly white and swayed. For a moment I thought he'd faint, and I got ready to catch him. But he stayed on his feet and tugged at his collar and pressed a palm to one cheek, as if stanching a wound.

'Oh, no.'

'I'm afraid so, Doctor. Did you know her well?'

222

'She worked for me. This is . . . hideous. My God. Come in.'

The penthouse was lots of wide-open space. A step-down conversation pit increased the size of the glass wall, magnified the view. No terrace on the other side of the glass, just air and infinity. One of the few walls was covered with metal shelving, filled with journals and books. No food smells from the open kitchen. No woman's touch or sign of domesticity. The first time I'd seen Dugger I hadn't taken a look at his hands. Now I did. No ring.

He sat down, hung his head, dropped it into his hands. When he looked up his eyes aimed for Milo; he still hadn't focused on me. 'For God's sake, what happened?'

'Someone shot her and dumped her in an alley, Doctor. Do you have any idea who would do something like that?'

'No, of course not. Unbelievable.' Dugger's chest rose and fell. Breathing fast. He shook his head. 'Unbelievable.'

'What kind of work did she do for you, sir?'

'She was a research aide on a project I'm conducting. I'm an experimental psychologist.'

'What kind of project, Doctor?'

Dugger's hand flapped distractedly. 'I run a small market research firm. We do mostly contract work with ad agencies – focus groups, limited-topic opinion surveys, that kind of thing . . . Poor Lauren. When did it happen?'

'Several days ago. When's the last time you saw her?'

'A couple of weeks. We're on hiatus . . . This is so . . .'

'What was Lauren researching?' said Milo.

'She wasn't actually – the study I hired her for is on interpersonal space,' said Dugger. 'Why does that matter?'

Milo's answer was a blank look. One of many tricks in his bag; it unsettles some people. It caused Dugger to shift his attention, and now he saw me and his mouth turned down. 'You were just in the elevator at my office. Have you people actually been *following* me? Why in the world would you *do* that?'

Milo and I had prepared for this. He said, 'First things first, sir. Please tell us about Lauren Teague's role in your research.'

Dugger kept his eyes on me for several moments. 'Lauren worked as an experimental confederate. But . . .' He shook his head. Still white.

'But what, sir?'

'I was going to say her job couldn't be relevant. But I'm sure my saying so means nothing to you.'

Milo smiled and took out his notepad. 'What's a confederate, sir?'

Dugger touched the chain of his eyeglasses. 'What psychologists call a plant.'

'I'm not a psychologist, sir.'

'She role-played.'

'Acting?'

'In a sense,' said Dugger. 'Lauren pretended to be an experimental subject.'

'But she was really in on the game?'

'Not a game, a study. Limited deception. It's standard operating procedure in social psychology.'

'Limited?'

'When the studies are over, we always debrief the subjects.'

'You tell them they've been fooled.'

'We— Yes.'

'How do people react to being fooled, Doctor?'

'It's no problem,' said Dugger. 'We pay them well and they're good-natured.'

'No one gets irate?' said Milo. 'No one who might want to take it out on Lauren?'

'No, of course not,' said Dugger. 'You can't be serious . . . Yes, I suppose you are. No, Detective, we've never had that kind of problem. We pretest our subjects, take only psychologically balanced people.'

'No weirdos even though it's a psychology experiment.'

'I don't deal with abnormal psychology.'

Milo said, 'The client doesn't want nutcases.'

Dugger scooted forward. 'We're not talking about anything strange here, Detective. This is quantitative marketing research.'

'Nothing sexy,' said Milo.

Dugger colored. 'Nothing controversial. That's the point, in marketing research one tries to establish norms, to define the typical. Deviance is our enemy. Nothing Lauren did for us could possibly have led to her death. Besides, her identity was always kept confidential.'

'But the subjects found out she'd fooled them.'

'Yes, but Lauren's name and personal information

were always kept confidential.' His chin quaked. 'I can't believe she's . . . gone.'

'Tell me more about the study, sir.'

'Nothing about it could possibly be important to you.'

'Sir, this is a homicide investigation, and I need to know about the victim's activities.'

The word *victim* made Dugger wince. His forehead was sweating, and he wiped it with his sleeve.

'Lauren,' he said. 'It's so . . . This is horrible, this is just horrible.' He shifted in his chair, played with his glasses. Stared at me and his eyes slitted. 'The study Lauren's been working on involves the geometry of personal space. How people configure themselves in various interpersonal situations. For example, if the client was a cosmetics company, they might want to know about the geometry of comfort zones.'

'How close people get to each other,' said Milo.

'How close people get to each other when they're in varying social situations. How people approach each other.'

'Men and women?'

'Men and women, women and women, men and men, the influences of age, culture, distraction, physical attractiveness. That's where Lauren fit in. She was very beautiful, and she served as our attractiveness confederate.'

'You wanted to know if guys got closer to good-looking as opposed to ugly women?'

'It's not that simple.' Dugger smiled weakly. 'Yes, I suppose that's basically it.'

'How'd you come to hire Lauren, sir?'

'She answered an ad in the campus paper at the university. The ad was actually soliciting subjects – we were going to use a modeling agency to get confederates – but when we saw Lauren, we realized she might fit.'

'We?'

'My staff and I.' Dugger looked pained. The sky behind him dimmed, turning the ocean black, graying his face.

'Because of her looks,' said Milo.

'Not just her looks,' said Dugger. 'It was also her bearing and her intelligence. She was – so bright. The experiment involves following complex sets of instructions that change from situation to situation.'

'Instructions about what?'

'Where to position oneself in a room, duration of pose, what to say, what not to say, nonverbal cues. There's some scripting involved – if the subject says one thing, you say another. When not to talk. We use a special room with grid sensors in the floor that are tied in with our computers, so we can track placement and movement directly—' Dugger stopped. 'You don't want to hear this.'

'Actually, we do,' said Milo.

'That's it, really. Lauren was attractive, extremely bright, able to follow directions, motivated, punctual.' Dugger's glance wandered to the ceiling, then lowered. His right hand slid over its mate, and both his knees began bouncing.

'Motivated how?'

227

'She expressed an interest in psychology. Was considering a career in psychology.'

'She talked to you about that.'

'It came up during the screening interview,' said Dugger. Another quick glance upward. A man with Dugger's training might have known, intellectually, about the telltale signs of evasion, but it didn't stop him. His knees bounced faster, and sweat beaded his upper lip.

Milo wrote something down, kept his eyes on his pad. 'So basically, you placed Lauren in this computerized room and measured how guys reacted to her.'

'Yes.'

'For how long were she and the subjects in the room?'

'That's one of the things we vary. Duration, temperature, music, dress.'

'Dress? She wore costumes?'

'Not costumes,' said Dugger. 'Different outfits. Varying colors, styles. In Lauren's case, she brought her own clothes, from which we selected what she wore.'

'Lauren's case?'

'It was actually Lauren's idea. She said she had an extensive wardrobe, suggested we might make good use of it.'

'Creative,' said Milo.

'As I said, she was motivated. Punctual, absolutely reliable, terrific with details. Plus she had the perspective of a researcher – intensely curious. So many people say they want to become psychologists because they have some ambiguous notion about helping people.

Which is good, nothing wrong with that. But Lauren went beyond that. She was extremely keen-minded and analytical. Had a very good *sense* of herself – socially poised, much more mature than other students we'd worked with.'

'Sounds like you came to know her quite well.'

'She worked with us for four months.'

'Since the summer.'

'Yes, late July. We ran the ad during the summer sessions.'

But Lauren hadn't been registered for the summer session. I kept silent.

'Mature,' said Milo. 'Then again, she was older than most students.'

'Yes, she was, but even so.'

'Four months . . . Full-time, every day?'

'Her work schedule was flexible. We run studies when we get enough subjects. Generally, I'd say it worked out to half-time – sometimes more, sometimes less.' Dugger wiped his lip with the back of his hand. His knees were still. Dealing with details had calmed him.

'How'd you reach her when you wanted her to come in?'

'We issued her a beeper.'

'When's the last time you beeped her?'

'That I couldn't tell you. However, if you call the Newport office tomorrow, I'll make sure her time cards are available.'

'Why Newport and not Brentwood?'

229

'The Brentwood office is new, not operational yet.'

'So you beeped Lauren and she drove down to Newport.'

'Yes.'

'How many other confederates are you using in this particular experiment?'

'Two other women and one man. None of them has met each other. None knew Lauren. We do that for contamination control.'

'And how many subjects did Lauren sit in a room with?'

'That I couldn't begin to tell you,' said Dugger.

'But the information is available.'

'You can't really expect me to hand over my subject list. I'm sorry, I really can't do that – Detective, I won't tell you how to do your job, but I'm sure there are more productive ways to solve your case.'

'Such as?'

'I don't know, I'm just saying it had nothing to do with the experiment— My God, the thought of someone destroying a life that vital is sickening.'

Milo got up, walked past him, stood near the wall of glass. A wisp of brass striped the northwest sky. 'Gorgeous view— Did you and Lauren have any personal contacts?'

Dugger's hands laced. Another ceiling glance. 'Not unless you call going out for coffee personal.'

'Coffee.'

'A couple of times,' said Dugger. 'A few times.' He'd gone pale again. 'After work.'

'Just you and Lauren?'

'Sometimes other members of the staff were there. When work ran late and everyone was hungry.'

Milo said, 'And other times it was just you and Lauren—'

'Hardly alone,' said Dugger, in a tight voice. 'We were in a restaurant, in full public view.'

'Which restaurant?'

'More like coffee shops – the Hacienda on Newport Boulevard, Ships, an IHOP—' Dugger's hands separated. He drew himself up, twisted in his chair, met Milo's gaze. 'I want to make this perfectly clear: There was absolutely nothing sexual going on between Lauren and me. If you had to characterize the meetings, I'd liken them to student-teacher chats.'

'About psychology.'

'Yes.'

'What aspect of psychology?' said Milo.

Dugger continued to stare up at him. 'Academic issues. Career opportunities.'

'Sometimes students confide in teachers,' said Milo, walking around so he faced Dugger. 'Did Lauren ever get into her personal life? Her family?'

'No.' Dugger wiped his lip again, and his knees began bouncing again. 'I'm a researcher, not a therapist. Lauren had questions about research design – excellent questions. Why we were structuring an experiment in a certain way, how we developed our hypotheses. She even had the courage to make suggestions.'

Dugger rubbed his thinning hair. His eyes were

231

feverish. 'She had terrific potential, Detective. This is just a god-awful *waste*.'

'Did she ever tell you about any other jobs she'd held?'

'That would be on her personnel form.'

'It never came up in conversation?'

'No.'

'I'd like to see her personnel form, sir. As well as any other data on Lauren you have at hand.'

Dugger sighed. 'I'll try to have them ready for you tomorrow. Come by the Newport office after eleven.'

Milo walked back to where I sat, remained on his feet. 'Thank you, sir . . . Apart from filling out the form, did Lauren say anything about her professional background?'

'Professional?' said Dugger. 'I'm not sure I understand.'

'Dr Dugger, can you think of *anything* that might help us? Anyone at all who resented Lauren or would've had reason to harm her?'

'No,' said Dugger. 'All of us liked her.' To me: 'How did you connect me with Lauren anyway?'

'Your name was among her effects,' said Milo.

'Her effects.' Dugger's eyes closed for a second. 'So . . . pathetic.'

Milo thanked him again, and we walked to the door. Before Dugger could get to the knob, Milo took hold of it. Held it in place. 'Are you married, Dr Dugger?'

'Divorced.'

'Recently?'

'Five years ago.'

'Children?'

'Luckily, no.'

'Luckily?'

'Divorce scars children,' said Dugger. 'Would you like to know my blood type as well?'

Milo grinned. 'Not at this point, sir. Oh – one more thing: the experiment – how long has it been running?'

'This particular phase has lasted around a year,' said Dugger.

'How many phases have there been?'

'Several,' said Dugger. 'It's a long-term interest of ours.'

'Interpersonal space.'

'That's right.'

'We found some notes in Lauren's effects,' said Milo. 'Your name and number and something about intimacy. Is that the same study?'

Dugger smiled. 'So that's it. No, it's nothing sexy, Detective. And yes, it's the same study. Intimacy – in a psychosocial sense – is a component of interpersonal space, sir. In fact, the ad Lauren answered *used* the term *intimacy.*'

'In order to . . .'

'As an eye-catcher, yes,' said Dugger.

'For marketing purposes,' said Milo.

'You could put it that way.'

'Okay, then.' Milo turned the knob. 'So you have absolutely no knowledge of Ms Teague's prior work history?'

'You keep coming back to that.'

Milo turned to me. 'Guess she wouldn't have brought it up with someone like Dr Dugger.'

'What are you getting at?' said Dugger.

'Your being her teacher and all that, sir. Someone she looked up to. You'd be the last person she'd tell.'

He opened the door.

'Tell what?' said Dugger.

Milo's big face took on the burden of so many sad Irish centuries. 'Well, sir, you're likely to read about it in the paper, so there's no sense avoiding it. Before Lauren showed up at your door – before she became a student – she had a history of exotic dancing and prostitution.'

A shudder ran down Dugger's body. 'You can't be serious,' he said.

'I'm afraid I am, sir.'

'Oh, my,' said Dugger, reaching for the doorpost. 'You're right . . . She never mentioned that. That's very . . . tragic.'

'Her death or working as a prostitute?'

Dugger turned away, faced the glass.

'All of it,' he said. 'Everything.'

sixteen

On the way out, Milo bellowed a cheery 'Bye-bye' to Gerald the doorman.

We drove up Ocean. Night had settled in, streetlights were hazed, the ocean was reduced to a slash of reflection.

'He blushed the first time you used the word *sexy*, and he was sweating,' I said. 'Did plenty of his own eye calisthenics, mostly when you suggested something personal between him and Lauren.'

'Yeah, but he looked genuinely shocked when he found out Lauren was dead.'

'Yes, he did,' I admitted. 'I thought he was going to fall down. Still, that's a strong reaction for an employer, wouldn't you say?'

He guided the wheel with one finger. 'So maybe he was screwing her – or wanted to. Doesn't mean he killed her.'

'True. Then again, he could be characterized as an intellectual with bucks – nice penthouse. Be interesting to get a look at his bankbook, see if there are any

235

withdrawals that match Lauren's deposits.'

'No way to do that,' he said. 'Not at this point. The guy's not even close to warrant material – at this point he's done nothing to even justify a reinterview. But after I have a look at Lauren's time cards tomorrow, I'll check out some of those coffee shops he mentioned. If anyone saw hanky-panky between him and Lauren, I'll start talking to the DA.'

'Want me there?'

He chewed his cheek. 'No, I think I'd better do this alone. Got to be careful procedurally.'

'He doesn't like me.'

'Well,' he said, smiling, 'I don't know how anyone couldn't *like* you, but right now I'm shining in comparison. Let me ask you about that experiment of his. Sound kosher?'

'Hard to say. I wonder who his client is.'

'What if Lauren did get to know one of the subjects – put two people in a room and who knows what can happen. Or suppose a subject got turned on to her, decided to pursue it and it turned ugly.'

'Or what you suggested: A subject found out he'd been conned, didn't like that one bit. He claims confidentiality, but how hard would it be for a guy to sit and wait for Lauren to come out.'

'I'd love to have his subject list, but unless he decides to cooperate voluntarily, forget it. Maybe I'll appeal to his sense of morality – he strikes me as someone who likes to think of himself as upstanding, buying stuff for poor kids. He's already been tenderized – maybe he'll bleed some.'

He turned right on Wilshire, cruised past the Third Street Promenade, glanced at shoppers strolling, panhandlers trolling.

'What about his ex-wife?' I said. 'If anyone's gonna debeatify him, who better?'

He smiled. 'You want to knock him off his pedestal.'

'Maybe I do,' I said. 'I guess something about him bugs me – too good to be true.'

'Tsk, tsk, such cynicism.'

'Comes from spending too much time with you.'

'About time you learned,' he said.

Lauren's murder rated three back-page Metro paragraphs in the next morning's *Times*. The story listed her as a student.

I'd woken up thinking, Benjamin Dugger. And Shawna Yeager.

The fact that Dugger's intimacy ad had run during the weeks before both women's disappearances – Milo was right about there being no logical connection, but rationality was his province; I was free to be foolish.

I turned it over for a while, decided to look for Adam Green, the student journalist who'd covered Shawna's story.

Back to the phone book, the four *Green, Adam*s. In 310; Lord knew how many others existed in the panoply of area codes that blanketed L.A. I began calling, got two wrong numbers, a disconnected line, then a phone message that sounded promising:

'This is Adam Green. I may be out seeking inspiration

or slaving away at my word processor or just pursuing pleasure. Either way, if you don't think life sucks, leave a message.'

Nasal baritone. Boy to man.

I said, 'Mr Green, this is Alex Delaware. I'm a psychologist working with the L.A. Police Department and would like to talk to you about Shawna Yeag—'

'This is Adam. Shawna? You've got to be kidding.'

'No, I'm not.'

'They're reopening Shawna? Unreal. Did something happen – did they finally find her?'

'No,' I said. 'Nothing that dramatic. Her name came up during another investigation.'

'Investigation of what?'

'Are you still a journalist, Mr Green?'

Laughter. 'A journalist? As in working for the *Cub*? No, I graduated. I'm a freelance write— Scratch that, that's pretentious, I write ad copy. "Golden Dewdrops, an organic breath of morning freshness." Half of that was mine.'

'Which half?'

'You don't want to know— So what's up with Shawna? What's this other investigation all about?'

'Sorry, I can't get into that,' I said. 'But—'

'But I'm supposed to talk to you.' He laughed again. 'Psychologist, huh? What is this, some kind of FBI profiling thing? Doing a special for A & E?'

'No, I really am working with LAPD. I was reviewing Shawna's case and came across your coverage in the *Cub*. You were more thorough than anyone else and—'

'Now you're butt-kissing. Yeah, I *was* good, wasn't I? Not that there was much competition. No one else seemed to give a damn. Too bad Shawna's dad wasn't a senator.'

'Big-time apathy?'

'I won't say that, but it wasn't exactly a task force offensive either. The unicops did their thing, but they're no geniuses. And the guy LAPD assigned was an old fart – Riley.'

'Leo Riley.'

'Yeah. Ready to retire – I always felt he was phoning it in.'

'Where'd you get the material for your coverage?'

'Hung around the unicop station – mostly watched them work the phones and tack up flyers. When I bugged them, they treated me like a pain-in-the-ass kid – which I was, but so what, I was still covering it. I got the distinct feeling I was the only one making a deal out of it. Except for Mrs Yeager, of course – Shawna's mother. Not that it did her much good – they shined her on too. Finally, she started complaining, and some dean and the head unicop met with her and told her they were really on it. She didn't think much of Riley either.'

He paused. 'I think Shawna's dead – I think she was dead soon after she disappeared.'

'Why do you say that?'

'It's just a feeling I have. If she was alive, why wouldn't she have turned up by now?'

'Could we talk about this face-to-face?' I said. 'Breakfast, lunch, or whatever?'

'LAPD's buying?'

'I'm buying.'

'Cool,' he said. 'Sure, my screen's blank, anyway – can't gear myself up for a go at "Ginkoba, Ginger Gumdrops." Let's see, what time is it – ten. Make it brunch, eleven. I'm over in Baja Beverly Hills – Edris and Pico, east of Century City. There's a Noah's Bagel right down the block – nope, too dinky. How about the kosher deli on Pico near Robertson?'

'Sure, I know the place.'

'Or maybe I should go for something even pricier.'

'The deli's fine.'

'Yada yada,' he said. 'Maybe I'll get an extra sandwich to go.'

I arrived ten minutes early, secured a rear booth, and nibbled sour pickles while I waited. The deli was clean and quiet. Two elderly couples bent over soup – one young, bewigged Orthodox Jewish mother corralled five kids under the age of seven, and a Mexican weight lifter in bicycle tights and a sleeveless sweatshirt trained on chopped liver and a rye heel and a pitcher of iced tea.

Adam Green showed up at 11:05. He was a tall, lanky, dark-haired kid wearing a black V-neck sweater over a white T-shirt, and regular-cut blue jeans that transformed to easy-fit baggy on his ectomorphic frame. Size-thirteen sneakers, gangly limbs, a face that would've been teen-idol handsome but for not quite enough chin. His hair was short and curly, and his sideburns dropped an inch lower than Milo's. A tiny gold hoop pierced his left eyebrow. He spotted me immediately, plopped down hard, and grabbed a pickle.

'Killer traffic. This city is starting to entropize.' He bit down, chewed, grinned.

'L.A. native?' I asked.

'Third generation. My grandfather remembers horses in Boyle Heights and vineyards on Robertson.' Finishing the pickle, he lifted a mustard jar, rolled it between his palms. 'Okay, now that we're auld acquaintances, let's cut to the chase: What's really up with Shawna?'

'Just what I told you.'

'Yeah, yeah, I know. Another investigation. But why? 'Cause some other girl dropped off the face of the earth?'

'Something like that,' I said.

'Something like that . . . Always thought it would make a good book, Shawna's story. Death of a Beauty Queen – something like that. You'd need an ending, though.'

A waitress came over. I ordered a burger and a Coke, and Green asked for a triple-decker pastrami-turkey-corned beef deluxe with extra mayo and a large root beer.

'And to go?' I said.

He showed lots of teeth and slapped his back against the booth. 'Don't think you're safe yet.'

When we were alone again, he looked ready to ask another question, but I got there first. 'So you think Shawna was dead soon after she went missing?'

'Actually, at first I thought she'd gone off with a guy or

something. You know – a fling. Then when she didn't show up, I thought she was dead. Am I right?'

'Why a fling?'

''Cause people do that. Am I right about her probably being dead?'

'Could be,' I said. 'Did you learn anything about Shawna that you didn't put in your articles?'

He didn't answer, had another go at the mustard jar.

'What?' I said.

He blew out air. 'It's like this. Her mom was a nice person. Basic – as in countrified. I don't think she'd been to L.A. in years – she kept talking about how noisy it was. So here she was, someone who'd grown up in this hick town, raised a daughter all by herself. Shawna's dad died when she was little – some kind of trucker. Just like a country song. And the daughter turns out to be gorgeous, goes on to become a beauty queen.'

'Miss Olive.'

'Shawna's idea – entering pageants. Her mom never pushed her – at least that's what she said, and I believe her. There was something about Mrs Yeager. Straight. Salt of the earth. She supported herself and Shawna waiting tables and cleaning houses. They lived in a mobile home. Shawna was her main source of pride, then Shawna wins that Olive thing, announces she hates Santo Leon, is going up to L.A. to study at the U. Mrs Yeager lets her go, but she worries all the time. About L.A., the crime. Then it *happens* – her worst nightmare comes true. I mean, can you think of anything worse?'

I shook my head.

He said, 'Mrs Yeager was *destroyed* – completely. It was pathetic. She comes up here by herself, no money, not a clue as to what things are like. The U— Just the *size* of it scared her. She hadn't made any plans to stay anywhere, ended up in a crappy motel. Near Alvarado, for God's sake. She was taking two-hour bus rides to Westwood, taking her life in her hands walking around MacArthur Park at night. No one's giving her guidance, no one's giving her the time of day. Finally, she gets her purse snatched and the U puts her in a dorm room. But still, no one's really paying her any attention. I was the only one.'

He frowned. 'To be honest, I went after the story in the beginning because I thought it was a cool human-interest hook. Then, after I met Mrs Yeager, I forgot about that— Mostly I sat there while she cried. It kind of soured me on journalism.'

He put the mustard jar down, finished his pickle, snagged another.

'You liked Mrs Yeager,' I said. 'That's why you didn't answer my question about material you kept out of your articles. You'd hate to do anything that compounded her grief.'

'The point is, what good is it gonna do? If no one's found Shawna yet, she's probably never going to be found. You're doing some profile thing to collect data, whatever reason, but you probably don't care either. So what's the point? Why add to Mrs Yeager's misery?'

'It might help solve another case,' I said. 'Maybe Shawna's too.'

He chewed noisily, lowered his head.

'It might, Mr Green.'

No answer.

'What did you find out about Shawna?' I said. 'It won't be released publicly unless lives are at stake.'

He looked up. 'Lives at stake. Sounds ominous.' His eyes were bright blue, charged with curiosity. 'Hey, here comes the grub.'

The waitress brought our sandwiches. My burger was good, and I ate half before putting it down. Adam Green's order was a massive thing dripping with cold cuts and coleslaw, and he chomped furiously.

'I still don't see why I should tell you anything,' he finally said.

'It's the right thing to do.'

'So you say.'

'Yes, I do.'

He wiped his lips, held the sandwich like a shield. 'Look, I need something out of this. If anything gets resolved – what happened to Shawna, or the other case you're working on – I need to know before any of the media. 'Cause maybe I *should* write a book. Or at least an article for a magazine.' He wiped his mouth. 'The truth is, it stayed with me – Shawna. She was so gorgeous, smart, had everything going for her – here she was, just a few years younger than me, and then it was all over for her. I've got a *sister* her age.'

'At the U?'

'No, Brown.' He placed what was left of his sandwich on his plate, reverentially, like an offering. 'We're talking great story elements here. If it's not a book, it could be a screenplay. You learn something, I've got to know. Deal?'

'If the case resolves, you'll be the first writer to know.'

'That sounds kind of ambiguous.'

'It's not,' I said, without taking my eyes off him. He tried for impassive, fell way short. Just a kid. I felt exploitative, told myself he was over twenty-one, had come here voluntarily, was trying his own wheel-and-deal.

'Okay, okay,' he said. 'It's no big thing anyway. The basic point is that Shawna might not have been such an innocent farm girl.'

He took another giant gulp of sandwich, washed it down with root beer. I waited.

'Shawna – and this isn't fact, it's just my assumption, that's why I never published it, along with not wanting to hurt Mrs Yeager. Also, I did tell Riley and the unicops and they ignored me. The fact that *you're* here tells me they never even bothered to put it in their file. Because obviously if they did, you'd have read it.'

'What did you learn, Adam?'

'Okay,' he said. 'Shawna might've posed nude. Done a photo shoot for *Duke* magazine – or what she thought was a shoot for *Duke* magazine, 'cause *I* think it might've been a scam.'

'When did she do this?'

'*Might've*,' he emphasized. 'And I don't know. Probably sometime during the first part of the quarter would be my guess.'

'Not long after she arrived.'

245

He nodded.

'How'd you learn this?' I said.

'I saw a picture – what I'm pretty sure was a picture of Shawna. And the way her roommate reacted when I brought it up told me I was probably right.'

'Mindy Jacobus.'

'Yeah, Mindy. I bugged her a lot, 'cause she was the last person to see Shawna alive. She never wanted to cooperate, said she and Shawna were close, she didn't want to bad-mouth Shawna. Maybe she was being sincere, but I also think she was a little jealous.'

'Why'd you figure that?'

'You've seen pictures of Shawna?'

I nodded.

'Mindy was cute, but she was no Shawna. I'm not saying there was overt animosity between them. But something about the way she talked about her – I couldn't put my finger on it, I just felt it. Whatever the reason, Mindy really didn't want to talk about Shawna. I kept bugging her – showing up at her dorm room, catching her in between classes, playing Ace Newshound.' He smiled wistfully. 'I must've been a real pain in the ass – today, she'd probably have me arrested as a stalker. But I was like . . . driven. Things bothered me. Like why didn't Shawna have a boyfriend? Mindy had a boyfriend. Any good-looking girl can have a boyfriend at the snap of a finger, right? Mindy's answer was that Shawna was a super-grind, end of story. Went to class, came back to the dorm and studied, went to the library and studied some more. But I checked out the grinds in all the libraries, and no one remembered seeing Shawna, and neither did the librarians. I also managed to get hold of Shawna's library records – big no-no, don't ask me how. Shawna hadn't checked any books out the entire quarter.'

'Your article said she was headed for the library the night she disappeared,' I said.

'That was the official story. Mindy's story. And the unicops believed it. But I'm not sure *Mindy* believed it. I think she was covering for Shawna. Because she got all shifty when I bugged her about it. And finally I got her to admit that the reason Shawna didn't have a boyfriend was because she liked older guys. Mindy had tried to fix her up with a buddy of her boyfriend, and Shawna had turned her down flat. Said she preferred older guys – "grown-ups" was the term she used.'

'You're thinking she was having an affair with an older man,' I said.

'It crossed my mind,' he said. 'But I was never able to take it any further. Mindy got all pissed off at me and got her boyfriend – he was this refrigerator-sized behemoth named Steve – to warn me off. I wasn't about to risk life or limb, so I backed off. I did suggest to the unicops that they check out whether Shawna had ever been seen with an older guy – maybe even a faculty member – but they brushed me off.'

'Why a faculty member?'

'Campus life is isolated. What other older men do students come in contact with? But no one cared – not even my editor. She pulled me off, said they needed to run more political stories.'

He shrugged. 'Being on the receiving end of all that apathy and hostility was an eye-opener. So now I write jingles, which is whoring but good-paying whoring. Douche and toothpaste don't slam the door in your face.'

'The photo you saw,' I said. 'Tell me about it.'

'It was the first time I went to the dorm to talk to Mindy – maybe two days after Shawna was reported missing. I don't know if you've seen the dorms, but the rooms are tiny – cells, really. Two people in an area barely big enough for one and not enough closet space, so you tend to keep your stuff out in the open. Shawna must have been a neat freak, 'cause she'd stored her junk on shelves above her bed. I was surprised the police hadn't confiscated it – doesn't that show you how seriously they were taking the case? Anyway, I stuck my hand up to pull down her stuff – I really had nerve – got hold of some books and saw this magazine in the middle of the stack. Recent copy of *Duke*. Which was kind of weird in a girls' room, right? I grabbed the stuff when Mindy had her back to me, then she turned and started screaming at me and knocked everything out of my hand. That's when the photos fell out of the *Duke*. Black-and-whites, clearly nudies. Mindy scooped them up too fast for me to get a good look at them, stuffed them back in the *Duke*, shoved all of it under her own pillow, continued screaming at me. It all happened really fast, but I did see a killer bod and big blond hair, and that would fit Shawna. Mindy starts shoving at me, yelling at me to get out, and I'm saying, What's with the skin shots? and she says it's none of my fucking business. Then she says it belonged to Steve and I'm out in the hall and the door slams.'

He took another bite of sandwich. 'It was almost as if she decided to give me *some* answer so I'd drop it. And maybe it was Steve's, but then what was it doing on Shawna's shelves? In the middle of Shawna's books.'

'Did you tell anyone about this?'

'The unicops and Riley, just like with the older-man theory. Same reaction: Thanks, we'll look into it. Maybe they did. Though my guess is if the pictures *were* of Shawna, Mindy might've gotten rid of them. To save Shawna embarrassment.'

'Any idea where Mindy is now?'

'She was older than Shawna, would be a senior by now. Don't imagine it would be that hard to find her.'

'You never tried.'

'I was out of it – did those few stories, then moved on. But like I said, Shawna stayed with me. Though I never thought I'd be talking about her again. Is our deal still on?'

'Sure,' I said.

'You think any of what I told you might mean something?'

'I'm not dismissing it, Adam.'

Older man, younger woman. Dugger's ad. Nude pictures. Sexual hang-ups.

I'd thought Dugger a prude, but prudes can have secret lives. Maybe Dugger's donation to the kids at the church had been a guilt offering.

Adam Green was staring at me.

I said, 'So maybe the older man in Shawna's life was a photographer. Someone who claimed to be working for *Duke*.'

'Why not? I mean, I can't see a sleazeball like that actually working for *Duke*, 'cause whatever else *Duke* is, it's bona fide, right? They'd have to be careful – couldn't assign some psycho to take pictures of young girls, right? But this is Hollywood – there've got to be armies of low lifes roaming around with cameras and bogus stories. Everyone says Shawna was smart, but she had gotten big-time strokes for her looks and she was still a country girl. How much of a stretch is it from posing in bathing suits and wearing a plastic crown to taking off the suit? And if Shawna did have a thing for older men, couldn't she have been vulnerable to some guy coming across mature and sophisticated?'

'Makes sense,' I said.

'You're not bullshitting me?'

'No. You've put together a logical scenario.'

He grinned. 'I do that once in a while. Maybe I *will* write a screenplay.'

seventeen

Wondering if Mindy Jacobus was also a psych major, I called Mary Lou at the department and asked her to look up Shawna's roommate.

'That girl,' she said. 'Lauren. I read about it— I'm so sorry, Dr Delaware. That poor mother. What does this Mindy have to do with it?'

'Maybe nothing,' I said. 'But you know how it is.'

'Sure – hold on.'

Several minutes later. 'She's not one of ours, so I called Letters and Science. She's an econ major – or was. She didn't re-enroll this year. You don't think she could also be . . .'

'No,' I said, feeling my heart jump. 'Was any reason given for her dropping out?'

'I didn't ask. If you can stay on, I'll call over there again.'

'Sure.'

A longer wait, then: 'Nothing ominous, Dr Delaware. Thank God. She got married, changed her name to Grieg, but the files didn't get put together. So we saved her some red tape. She's only enrolled in one business class this quarter, has a job at the Med Center in public relations.'

I thanked her and hung up. Even if I reached Mindy Jacobus Grieg, what would I say to her? 'Fess up about your missing roommate's secrets?

No reason for her to respond with anything other than a call to Security.

There was another reason not to confront her. I was off my game. My surveillance of Benjamin Dugger had turned out to be an amateurish fumble. Milo'd been gracious enough not to point that out, and when Dugger had confronted me, he'd steered the conversation in another direction. But no sense adding to my list of gaffes. I'd check in with the pro, see what he thought about talking to Mindy. Later. At the end of his workday, when leads had either borne fruit or dead-ended.

No way to know how Milo would react to what I'd learned about Shawna's posing for skin shots. He was reluctant to consider her as a factor in Lauren's death, and all I really had to fuel my suspicion was a college newshound's hunch. But as I sat there mulling, Adam Green's intuition refused to fade.

Maybe because it fit my own premonitions. Shawna's venture into the skin trade firmed the linkage between her and Lauren. So did the fact that both girls had studied psychology, talked about becoming doctors. Grown up deprived in the Daddy department – in Shawna's case literal fatherlessness, in Lauren's a cold, hostile relationship with Lyle Teague. I'd treated enough girls in similar situations to understand where that could lead: the search for the Perfect Father.

And who better than a seemingly gentle older man like Dugger – a man with a psychology doctorate, no less – to fill the void?

Shawna's beauty pageant appearances would have put her in front of an appreciative crowd while still in her teens. Stripping and hooking and runway modeling had done the same for Lauren. I thought of her and Michelle, youth and agility and sexuality playing to a sea of middle-aged leers.

The following day Lauren had talked about the power.

During my attempt to treat Lauren – those few, pitiful hours – she'd been uncooperative, passive-aggressive, seductive. During her final visit sullenness had erupted into outright hostility. Yet Jane claimed she'd admired me, that I'd meant a lot to her and knowing me had fueled her career choice. And Andrew Salander had backed that up.

It was precisely the ambivalence you'd expect from a girl with a father like Lyle Teague. Could I have been smarter . . . ? Then I thought of something else: Jane Teague had also found solace with an older man. Perhaps Lauren hadn't veered as far from maternal influence as she'd thought.

Lauren and older men . . . Gene Dalby had thought Lauren older. She dressed older. Playing for someone sophisticated?

When Lauren had vented at me, I'd sat there and taken it. Because that was part of my job. And because my shame at being at the party still resonated. But another man – a man who'd contracted to lease Lauren's body – might not have been so understanding if Lauren's ambivalence had twisted into verbal abuse.

Gretchen Stengel had put it perfectly: Men paid to have it on their terms. And challenging the rules – or trying to leave the playing field – just wouldn't do.

Lauren had never been anything but a pawn, but her bravado – *I do great with tips* – said she'd fooled herself into thinking she was a queen.

The way she'd died – trussed, shot in the back of the head – spelled out cold execution. The killer making it clear that he was in charge.

The hallmarks of a professional job because the killer wanted to make it look like that. Or was he the type of man who kept his hands clean and hired professionals?

Just another business deal . . . Superficially, it was hard to see Benjamin Dugger – he of the frayed collar, delivering goodies to children – engaging in something like that. But if the man had sexual hang-ups and money, just because he affected a professiorial stance didn't mean he wasn't capable of the worst kind of cruelty.

Either way, someone had been there to teach Lauren a final, horrible lesson: Self-delusion was the mother's milk of prostitution, and fantasies of control were no protection against the worst kind of sore loser.

I made the call to the West L.A. station at five P.M. Milo was away from his desk, and a detective named

Princippe told me he'd gone out on a call.

'Any idea where?'

'Nope.'

I left my name, hung up, and went out for a run. When I got back the sun had set and Milo hadn't called back. I showered and changed, and Robin phoned a few minutes later, telling me she'd gone out to Saugus to look at a rumored store of seasoned Tyrolean violin maple that had turned out to be wormed and worthless – and oak to boot.

'Now I'm stuck on the freeway,' she said.

'Sorry.'

'Guess it's not a bad day compared to other people's.'

'Like who?'

'You don't know?'

'Good point,' I said.

'You all right, hon?'

'I'm fine. Want to go out or should I fix dinner?'

'Sure.'

I laughed. 'Which?'

'Either. Just feed me.'

'That seems reasonable,' I said.

'You're not getting into anything iffy, are you?'

'No. Why should I?'

'Good question.'

'I'm fine,' I said. 'Love you.'

'Love you, too,' she said. But there was something other than affection in her voice.

I was grilling steaks and feeling quite useful when the

phone rang again and Milo said, 'What's up?'

'Anything new on Dugger?'

'Talked to his ex-wife,' he said, sounding rushed. 'Located her in Baltimore – English professor at Hopkins. And guess what: She loves the guy. Not romantically. As a *person*. "Ben's a terrific *person*." No serious personality defects that she was willing to divulge.'

'Why'd they divorce?'

' "We grew in separate directions." '

'Sexually?' I said.

'I didn't ask, Professor Freud,' he said with exaggerated patience. 'It wasn't appropriate. Bottom line: She was amused that the police would be interested in him.'

'He probably alerted her to the fact that you'd be calling.'

'As a matter of fact, I don't think he did. She sounded genuinely surprised. Anyway, something else just came up. Citywide homicide sheets came in this afternoon, and a downtown case caught my eye. Two bodies left in an alley near Alameda late last night or during the early morning, the industrial area east of downtown. Man and a woman, shot in the head, then doused with lighter fluid and torched. The woman had only one arm. The right one. At first they thought it was burned off, but the bodies hadn't burned long enough to do that.'

'Michelle.'

He kept reciting: 'Coroner says an old amputation, they're trying to roll prints off what's left of the right hand, but whatever skin hasn't been broiled is sloughed and messed up and it doesn't look promising. Hopefully, she's got a dentist.'

'The day after we talked to her.'

'Same thing vis-à-vis prints on the male, but they did find some scorched blond hairs. White male, six foot or so.'

'The junkie she lived with,' I said. 'Lance.'

'I asked Ramparts Narcotics to pull up users named Lance. Hopefully I'll have something soon.'

'You're talking as if there's a doubt,' I said.

Silence. 'It's them and I'm wondering if my visit signed their death warrant.' Using the singular. Shouldering the blame.

'Someone who didn't like Michelle talking about Lauren?'

'On the other hand, a girl like Michelle could've been into anything. That place she lived, dope was flowing in and out, those tough guys next door. Or someone was watching her apartment, made me for what I am, figured Michelle had squealed. I wouldn't have noticed – I wasn't looking out for surveillance.'

I said, 'Gretchen knew you were looking for Michelle. She gave you nothing, but Ingrid came up with Michelle's last name. It's not a stretch to think Ingrid told Gretchen.'

'Yeah,' he said, with forced calm. 'The possibility occurred to me, so I called in a favor, asked one of the other detectives in the office to keep an eye on Gretchen's movements for the next day or so. So far, it hasn't come to much. She had a late lunch at the same place, again with Ingrid, went back to her boutique, stayed till three, then got in her little Porsche Boxter and drove to the beach—'

'Dugger's place?'

'No, no, hold on. She bypassed Santa Monica completely, took Sunset straight to PCH, broke the speed limit all the way to Malibu, turned off at Paradise Cove. One of those big gated estates that front the highway. The top was down on the Boxter, the whole time she was gabbing on the cell phone, looking carefree. Even when she was waiting at the gate she was yapping. It didn't take long for her to get buzzed in. And my guy didn't need a map to know where he was. He'd worked security for a party there several times. The Duke estate – the palace Tony Duke built on mammaries. Talk about your Silicone Valley. Apparently Duke hires off-duty cops all the time. Contributes to the police benevolent fund, part of the whole respectability thing. I guess it's no surprise Gretchen would know Duke. Back when she was riding high, she was on every A party list.'

'Tony Duke,' I said. 'Maybe there's more to it.' I told him what I'd learned from Adam Green.

'You've been busy too,' he said evenly.

'I didn't see the harm.'

'No harm done,' he said. 'All this kid saw was some skin shot, he doesn't know they were for Duke.'

'Shots hidden in an issue of *Duke*. Tony Duke has a thing for young blondes, doesn't he? Both Shawna and Lauren fit that bill.'

'I'm sure Tony Duke has blondes lining up to be Treat

of the Month, but his rep is for screwing them, not killing them. And why would he go for a call girl like Lauren?'

'No accounting for taste,' I said.

'I suppose, but some college kid's screenplay fantasies and Gretchen taking a drive to Malibu doesn't exactly get my heart beating.'

'Malibu's where Lauren placed those calls to the pay phone.'

'Exactly. You see Tony leaving Xanadu to take calls at a gas station?'

'Can you tolerate more hypotheses?'

'Sure, hit me.'

I gave him my older-man theory, rambled about power and dominance, the vulnerability that Shawna and Lauren might've shared.

'Tony Duke,' I ended. 'Talk about an older man.'

'So you're trading Dr Dugger for the Sultan of Skin?'

'I adapt to changing circumstance. Fifty plus thousand in Lauren's account would be chump change for Duke. He'd also have a good reason to want her laptop.'

Milo didn't reply. In the background a siren wail climbed like a slide trombone solo, then dopplered into silence.

'Tony Duke,' he finally said. 'Christ, I hope you're wrong. That's just what I need.'

'What's that?'

'Big game, small gun.'

eighteen

For forty years Tony Duke had preached the gospel of meaning through pleasure, converting a generation and scooping millions from the collection plate.

The easy life was his creed. For forty years every issue of *Duke* had splayed that dogma above the masthead.

Over four decades *Duke* pictorials had grown a bit more daring, but the magazine's format hadn't changed much since its first issue: golden-toned, milk-fed female nudity personified by the Treat of the Month, combined with suggestive cartoons, big-brotherly advice on dress, drink, and the acquisition of toys, token ventures into political journalism.

When Duke published his maiden issue, photographic essays of bare breasts, pouting lips, and willing thighs were nothing new. Pinup calendars had been gas station fixtures for years, and 'nature pictorials' had occupied a stable market niche since the invention of the camera. But all that was under-the-counter stuff, supposedly for guys in raincoats and lowered fedoras – sex as dirty, in the finest American tradition. Marc Anthony Duke's revolutionary act had been to veneer the skin rag with respectability. Now Suburban Dad could purchase T & A at the corner newsstand and be regarded as classy rather than creepy.

With its winking scamp logo and gloriously uddered, fresh-faced models, *Duke* magazine had been a major force in the crumbling of sexual censorship barriers, and Tony Duke had fought his share of legal battles. But his victories in court proved, ultimately, to be market-share defeats as each landmark decision allowed successively raunchier publications to achieve legitimacy. Now, in a world where hard-core porn rentals were the number-one video-store commodity, *Duke*'s airbrushed sensibilities seemed almost quaint. When Tony Duke hit the papers these days, it was usually because he'd thrown a fund-raiser for some worthy cause.

All this and whatever else I thought I knew about him had been gleaned from the papers: California farm boy morphed to starving bookkeeper to failed Hollywood scriptwriter to the author of a dozen forgettable science fiction paperbacks, then finally to head of the gutsy publishing venture that had earned him twenty beach-front acres and the kinds of toys his readers could only dream about. But the papers printed what you gave them, and no doubt Duke employed a fleet of publicists.

He had to be what – seventy by now?

Older man.

As far as I knew he'd never been implicated in anything violent. On the contrary, he had a reputation as someone who genuinely loved women. Years ago I'd

caught the tail end of a televised interview with him –
some biographical feature on a network that deluded
itself as substantive. Duke had come across still boyish, if
a bit frail. A small, narrow-shouldered, goateed, ludicrously tanned elf of a man with an easy-to-listen-to
drawl and friendly brown eyes.

Small brown face under a steel-hued hairpiece. Your
eccentric favorite uncle, on shore leave from his latest
jaunt to *locales exotique*, brimming with ribald anecdotes,
naughty jokes, and the unspoken promise that he might,
one day, take you with him.

As I watched the steaks sizzle, I continued to wonder.
About Marc Anthony Duke and Lauren Teague and
Shawna Yeager.

A few years ago, when our house was being rebuilt,
Robin and I had rented on the beach in western Malibu.
During that year I must've zipped past the Duke estate
hundreds of times, never thinking about what went on
behind those foliage-shielded walls. I had only the faintest memory of a green expanse: palms and pines, banks
of devil ivy, geraniums, rubber plants. The gate that had
admitted Gretchen Stengel.

Tony Duke had made a fortune knocking down barriers, but he hid behind high walls. Milo was right: If
Duke was involved it was a whole new game.

I made a salad, mixed iced tea, set the table, tempted
Spike outside with porterhouse, and bolted the dog
door. Robin came home just as I had everything in place.
She looked tired and pale, and her hair was half tied, half

loose. A beautiful woman anyway, but I wondered if Tony Duke would've noticed.

'This is wonderful,' she said, washing up and pecking my cheek.

I took her in my arms, kissed her face, rubbed her back, ran my fingers through her curls, gently, so as not to snag. The sounds she made and the way she melted against me said I was doing okay, even though most of my concentration was spent blocking out the faces of dead people.

She found a bottle of Cabernet that I'd forgotten about, and as we ate and drank my appetite returned. We did the dishes together, took a walk without Spike, holding hands, not saying much. The night was cold enough for visible breath, and the smog had traveled somewhere else. Winter, California style, was finally arriving. I'd check the garden tomorrow, maybe cut back some roses, see what the pond needed. Basic stuff. Concrete stuff. Time to get away from being useless.

When we got back home I got another peck on the cheek and a tired smile. Robin got into bed with a stack of magazines, and I went to my office and switched on the computer.

Marc Anthony Duke's name pulled up sixteen quick hits, mostly press pieces and the official *Duke* magazine website, decorated with grinning portraits of the man himself and thumbnails of pastied and G-stringed Treats Through the Years that could be enlarged with a click.

I scanned for a while, learned only one new fact: Two

years ago Tony Duke had gone into 'ultraleisure mode' and passed the day-to-day operations of Duke Enterprises to his daughter Anita. The accompanying PR photo showed an indigo-robed Duke posing proudly with a sternly attractive brunette in her thirties wearing a strapless black evening gown. Anita Duke was taller than her father by several inches, a shapely woman with smooth, bronze shoulders and nice teeth displayed by a tentative smile that appeared anything but happy. Described as 'an investment banker with a Columbia University MBA and ten years' experience on Wall Street'; 'These will be years of market growth and consumer-sensitivity for Duke Enterprises,' she predicted. 'Soon we'll be moving full-force into cyberspace.'

I searched for something less laudatory, found a couple of Bible Belt organizations listing Duke Enterprises as 'a tool of Satan.' Then some paeans from fans – do-it-yourself stuff, with Tony Duke featured high on most-admired lists. From one of these I learned that Duke had been widowed two decades ago and remained single until four years ago, when he'd hooked up with a former Treat with the improbable name of Sylvana Spring ('the girl who tamed Tony!'), with whom he'd sired two children.

Any taming, though, had been short-lived. Duke and Sylvana had concluded an 'amiable divorce' last year. The kids were proof, claimed the admiring webmaster, of 'Tony Duke's Eternal Virility – eat your hearts out, Viagra-chompers! Beautiful Sylvan and the rugrats still live in a guesthouse right their on T.D.'s palatiol Malibu spreadorama! The Man is ultra-gennerous and too-cool!'

Then pages of downloaded cartoons and centerfold photos, copyright infringements I supposed Duke tolerated. One unlined, doe-eyed, pouty-lipped face after another, sponge-rubber buttocks, geometrically barbered pubic triangles. And breasts. Peach-toned and pink-nippled, identically upswept, pneumatic in a way that Nature had never conceived.

I logged off, returned to the bedroom. Night chill had seeped in, and Robin was wearing a flannel nightgown, buttoned to the neck.

'I was just about to get you,' she said. 'Ready to go to sleep? I am.'

Her hair was pinned, and she'd scrubbed her face clear of makeup. Her eyes still looked tired, and her lips were chapped. A tiny pimple that I hadn't noticed before had sprouted on her forehead. I got into bed, rolled next to her, smelled toothpaste breath, the merest eau of perspiration. As she began to stretch away from me, I kissed her, touched her.

She said, 'I look horrid – wasn't planning to . . .'

Then she sighed, hiked up her gown, drew me to her, held me tight. She was wet when I entered her, came quickly, chewed on my nipple, and rocked the pleasure out of me. When her body peeled away from mine, she was already asleep. I lay there on my back, feeling the thump of my heartbeat, feeling alone. She began snoring lightly, and her hand snaked across the bedsheet, touched my arm, found my index finger. Her pinkie curled around the digit and held on.

Deep in slumber but gripping my finger hard.

Not daring to move, I waited for sleep.

I awoke the next morning knowing I'd dreamed but struggling to retrieve the details. Something to do with a party . . . palm trees, blue water, naked flesh. Or was I imagining that?

I took a very hot shower, dressed, made coffee, and brought it to Robin's studio. She was goggled and gowned, about to enter the spray booth with a new mandolin, feigned patience when she saw me. After a few minutes of sipping and chat, I let her be and returned to the house. Thinking about parties again. Tony Duke's lifestyle. The kind of opulence that might attract a girl like Lauren. Would be even more of a lure for the Olive Queen of Santo Leon. Had Shawna Yeager covered for a bash at the Duke estate with a story about going to the library?

I drove to the U, hurried into the research library, checked out spools of *L.A. Times* microfiche, and searched the social calendar for mention of any parties thrown by Tony Duke over the last year.

Nothing.

Given Duke's reputation that seemed odd, and I retrieved the previous year's worth of spools, covered another six months with still no mention of bashes or fund-raisers at the Malibu estate.

Maybe there were certain parties Tony Duke kept out of the papers. Or maybe, finding himself a father again, the King of the Easy Life had changed his ways.

I kept searching, finally found something nearly two years ago. A 'star-studded' benefit for a free speech organization that had earned Duke two paragraphs in the social pages and was accompanied by photos of the Man, gaggles of Treats, and various screen-famous faces – a plastic surgeon's bragging session. Anita Duke, too, standing behind her father wearing a conservative dark pantsuit and that same edgy smile as she looked down at her father.

His attention was elsewhere. He held two children in his lap – a plump-looking baby not more than a few months old and a two-year-old boy with a chubby face surrounded by cloud puffs of vanilla ringlets. No lounging duds for Dad – he wore a dark suit, white shirt, dark tie. The toupee was gone, and his bald head was exposed in full, iridescent glory. Older and smaller than in the official *Duke* shots – as captured by the paper, the Man resembled nothing but a model grandfather.

'Paternal pride' read the caption. 'Magazine mogul Marc Anthony Duke relaxes with daughter Anita and her half-sibs, tykes Baxter and Sage. Only the absence of son Ben prevented the evening from being a complete family reunion.'

Son Ben.

I hurried out of the microfilm room, raced to the reference stacks, found *Who's Who*, pulled out the most recent copy, and paged furiously to the *D*s.

Duke, Marc Anthony (Dugger, Marvin George)
b. Apr. 15, 1929.

par: George T. and Margaret L. (Baxter).
m. Lenore Mancher, June 2, 1953 (dec. 1979)
children: Benjamin J., Anita C.
m. Sylvana Spring (Cheryl Soames) June 2, 1995 (div.)
children: Baxter M., Sage A. . . .

The rest didn't concern me.

Son Ben.

Professor Monique Lindquist's laughter rang in my ears.

The sex angle – if that's what you want from Ben Dugger . . .

Dugger dressed and drove below his means, used his father's real surname, eschewed the camera. Casting off notoriety? Rejecting what his father stood for? Both?

Now his research made sense.

The mathematics of intimacy.

Reducing sweat and libido to grids and statistics.

The anti-Duke. Sins of the fathers . . . bearing some kind of guilt – had his church visit been part of a chronic quest for absolution?

An older man. Filling the Daddy void.

When I'd learned about Gretchen's visit to his father's estate, I'd veered away from Dugger, but now I was right back where I'd started.

Maybe it hadn't been Tony Gretchen had come to see.

Shawna Yeager posing for *Duke* magazine. Lauren, reminding herself to call 'Dr D.' to talk about intimacy. Getting a job with Dugger, spending time with him in Newport Beach coffee shops – meals Dugger claimed were no more than vocational guidance. Dugger blushing and sweating as he insisted intimacy hadn't crept into *his* time with Lauren. But pseudointimacy was exactly what Lauren had sold, and a man could be forgiven for failing to see the truth.

Self-delusion . . . Lauren, shot to death. Michelle, shot to death, maybe because Lauren had confided in her. Shawna, posing for someone who claimed to be working for Duke.

There had to be a syllogism floating somewhere in that tangle.

I had bad news for Milo.

nineteen

Shortly after five P.M. he called me back.

'Official confirmation on Michelle and the boy-friend.' No triumph in his voice. 'His full name's Bartley Lance Flowrig. Bachelor's degree in shoplifting and burglary, mostly real dumb stuff, no violence. Maybe he and Michelle got desperate and tried to break into the wrong house. Neighborhood like theirs, that could be dangerous.'

'Maybe,' I said. 'But guess what?'

He took the news of Ben Dugger's lineage more calmly than I expected.

'So maybe Lauren told Michelle about something Dugger would like kept private – a nasty kink, something at odds with his nice-guy image. Something that could damage him as well as his dad. Or expose the link to his dad – he seems to be doing his best to hide his family background. Once Lauren was gone, Michelle and Lance decided to profit from the information. Gretchen knew you'd get to them eventually, tipped off someone at the Duke estate.'

He let out a long, low whoosh of resignation, then laughed. 'Tony Duke and Dr Ben. No way I'd have made that connection.'

'That's exactly the point. I picked up some kind of sexual hang-up, and I'll bet I was right. Dugger wears frayed shirts, distances himself from his father and everything his father stands for. But maybe it's a case of protesting too much.'

'Running from his own quirks . . . So you're back on Junior. What about Senior?'

'Who knows?' I said. 'But at this point that visit to Newport doesn't seem like a bad idea. Not that Dugger won't be prepared – he just about invited you to drop by. But throw out Shawna's name at a strategic moment and see how he reacts. And check out the staff – see if anyone looks antsy.'

'Shawna,' he said. 'Who might've posed for *Duke*.'

'Or someone she believed was working for *Duke*. What if Dugger only used his connections once in a while – to attract young, gorgeous blondes. Not a bad ploy at all, especially when he had a genuine link to back it up, could throw in a visit to the estate. And maybe he scammed Lauren too. Despite her years on the street, she could've been seduced by big bucks. Maybe those calls to Malibu were hooking up with Junior, his not wanting her to call him at either his home or Daddy's. Someone as nondescript as Dugger could've used that phone booth without being noticed.'

'A rich kid,' he said. 'Pretending to be regular

folks . . . Okay, let's do Newport tomorrow. I love Orange County – how can you not dig a place that names its airport after John Wayne?'

'Sure you want me along?' I said. 'To Dugger I'm the bad cop.'

'Exactly.'

At nine A.M. Milo rolled onto my property. I had my keys out and headed toward the Seville.

'No,' he said, slapping the driver's door of the unmarked, 'we'll take the Ferrari. I want this to look official. Hence the tie – excellent choice, by the way. Nice power stripes – Italian?'

I checked the label. 'So it says.' I regarded the blue polyester ribbon riding his paunch. 'Where's yours from?'

'The Planet Vulgaro.' He tugged at the knot, licked his pinkie, pretended to slick his hair. 'Spiffed and ready for action. What a team.'

As he drove past the gateposts I said, 'You tell Dugger we were coming?'

He nodded. 'Mr Cooperative. Sounds a little depressed, though. I seem to have that effect on people.'

When we reached Sunset I said, 'Leo Riley.'

'What about him?'

'How would you rate him on the ace detective scale?'

'Average. Why?'

'Adam Green had the feeling Riley was phoning in the investigation on Shawna, just biding his time till retirement. Then again, he's kind of a mouthy kid and had nothing to offer Riley but guesses about an affair with a professor.'

'Leo . . . I called him a few days ago – he's living out in Coachella. Because I did look up the Yeager file, and there's not much in it. Left a message – he hasn't called me back.'

'Not much in the file because there wasn't much to know – or was Green right about Riley?'

'Maybe both,' he said. 'No, Leo was no workaholic . . . Still, there wasn't much to go on. She told her roommate she was going to the library and never came back. Like I told you before, Leo figured it for a psycho sex thing, and I can't say I argued with him. He even made some crack about it turning into a serial killer, and by that time he'd be playing golf in the desert and growing skin cancer. Let's see what he says when he does call back. Meanwhile, I've been thinking about Gretchen's trip to Duke's place. What do you think – collecting for services rendered?'

'Gretchen's never been picky about what she sells.'

'Something else,' he said. 'What Salander said – the whole deal about Lauren not wanting to be controlled by her mom. During the notification interview Jane Abbot did all the right things grief-wise. But basically she gave us nothing. Usually the family throws something at you – wild guesses, suspicions, useless stuff, sometimes a real lead. Jane cried a lot, but there was none of that from her. So I called her last night, left a message.' His eyes shifted toward me. 'She still hasn't gotten back to me. Which leads me to the fact that she hasn't called me once since the notification. That is *also* not typical, Alex. Your usual middle-class homicide, I get *bombarded* with messages: what progress has been made, how soon's the autopsy gonna be over, when can we claim the body, have a funeral. Generally, my problem is playing shrink and clerk and still trying to do my job. This lady – not only doesn't she get in touch on her own, she doesn't take the time to call *back*.'

'Meaning?'

'Meaning is there anything more I should know about her?'

'No,' I said. 'I barely knew her. Barely knew Lauren.'

He gave a cold smile. 'And look where that got you.'

'The price of fame.'

'Yeah— Alex, I guess what I'm saying is there's something about Jane – like maybe she knows something she isn't letting on. The Duke angle's nice and juicy, but what if this all traces back in some way to Lauren's family – Jane, that asshole dad, whatever. I did some checking on ol' Lyle. Couple of DUIs, but that's it. Still, you know better than anyone, this was not one happy family. Is there anything I should be looking at?'

I thought about that as Sunset sloped upward and the 405 on-ramp appeared. Milo pushed down harder on the accelerator, and the unmarked kicked, shuddered, and jammed into high gear.

'Maybe Jane hasn't called back because she's gone into seclusion,' I said.

'With Mel? Where? They both check into some rest

home? So that's my answer, huh? Don't waste my time in the Valley.'

'I can't think of anything.'

'Fair enough.' His hands were white around the wheel as he sped onto the freeway, narrowly passing a Jaguar sedan and eliciting angry honks. 'Fuck you too,' he told the rearview mirror. 'Alex, let's say there is no big family issue. But what if Lauren got hold of juicy info on Dugger or Duke or whoever and passed it along to Jane? Maybe Jane reacted strongly – told her to keep her mouth shut, whatever, and that was the control thing Lauren talked about to Salander.'

'Lauren had been out of the house for years,' I said. 'Had just reconnected with Jane. Their relationship was still thawing. That doesn't mesh with her confiding something explosive, but maybe. When times get rough sometimes the chicks return to roost.'

'So maybe Jane hasn't been in touch with me because she's scared. Has an idea what led to Lauren's death and is worried it could be dangerous for her too. That would be enough to get her to hold back on a lead to Lauren's murder— I know, I know, now it's me who's hypothesizing. But when I'm finished with Dugger, I definitely want another try at her.'

'Makes sense,' I said.

He grinned fiercely. 'Makes no sense evidence-wise, but thanks for the emotional validation. I'm flopping around like a fish on the pier— I know you like Dugger, but he just doesn't bother *me*. I don't pick up any guilt vibe. Sure, he reacted strongly to the news of Lauren's death, but my immediate impression was it was just that: news. Okay, he was sweating, and maybe he and Lauren *were* doing the dirty— Let's see if any of those Newport restaurants remember serious smooching. But still, he doesn't give off any of that fear-hormone stink. He's depressed, not spooked . . . What the hell, he could be a primary psychopath – hog-tied her, shot her, dumped her, and ate a candy bar afterward, and I'm being played like a cheap harmonica. Have you seen anything that points to that level of disturbance? I mean, you should've heard the ex-wife – ready to beatify the guy.'

'Psychopaths don't get anxious, but they do get depressed. Let's take a closer look at him today.'

Milo frowned, rubbed his nose. 'Sure. What the hell, at least we'll get another trip to the beach.'

Just before LAX the freeway clogged. We rolled slowly toward El Segundo, and when the clog gave way Milo said, 'What do you think Tony Duke's worth – couple of hundred million?'

'The magazine's not what it used to be,' I said, 'but sure, that wouldn't surprise me. Why do you ask?'

'I was just thinking. Big stakes if something Dugger *did* do placed the old man in jeopardy. As in sexual violence. 'Cause *Duke*'s image is good, clean licentiousness, right?'

A few miles later: 'Think about it, Alex: John Wayne Airport . . . The guy spent World War Two on the Warner's lot and he's a combat hero . . . Welcome to the land of illusion.'

'Maybe that's why Dugger likes it here.'

Newport Beach sits forty miles south of L.A. Milo violated as many traffic laws as he could think of, but the LAX slowdown turned the trip into a full hour. Exiting at the 55 south, he stayed on the highway as it became Newport Boulevard, sped past miles of basic SoCal strip mall and some spanking new shopping centers with all the charm of theme parks on Prozac. The first evidence of maritime influence – boat brokers – appeared as we switched to Balboa, and soon I was seeing lots of anchor motifs, restaurants claiming FRESH FISH! and HAPPY HOUR! and people dressed for the beach. A silvery winter sky said the sand would be gray and cool, but there was no shortage of bare skin. I opened the window. Ten degrees warmer than L.A. Salt smell, clean and fresh. Between this and Santa Monica, Ben Dugger's lungs would have to be pink and pretty.

A few blocks later Balboa turned narrow and residential: beautifully landscaped two-story homes lining both sides of the boulevard, beach view to the west, marina vista across the street. A turn onto Balboa East took us past more sparkling windows, bougainvillea flowing from railings, Porsches and Lexuses and Range Rovers lolling in cobbled driveways. Then a two-block, low-profile commercial stretch appeared, and Milo said, 'Should be right around here.'

The shop fronts were shaded by multicolored awnings. More shade from street trees, immaculate sidewalks, easy parking, bird chirps, the merest drumbeat of the tide rolling in lazily. Cafés, chiropractors, wine merchants, beachwear boutiques, a dry cleaner. The address Dugger had given for Motivational Associates matched a one-story, seafoam green stucco structure near the corner of Balboa East and A Street. No signage, just a teak door and two draped windows. The immediate neighbors were a dress shop with a window full of chiffon and a storefront eatery labeled simply CHINESE RESTAURANT! Behind the glass front of the café, an Asian man played the deep fryers at warp speed as the woman next to him chopped with a cleaver. The aroma of egg rolls mingled with Pacific brine.

We parked, got out, and Milo knocked on the teak door. The wood was highly varnished, like a boat's deck; with so many coats laid on the thump barely resonated. Ben Dugger opened and said, 'You made good time.'

He wore a white shirt under a gray crewneck, wide-wale green cords, brown moccasins with rawhide laces. The sweater showcased dandruff flecks. He'd shaved recently, but not precisely, and dark hairs hyphenated a raw-looking neck. Behind the thick lenses of his glasses, his eyes were bloodshot and resigned, and when they met mine the pupils expanded.

I smiled. He turned away.

Milo said, 'Easy ride. Scenic.'

Dugger said, 'Come on in,' and admitted us into an off-white anteroom set up with cream canvas chairs and tables piled with magazines and hung with photos of the ocean in various color phases. An unmarked door at the back took us into a larger space, empty and silent and

279

lined with a white door on each wall. The entrance to the left had been left open, revealing a very small, baby blue room furnished with a single bed draped by an Amish quilt and a plain pine nightstand. Stacks of books on the stand, along with a cup and saucer and a pair of glasses. Dugger continued toward a door to the right, but Milo paused to look into the blue room.

Dugger stopped and raised an eyebrow.

Milo pointed at the blue room. 'You've got a bed in there. Sleep research?'

Dugger smiled. 'Nothing that exotic. It's a genuine bedroom. Mine. I sleep here when it's too late to drive back to L.A. Actually, this was my home until I moved.'

'The whole building?'

'Just this room.'

'Kinda cozy.'

'You mean small?' said Dugger, still smiling. 'I don't need much. It sufficed.' He crossed to a closed door and took out a key ring. Double dead bolts, a sign marked PRIVATE. He'd unlatched the first bolt when Milo said, 'So how long ago did you move to L.A.?'

The keys lowered. Dugger took a deep breath. 'All these questions about me. I thought this was about Lauren's employment.'

'Just making conversation, Doctor. Sorry if it makes you uncomfortable.'

Dugger's lips curled upward, and his long, grave face managed a low, inaudible laugh. 'No, it's fine. I moved a couple of years ago.'

'Newport too quiet?'

Dugger glanced at me. Again I smiled, and again his eyes whipped away. 'Not at all. I like Newport very much. But things came up, and I needed to be in L.A. more, so I opened the Brentwood office. It's not really in full gear yet. When it is, I may have to close this place down.'

'Why's that?'

'Too much overhead. We're a small company.'

'Ah,' said Milo. 'Things came up.'

'Yes,' said Dugger, releasing the second bolt. 'Come, let's meet the staff.'

On the other side of the door was a large, bright office pool partitioned into workstations. The usual off-white blandness, computers and printers and bracket bookshelves, potted plants and cute calendars, stuffed animals on shelves, the smell of lilac air freshener, Sheryl Crow from a cassette player over the watercooler.

Four women stood by the watercooler, all blandly attractive, ranging from mid-twenties to mid-thirties. Each wore a variant of sweater-and-pants, and it came across as a uniform. Dugger rattled off names: Jilda Thornburgh, Sally Patrino, Katie Weissenborn, Ann Buyler. The first three were research assistants. Buyler, the secretary, was already equipped with Lauren's time cards.

Milo flipped through them, began questioning the women. Yes, they remembered Lauren. No, they didn't know her well, had no idea who would have wanted to hurt her. The word *punctual* kept coming up. As they talked to Milo I searched for signs of evasiveness, saw only the discomfiture you'd expect from honest people confronted with murder. Ben Dugger had retreated to a cubicle dominated by a large, framed zoo association poster – koalas, cute and cuddly – and had turned his back to us.

Occasionally, one or more of the women looked his way, as if for support.

The women.

Surrounding himself with females.

Like father, like son?

Milo said, 'Dr Dugger? If you don't mind, I'd like to see that room – the one where Lauren worked.'

Dugger turned. 'Certainly.'

As he walked toward us Milo said, 'Oh yeah, one more thing, gang. Shawna Yeager. Anyone by that name ever work here?'

Four headshakes.

'You're sure?' said Milo. 'Not as a subject or a confederate or anything else?'

Dugger said, 'Who?'

Milo repeated the name.

'No,' said Dugger, eyes steady. 'Doesn't ring a bell. Ann?'

Buyler said, 'I'm sure, but I'll check.' She pecked at her computer keyboard, called up a screen, manipulated the mouse. 'No. No Shawna Yeager.'

'Who is she?' Dugger asked Milo.

282

'A girl.'

'So I gathered, Detective—'

'Let's see that room,' said Milo. 'Then I don't need to waste any more of your time.'

twenty

Back in the inner lobby Milo said, 'So who're your clients?'

'You're not thinking of contacting them,' said Dugger.

'Not unless the need arises.'

'It won't.' Dugger's voice had grown sharp.

'I'm sure you're right, sir.'

'I am, Detective. But why do I get the feeling you still suspect me of something?'

'Not so, Doctor. Just—'

'Routine?' said Dugger. 'I really wish you'd stop wasting your time here and go out looking for Lauren's killer.'

'Any suggestions where?' said Milo.

'How would I know? I just know you're wasting your time here. And as far as clients go, in terms of the intimacy study there isn't one. It's a long-term interest of mine, goes back to graduate school. Our commercial projects tend to be much shorter – attitudinal focus groups, a specific product, that kind of thing. We work on a contractual basis, the timing's irregular. When we're in between projects, I focus back on the intimacy study.'

'And now's one of those times,' said Milo.

'Yes. And I'd appreciate it if you don't talk about clients to the staff. I've assured the women that their jobs are secure for the time being, but with the move . . .'

'You may be revamping. So you're financing the intimacy study on your own?'

'There isn't much expense,' said Dugger. 'That woman you mentioned – Shawna. Was she murdered as well?'

'It's possible.'

'My God. So this— You're thinking Lauren could've been *part* of something?'

'Part, sir?'

'A mass murderer – a serial killer, pardon the expression.'

Milo jammed his hands into his pockets. 'You don't like the term, Doctor?'

'It's a cliché,' said Dugger. 'The stuff of bad movies.'

'Doesn't make it any less real when it happens though, does it, sir?'

'I suppose not— Do you really think that's what happened to Lauren? Some psychopathic creep?' Dugger's voice had risen, and he was standing taller. Assertive. Aggressive. Locking eyes with Milo.

Milo said, 'Any tips in that regard – speaking as a psychologist?'

'No,' said Dugger. 'As I told you before, abnormal psychology's not my interest. Never has been.'

'How come?'

'I prefer to study normal phenomena. This world—
We need to emphasize what's right, not what's wrong.
Now, I'll show you my room.'

Ten by ten, sand-colored walls, matching acoustical tile
ceiling, the same kind of canvas chairs as in front, similar
coffee tables but no magazines, no pictures. Dugger
peeled back a corner of the carpet and exposed a series
of stainless steel slats bolted to a cement floor. Soldered
to some of the panels were wires and leads and what
looked like integrated circuit boards.

'So they just sit here and you measure them?' said
Milo.

'Initially, we tell them they're here for marketing
research and they fill out attitude surveys. It takes ten
minutes on average, and we leave them in here for
twenty-five.'

'Fifteen extra to get acquainted with the confederate.'

'If they so choose,' said Dugger.

'How many do?'

'I can't give you a precise number, but people do tend
to be social.'

I watched his lips, listened to his words for import.
Flat tone, no commentary implied or expressed. Maybe
that said plenty.

Milo walked around the room, seemed to fill it with
his bulk. Running his hand along a wall, he said, 'No
one-way mirrors?'

Dugger smiled. 'Too obvious. Everyone watches TV.'

'Set me straight on procedure, Doctor,' said Milo.

'How do you ensure that the subjects and the confederates don't meet after the experiment's over?'

'The subject leaves the room before the confederate. While the subject is debriefed, the confederate is moved to a private waiting area – behind the main office. And we monitor subjects' exits – walk them out, watch them drive away. There's simply no opportunity for subsequent contact.'

'And there's no one – a loose cannon, a subject who resented being deceived – who might've wanted to harm Lauren?'

'No one,' said Dugger. 'We prescreen with a basic test of psychopathology.'

'You don't like abnormal psychology but you recognize its worth.'

Dugger twisted his collar. 'As a tool.'

Milo paced some more, scanned the ceiling. He stopped, pointed to a small metal disc in the corner. 'Lens cover? You film them?'

'We're set up for video and audio recording. It's an option.'

'Do you keep the tapes?'

'No, we transcribe the data numerically, then reuse the tapes,' said Dugger.

'Nothing you'd want to hold on to?'

'It's a quantitative study. The main findings are the informational bits that transmit from the grids to our hard drives. As well as the confederates' observations.'

'The confederates report back to you?'

'We interview them.'

'About what?'

Dugger's lips tightened. 'Qualitative data – variables that can't be numericized.'

'Weird behavior?'

'No, no – nuances. Observational impressions. Measures the grids can't pick up.'

'And you have no interest in abnormality.'

Dugger pressed himself against the wall. 'I really don't see the need to discuss my research interests.'

'The fact that Lauren was murdered—'

'Sickens me. Just *knowing* someone who's been murdered sickens me, but—'

'How well did you know her, Doctor?'

Dugger stepped away from the wall. His eyes rose to the ceiling. 'Look, I know what you're after, and you couldn't be further off the mark. I told you the first time, I never slept with Lauren. The idea is ridiculous and disgusting.'

Milo's shoulders bunched like a bull's as he stepped closer to Dugger. Dugger's hands rose protectively, but Milo stopped several feet away. 'Disgusting? A beautiful girl like Lauren? What's disgusting about sleeping with a beautiful girl?'

Once again sweat beaded Dugger's upper lip. 'Nothing. I didn't mean it in that sense. She was – a lovely girl. It just wasn't like that. She was an employee. It's called professionalism.'

'An employee with whom you had dinner, several times.'

'Jesus,' said Dugger. 'If I'd have known that would set

you off, I'd never have mentioned it. We talked about psychology, her career plans. That's it.'

'Beautiful girls aren't your thing either?'

Dugger's hands lowered, curled into fists, opened slowly. He smiled, brushed dandruff from his sweater. 'As a matter of fact they're not. Per se. I'm sure you're constructed differently, but external beauty means very little to me. Now please leave – I insist you leave.'

'Well,' said Milo, remaining in place. 'If you *insist*.'

'Oh, come on,' said Dugger. 'Why does this have to be adversarial? I realize it's an occupation hazard, but straighten your sights. Lauren deserves that.'

His head dropped, and he covered his eyes. But I saw what he was trying to conceal. The glisten of tears.

Before we got back in the car we stopped at the Chinese restaurant, got some egg rolls and wontons to go, showed the proprietors Lauren's picture.

'Yes,' said the cook, in perfect English. 'She came in here a few times. Chicken fried rice to go.'

'Alone?'

'Always alone. Why?'

'Routine investigation,' said Milo. 'What about Dr Dugger? From next door.'

'No,' said the cook. 'All these years we've been neighbors, and he's never come in. Maybe he's a vegetarian.'

Milo drove six blocks, pulled over, ate a roll in two bites, scattering crumbs and not bothering to brush them off. I got to work on a wonton. Greasy and satisfying.

'How'd he react when I popped Shawna's name? I didn't pick up anything striking.'

'No reaction at all,' I said. 'Which is interesting in itself. Wouldn't you expect some puzzlement?'

'Or, as you remind me from time to time, sometimes a cigar is just a cigar.' He opened the envelope with the time cards that Ann Buyler had given him, and I read over his shoulder. Ten to twenty hours a week, the last pay period three weeks ago.

I said, 'So either Dugger's concealing something or Lauren lied to Salander about going to work during the break.'

'Dugger concealing? What, you don't believe him about no hanky-panky with the help, no attraction to mere physical beauty?'

'He was sweating again.'

'Noticed that. And did you see those tears when he went on about Lauren? What's with the guy?'

'He's holding back something.'

Still eating, he pulled away from the curb, and I slapped his sleeve lightly. 'Mean, bad policeman. You made him cry.'

'Jesus, you've turned into a hard case,' he said, finishing another roll and reaching for a third.

'That marketing company of his,' I said. 'There's a phony feel to it— He got really defensive when you asked him about clients, claimed to be between jobs. Maybe because he doesn't get many. Doesn't need to, because he's got funding from the Duke Foundation – overtly or otherwise. And that would've raised the blackmail stakes:

What if the old man's getting tired of financing Junior's supposedly pure lifestyle? Especially with Ben distancing himself from all Tony Duke regards as holy. But still takes the money. What if Duke's looking for an excuse to cut Ben off? A nasty scandal would play nicely into that. More than Dugger's reputation could be at stake.'

'Well, let's see if anyone around here remembers him doing anything scandalous. With Lauren or anyone else.'

We spent the next two hours cruising Newport and showing Lauren's photo to restaurant servers and hosts, dropping Ben Dugger's name, getting absolutely nothing. More than once someone said, 'A face like that I would've remembered.' A kid in a seafood joint said, 'If you find her, can I have her number?'

As we left the final restaurant Milo said, 'If Dugger and Lauren were trysting, they weren't doing it over food.'

'Maybe food's not his thing either. How about motels?'

He groaned but nodded. Another hour was lost questioning desk clerks. Same result. Milo cursed all the way back to the 55.

'Maybe the guy's gay,' I said. 'You sense any hint of that?'

'What, I'm supposed to have gaydar?'

'Touchy.'

'Low blood sugar – anything left in that bag?'

'One wonton.'

'Hand it over.' Between mouthfuls: 'Maybe he is gay. Or asexual, or virtuous, or Lord knows what.'

'Asexual,' I said. 'Wouldn't that be something? The Grand Stud spawns a son who's anything but.'

'You don't like him. I wouldn't wanna go bowling with him either – guy's a priss. But being Tony Duke's kid isn't grounds for a warrant. He's untouchable with regard to Lauren, and so's all his intimacy data. When we get back I'm getting on the horn to Central and the coroner, see if anything's come up on Michelle. If they pull a bullet out of her head and it matches the nine millimeter in Lauren's, maybe I can talk to someone about leaning on Gretchen. Right now, it's time for that second face-to-face with Jane Abbot. Speaking of which.'

He placed another call to the Sherman Oaks number, got another taped reply. This time he hung up without leaving a message.

'I've also got a call in to Westside Vice about Gretchen. Be interesting if she's gotten active again. If anything leads back to her and Duke, I'll be on Junior like a rash. Let's hit the Abbot house, see if the neighbors know where Jane and Mel are. I'll leave my card in the mailbox, and if she doesn't respond to that, I'll really want to know why.'

'Would you consider a detour to Westwood?' I said. 'Mindy Jacobus works at the Med Center in public relations. Adam Green feels she didn't want to be helpful. Any statements from her in Riley's file?'

'Just the library story.'

'Green checked out the library. No one remembers Shawna ever being there.'

He looked at his watch, gazed through the windshield

at the clear stretch of freeway. Midday lull: just a few trucks and cars, and us in the fast lane, under a browning sky that mocked the virtues of progress.

'Nice little off-ramp in Westwood,' he said. 'Why the hell not?'

Adam Green had described Mindy Jacobus as 'no Shawna,' but she turned out to be a stunning young woman with flawless, lightly tanned skin and one of the healthiest heads of glowing black hair I'd ever seen. A tall, long-legged sylph in a pale blue knit dress and high-heeled white sandals, she strode out of the public relations office into a hallway that reeked of rubbing alcohol carrying a gold Cross pen, moving with a confidence that made her seem older than twenty.

More planes than curves; Tony Duke would probably have walked past her, so maybe that was what Green had meant. But her stride was a hip-swiveling sashay that transcended lack of flesh.

'Yes?' she said with a publicist's ready smile. Her ID tag read, M. JACOBUS-GRIEG. ASSISTANT PUBLICIST. Milo had given the front desk his name only, no title. The smile wavered when she got a good look at him. No way could that face – that tie – mean philanthropy or any other brand of good news.

When he flashed the badge her confidence shut down completely, and she looked like an overdressed kid. 'What's this about?'

'Shawna Yeager, Ms Jacobus-Grieg—'

'How *weird*.'

294

We were in an administrative wing of the Med Center, far removed from clinical care, but the hospital smell – that alcohol *stink* – brought back memories of mass polio vaccinations in school auditoriums. My father accepting the needle with a smile, biceps tensing so hard the blood ran down his arm. I, five years old, fighting to squelch my tears as a white-capped nurse produced a frigid cotton swab . . .

'Weird?' said Milo.

Mindy Jacobus-Grieg's fine-boned hand clutched the pen tighter. Closing the door behind her, she moved several feet down the hall and settled a lean rump against pale green plaster. The decor was photos of med school deans and famous benefactors at black-tie galas. Some of the angels were showbiz types, and I searched for Tony Duke's face but didn't find it.

'Hearing Shawna's name again,' she said. 'It's been over a year. Has something finally— Did you find her?'

'Not yet, ma'am.'

Ma'am made her flinch. 'So why are you here?'

'To follow up on the information you gave during the initial investigation.'

'Now? A year later?'

'Yes, ma'am—'

'What could I tell you that I didn't already say back then?'

'Well,' said Milo, 'we're new on the case, just doing our best to see what we can learn. And you were the last person to see Shawna.'

'Yes, I was.'

295

'Just before she left for the library.'

'That's what she said.' She glanced down at her left hand. The third finger was circled by a gold wedding band and a one-carat diamond ring. She rubbed the stone – reminding herself she'd made progress since then?

Milo said, 'Newlywed?'

'Last June. My husband's a rheumatology resident. I dropped out temporarily to help pay some bills— Does Shawna's mom know you're back on the case?'

'Are you in contact with Shawna's mom?'

'No,' she said. 'Not any longer. I did stay in touch for a while – a few months. Agnes – Mrs Yeager – moved to L.A., and I tried to help her get adjusted. But you know . . .'

'Sure,' said Milo. 'Nice of you to help her.'

A tiny pink tongue tip darted from between Mindy's lips, then retracted. 'She was pretty destroyed.'

'Any idea where she can be reached?'

'She's not working at the Hilton anymore?'

'Beverly or Downtown?'

'Beverly,' said Mindy. 'That's not in the file? You must be missing a bunch of stuff. That other detective – the old one. He seemed a little . . . Is he your friend?'

Milo smiled. 'Detective Riley? Yes, he did tend to get a little distracted.'

'I never felt he was really paying attention. Anyway, that's where Agnes worked. I was just thinking about her on Christmas. Because Shawna's birthday was December twenty-eighth and I knew her mom must be going through hell. I would've invited her to my parents' house, but we all went to Hawaii . . .'

'What did Mrs Yeager do at the Hilton?'

'Cleaned rooms. She needed something so she could stay in L.A., and she couldn't find any decent waitress jobs. The U let her stay in a grad student dorm for a few weeks, but then she had to leave. She didn't know the city at all, almost ended up near MacArthur Park. I told her to stay as far west as she could, and she found herself an apartment near La Brea and Pico – Cochran south of Pico.'

'So she stuck around.'

'For a few months. Maybe she moved back home – I don't know.'

'Back to Santo Leon,' I said.

'Uh-huh.' She rolled the pen between her fingers.

Milo said, 'So the last time you saw Shawna was that night she said she was going to the library. Remember what time that was?'

'I think I said eight-thirty. It couldn't have been too much earlier 'cause I was out with Steve – my ex-boyfriend.' Tiny smile. 'He had football practice until seven, and I used to pick him up and we'd have dinner in the Coop and then he'd walk me back to the dorms. Shortly after I got back, Shawna left. I studied for a while, went to bed, and when I woke up she still hadn't returned.'

'Was the library a usual place for her to study?'

'I guess.'

'You're not sure?'

The hand clutching the pen tightened. 'In the papers – the campus paper mostly – they said no one remembered Shawna in any of the libraries. Trying to make out like Shawna had lied. But the libraries are huge, so what does that prove? I had no reason to doubt her.'

Footsteps and laughter caused her to gaze down the hall. A group of people in suits passed, and someone called out her name. 'Hey, guys,' she said, flashing the sunny smile, then turning it off as she faced us. 'Is that it?'

'When Shawna left was she carrying books?'

'She'd have to be,' said Mindy.

'She'd have to be?'

'Even if she wasn't telling the truth about studying, she would've covered herself, right? I mean, with no books, I'd have said something. And I didn't. So, sure, she must've had books. I would've noticed if she hadn't been.'

'Logical,' agreed Milo. 'But do you specifically recall seeing books?'

Blue irises bobbled. 'No, but . . . why do you doubt her?'

'Just trying to collect as many details as I can, ma'am.'

'Well no way I can give you details after all this time, but the logical thing was she had books. Probably psych books. That's all Shawna read, she was really into it – psychology, medicine. All she did was study.'

'A grind,' I said, remembering the phrase she'd used with Adam Green.

'Not in a dorky sense. She was just serious about her

grades . . . Do you think she could still be alive?'

Milo said, 'Anything's possible.'

'But unlikely.'

Milo shrugged.

Mindy shut her eyes, opened them. 'She was so beautiful.'

'If Shawna did make up the story about going to the library, what do you think she was covering for?'

'I don't think she was covering, and if she was I wouldn't have the faintest.' The pen slipped from her grasp. She moved fast and caught it.

'Could she have been hiding the fact that she had a boyfriend?' said Milo.

Mindy licked her lips. 'Why would she hide that?'

'You tell me,' said Milo gently.

Mindy edged away from him. 'I have no idea.'

'*Did* Shawna have a boyfriend, Ms Jacobus-Grieg?'

'Not that I knew.'

Milo consulted his pad. 'Funny, going over the file, I copied down something about a boyfriend . . . For some reason I thought that came from you.'

'No way. Why would I tell anyone that?'

'Must be a mistake, then. Oh, well.'

The smooth skin behind Mindy's ears had pinkened. Milo began paging through his pad. Blank pages. From where Mindy stood, she couldn't see that. 'Here it is . . . "Possible boyfriend. Maybe older guy." Per MJ.' Looking up, he favored Mindy with an innocent look. 'I assumed "MJ" was you, but maybe something got scrambled.'

'Probably.' The flush had spread to Mindy's jawline.

Milo kicked the wall lightly with the back of his shoe. 'Let's talk theoretically, okay? If Shawna did have an older boyfriend, any idea who he coulda been?'

'How would I know?'

'I just thought, the two of you living together, being close—'

'We lived together, but we weren't close. Anyway, it was only for a couple of months.'

'So you guys weren't real friends?' I said.

'We got along but we were different. For one, I was older. A screw-up landed me in a room with a freshman.'

'Different worlds.'

'Exactly,' said Mindy, relieved at being understood.

'Different how?' asked Milo, smiling.

'I'm social,' she said. 'I like people, always had lots of friends. Shawna was more of a loner.'

'Interesting trait for a beauty queen.'

'Oh, that – well, that was back in Santo Leon.'

'Didn't count?'

'No, no, I'm not putting it down – it's just I gathered that back home Shawna was pretty important, but up here she was just another freshman. I went to Uni, had tons of friends here from high school, she didn't. I tried to— She didn't make too many of her own friends. I mean she probably would've – it was only the beginning of the quarter.'

'Not too social?' I said.

'Not too.'

'So back in Santo Leon she'd been a big fish in a small pond, but in L.A. she had trouble distinguishing herself.'

'Yes— I mean she *was* beautiful. But kind of . . . country. Unsophisticated. Also, her basic personality was – I don't want to say stuck up, more like private. She *did* like to keep to herself. Like when Steve would come over, Shawna would ignore him or leave— She said she wanted to give us space. But . . .'

'You thought maybe she was being a bit antisocial,' I said.

'To be honest? Kind of. That's why I didn't pay much attention that night when she left for the library. She was gone a lot.'

'A lot?'

'Yes.'

'Nights?'

'Nights and days. I really didn't see her much.'

'Did she spend nights away from the dorm?'

'No,' she said. 'She always was there in the morning. That's why when I woke up and she wasn't, I thought it was weird. But still . . .'

'Still what?' said Milo.

'I didn't freak or anything. You know – this was college. We were supposed to be grown-ups.'

Milo twirled his own pen. Blue plastic Bic. 'So there was no boyfriend you know of.'

'Right.'

'And this other note I've got – about maybe it being an older man. Did Shawna ever say anything about liking older men?'

Mindy's back was flat against the wall. Another upward glance. Both of her hands clenched the pen.

301

'Ms Jacobus-Grieg?'

'Is this – is all this going to be publicized?'

'That's not our priority.'

''Cause it was really no big deal. And Agnes . . .'

'What was no big deal?'

Mindy shook her head. 'I told a reporter – some pest from the *Cub* – and he told the police about a conversation Shawna and I had.'

'A conversation about what?'

'Guys – what girls talk about all the time. I shouldn't have opened my mouth. And that pest shouldn't've repeated it.'

'Repeated what, Mindy?'

Mindy rubbed one pump against the other. 'I wouldn't want to ruin Shawna's reputation.'

'Ruin it in what way?'

'Raising rumors – because what's the point, a year later? Why should her mom read it and get upset?'

Milo moved closer to her, placed his weight on one foot, looking very tired. 'What hurts Mrs Yeager the most is not knowing what happened to Shawna. That's the ultimate hell for a parent, so anything you can do to clear it up would be a good deed.'

Mindy bit back tears. 'I know, I know, but I'm sure it's nothing—'

'Indulge us. Unless it leads to a solution, we'll keep it close to the vest.'

The flush had overtaken Mindy's face. Coppery glow beneath the tan, but nothing healthy about it.

'It was really just a single conversation,' she said,

swiping at her eyes again. 'Maybe three weeks into the semester. Steve had a friend who thought Shawna looked hot, and he asked if Shawna wanted to be fixed up. Shawna said no, she had too much studying, but then she went out – and not to the library, this was a Friday morning and she said something had come up suddenly, she had to leave early for the weekend. Something back home in Santo Leon. But the thing is, she was all dressed up and made up – nothing like what you'd expect just to take the bus home. So I asked her who the guy was, said she wasn't wasting stockings and all that lip gloss on some campus loser. And she gave me this – I can only call it an *off* look, know what I mean? Real serious – almost angry. But not angry – upset.'

'Like you'd hit a nerve,' I said.

'Exactly. She gave me the off look and said, "Mindy, I would never date anyone my age. Give me an older guy any time, 'cause they know how to treat a woman." And that's when it hit me: the way she was dressed. A suit – all that makeup. It's like she was trying to make herself *look* older, so I wondered. And that's what I told that pest from the *Cub*. Which is probably what you've got in there.' Pointing to the pad. 'But I don't know for sure,' she added.

'You didn't ask her?' said Milo.

'I tried— I can be nosy, I admit it. But like I said, Shawna was private. She just kind of blew me off, picked up her suitcase and left.'

'So older men know how to treat a woman,' said Milo. 'You think she meant financially?'

'That's the way I took it. 'Cause Shawna liked *things*. Talked about becoming a psychiatrist or a plastic surgeon, getting herself a big house in one of the Three Bs – Brentwood, Bel Air, Beverly Hills – like she'd read about that in some magazine. I mean, she actually took the bus into Beverly Hills once, walked up and down Rodeo Drive – unsophisticated. Kind of adorable, really.'

'Into stuff,' said Milo.

'Clothes, cars – she said one day she'd drive a Ferrari.'

'From being a plastic surgeon or marrying one?'

'Maybe both,' said Mindy.

'She ever talk about any professors she really liked?'

'What, you think it was a professor?'

'They're the older men on campus.'

'No, she never said.'

'Okay, thanks for your time,' said Milo, flipping through his pad, then slipping it into his pocket. Mindy smiled, and her posture had just loosened when he said, 'Oh, one other thing – and this'll stay as private as possible too. There was mention of some photos Shawna might've posed for, for *Duke* magazine—'

'Oh, please,' snapped Mindy. 'That stupid *idiot* – the weirdo from the *Cub*.'

'Weird, how?'

'Obsessive. Like a stalker. He wouldn't leave me alone. Kept dropping in at the dorm, doing his big reporter thing. The last straw was when he barged right past me, started poking around our stuff. The whole *Duke* thing came up because Steve had left some magazines around – *Sports Illustrated*, *GQ*. And, yes, some *Playboy*s and

*Duke*s too – you know guys. And the idiot has the nerve to start poking around in the stack and these loose pages fall out of the *Duke* and Green – the idiot – grabs them and says, "Whoa, is this Shawna?" I grab them back and tell him to keep his filthy mitts off and his mind out of the gutter. And he gives me this knowing smile – this smirk – and he says, "What's the matter, Mindy? Why shouldn't Shawna pose? God gave her the bod and the hair—" disgusting talk. That's when I threatened to scream and he left, but he kept hassling me, and I had to get Steve to warn him off. Maybe you should be looking at him.'

'Did he know Shawna before she disappeared?' I said.

'No – I don't think so. I was just talking in the sense that he was weird. Anyway, that's where that *Duke* stupidity came from.'

'So Shawna never posed.'

'Of course not. Why would she do that?'

'Same reason any girl does. Money, fame – or maybe she'd met an older guy who was also a photographer.'

'No,' said Mindy, 'no way. Shawna wanted to be a *doctor*, not a centerfold. That's not the kind of money and fame she wanted. None of us want *that*. It's demeaning.'

'Shawna entered beauty contests,' said Milo.

'And hated it – Miss *Olive* Oil, whatever. She told me she only did it for the prize money and because she figured it would look good on her U application. She wasn't that kind of girl.'

'What kind is that?'

'A bimbo. She was smart.' Another quick study of the ceiling. White knuckles around the gold pen. One hand let go and began tracing the outline of her narrow hip. Her face had turned salmon pink. Her eyes jumped around like pachinko balls.

'Demeaning,' she said.

Milo smiled at her. Let it ride.

twenty-one

A s Mindy returned to her office the corridor filled
with people.

Milo said, 'That Chinese food made me thirsty.'

We rode a crowded elevator down to the Med School
cafeteria. Amid the clatter of trays and the odors of mass
fodder, we bought Cokes and settled at a rear table.
Behind us was a cloudy glass wall looking out to an
atrium.

'So,' he said. 'Mindy.'

'Not a terrific liar,' I said. 'Her complexion wouldn't
cooperate, and she was squeezing that pen hard enough
to break it. Especially when she talked about the
photos. Adam Green said they were loose black-and-
whites, not magazine pages. Mindy tried to make him
out as some nut, but he seemed pretty credible to me.
And Mindy's explanation makes no sense. Why would
her boyfriend keep skin mags in *her* room? Green
wondered if both Shawna and Mindy had followed up
on a solicitation to pose. That would explain Mindy's
nervousness.'

He nodded. 'Especially now that she's an old married woman.'

'You didn't press her on it.'

'I felt I'd gone as far with her as I could. For the time being. Even if Shawna did pose for nudies, there's no proof it was really a *Duke* gig, and not some con man with a business card. Fact is, I can't see *Duke* using some psycho photographer – too much at stake. And I can't exactly march into Tony's corporate headquarters and demand access to the photo archives.'

His beeper went off. He read the number, cell-phoned, couldn't get a connection, and stepped outside the cafeteria. When he returned he said, 'Guess who that was? Lyle Teague. Mommy doesn't call me, but Daddy does.'

'What did he want?'

'Have I gotten anywhere, was there anything he could do? Forcing himself to be polite – you could just about see his hands clench through the phone lines. Then he slips in a question about Lauren's estate. Who's in charge, what's going to happen to her stuff, do I know who's handling her finances?'

'Oh, man.'

He shook his head. 'The vulture circles. When I told him I had no idea about any of that, he started to get testy. Poor Lauren, growing up with that. Sometimes I think your job's worse than mine.'

He bought another Coke, emptied the can.

I said, 'The one thing Mindy did confirm was Shawna's attraction to older men. That and a *Duke* angle –

real or not – does provide a possible link between her and Lauren.'

'Dugger,' he said.

'Older man, rich, smart. A psychologist, no less. He fits Shawna's list. And talk about business cards – he's got paternity to back it up. For all we know he uses the magazine as a lure. Same for the intimacy study.'

'Double life, huh? Mr Clean by day, God knows what after hours?'

'Even by day he's strange,' I said. 'He has no current clients but keeps that lab going. Putting people in a strange little room and measuring how close they get to each other. Sounds more like voyeurism than science to me. And he was running ads prior to both Shawna's and Lauren's disappearances.'

'His staff said Shawna had never been to Newport.'

'So he destroyed records. Or met Shawna another way. Taking glam pictures, or he used some other premise. Mindy said Shawna got all dressed up for that weekend thing back home. She didn't buy the story, assumed the obvious: a date. Shawna was eighteen years old, hungry for the finer things, talked openly about digging older guys. It wouldn't take a genius to seize upon that and exploit it. And here's something else to think about: A year has passed between Shawna's disappearance and Lauren's death, but that doesn't mean there've been no victims in the interim.'

'I checked for that,' he said. 'Right after you told me about Shawna. No obvious similars.'

'Things happen,' I said. 'Stuff no one knows about.

Especially when there's money involved.'

He didn't answer. But he didn't argue.

We left the Med Center and walked to the no parking zone in front, where he'd left the unmarked. A parking ticket flapped under the windshield wipers. He crumpled it and tossed it in the car's backseat.

I said, 'At the very least, it would be worth talking to Shawna's mother. She might be able to confirm or deny the weekend event in Santo Leon. Maybe she's still working at the Hilton.'

'Someone else to make miserable,' he said. 'Yeah, yeah, let's blow by. After that, I'm heading out to Sherman Oaks to see Jane Abbot. Happy Mother's Day.'

The Beverly Hilton sits at the western edge of Beverly Hills, just east of where the L.A. County Club begins its dominance of Wilshire. The drive from Westwood was five minutes. The hotel's personnel office was cooperative but careful, and it took a while to find out that Agnes Yeager had left the Hilton's employ nine months ago.

'She didn't stay long,' said Milo. 'Problems?'

'No problems at all,' said the assistant personnel manager, Esai Valparaiso, a small, friendly man in a tight brown suit. 'We didn't dismiss her, she just left.' Valparaiso's thumb flicked the edge of the folder. 'Without notice, it says here.'

'Any idea where she went?'

'No, sir, we don't follow them.'

'And her job was to clean rooms.'

'Yes, sir – she was a Housekeeper One.'

'Could I have her most recent address?'

Valparaiso's hands spread atop his desk. 'I hope she hasn't done anything that reflects upon the hotel.'

'Not unless grief's bad for your image.'

'Twelve hundred Cochran,' Milo said, reading the slip as we headed for the car. 'The place Mindy told us about.' He plugged Agnes Yeager's name into DMV. 'No wants, warrants, violations, but the address is back in Santo Leon.'

'Maybe she gave up, moved back.'

He got the area code for the farm town, called Information. 'Not listed— Okay, let's have a look at Cochran.'

The apartment was a six-unit dingbat just south of Olympic, on the east side of the street. White-stucco box faced with blue diamonds, remnants of sparkle paint glinting at the points, an open carport packed with older sedans, and a spotless concrete yard where there should've been lawn. No Yeager on the mailbox in front, and we were about to leave when an old black man leaning on a skinny chromium cane limped out of the front unit and waved.

His skin was the color of fresh eggplant, shaded to pitch where a wide-brimmed straw hat blocked the sun. He wore a faded blue work shirt buttoned to the neck, heavy brown twill trousers, and bubble-toed black work shoes with mirror-polished tips.

'Sir,' said Milo.

Tip of the hat. 'So who did what to who, Officers?' The cane slanted forward as he limped toward us. We met him midway to the carport.

Milo said, 'We're looking for Agnes Yeager, sir.'

Cracked gray lips canted downward. 'Agnes? Is this about her daughter? Something finally happen with that?'

'You know about her daughter.'

'Agnes talked about it,' said the man. 'To anyone who'd listen. I'm around all the time, so I ended up doing lots of listening.' Bracing himself on the cane, he held out a horned hand, which Milo grasped. 'William Perdue. I pay the mortgage on this place.'

'Detective Sturgis, Mr Perdue. Nice to meet you. You're talking about Mrs Yeager in past tense. When did she leave?'

Perdue worked his jaws and placed both hands on the cane. The straw of his hat brim had come loose near the band, and the sunlight poking through created a tiny lavender moon under his right cheekbone. 'She didn't leave of her own will – she got sick. Nine or so months ago. Happened right here. My niece was down visiting me from Las Vegas. She's a traffic dispatcher for the police there, works the morning shift and tends to get up early, so she was out that morning just before sunrise. She heard it – a big noise from Agnes's apartment.' Twisting slowly, Perdue pointed to the ground-floor unit across from his. 'Agnes fell down, right inside her door.

The door was open, and the newspaper was on the floor next to her. She went outside to fetch it, took a step back inside, and collapsed. Tariana said she was breathing, but not too strong. We called 911. They said it looked like a heart attack. She didn't smoke or drink – all that sadness was probably what caused it.'

'Sadness over her daughter.'

'It cut her to the bone.' The cane wobbled, but Perdue managed to draw himself up.

'Any idea where she is, Mr Perdue?'

'They took her right down the block – to MidTown Hospital. Tariana and I went to see her there. They had her in the intensive care and we couldn't get in. She didn't have insurance, so a while later they moved her to County Hospital for evaluation. That's a far trip for me, so I just called her. She wasn't in much of a state for talking, said they still didn't know what was wrong with her, but she'd probably be moving out, she'd send someone for her things, sorry about the rent – she owed a month. I said not to worry and don't be concerned about her things either— There wasn't much, she rented the place furnished. I had everything packed up – two suitcases – and Tariana brought them over to County Hospital. That's the last I heard from her. I know she was discharged from County, but no one would tell me where.'

'Mr Perdue,' said Milo, 'did she have any ideas about what happened to Shawna?'

'Sure did. She figured Shawna had been killed, probably by some man who lusted after her.'

'She used that word, sir? "Lusted"?'

Perdue pushed up the brim of his hat. 'Yes, sir. She was a pretty religious woman, one of those with a strong sense of sin— Like I said, no drinking or smoking, and once she got home from work, she sat and watched TV all night.'

'Lusted,' said Milo. 'Did she tell you why she thought that?'

'It was just a feeling she had. Shawna meeting up with the wrong gent. She also said the police weren't doing much – no offense. That the officer in charge didn't communicate with her. One time I met her out back. We were both taking out the garbage and she was looking sad and I said what's wrong, and she just started bawling. That's when she told me. That Shawna had been a little difficult back home and that she'd tried her best but Shawna had a mind of her own.'

'Wild in what way?'

'I didn't ask her, sir,' said Perdue, sounding offended. 'Why would I pour salt in her wounds?'

'Of course,' said Milo. 'But she didn't give you any details?'

'She just said she regretted the fact that Shawna's daddy died when Shawna was a baby. That Shawna never had any father, didn't know how to relate to men properly. Then she started crying some more, talking about how she'd done the best she could, how when Shawna announced she was moving down here to go to college it had scared her 'cause Shawna was all she had. But she let her go, because you couldn't say no to

Shawna – she'd do what she pleased, like entering those beauty contests. Agnes never approved of that, but Shawna wouldn't be refused. Agnes figured you had to cut the apron strings. "Now look what's happened, William," she told me. Then she just cried some more. Pitiful.'

Perdue ran a finger over his upper lip. The nail was hardened, cross-grained like sandstone but carefully shaped. 'I told her it wasn't any of her fault, that things just happen. I lost a boy in Vietnam. Three years I spend fighting Hitler's war, and I came back without a scratch. My boy flies over to Vietnam, two weeks later he steps on a mine. Things happen, right?'

'They do, sir,' said Milo.

'They do, indeed.'

We drove to Crescent Heights, crossed Sunset as the street shifted to Laurel Canyon, and headed for the Valley.

'Woman with a heart condition,' said Milo. 'I'm gonna kick her off the ledge?'

'What do you think about what she told Perdue?'

'About Shawna being wild?'

'Wild because she had no father in her life,' I said. 'Wild in a specific way. I think her mother knew of Shawna's attraction to older men. Meaning maybe Shawna had older boyfriends back home.'

'Maybe,' he said. 'But that could also mean that Shawna's story about heading home for the weekend was true. She got dolled up for some Santo Leon Lothario, it went bad, he killed her, dumped her somewhere out in the boonies. That's why she's never been found. If so, there goes the Lauren connection.'

'No,' I said. 'Agnes might've been aware of Shawna's tendencies, but I doubt she knew about a specific hometown boyfriend. If she had, wouldn't she have given his name to the police? Even if the police weren't listening.'

'Leo Riley,' he said. 'SOB still hasn't called back.'

'He probably couldn't tell you much anyway. Milo, I think Agnes Yeager knew Shawna's pattern and suspected history had repeated itself in L.A., but she didn't know the specifics.'

'Could be . . . The thing that bothers me is that whoever made Shawna dead really didn't want her to be found. But just the opposite's true of Lauren, and Michelle and Lance. We're talking bodies left out in the open, someone flaunting – maybe wanting to set an example, or scare someone off. Something professional. None of that fits with a sex crime.'

'So the motives were different,' I said. 'Shawna was a lust killing, the others were eliminated to shut them up.'

We passed the Laurel Canyon market, and the road took on a steep grade. Milo's foot bore down on the accelerator, and the unmarked shuddered. As the trees zipped by my heart began racing.

'Oh, man.'

'What?'

'What if Shawna's death *is* the secret? Lauren found

out somehow, tried to profit from it. Talk about something worth killing for.'

He was silent till Mulholland. 'How would Lauren find out?'

I had no answer for that. He began pulling on his earlobe. Took out a panatella. Asked me to light it and blew foul smoke out the window.

'Well,' he finally said, 'maybe Jane can elucidate for us. Glad you're here.' Angry smile. 'This might require psychological sensitivity.'

We drove up to the gates of the Abbot house just before four P.M. Both the blue Mustang convertible and the big white Cadillac were parked in front, but no one answered Milo's bell push. He tried again. The digital code sounded, four rings. Broken connection.

'Last time it was hooked up to the answering machine,' he said. 'Cars in the driveway but no one's home?'

'Probably just as we thought,' I said. 'They went away, took a taxi.'

He jabbed the bell a third time, said, 'Let's talk to some neighbors,' and turned to leave as the third ring sounded. We were nearly at the car when Mel Abbot's voice broke in.

'*Please . . . this is not . . . this is . . .*'

Then a dial tone.

Milo studied the gate, hiked his trousers, and had taken hold of an iron slat. But I'd already gotten a toehold, and I made it over first.

twenty-two

We ran to the front door. I tried the knob. Bolted. Milo pounded, rang the bell. 'Mr Abbot! It's the police!'

No answer. The space to the right of the house was blocked by a ficus hedge. To the left was an azalea-lined flagstone pathway that led to the kitchen door. Also locked, but a ground-floor window was half open.

'Alarm screen's in place,' said Milo. 'Doesn't look like it's been breached. Wait here.' Unholstering his gun, he ran around to the back, returned moments later. 'No obvious forced entry, but something's wrong.' Replacing the weapon and snapping the holster cover, he flipped the screen on the partially open window, shouted in: 'Mr Abbot? Anyone home?'

Silence.

'There's the alarm register,' he said, glancing at a side wall. 'System's off. Okay, boost me.' I cupped my hands, felt the crush of his weight for a second, then he hoisted himself in and disappeared.

'You stay put, I'm going to check it out.'

I waited, listening to suburban quiet, taking in what I

could see of the backyard: a blue corner of swimming pool, teak furniture, old-growth trees screening out the neighboring property, pretty olive green shadows patching a lawn skinned in preparation for fertilizer . . . Someone had plans for a verdant spring.

Eight minutes passed, ten, twelve. Why was he taking so long? Should I return to the car and call for help? What would I tell the dispatcher?

As I thought about it, the kitchen door opened and Milo beckoned me in. Sweat stains had leaked through the armpits of his jacket. His face was white.

'What's going on?' I said.

Instead of answering he showed me his back and led me through the kitchen. Blue-granite counters were bare but for a carton of orange juice. We hurried through a floral-papered breakfast nook, a butler's pantry, the dining room, past all that art, and Milo ran past the elevator into the living room, where Melville Abbot's trophies were gloomed by blackout drapes.

He vaulted up the stairs, and I followed.

When I was halfway up, I heard the whimpering.

Abbot sat propped in bed, cushioned by a blue velvet bed husband, hairless skull reflecting light from an overhead chandelier, slack lips shellacked with drool.

The room was huge, stale, someone's vision of Versailles. Gold plush carpeting, mustard-and-crimson tapestry curtains tied back elaborately and topped by fringed valances, French Provincial replica furniture arranged haphazardly.

The bed was king-sized and seemed to swallow Abbot. The bed husband had slipped low against a massive swirl of rococo headboard of tufted yellow silk. Lots of satin pillows on the bed, several more on the carpet. The chandelier was Murano glass, a snarl of yellow tendrils crowned by multicolored glass birds. A small Picasso hung askew above the crest of the headboard, next to a dark landscape that could've been a Corot. A folded wheelchair filled one corner.

The straggling white puffs of Melville Abbot's hair had been battened down by sweat. The old man's eyes were vacant and frightened, lashes encrusted with greenish scum. He wore maroon silk pajamas with white piping and LAPD-issue handcuffs around his wrists.

To his left, a few feet from the bed, red-brown splotches Rorschached the gold carpet. The largest stain spread from under Jane Abbot's body.

She lay on her left side, left arm stretched forward, legs drawn upward, ash hair loose and fanned across the thick pile. A silver peignoir had ridden up, exposing still-sleek legs, a sliver of buttock swelling beneath black panties. Bare feet. Pink toenails. Graying flesh, green-tinged, purplish suggestions of lividity at ankles and wrists and thighs, as dead blood pooled internally.

Her eyes were half open, filmed, the lids swollen and blueing. Her mouth gaped, and her tongue was a gray garden slug curling inward. One ruby-crusted hole blemished her left cheek; a second punctuated the hairline of her left temple.

Milo pointed to the floor next to the nightstand. A gun, not unlike his 9 mm, near the draperies. He drew the clip from his trouser pocket, put it back.

'When I got here, he was holding it.'

Abbot gave no indication of hearing. Or comprehension. Saliva trickled down his chin, and he mumbled.

'What are you saying, sir?' said Milo, drawing closer to the bed.

Abbot's eyes rolled back, reappeared, focused on nothing.

Milo turned to me. 'I walk in and he points the damn thing at me. I almost shot him, but when he saw me he let go of it. I kept trying to find out what happened, but all he does is babble. From the looks of her, she's been dead several hours. I'm not pushing him without a lawyer present. It's Van Nuys's case. I called them. We should have company soon enough.'

Mel Abbot groaned.

'Just hold on, sir.'

The old man's arms shot out. He shook his wrists, and the cuffs jangled. 'Hurts.'

'They're as loose as they can be, sir.'

The chocolate eyes turned black. 'I'm *Mr* Abbot. Who the hell are you?'

'Detective Sturgis.'

Abbot stared at him. 'Sherlock Bones?'

'Something like that, sir.'

'Constabulary,' said Abbot. 'State trooper stops a man on the highway – have you heard this one?'

'Probably,' said Milo.

'Aw,' said Abbot. 'You're no fun.'

twenty-three

M ilo scanned the bedroom as we waited. I could see
nothing but tragedy, but his trained eye located a
bullet hole on the wall facing the bed, just to the right of
the wheelchair. He drew a chalk outline around the
puncture.

Mel Abbot continued to hunch stuporously in the bed,
cuffed hands inert. Milo wiped his chin a couple of
times. Each time Abbot yanked his face away, like a baby
repelling spinach.

Finally, the howl of sirens. Three black-and-whites on
Code Two, a Mutt-and-Jeff detective duo from Van
Nuys Division named Ruiz and Gallardo, a squadron of
cheerful, bantering paramedics for Mel Abbot.

I stood on the landing and watched the EMTs set up
their mobile stretcher. Milo and the detectives had
moved out of the bedroom, out of the old man's earshot,
talking technical. Sidelong glances at the old man. A
moist slick of snot mustached Abbot's upper lip. Jane's
corpse was within his line of vision, but he made no
attempt to look at her. A paramedic came out and asked

the detectives where to take him. All three cops agreed on the inevitable, the prison ward at County General. The short D, Ruiz, muttered, 'Love that drive to East L.A.'

'No place like home, *ese*,' said Gallardo. He and his partner were in their thirties, solidly built, with thick black hair, perfectly edged and combed straight back. He was around six-two, Ruiz, no more than five-eight. But for the height differential they could have been twins, and I began thinking of them as outgrowths of some Mendelian experiment: short detectives, long detectives . . . Anything to take my mind off what had happened.

It didn't work – my head wouldn't shake off images of Jane Abbot's final moments. Had she known what was coming, or had the flash of the gun been sensation without comprehension?

Mother and daughter, gone.

A family, gone.

Not a happy family, but one that had cared enough, years ago, to seek help . . .

A restraint strap unbuckled with a snap, and the EMTs advanced on Abbot. He began to cry but offered no resistance as they eased him onto the stretcher. Then he gazed down at the body and screamed, and waxy arms began striking out. One paramedic said, 'Now, come on,' in a bored voice. *Snap snap.* The paramedics went about their work, speedy as a pit crew, and Abbot was immobilized.

I ran downstairs, retraced the path through the house

and out the kitchen door to the flagstone pathway. The sun was relenting, and the lowest quadrant of the sky was striped persimmon. A few neighbors had come out to stare, and when they saw me they edged closer to the gates. A uniform held them back. Someone pointed, and I ducked out of view, stayed close to the house, which was where Milo found me.

'Taking the air?'

'Breathing seemed a good idea,' I said.

'You missed the fun. Abbot managed to slip an arm out and grab hold of one of the EMTs' hair. They shot him up with tranquillizer.'

'Poor guy.'

'Pathetic but dangerous.'

'You really think he did it?'

'You don't?' He slapped his hands on his hips. 'I'm not saying it was premeditated, but hell, yeah. He was holding the gun, and that hole in the wall fits with a shot fired from the bed. My best guess is it happened last night. They probably had the gun in a nightstand, somehow he found it, was using it as a teddy bear, Jane entered the bedroom, freaked him out, and boom.'

'Suburban security goes bad.'

'We see it all the time, Alex. Usually with kids. Which is what Abbot really is, right? The nightstand drawer's within arm's reach. There's another gun in there – older revolver, a thirty-eight, unloaded. So maybe Jane was being careful. But not careful enough. She forgot about the clip in the gun.'

'Tragic accident,' I said. 'You're the detective.'

He stared at me. 'Spit it out.'

'Jane was an experienced caretaker. I can't see her letting him get near a gun.'

'She had her hands full, Alex. People get careless. Perfectly competent parents turn their backs while Snookums toddles over to the pool.'

He stared down the length of the house. 'There're no signs of forced entry, there was a box of loose jewelry in Jane's dresser and a nice fat safe in the bedroom closet, combination-locked. Not to mention all those paintings. Ruiz and Gallardo's first order of business will be to see if the gun was registered. Solid citizens like them aren't likely to own an illegal piece. If it was theirs, that pretty much clinches it.'

He took baby steps, turned in a small, tight circle, hitched his trousers. 'Least I know why she didn't return my calls.'

'You're right about the art,' I said. 'If it's real, it's worth a fortune. One hell of an estate. One hell of a community property. I wonder who inherits.'

He rotated, faced me, eyes half closed but alert, like those of a resting guard dog. 'And the point is . . .'

'Mel Abbot's only child died ten years ago, Jane's, just a few days ago. Now Mel will be declared incompetent and someone else will be placed in charge of all the assets. Probably a court-appointed conservator. My guess is relatives will start lining up. I wonder who's next in line, from a legal standpoint.'

'Some cousin from Iowa. So what?'

'Maybe not,' I said. 'Jane mentioned a prenup, but

that could've applied only to divorce, not death. If Mel's will signed everything over to Jane, that would've put Lauren in place to inherit. But with Lauren dead, *her* closest living relative could step up to the plate. And look who just called you and asked about Lauren's finances.'

His head shot forward, and the eyes opened wide. 'Daddy dearest— Oh, man, you have a devious mind.'

'He *did* call. Hours after Jane died.'

'Jane and Lauren both hated his guts. There'd be no reason for him to think anyone made him a beneficiary.'

'Any will come up for Lauren?'

'Not yet.'

'If she died intestate,' I said, 'her estate will end up in probate and be up for grabs. I'm no lawyer, but my bet is that, as her closest living blood relative, Lyle will have a strong claim. Sure, getting through the paperwork will be a hassle, and there'll be estate taxes to pay, but if those paintings are real, even a chunk would be serious money. Lyle's hurting financially. A Picasso or two would do wonders.'

'He offs his ex and plants the gun in the old guy's hand?'

'Like you said, no love lost between them.'

'C'mon, Alex. He can't be stupid enough to do it and call me the same day. Talk about obvious.' He frowned. 'But it *wasn't* obvious, was it? Not till your warped mind seized it. You are one creative puppy.'

He began pacing along the side of the house. Low chatter from the front of the property created an irritating soundtrack: noise but no reason.

'Lyle's calling you *was* blatant,' I said. 'But, like you said, people get careless. Did he seem the subtle type to you? The guy's angry, depressed, out of work, drinks, stomps around his property with a loaded shotgun. If that's not a recipe for violence, I don't know what is.'

'You're saying he did Jane and Lauren? No big bad Duke conspiracy or Shawna cover-up?'

'Who knows?' I said. 'The other thing to think about is everyone around Lauren is dying. Which fits with Jane not being more forthcoming because she did know something explosive. Either way, pinning it on Abbot seems awfully convenient.'

'For argument's sake, let's say Lyle was the shooter. He shows up and Jane just lets him in?'

'She might've. Even with tons of hostility, there was that early bond – the years they'd been together, familiarity, chemistry. I've seen it plenty of times working custody cases. The nastiest divorces. Two people trying to rip each other's hearts out in court, then they find themselves alone and end up in bed. Maybe Lyle put on a big show of grief – that's the one thing they shared. Lauren's death. For all we know he didn't even come to kill her. They started talking, Lyle segued into money talk like he did with you, Jane lost it, and one thing led to another.'

'So why's the old guy still breathing?'

'Because Lyle's no genius, but he did have an inspiration. Picture it this way: The argument begins downstairs. Jane orders Lyle out, he refuses. She rushes upstairs, thinking to lock herself in the bedroom, then call the police. Lyle goes after her, gets in the bedroom, shoots her. It's dark, they could've wrestled from a spot near the bed – the hole in the wall. He misses that time but hits his mark twice, and Jane goes down. Abbot's asleep – maybe deeply, he's probably on medication. The gunshot wakes him up. He sits up. Disoriented. A senile old man confronted with sudden loud noise and darkness. His consciousness is clouded anyway. He wouldn't have focused immediately – where were his glasses?'

'On his nightstand.'

'He could've seen nothing. Lyle spots him, considers killing him, realizes Abbot's no direct threat, and comes up with a better idea: plant the gun near or in Abbot's hand and leave quietly. He might've even pressed Abbot's finger on the trigger and fired and that's where the hole in the wall came from. Even if Abbot's head does clear and he recalls some details, who's going to believe him? What's his story? A mystery intruder with no signs of forced entry? A bogeyman who leaves his weapon behind? But I'll wager Abbot comes up with nothing. He's out of it. A few days in the prison ward at County and he'll probably be completely vegetative.'

A door slammed at the front of the house. We stepped forward to see the paramedics trundle Abbot out. The old man lay strapped on the stretcher, eyes closed, mouth agape. As the EMTs carried him across the motor court, they chatted and seemed relaxed. No threat from the cargo. Neighborly necks craned as Abbot was loaded into the ambulance. Siren sonata as the uniform at the gate cleared an exit path and the ambulance sped away. Two vans drove up. One white, with the coroner's logo on the door, was allowed through the gates. The silver one with a network affiliate's call letters on the roof next to a satellite antenna was waved to the curb.

'The party begins,' said Milo. 'At least it's Ruiz and Gallardo's bash.'

'I can just hear tonight's broadcast,' I said, as a young redhead in a yellow pantsuit stepped out of the news van. ' "A Sherman Oaks man was arrested today on suspicion of murdering his wife. Neighbors described Melville Abbot as friendly but feeble—" '

'That's still where the facts point, Alex.'

'Guess so,' I said. 'And Ruiz and Gallardo do seem like nice guys. Why complicate their lives?'

'Oh, my,' he said. 'What the hell went down during your childhood to make you enjoy complications?'

'When my mother was pregnant with me she got startled by an obsessive-compulsive pit bull.'

The woman in yellow approached with a cameraman and a soundman in tow. The boom hovered over her coiffure as she flirted with the uniform at the gate. Smiles all around, then the cop shook his head and the reporter pouted and the news crew drifted toward the growing clot of suburban observers.

Milo said, 'Let's get the hell out of here. Just walk straight through and don't make eye contact. If Ms Bubblehead chirps, remember she's a vulture, not a canary.'

'You heading home?'

He laughed harshly. 'You kidding? I *love* the goddamn

Valley – hey, how about a nice little jaunt to *Reseda*?'

The commuter rush. Ventura Boulevard was consti-pated, and a glance at the freeway overpass revealed a chromium still life. Milo stayed on surface streets, sitting too straight in the driver's seat, jaw muscles pumping, lips twisting, one big hand shoving aside the hair lick that shadowed his brow – repeating the futile gesture over and over.

Silent, talking to himself. Assessing the possibilities I'd inflicted upon him.

I might've felt guilty, but my mental camera was working overtime too. Flashing images of Jane Abbot's gray-green corpse. Then: the trussed bundle of ruin that had been Lauren's final pose.

I tried to switch channels, but the alternative fare wasn't any prettier. Michelle and Lance, burned to cinders. Shawna Yeager brutalized unthinkably, then kicked into a hidden grave. Agnes Yeager probably still pictured her only child's beautiful face, but by now Shawna would be nothing more than bones.

Mothers and daughters. Entire families, disap-peared . . .

Past Haseltine the traffic eased up. Milo said, 'Finally.'

The same soil-and-paint smell, the same irate dogs.

When we reached the chain link around Lyle Teague's property, the sun was a brick-colored skullcap on a flat, gray pate of horizon, and the smear of illumination in the lower sky had dulled to excremental brown.

Grimy chemical light revealed the shabby neighbor-hood at its worst. A few kids with shaved heads lounged in front of the apartments across the street, slouching and drinking, enjoying delusions of immortality. Their grins shifted to fear and distrust as we pulled up. When Milo parked a bottle shattered against the curb. By the time we got out of the car, the kids were gone.

The beefy padlock on Teague's front gate was in place, but the pickup with the chrome pipes and the overgrown tires was missing, and we had a view of the carport littered with machine parts and broken toys.

'Gone,' I said.

Milo peered through the chain-link diamonds. 'This one I don't scale. Let me call his number.'

As he reached for his cell phone, the house's front door opened a crack, then wider as Tish Teague stepped out into the dirt, holding the hand of a brown-haired girl around five years old. The child's eyes were open, but she looked sleepy. The second Mrs Teague wore a baby blue tank top and too-tight white shorts that sausaged her hips. Her bra strap did the same for her torso, turning her into a mass of soft rolls supported by pasty, dimpled legs. Blue tattoo on the left biceps. Her hair was drawn up at the top, rubber-banded to an off-center thatch.

Milo waved, but she just stood there, bland, pale pudding of a face aiming for stoic.

'Mrs Teague,' Milo called. 'Is your husband home?'

Headshake. Her mouth formed 'No,' but the sound failed to make it across the yard.

'Where is he, ma'am?'

Instead of answering Tish returned inside, came back minus the child and with her hair loosened. Walking halfway across the dirt, she stopped, folded her arms under her bosom, and shouted, 'Hunting.'

'Hunting what?'

'Usually he brings back birds. Or a deer.'

Milo muttered, 'Dan'l Boone.' To Tish: 'Where's he hunt, ma'am?'

'Up near Castaic. What do you need him for?'

'Doing some follow-up, ma'am— May we come in?'

'Follow-up on what?'

'Your husband phoned me today, and I was getting back to him. How long's he been gone?'

Tish blinked three times. 'Coupla days.'

'So he must've called me from somewhere else. He have a cell phone?'

'Nope.'

'But he did take camping gear.'

'Yeah.'

'Guns too.'

'He's hunting,' said Tish.

'What, the shotgun?'

'I don't know what he takes. He wraps everything up in plastic. I don't pay attention to guns— Why all these questions?'

'Just curious.'

'What, you're saying Lyle could shoot someone?'

Milo paused. 'Has that been on *your* mind, ma—'

'No way,' she said. 'He keeps that stuff just for home

protection and hunting – that's all, and I like that. He's a good man, why're you hassling him?'

'I don't mean to hassle, ma'am. So you haven't heard from Mr Teague in two days?'

'I told you, he don't have one of those.' She pointed to the cell phone. Her tone said the deficiency was a crime for which someone needed to be blamed.

'Hmm,' said Milo. 'Well, he did call me.'

'Well, he *didn't* call *me*.' Tish aimed for defiance, but her gray eyes filled with hurt. She stepped a few yards closer. 'Sometimes he uses a pay phone— What did he want?'

'To talk about Lauren.'

'*Her?* What for?'

'She *was* his daughter, ma'am.'

'Not if you asked *her*.'

'What do you mean, ma'am?'

Crossing her arms, she covered several more feet, stopped well before the gate. Bare feet, toes grayed with dust. The nacre of chipped pink polish glinting through. 'She wasn't nice to us.'

'Lauren wasn't?'

'Not to me or him or the girls.'

'I thought she brought the girls Christmas presents.'

Tish smirked. 'Oh, *sure*. Big *deal*. She comes in wearing her *cool* clothes and her *cool* makeup and hypers them up with all that candy and junk, and then when she leaves I'm nice enough to thank her and say she can take home some of the apricot pie I baked from fresh apricots because that's the kind of person I am. She laughs at me and looks down at the pie slice I'm offering her and says, "No, thanks." Like I stuffed shit in a crust or something. Then she says, "At least you've got better manners than *him*. *Thanking* me. Which you should, 'cause I didn't have to do this." And I'm like, "What do you mean?" And she's like, "You better *believe* you should thank me, 'cause you don't deserve a damn thing from me – you're not even my family and neither is he and neither are your rugrats." '

Tish's lip trembled. 'Just like that. Nasty mean. One minute she's playing with the girls, and then she's insulting us. I could've trashed her back, but I just said, "Well, sorry you don't like apricot pie. Goodbye." And she laughed again and was like, "I came here 'cause I've got *class* – something you'll never know, chubby." Then she prancie-pranced out the door.'

Tish released her arms, let the wrists go limp. 'She prancie-prances around like she's doing one of her strip dances – which is the class *she* had, a stripper and a whore. So who's she to be snobbing and styling on me? I was so mad, it gave me a migraine, but at least she was out of here. Then, just as I'm closing the door, she turns around and starts coming *back* and I'm like, Okay, Tish, you controlled yourself good, but she's asking for it. I really thought we were gonna get into it, and I tell you, I was ready. But she musta figured that out or maybe it was the girls, running around the house, in and out of rooms, screaming and wild, all hypered up 'cause of her. Or maybe she was just a chicken – whatever.'

'She didn't come back.'

'She didn't come back all the way – just stopped in the middle, right back there.' Gesturing behind her. 'Then she gives me a *look* and laughs and shakes her ass outta here. Laughing – loud, so the neighborhood could hear. That's what she was after – to *humiliate* us.'

Milo said, 'So what do we do for the next round of yuks?'

'Try to find Lyle?'

We got in the unmarked, and he drove back to Ventura Boulevard. 'Sure,' he said. 'Let's call out the hounds and track the sonofabitch. And when we find him, we'll have a weenie roast and tell ghost stories. While we're at it, we can work in some fishing.'

'Fishing and hunting,' I said. 'Wonder how many firearms he's packing.'

'Given that bad eye of his, he wouldn't be much good with a bow and arrow.'

'Jane's dead, and he just happens to be gone,' I said.

'I'll call the sheriffs up at Castaic, see if they can locate him, but I'm not putting in a requisition for a search party. Lyle may have all the charm of a warthog with piles, but at this point, before the ballistics and the registration on the gun that did Jane come in, he's no *suspect*. And her other husband *is*. Ruiz and Gallardo should have word soon enough on all of it.'

'Even if the gun was registered to Jane or Mel,' I said, 'that doesn't rule out an outside shooter. Let's say Jane was afraid, made a run for the bedroom, and grabbed her own gun, but whoever frightened her got hold of it.'

'When it comes to theories, you are human flypaper,

my friend. First Dugger for Dr Bloodlust, now Father of the Year for Lyle.'

'I've always been goal-directed.'

'Me too,' he said. 'Least that's what my third-grade teacher said. But screw goals. I need to connect the dots, and right now I don't even have a pencil.'

At White Oak he said, 'The thing that bothers me is maybe I narrowed my focus too quickly. I'm not saying the Duke thing or Lyle is wrong, but there's always the danger of tunnel vision.'

'What do you mean?'

'I know Lauren . . . meant something to you, but the hard truth is she sold her body for a living, and women who do that live dangerously. The whole thing could track back to some other john. Hell, I haven't even followed up on her supposed modeling – the garment industry connections. There's a real clean business for you – sweatshops and kickbacks.'

'What about Shawna and *Duke*?' I said.

He rotated his head, winced, rubbed his face. 'I don't know, Alex. My gut still tells me Shawna isn't related to the rest of it.'

'Your gut's worth listening to.'

'Thanks, Doc – see you next session.'

We traveled in silence all the way to Beverly Glen and Valley Vista, where Milo began the trip back to the city.

He let out a long, raspy sigh. 'I respect your intuition also, Alex, but even an O-C pit bull takes a breather between bouts. Let's both step back for a while. Maybe try to relax.'

twenty-four

Robin said, 'First the daughter, now the mother?'

We were on the big couch in the living room. She was sitting at the far end, just out of reach, still wearing her work overalls and her red T-shirt. I'd come home determined to put everything aside, had ended up talking about all of it: Lauren's aborted therapy, Phil Harnsberger's party, Michelle, Shawna, Jane Abbot, Mel Abbot's senescent terror.

Death kills confidentiality.

'You're making it sound like a confession,' she said.

'Whose?'

'Yours. The whole sordid tale. As if you've done something wrong. As if you're a main player in all of it and not just an extra.' She looked away. 'It's almost as if she's seduced you – Lauren. Not sexually – you know what I mean. I guess I shouldn't be surprised. Seduction's how she made a living.'

'I don't see that at all.'

She got up, went into the kitchen, returned with two bottles of water, and handed me one. Sitting just as far.

'What's wrong?' I said.

'You saw this girl, what – twice, ten years ago? – yet you've convinced yourself that you're obligated to clarify every detail of her life. People like that don't lend themselves to solutions. For them it's always problems.'

'People like that.'

'Outcasts, troubled souls – *patients*, call them what you will. Didn't you tell me one thing you had to learn so as not to become a toxic sponge was how to let go?'

'It's not a matter of letting go—'

'What, then, Alex?' Her voice was low, but there was no mistaking the edge.

'Is there anything else that's bothering you?' I said.

'That,' she said, 'was very shrinky.'

'Sorry—'

'Your mind's a fine piece of machinery, Alex. I've never encountered anything like it. You're like a precisely tuned watch, always ticking – relentless. But sometimes I think you use what God gave you to dig ditches. Lowering yourself . . . these people . . .'

I reached for her, and she allowed me to touch her fingertips. But she exerted no stretch that would have allowed me to hold her.

'The thing is,' she said, 'you get yourself on a track and you just keep running. People around this girl tend to *die*, Alex, and you haven't even considered the possibility that you might be in danger.'

'The people who've died knew her well—'

She sighed and got up. 'Listen, I've got work to catch up on – catch you later.'

'What about dinner?'

'Not hungry.'

'You are *not* happy with me.'

'On the contrary,' she said. 'I'm very happy with you. With us. That's why I'd like us both to keep breathing for a while.'

'There's no danger. I wouldn't do that to you again.'

'To me? Why don't you start thinking of yourself? Check out your own boundaries – what you'll allow in and what you won't.'

She bent and kissed my forehead. 'I don't mean to be cruel, baby, but I'm weary of all this surmising and ugliness. You did what you could. Keep telling yourself that.'

I spent the night alone, listening to music but ingesting no harmony, trying to read – anything but psychology – waiting for Robin to come back in the house. By eleven she hadn't, and I went to bed – early for me – and woke at 4:30 A.M., fighting the urge to bolt, exhausted yet charged, using every relaxation trick in my repertoire to fall back asleep. I endured the tension for two more hours until Robin's eyes opened and I pretended to be ready to greet the day.

She smiled at me, tousled my hair, showered alone but made coffee for both of us and sat down with the first section of the papér. If Jane Abbot's murder had made the edition, she didn't say. I took the Metro pages. Nothing there.

By eight she'd headed back to the studio and I was

running up in the hills, harder than usual, punishing my joints, trying to sweat off adrenaline. I'd promised myself to avoid the paper, but when I got back I thumbed quickly and found the summary of Jane Abbot's death on page twenty-five. Worded nearly exactly as I'd predicted: senile husband, shocked neighbors, domestic tragedy, investigation pending.

I finished up some court reports – a couple of personal injury cases where kids had experienced psychological sequelae and a custody battle with wealthy protagonists that might never end unless the principals died. Printing, signing, sealing, and addressing my findings to various judges, I reviewed my ledger books and tried to figure out if I'd owe taxes in April. By eleven I still hadn't figured it out. By eleven-thirty Robin bopped in, Spike in tow, and informed me she had to deliver two repaired D'Angelico archtops to the Los Feliz home of a movie star who was considering playing Elvis in an upcoming flick.

'Elvis never played D'Angelicos,' I said.

'That should be the worst of it. This guy's got a tin ear.' A peck on the cheek – hard, maybe dismissive – and she was off.

By noon I was jumping out of my skin.

At twelve-eighteen I gave up, and drove away.

West. Toward Santa Monica. The ocean. Figuring I'd just cruise by Ben Dugger's high-rise, then take a nice, relaxed drive north on Ocean Front, down the ramp to Pacific Coast Highway.

Malibu. Day at the beach. Nothing to do with Lauren, because Lauren had left no clues in Malibu, and why should I avoid an entire coastline?

I could be as Californian as anyone.

But when I passed the building, Dugger was standing out in front, and I reduced my speed to a crawl.

Standing alone. Checking his watch. Looking rumpled and tense in a tan corduroy sport coat, white shirt, gray slacks. Flicking his wrist again. Glancing at the ramp of the underground parking garage.

Circling the block, I returned, cruising as slowly as I could without drawing the ire of other motorists. That left me mere seconds to stare, but it was enough to catch a glimpse of a green-jacketed figure – the diminutive Gerald – pulling up in Dugger's old white Volvo, getting out, saluting, opening the door for Dugger.

Dugger gave him a tip and got in.

I drove fifty feet, veered to the curb, parked in front of a hydrant, waited until the Volvo chugged by. Allowing three cars to get between us, I began the tail, knowing this time I couldn't risk discovery. Figuring I could pull it off. No reason for him to suspect.

He turned right onto Wilshire, headed east to Lincoln, picked up the 10 east freeway and transferred to the 405 south. The route to Newport Beach. Probably just checking out the office; soon the Seville and I would be several dozen miles older with nothing to show.

It beat sitting around the house working at mellow.

But instead of continuing to Orange County, he exited at Century Boulevard and continued west.

LAX signs all over. Flying somewhere? I hadn't seen luggage, but perhaps the car was already packed.

He headed into the airport. Maintaining the three-car shield, I stayed with him as he entered a parking lot opposite Terminal 4. Several airlines shared the lot, most prominently American. The driver in front of me had trouble figuring out how to take the ticket from the machine, and by the time I got inside the Volvo was nowhere in sight.

No parking spaces on ground level, and I took the ramp down, hoping Dugger had done the same. Sure enough, I spotted the Volvo's square back just as Dugger nosed into a corner space between two SUVs. He got out and alarm-locked the car, carried no luggage as he headed for the elevators. I chanced parking the Seville in an illegal space and hurried after him.

I hid behind a concrete pylon as he stepped into the lift. Ran over in time to read the illuminated numbers. Two flights up. The footbridge to American Airlines. Vaulting up the stairs, I cracked the stairwell door and saw him lope past. But he didn't take the right turn toward the escalator that led down to the ticket gates. Continuing straight toward the army of phony nuns and preachers hawking for nonexistent charities, he dropped a coin in a cup, and walked hurriedly to the metal detectors.

Long queue of travelers at the single device in service and one sleepy-looking security attendant, so no problem putting space between us there. I watched Dugger place his wallet and keys in a plastic dish and keep his eyes on them as he sailed through. But the two people in front of me set off the machine, and I was forced to cool my heels as Dugger disappeared around a bend.

Finally, I got through and walked briskly through hordes of travelers and loved ones, flight attendants and pilots. No sign of Dugger. During the moments I'd lost sight of him he could've gone anywhere – the men's room, a shop, any of the gates.

I strolled up the corridor trying to look casual, searching for a flash of tan jacket. Then I came to an elevator that led to the private lounge – the Admirals Club. Members Only. A woman sat behind a counter to the right, busy at her computer.

Dugger was a rich kid – why not? Affluence could also explain no luggage: He might have turnkey access to hideouts in Aspen, the Hamptons, Jackson Hole, Santa Fe.

As I approached the elevator the woman behind the counter smiled. 'May I please see your membership card, sir?'

I smiled back and walked away. The elevator was in open view of the terminal's main artery. If Dugger was in there, I had no way to observe his comings and goings without being spotted myself . . . No, *there* he was, twenty feet in front of me, stepping out of a men's room.

I ducked behind an automated insurance machine and pretended to estimate actuarial odds as Dugger whipped out a handkerchief and blew his nose. A nice, heavy rush of newly arrived travelers added further cover. Dugger stashed the hankie and consulted his watch again. Paused at a bank of TV monitors set into the wall, resumed walking.

Checking arrivals.

Not going anywhere. Meeting someone.

I stayed behind Dugger as he entered the main reception area – a wide, circular, noisy space around which the big-bodied jets docked. He bought a pretzel at a kiosk, took a nibble, frowned, tossed what was left into a trash basket.

Yet *another* consultation of his watch.

Nervous.

A newsstand–sourdough bread outlet occupied the center of the terminal, and I stationed myself at the paperback rack, pulled out a Stephen King, and stuck my nose between the covers. I had a good clear view of Dugger as he commenced to Gate 49A, walked up to the glass wall that offered a view of the landing strip, and peered through. A big, fat 767 sat in the bay.

He walked over to the desk, asked the ground clerk something, remained expressionless as she nodded. Plenty of empty seats in the arrival lounge, but he stayed on his feet. Paid further homage to his watch. Took another gander at the plane.

Very nervous.

I was too far away to read the flight information at 49A. Placing the book back on the rack, I edged closer.

The flight numbers remained blurry, but I was able to make out 'New York.'

Dugger remained near the glass wall for a while before pacing more. Tugging at his collar. Rubbing the crown of his scalp where the hair had deserted it. When the door to 49A finally opened, he gave a small start and hurried forward.

He edged to the front of the greeting crowd, standing with three uniformed livery drivers holding signs and a young, shapely woman rocking two-year-old twins in a dual stroller.

The limo drivers' clients emerged first – a white-haired couple, a bespectacled black giant in a five-button cream-colored suit, and a bedraggled, sallow, unshaven wraith in his twenties, wearing dark shades and a food-stained T-shirt, whom I recognized as an actor on a cheesy TV comedy.

Then Dugger's quarry.

Thickset, swarthy man in his mid-forties, wearing a well-cut black suit and glossy black silk shirt, buttoned to the neck. Black hair in a dense, dark crew cut. Beetle brows, simian hairline – only inches from the shelf of his brow.

Not tall – five-eight or nine – but at least one ninety, maybe more. A dense, cubic mixture of muscle and fat. His brown neck bulged over the collar of the silk shirt. Suggestions of upper-body bulk and massive strength were enhanced by good tailoring. Flat, prizefighter's nose. Huge hands. Squinty eyes, thin lips.

He toted a single piece of carry-on: a sleek black-leather bag that Dugger offered to take.

Black Suit refused, scarcely nodded at Dugger. Barely touched Dugger's hand as they shook. No smiles exchanged, just a curt nod from Black Suit and the two of them were off, Black Suit running a palm over his bristly head.

Dugger hurried to keep pace as the stocky man pressed toward the GROUND TRANSPORTATION/BAGGAGE CLAIM sign. Then Black Suit pointed to the newsstand. Looked right in my direction. Said something. Changed direction and headed toward me.

How could he have seen me— No, there was no alarm in his eyes, just that same stolid . . . flatness.

I backed away just in time to find an observation point behind a support column as the two of them reached the newsstand. They didn't enter, remained near the register – in front of the candy rack, where Black Suit stopped and considered chewing gum options. Lifting packs, reading ingredients. Finally, he settled on a double-decker Juicy Fruit, popped two sticks in his mouth, pocketed the wrappers, chewed energetically as Dugger paid the cashier.

The two of them exited the reception hall.

Black Suit's luggage was among the first to bounce down the ramp onto the carousel. A pair of midsized valises in that same expensive-looking ebony leather. Probably calfskin. First Class tags. Once again Black Suit rebuffed Dugger's attempt to tote, swinging the strap of the carry-on over his shoulder and hefting a suitcase in each hand with no apparent strain. I'd hovered at the neighboring carousel, well-concealed among a group of arrivals from Denver. Keeping Dugger and Black Suit in steady view – trying, without success, to read their lips.

Very little conversation anyway. Mostly one-sided: Dugger made an occasional comment while Black Suit chomped his gum and played Sphinx.

I stuck with them on their rapid march to the parking lot, was two minutes behind the Volvo as it left the airport.

Back on the 405 freeway. North. Return to L.A.

This time Dugger took the Wilshire west exit and drove into Brentwood, and I assumed he'd be heading for his L.A. office – soon to be the exclusive headquarters for his alleged consulting group.

But once again he proved me wrong, passing the black-and-white office building and continuing into Santa Monica. Back to the Ocean Front high-rise? Then why hadn't he switched to the 10 west? No, he was swinging a quick right onto Nineteenth Street.

I turned too, in time to see him hook another right.

Nosing into an alley that fed into a parking lot behind several storefronts. Stationing the Volvo in an empty slot behind a rear door.

Red, white, and green sign: BROOKLYN PIZZA GUYS. Plastic pie above the lettering.

I stopped, backed up to the mouth of the alley, the Seville's grille barely extending past a drive-up dry cleaners, just close enough to see the white car.

Dugger stepped out of the Volvo, looked at his watch yet again. Black Suit was more relaxed than he'd been at the airport, swinging his legs out with unexpected grace, looking up at the sky, stretching, yawning. Still chewing like mad.

Dugger made for the door to the restaurant, but Black Suit just stood there, and Dugger stopped.

The thickset man squeezed his eyes into slits. Scratched his head. Buttoned his suit jacket and rolled his neck. Working out kinks after the cross-country flight. But other than this gesture showing no signs of discomfort. No anxiety, either, on his broad, brown mask of a face. Mr Tough Guy.

He said something to Dugger, who returned to the car and produced a white tissue. Black Suit extricated his gum, wrapped it in the paper, placed the paper in his pocket. Then he nodded, waited as Dugger held open Brooklyn Pizza Guys' back door and passed through with an imperial air.

Gourmet lunch for a goombah? The guy had Brooklyn all over him.

The way she was hog-tied and head-shot told me this was all business.

Central casting goombah. I was willing to bet the pizza joint sported checked tablecloths and straw-wrapped Chianti bottles hanging from the ceiling. Sometimes people defy stereotypes. Mostly, they lack imagination.

Goombah traveling first-class with expensive luggage.

High-priced specialist. A guy who lived well when a well-heeled client was paying the bills.

I drove up the alley, exited at Twentieth Street, drove to the drugstore where Dugger had bought goodies for the church-school kids, and bought a cheap camera. The wonders of technology – for a few bucks you could get one with a zoom.

Then back to Nineteenth, where I parked on the street and returned on foot to Brooklyn Pizza Guy's alley entrance. Stationed myself behind a dumpster and hoped no one would spot me. I was lucky. The neighboring businesses were a hearing-aid store and an employment agency, and neither seemed to be meriting any rear-entrance traffic. But the dumpster reeked of rotten produce, and it was thirty-three smelly minutes before Dugger and Black Suit reemerged.

The restaurant's air conditioner chugged away, more than loud enough to cover the sound of my *click click click*.

Nice, clear medium shot of the two of them, side by side.

Close-up of Dugger, biting his lip.

Then one of Black Suit's impassive face and flat, dark eyes.

I kept the camera going as they made their way back to the Volvo, filling the roll with side- and rearviews. Caught them walking in step. No amiability. All business.

Dugger backed the Volvo diagonally across the alley and aimed it west. I gave him a two-minute lead before starting my own engine.

twenty-five

Dugger drove all the way to Ocean Avenue. Bringing a hit man home? That surprised me.

But instead of turning left toward the high-rise, he made a right and swung into the left-turn lane. Only a truck between us now, but the height of the cab kept me safely out of view as we sped down toward PCH.

I switched to the right lane, got close enough to see Dugger behind the wheel, sitting straight, head not moving. Black Suit turned from side to side. Catching an eyeful of the mansions lining Santa Monica's Gold Coast, the white-clapboard palace William Randolph Hearst had built for Marion Davies, now a crumbling mass of planks, generous expanses of beach parking lot that afforded a clear view of the Pacific, churning and silver under a charcoal cloud bank. Gulls flecked the clouds with avian static. A few wet-suited surfers had paddled out yards from the tide line, despite breakers that degraded to a dribble.

The ocean is never anything but beautiful.

Black Suit taking it all in.

Sightseeing.

Dugger stared straight ahead and put on speed.

He sped through the Palisades and into Malibu, past the latest slide zone and Caltrans's feeble attempt to battle nature with concrete barriers and sandbags and pink, gritty fiberglass slopes as genuine as Caltrans's promises. A few more wet winters and the coastline would look like Disneyland. Black Suit's head had stopped swiveling – fixed on the ocean. Easy choice: The land side was shopping centers and pizza joints and schlock shops not much different from what he'd encounter in Brooklyn.

I followed the Volvo through Carbon Beach, La Costa, past the private road that led to the Colony, the emerald hills of Pepperdine University, where the commercial clutter gives way to brown mountains, black gorges, orange poppies, and more than a hint of what Malibu must have been like when the Chumash Indians roamed.

Latigo Beach, the Cove Colony, Escondido. No suspense: I knew exactly where Dugger was headed and was ready well before his left-turn signal flashed and he pulled into the center turn lane.

He stopped a quarter mile before the Paradise Cove intersection and Ramirez Canyon. A towering plastic sign advertised the Sand Dollar Restaurant and the trailer park that bordered the restaurant's private beach.

Malibu's estate zone. A half mile broken by a handful of gates, each handcrafted and unique and flanked by old trees and hedges, too-perfect beds of flowers, closed-circuit TV cameras, No Trespassing warnings.

Prime of the prime: the few multiacre Malibu properties blessed with sheltered coves and sandy beach and
views of the shipping channels that lead to Asia.

The gate that held Dugger's interest was a tangle of
burnished copper tentacles shadowed by the palms and
pines I remembered, as well as gigantic rubber trees and
schefflera and sagos and birds-of-paradise blazing flame-
like in the afternoon sun. He must have had a remote-
control unit, because before he completed the turn
across PCH the octopus arms swung open and he sailed
through. I had my cheapie camera ready and hustled for
shots of the Volvo's rear end as it vanished into green.

Click click click.

The gates closed. I was going no further.

But Dugger had a busy day lined up.

Chauffering Black Suit to Daddy's place. The pleasure
dome conceptual light-years from the little cell in Newport that Dugger had once called home. For all his
rumpled guy pretense – attempts to distance himself
from his father and what his father represented – when
things got rough Junior returned with the volition of a
homing pigeon.

Walking in step with a cold-faced man in a black suit.

Business. Tying up loose ends.

Who was next?

I returned to Santa Monica, found a MotoPhoto with a
'FREE DUPLICATES!' banner, had a cup of coffee while
my film developed, then inspected my handiwork. Most
of the roll was taken up by rear shots too distant to be

useful, but I had managed to snag Dugger and Black Suit together in full-frontal midrange and in two individual close-ups. Nice clear view of the Volvo passing through the coiling copper gates but, once again, too far to catch the license plate. Tony Duke's address was partially obscured by greenery, but no matter: Those tentacle gates were unique.

I drove home. Robin's truck was gone, and I was ashamed for being happy about that. Hurrying into my office, I called Milo.

'The gun that killed Jane was registered, all right,' he said. No greeting, no preliminaries. 'And guess who?'

I said, 'Charles Manson.'

'Lauren. She bought it two years ago at a Big Five on San Vicente – not far from her apartment. She probably figured in her line of work, she could use protection. Or maybe she was just another single woman wanting the security of firepower. Looks like she lent it to her mother, and stepdad got hold of it.'

'Another unfortunate accident.'

'So far, that's how it's going down, Alex.'

'What will Mel Abbot be charged with?' I asked.

'The DAs office is brainstorming because it's a tricky situation – old helpless guy like that. No one dares question Abbot until he has a lawyer, but he's in no shape to hire one of his own volition. He's also too rich to qualify for a public defender, but they may assign him a temporary PD anyway. In addition to an advocate from competency court. Ruiz and Gallardo are searching for relatives, someone willing to assume responsibility.

Meanwhile, Abbot's got a comfy bed in the jail ward at County, and the shrinks say it'll be a few days before they can even try to get an accurate picture of his mental status.'

'Once he gets an attorney, then what?'

'No one's eager to make a show case out of it. My guess is he'll be quietly committed.'

'Nice and neat,' I said.

'If you call a dead woman and a pathetic old guy ending his days on the funny farm neat.'

'Everything's relative,' I said. 'Unfortunately, I just made a mess.'

'What are you talking about?'

I described my afternoon.

He didn't answer, but I had a pretty good idea about the look on his face.

Finally: 'You followed him *again*?'

'I know,' I said. 'But this time, I was really careful. He definitely didn't see me. The main thing is what *I* saw.'

'You think Dugger's personally escorting a hit man.'

'You had to see the guy. He sure doesn't look like a brain surgeon—'

'Whatever he is, Alex, if he flew in today from New York, he didn't kill Jane last night in Sherman Oaks.'

'Granted. But he could've killed Lauren. And Michelle and Lance. Maybe there's a team.'

'Musical mafiosi,' he said.

'That's how I'd do it if I had the money. Use pros the locals don't know, cover my tracks by transporting them back and forth.'

'All that flying means paperwork, Alex. If the guy is a professional – a really heavy hitter – he'd have to worry about that. And like I said, if you're the contractor – a supposedly law-abiding fellow like Dugger – why would you also pick the guy up at the airport *yourself*? Take him out to lunch in plain view and truck him straight to Daddy's place in broad daylight and give someone the opportunity to snap pictures?'

'So you have no interest in looking at the passenger list?'

'That,' he said, 'would require a warrant. And grounds—'

'Okay, fine,' I said. 'He likes black 'cause he's a priest, lost his collar. Tony Duke flew him out for spiritual guidance.'

'Listen, Alex, I appreciate all you've—'

'Want me to toss the photos?'

Pause. 'You have clear shots of this joker's face.'

'Clear enough. In duplicate.'

He made a sound – not a sigh, too weary for a sigh. 'I'll come by tonight.'

He didn't.

twenty-six

By ten the following morning my phone was still silent.

Either my Brooklyn Pizza lens work had paled in comparison to some new lead Milo was chasing or, given the benefit of a good night's sleep, he'd decided the snapshots were a waste of time. Still, it was unlike him not to call.

Robin was smiling again, and we'd made love this morning – though I'd felt some distance. Probably my imagination.

When in doubt, torment your body. I put on running clothes, stepped out into a cold, wet morning, and struggled clumsily up the canyon. Shoes squeaking on still-dewy vegetation, stumbling along the earthen patchwork laid down by a fast-shifting sky.

When I returned the house was echoing hollowly, silent but for the whine of the circular saw from Robin's studio. I changed into a sweatshirt, old jeans, and grubby shoes, stuck a Dodgers cap on my head, and left.

The air had chilled even further, and the sun hid

behind a big, iron saucer of the same sooty hue as yesterday's cloud bank. A tongue of wind whipped past me, rattling trees, twanging shrubs. The earth smelled of loam and iron. Not winter in any real sense, but in L.A. you learn to live with pretense.

On days like this, the ocean was still beautiful.

I took Sunset to the coast highway, encountered no obstruction, and was speeding past Tony Duke's copper octopus by twelve-thirty. No cars were parked on the shoulder, and all the gated estates looked forbidding. Continuing to the Paradise Cove intersection, I turned onto the speed-bumped asphalt that dips down past Ramirez Canyon and ends at the beachfront clearing where the Sand Dollar sits. As I passed the restaurant's plastic sign, I noticed a rectangle of whitewashed plywood staked a few feet in, painted crudely in red:

The Dollar's Renovation Continues.
Sorry, Folks. Please Remember Us
When We Re-open This Summer

I bumped my way past the oleander-planted berms that nearly concealed the trailer park on the north side of the cove. No chain had been slung across the blacktop, and the splintered placard warning that beach parking was twenty bucks a day if you weren't eating at the restaurant appeared in its usual spot, bottomed by the halfhearted announcement BOOGIE BOARD, SNORKEL, and KAYAK RENTALS. So far, so good.

West of Spring Street, renovation usually means extinction. The Dollar was going the way of all L.A. landmarks, and I didn't know how I felt about that.

It had been nearly three years since I'd tackled a fisherman's breakfast from the red-vinyl cradle of a Sand Dollar window booth. Back in the days when Robin and I had rented a drafty beach house ten miles up the coast, as we waited out the reconstruction of our burned-out home. Then a patient's childhood nightmares drew me into a long-unsolved abduction and murder, and the victim turned out to be a waitress at the Dollar. The questions I'd asked had overridden six months of generous tips. Some time later I'd dropped in for breakfast again, hoping all had been forgotten. It hadn't, and I never returned.

I drove fifty more yards, and the shack that serves as the Paradise Cove guardhouse came into view. The lowered gate arm was more symbolic than functional – I could've lifted it by hand, squeezed the Seville through – I wondered if it would come to that. Then I saw movement through the shack's window, and the attendant was ready for me when I drove up, shaking his head and pointing at yet another sign that reiterated the twenty-dollar tariff. Older man – seventy-five or so – with blue eyes and a beef-jerky face shielded by a battered canvas hat. Big band music played from a tape deck in the shack.

'Closed,' he said.

Down below, through the twisting branches of giant sycamores, I could see ocean and what remained of the restaurant: The redwood façade and half of the shingle roof were in place, but empty holes gaped ulcerously where the windows had been, and through the wounds was a clear view of walls stripped to the studs and snarls of severed electrical conduit. What had once been the parking lot was now a table of raked brown dirt filled with backhoes, tractors, and trucks, sheets of plywood, stacks of two-by-fours. No workers in sight, no construction noise.

'Big project,' I said.

'Oh, yeah,' said the old man, stepping out of the shack. He wore a khaki shirt and gray twill pants cinched tight by a skinny maroon vinyl belt. 'Didn't see the sign, huh? They should stick it right out front on the highway, so folks don't bother to turn. I'll raise the yardarm and you can swing a U-ey.'

'I saw the sign,' I said, and held out a twenty.

He stared at the bill. 'There's nothing to do down there, amigo.'

'There's still the beach.'

'Not much of it. They got wood and cement blocks and all kinds of garbage piled all over the place. Haven't even had a decent film shoot in months – only thing they could film right now would be a disaster movie. They might be hotshots, but *someone's* not making money.'

'They?'

'Corporate syndicate.'

'How long's it been going on?'

'Months. Almost a year.' He looked back at the site. 'Owner died, kids inherited, squabbled, sold out to some chain seafood outfit, and *they* sold to some holding company. They say they're gonna preserve it, make it even better. Mostly, I see guys in suits driving in and out. Every so often they bring in a squad of Mexicans and there's some hammering and nailing for a few days, then weeks of nothing. But they keep paying me, and they don't bother the rest of us who live up there.' His thumb hooked toward the mobile homes. 'Be nice, though, to have somewhere to eat out without driving to Malibu Road.'

'Yeah,' I said, waving the twenty. 'Gonna take a look, anyway. For old times' sake.'

'You're sure? I don't even think the Porta Potties are working.'

'I can handle it.'

'Wait till you're my age— Nice car. Take much maintenance?'

'Just a bit. It's old but it works.'

He smiled. 'Like me.' He started to take the money, shook his head. 'Aw, hell, forget it – someone asks you, though, you paid.'

'Thanks.'

'Don't thank me, just change the oil every two thousand miles and keep that thing alive.'

I parked south of the construction zone, well away from the heavy machinery. Gulls picked and pecked in the dirt, and a dozen more birds perched noisily atop what was left of the roof. The shingles that remained were wind-warped and salt-grayed and shit-specked. The birds looked happy enough, squawking and jockeying for space.

I got out, righted my baseball cap, and ambled south along the cove, veering diagonally toward the waterline. Medium tide. No beach chairs like in the old days, just plenty of open, creamy sand. The ocean was even lazier than yesterday, oozing in slowly like a giant glue spill, its retreat discernible only as the gradually deepening stain of water-saturated silica. Off at the southern edge was another shack, white-frame like the guardhouse and not much larger. The blackboard bolted above the door was crowded with sloppy script in that same bright red, proclaiming, KAYAKS! SNORKELS! WET SUITS! COLD DRINKS! Rusty hasp, bolted. I kept walking. Walls of bluff rose behind me. Against the dirt stood a bank of five bright blue plastic Andy Gumps – three of the latrines marked HIMS, two, HERS. Next to the male loos was a large pile of something under layers of bright blue tarp.

I headed toward what was left of the Paradise Cove pier. A few storm seasons ago the gangly structure had been wind-sheared in two, the jutting face washed out to sea and never replaced. Now the remains, condemned and blockaded by county chain link, were a listing, bleached skeleton, the vantage point for yet more noisy gulls and a big, solitary, dignified-looking pelican who'd distanced himself from the din.

A squirt of light hit me full-face as I walked across splotches of yellowed sand. The glare made me squint and lower the brim of my cap. False dawn in the afternoon. The flying saucer cloud bank had reversed direction – gliding out toward Japan and leaving behind a pink-pearl residue through which sun struggled to leak. The light that made it through was glossy, almost liquid – squibs of golden ointment.

Even in this ruinous state, the cove was a glorious bit of geography. Thinking of what Tony Duke and his neighbors owned, I sighted down the coast, aiming for a glimpse of the beach estates that claimed the bluffs. But the shoreline curved sharply, and the only home I spotted was a single glass-and-wood thing on stilts, squat and aggressive, ovoid as the cloud bank.

A door slamming from the direction of the latrines made me turn, as a voice behind me said, 'Cool, huh?'

I completed the swivel, focused on a red-tan stubbled face. A wiry, midsized man wearing only baggy red swim shorts, standing a few feet away, swinging a key chain. Fat-free torso, corded arms, knees deformed by calcium knots. Coarse peroxided hair with black roots was a crown of thorns above his narrow face. His sharp nose was crooked and zinc-whitened and a puka shell necklace circled a gullet starting to sag. The stubble on his chin was white as the zinc. Forty, maybe older.

'You were checking out that Starship *Enterprise* deal, right?' he said, eyeing the house on the sand. 'Know who owns it?'

'Who?'

'Dave Dell.'

'The game-show host?'

'The game-show host and mega-gazillionaire – guy started out as an AM disc jockey, bought up Malibu land back when Lincoln was president, got himself a sweet chunk of bluff, man. He's partnering with the dudes who're doing that.' Cocking his head at the restaurant renovation. 'Downtown dudes.'

'Nice investment,' I said.

'That's what they live for – more and more and more. Borrowing someone else's money.' He laughed. 'Thing is, except for that house of his – Dell's – all those humongoid things are on bluffs and most of them got no beach at all. They got their views to China, but they don't have serious *sand* because of the way Paradise is shaped. Even the ones that do got some, and even at low tide, it ain't much – little squares where you can sit and watch your money wash away. 'Cause the whole damn beach is disappearing.'

'Really?'

'You bet, man. Inches each year, maybe more – you never heard about it?'

'Sounds familiar,' I said. 'Global warming or something. I wasn't sure it was true.'

'Oh, it's true all right. Global warming, El Niño, La Niña, La Cucaracha, the ozone layer, all that shit. One of these days, we're gonna have this conversation from La Brea.'

He laughed again and shook his head. The yellow thatch was salt-stiff, and it didn't vibrate. 'Meanwhile, a bum like me's got all this sand for free, and *they* got their little private patches of nothing— You actually pay twenty bucks to come down here? Didn't Carleton tell you everything's closed up?'

'He did, but I wanted to see it anyway.' I pointed down the coast. 'Still beautiful.'

'Yeah.' Another grin. Sly. 'You're bullshitting me, man. Carleton don't charge no one no more. He and the other trailer folk are pissed about what they done to the Dollar, and I can't say I blame them, so they let anyone in free who wants to. Which isn't too many.' He shrugged, and the puka necklace rattled. 'Used to be, you couldn't find a parking space and they were filming commercials all the time. Now it's El Quieto, which is fine with me. Things change and then you die. Bye, man. Enjoy.'

As he walked away from me, I said, 'I heard Tony Duke lives in one of those bluff houses.'

He stopped, turned. 'Hell, yeah. It's nothing but his type and Hollywood assholes up there.' He rubbed his chin, looked up into the sun. In the full light I saw a canker sore sprouting under his lower lip. Raw spots on his forehead glistened precancerously. 'Duke's place is about five properties down. I swam by a few times, seeing if I could maybe catch a look at some of those girls he keeps there. No luck.'

'Too bad.'

Snort. 'Like I'd know what to do if I found something.'

'How'd you know which place is his?'

'Easy. You can't see the house – it's set far back, like most of them. But Duke's got this wooden cable-car doohickey running along the side of his bluff. Little box on tracks that goes up and down. Everyone else has steps, but he's got that. Guess the guy's serious about leisure, like he says – wants to waste his calories on pussy, not climbing stairs. It's a cool little deal, that car, but I never seen anyone actually using it.'

'A funicular,' I said.

'If you say so. Other of the guys have gone by there too – swimming, kayaking. Especially when Duke's got a party going. Everyone wanting an eyeful of pussy, maybe catch some looker sucking dick – something you could take a picture of and send home to Mom.' He laughed. 'The gizmo's always at the top of the bluff, locked up, and when Duke's partying, there's bouncers there – big meat, like iron pumpers, standing on top of the cliff like they're waiting for someone to piss 'em off.'

'I hear he uses off-duty cops for that.'

'Wouldn't surprise me – even scarier, right?'

'Right.'

'Anyway, no one ever gets to see any girls.'

'Does Duke throw lots of parties?'

'He used to. Like every two months. You'd see the superstretches lined up on PCH, valets, heat lamps, caterers' trucks, the works. But not in a long time.' He thought. 'Not in a real long time – a year, maybe more. Maybe he's getting too old for it – that would be a hell of a thing, wouldn't it? Cool old dude like that, living on caviar and Viagra, surrounded by pussy but losing the desire. 'Cause it wouldn't matter how wrinkled his nut bag was and how far down it hung. There's one perfume that opens up pussy faster than Kama Sutra Love Oil.' He rubbed his index finger with his thumb and sniffed.

'Money,' I said.

'Eau de cash,' he assented. 'Does it every time.'

'So old Tony's on Viagra,' I said. 'That a fact?'

'I don't know if it's a fact, man, but that's what you hear. Look, the dude's got to be what – seventy, eighty, a hundred fifty? My *dad* used to buy his magazine. Hell, maybe the lead in his pencil still is righteous – he's got a young wife, I seen her, she comes in once in a while to the Dollar for breakfast – used to, when there was a Dollar.' He cupped his hands six inches from his chest. 'Rack on her. Never looked happy, but I heard she popped a coupla kids for Old Tony.'

'What was she unhappy about?'

'Who knows? The dudes who used to work the parking lot said she'd style up in this very cool Expedition – black with gray trim on the bottom, big tires, righteous running boards, chrome wheels – always open her own door before they could reach her, then act pissed that they hadn't got there in time. Always in a big hurry. The parking dudes used to joke about that – she had to rush because the old guy needed her home by the time the Viagra kicked in. 'Cause that's the way that stuff works, you know? You drop a pill, wait for the old pecker to salute the flag, but you only got so much time to pour the pork before it's back staring at your shoes.' He lowered his hand in a long, slow flutter. 'Maybe that's how the Viagra thing started – 'cause she was always in a hurry. Anyway, money don't buy everything, right? Give me my sand, a few waves, and *I'm* styling.'

He pinched his Adam's apple and touched the canker

sore briefly. I looked for a surfboard, didn't see one.

'You ride, huh?' I said.

'When I can.'

'No shape today.'

He laughed hard. 'Never any shape, here. You don't surf *Paradise*, man. This is work. That's my *office*.' Pointing to the rental shack.

'Thought everything was closed.'

'Hey, they pay me to show up, I show up.' He swung the key ring in a wobbly arc.

'You open for any business at all?' I said.

'I wouldn't snorkel out there, man. Too much silt, and a sky like this is gonna reduce your visibility to zippo.'

'I was thinking a kayak.'

The crooked white nose lowered as he gave me a long, appraising look. 'You don't know squat about waves, but you don't have that tourist smell about you either.'

'Tourist from L.A.,' I said. 'I used to live in Malibu. Out past Leo Carrillo. Came back for old times' sake.'

'Over by El Pescador?'

'Past El Pescador. Over the county line, near Neptune's Net.'

'Livingston Beach,' he said. 'Cool riding zone – prime shape – you ever try to surf?'

'Did some boogie boarding,' I said.

'I graduated that when I was in third grade, man. Moved right on to the heavy stuff. I was a hotdogger back in high school – got three minutes of footage in *Water Demons II*. Then my ears went – chronic infections, the doctor said no more. I said screw the doctor, but now my head hurts all the time no matter how much Advil I drop, so I hold down the rides to once a week. You serious about a kayak?'

'Sure, why not?'

He looked me up and down again. 'Guess no reason. It's cold out there, but it's glass, except for the rips. Which way you gonna go?'

'South.' I smiled. 'Maybe catch a look at Old Tony's place.'

He laughed. 'Figures. But don't get your hopes high.'

He led me toward the rental shack, said, 'It's a pretty easy day for paddling, but going south you are gonna be pushing against the currents. You look like you got the shoulders to handle it, but just know that, okay? We're not talking Lake Arrowhead. Also, there are some rip-tides along the way – small ones, but they'll bump the boat, so don't be looking for tits and ass and start getting pushed out further than you wanna be.'

'Thanks for the advice. How much is the rental?'

'Hold on,' he said. 'Another thing: No matter how glassy it looks and how good a rower you think you are, your clothes are gonna get soaked. I tell people all the time but they never listen and sure enough they come back with their clothes all stuck to them, pissed off. Only way to stay dry is use a wet suit, man. I can rent you that too.'

'Make it a combo,' I said. 'How much?'

He licked his lips, peeled a speck of zinc from his nose. 'First I gotta unlock the place, then I gotta find a flashlight so I can check the suits, make sure there's no cracks from all the time they been sitting there. *Then,* I gotta check 'em for spiders and scorpions crawling in – 'cause we get them, here.'

'Scorpions?' I said. 'Near the beach?'

'Little black nasty ones. You think of 'em as desert dudes, but they're here, man, hibernating or whatever. Probably hitched a ride in on some truck from T.J. So I gotta stick my hand in and shake out the suit.'

'I appreciate it. Exterminator fees gonna cost me too?'

He laughed. 'Well,' he said, 'normally it's twenty bucks an hour for the boat, twelve for the suit, six for mask and fins, so that would be thirty-eight up front, and we usually take a driver's license for deposit.'

'No mask and fins,' I said. 'Just the boat and the suit.'

'Your feet are gonna get cold.'

'I can live with it.'

'Your choice, man – okay, how long you planning on staying out? 'Cause I wasn't planning to be here all afternoon. I mean, I show up, but I don't make a big thing out of it, know what I mean?'

'Couple of hours at the most.'

'Couple of hours – yeah, I can handle that. So that would be sixty-four bucks, but for you, let's make it a package – say fifty-five even, and I won't even take no deposit, 'cause where the hell are you gonna go? If it's cash.'

Wink, wink.

'Cash it is,' I said, reaching for my wallet.

He selected a key from the ring, slipped it into the lock on the rental shack's door. 'Rusty. The ocean never stops eating – kind of freaky, idn't it? Cool, too. The ocean's gonna be here for a billion more years, and we're not. So why worry about anything?'

The kayaks made up the mass beneath the blue tarp, and he pulled a yellow-trimmed, white single-rider and a paddle from the shack. I stripped behind the tiny building as Norris – after I paid him he volunteered his name – readied the kayak. Standing naked and shivering in the frigid air, I double-checked the suit's neoprene sleeves and legs for creepie-crawlies. Once I slipped into the rubber sheath, the warmth was nearly immediate.

'Hey,' said Norris, as I emerged. He was kneeling next to the boat and wiping down the interior with a filthy-looking rag. 'Mr Lloyd Bridges, man. There's a zip compartment on the left leg for your wallet and keys. You can leave the rest of your stuff in your car – cool car, by the way. Long as you get back in time, I won't steal it.' Jamming the rag in the rear pocket of his shorts, he slapped the boat's fiberglass flank. 'Picked you a good one. You ever done this before?'

'Yup.'

'So you know that even when they feel like they're tipping over, they're probably not. If you wanna pick up speed, just keep that rhythm going – hand over hand. And don't let go of the paddle. It'll float, but it can get away from you, and if it does, I got to charge you.'

We toted the kayak to the water's edge, then he

eased it into the ocean and held it steady as I climbed in.

'Go for it, man,' he said, shoving me off. 'You see any serious pussy, I want to hear about it.'

twenty-seven

The placid ocean meant broad shallows, and I had to maintain a twenty-foot distance from the shore to keep the kayak out of sand. As I cut through the water, a weak, misty breeze washed my face. After this morning's clumsy jog, working my arms felt good, and so did being alone in the vastness of the sea.

I picked up speed as I passed Dave Dell's glass bowl. The house was huge but shabby from up close – gray paint scarred by wind and salt, lowered curtains, no signs of inhabitance. The next property meandered along the bluff, fronted by clumps of rough-cut shrubbery and backed by pines twisting spastically. Rickety steps to the beach dangled – the bottom dozen steps had been sheared off.

As I continued south the breeze picked up, and now I was working a bit just to keep from veering back toward land. A few minutes later the first sign of riptides appeared – narrow pipes of coiling water braiding the skin of the Pacific. As I passed over them the kayak bucked, then settled down gently.

377

Three more estates, two with intact steps so steep they were little more than ladders. Norris's tale of a fast-vanishing beach might have been hyperbole, but signs of erosion were obvious in the furrows that corrugated the bluffs. An outcropping of rock fingers stretched into the water, and I pushed the kayak farther out to sea, skimming the eastern border of a floating mass of kelp. Suddenly, the sun hid itself again and the water got dark. I was a good fifteen yards from the tide line when Tony Duke's funicular came into view.

Duke's property was wider and higher than those of his neighbors, and his property line was more sinuous – a series of S-curves created as the cliff twisted and relented. The hillside had been planted with succulents, but all that remained were scraggly gray-green patches, and the erosion scars were long and deep, impossible to mistake for anything but inevitable. Down below was Duke's patch of beach, a spoon-shaped hollow visible only from the water. The funicular was a low-key affair, redwood car and dark metal tracks blending in with the mountainside. The passenger compartment rested atop the cliff, shadowed by a brown metal arch that I assumed was some kind of power source. The tracks dropped from the hilltop to the sand in a near-vertical drop, adhering to the dirt as if by magic. If plants couldn't take root, could metal bolts be trusted?

Someone thought they could. Nestled in the spoon were a woman in a beach chair and two small white-blond children. I was too far to make out the woman's age. Her big straw hat and blowsy white dress provided no help. The kids looked to be around three or four. The smaller one – a girl in a pink one-piece bathing suit – sat in the sand, legs splayed, digging with a bright orange shovel and adding sand to a green bucket. Several feet in front of her a naked boy ran along the shore, kicking water, picking up clumps of seaweed and tossing them ineffectually at the ocean.

The woman's body was loose in a way that could mean only sleep or hypnosis. In the sand near her right arm, something glassy kicked back reflection.

I stopped rowing, backpaddled to remain in place, and watched them. The naked boy saw me, stared back, raised his arm. Not a greeting – a tight-fisted wave, combative. The woman didn't move. I resumed rowing – slowly. The breeze bumped me over a riptide, and water splashed into the boat. The air was colder, and the pool around my bare feet had become an ice bath. When I was well past the Duke estate, I looked back. The little boy had lost interest in me, was in thigh-high water, splashing.

I drifted past several more properties, caught sight of a couple of cathedral-sized houses but no people. The wind had grown adamant, and my feet, immersed in salt water, were numb. I crossed a few more rips, found easy water, sat there for a while, bobbing and staring out across the ocean, wondering why I'd come. A shadow passed over the kayak as a pelican – a big, fat, gray creature, maybe the bird I'd seen atop the pier – glided toward the horizon. I watched the bird cross the kelp bed and settle. Waiting. Dipping, retrieving, gulping. Oblivious to anything but the task at hand, a jowly monarch.

I rowed a bit more, hit increasingly angry waves. Fifty minutes had passed since I'd slipped into the wet suit. Time to get back.

I'd be bringing back no tales of naked babes for Norris and nothing of an evidentiary nature for Milo. The little towheads were most likely Tony Duke's second installment of offspring, and the woman could be anyone.

As I began to row back I decided not to tell Milo of my little ride. Maybe he'd call today, maybe not. One-handing the kayak into reverse, I began my return trip. Rowing faster and staying as close to the shore as the shallows would allow, because the wind had kicked up the waves. Working up a chilly sweat by the time the funicular appeared.

The cable car remained at the top, inert. But the woman in the white dress was on her feet now, hatless, running, golden hair streaming, arms spread wide. Her mouth open too, as she raced for the water.

I was too far to make out the words, but I could hear her scream and the tone was unmistakable: panic.

The little girl in the pink bathing suit hadn't budged, and the orange shovel was still in her hand. But no sign of the naked boy.

Then I saw him. A little white dot bobbing in the water, maybe twenty yards due north of the kayak.

Just a towhead, no arms. Bouncing like a ping-pong ball, so insignificant that I might have mistaken him for flotsam – a stray bit of styrofoam.

The golden-haired woman ran into the ocean just as the ocean swelled and the boy disappeared. I rowed toward the spot where I'd spotted him. Saw the riptide – tight, luminous, funneling.

No sight of him.

The woman was in the water. The little girl had gotten to her feet and was toddling after her.

I began rowing frantically, found my progress too slow, wormed my way out of the kayak and dove into the icy water.

Even a quiet ocean can make a man feel weak. This ocean cared nothing for my self-esteem.

I dove, stroked, dove, stroked, fixing my eye on the spot where the boy had gone down. Thrown off by the rips and by waves, now freshly stoked by a full-force wind. The funnels weren't strong enough to pose a danger to someone of my size, but they slowed me down, made it harder to focus on my destination.

I swam as hard as I could, got close to the spot – still no sign of the boy – *there* he was, ten yards farther out, face whitened by sunlight, bouncing – no sign of his arms, but he seemed to be staying afloat – treading water, good swimming skills for his age, but how long could he last? The water was icy, and I felt my own muscles clog. I threw myself into the currents, concentrated on keeping his blond head in my sights. Watched helplessly as he went under again, and when he resurfaced he was five yards farther from shore – being rolled out to sea, slowly but inexorably. The woman's screams sounded behind me, audible above the roar of the tide.

I changed course, widening the angle of juncture as I estimated where the rips would take the boy and swimming toward that point. Thinking about all those drowned kids I'd evaluated at Western Peds. Active little boys, mostly. Survivors with damaged brains . . .

I reached the spot. No boy. Had I miscalculated? Where the hell was he? A quick glance back at the shore told me I hadn't lost my bearings – the woman in the white dress was swimming too. But she'd covered only a third of the distance, was having trouble as the garment bloused about her like a deflated parachute. Behind her, the chubby little girl edged toward the water . . .

I started to warn her, caught sight of the boy's head, then his entire body – fifteen feet ahead – tossed like a scrap of kelp as a wave pushed him up and dunked him out of sight, and now he looked scared. I raced toward him, only to see gravity return him to the depths yet again. His arms were thrashing wildly – losing control.

Flinging myself across the riptide that had snared him, I reached out, got hold of wet hair, a skinny arm, then a small, bony torso that writhed in my grip. Circling his body with one arm, I held his head above water and began paddling back toward land.

He fought me.

Kicked my ribs, butted my chest, shouted in my ear. Tiny teeth bit down on my earlobe, and it was all I could do not to let go.

Strong for his size, and despite his ordeal he was feisty. Growling and spitting, intent on chomping my ear again.

I managed to pinion both his arms and forced his head away from mine using my chin as I continued toward the beach. He howled and bucked and butted his little skull against my collarbone.

When the water shallowed sufficiently, I stood and held his thrashing little body at arm's length. His scrunched-up, triangular face emitted a hoarse cry of outrage. Good strong lungs, nice-looking kid. Four or five.

'Down!' he screamed. 'Put me down, shit-poop asshole! Down!'

'Soon enough, my little gentleman,' I said, catching my breath.

Behind me a woman sobbed, 'Baxter!' and slender white hands tipped by long red fingernails yanked the boy from me.

I searched for the little girl.

In the water up to her knees. The woman in the white dress was hugging the boy, her back to the little girl.

I pointed. 'Should I get her, or you?'

The woman swiveled sharply. Young – very young, same triangular face as Baxter. Green-blue eyes followed my finger, and she froze. The baggy dress had soaked her to the skin, gauzy white cotton deepening to flesh tone as it clung to her torso, outlining too-full breasts, the grayish purple assertion of nipples, a sweep of abdominal swell, tiny tidepool of navel pit, the stippled outline of white lace bikini panties, labial cleft visible beneath the lace.

'Oh!' she said, but she still didn't move, and the

toddler was now up to her waist, laughing and splashing. Tiny little thing – two and a half was my guess – with plenty of baby fat, a convex tummy, a bud-mouth open in wonderment. White hair top-knotted, sand crust on her belly. The wind was strong enough to rustle the trees along the bluff, and foot-high breakers slapped the sand.

'Baxter,' said the woman, voice quivering. 'Look at what Sage is doing. You guys are going to kill me.' Still holding the boy, she moved toward the girl, tripped, fell, dropped the boy, who ended up with a mouthful of sand and began choking and screaming.

I hurried toward Sage. Hearing the woman call out, 'Ohmigod, I'm so stooopid!'

I reached the child just as she fell on her rear and gulped water and broke into sobs. When I swooped her up, she stopped crying immediately. Giggled. Touched my lip with a tiny, gritty finger. Giggled again and tried to poke my eye.

'Hey, cutie,' I said.

'*Cootie. Heh heh.*' Poke, poke. I restrained the finger, and she found that hilarious.

I carried her back to the blond woman, and handed her over. Baxter's mouth was clean and grinning crookedly. He glared at me, proclaimed, 'No fish,' and shook his fist.

'He thinks he was fishing,' said the woman. 'He thinks it's your fault he didn't catch anything.'

'Sorry,' I said.

Baxter scowled.

'Big fisherman,' said the woman. 'I can't believe he actually did that. He never did it before.'

'That's kids,' I said. 'Always something new.'

'No fish,' opined Baxter.

'*Fiss*,' echoed Sage.

'What, you have an opinion too, you little wild thing?' said the woman. She bent and stared at both kids. 'That was silly – really *silly*. Both of you were silly, right?'

No reply. Baxter had turned profoundly bored, and his sister's attention was taken up by the sand at her feet.

The woman said, 'You wild, wild things – for all I know there are sharks out there that could *eat* you! *Sharks!*' To me: 'Isn't that true?'

Before I could answer she repeated, 'Sharks! To *eat* you!'

The possibility made Baxter smile wider. But for a few sand scratches on his chest, he looked unscathed.

'Oh, you think it's funny. Would you *like* that? Huh? *Would* you? To be eaten by a shark – gobbled up like you're his Big Mac or something? Would either of you like to be a Big Mac?'

'No way,' said Baxter, cocking one leg. 'I eat him.'

The little girl giggled.

'You're impossible,' said the woman. 'You're both impossible.'

She straightened, folded her arms under her breasts, turning the nipples into twin torpedoes. She had a husky but girlish voice, beautiful, lightly freckled white skin, looked barely out of her teens. Full, soft lips, dainty chin, long neck, and the green-blue eyes were enormous and widely spaced under plucked eyebrows. No makeup, but for the extravagant red talons and toenails glossed in the identical shade.

'Fuckin' shark,' said Baxter.

'*Fug shaaf,*' said the girl.

'Oh, Jesus,' said the woman, grabbing each of them by the hand and shaking her head. Breathing hard and fast, but her breasts barely moved. Too big and too firm, and the rest of her was too slender to support a chest that robust. Solidity, courtesy the scalpel.

I don't think I stared, but maybe I did, because she seemed suddenly to become aware of her body – of being, for all intents, stripped naked by the second-skin wet dress. She gave a tiny, knowing smile, flipped her hair, peered into my eyes as I forced them to keep away from the curves below. Trailing *her* eyes – now I saw flecks of amber in the big, clear, green-blue irises – down her own body. Then her gaze shifted to me as she conducted a quick appraisal of my wet suit. Smiling again, she turned and, clenching a child in each hand, dragged them back to the spot where she'd fallen asleep. Walking slowly, with a swivel-hipped, tiptoe prance that jiggled her rear.

I followed, and she had to know that, but she paid me no mind all the way to her beach chair. The straw hat lay half buried in the sand. The shiny thing I'd seen from the kayak was an Evian bottle. I realized I'd forgotten about the kayak and turned sharply.

The boat had come aground, upended, almost square with the spot where I'd brought Baxter the ear biter to shore. I jogged over, pulled it out of the tide's way, became aware of the throbbing in my ear, touched the lobe, inspected my finger. No blood, but those little teeth had done their job and the flesh was still dimpled and hot.

Back in the spoon-shaped shelter, the woman in the wet dress remained on her feet, saying something to both kids. Sage looked up at her, but Baxter's attention had drifted back to the ocean, and when he moved toward the water the woman held him back.

Then she waved at me. I jogged back.

'Please tell him,' she said, when I arrived. 'There are sharks out there. Right?' Smoothing down the soaked dress, pressing the fabric flush against her skin.

'Fuckin' shark,' said Baxter, growling happily and gnashing those killer teeth. 'Eat eat eat eat eat! Grrr!'

Sage laughed.

'Well, *aren't* there?' the woman demanded of me. 'Big killer whites or whatever – as big as dragons – like from *Jaws*?' She gnashed too. Small, sharp white incisors of her own. Her nipples had swelled to cherries.

'There just might be some kinds of sharks in there,' I said to the kids. 'Sharks and all kinds of other fish.'

'There you go,' said the woman. 'Listen to this man, Bax, he knows. With all those sharks and fish and sea monsters in there, you'd be nothing but food, right?'

The boy chortled and tried to break free once more. The woman held on to him and whined: 'Stop, you're hurting my arm – you are *really* going to kill me. *Wild* thing – and *you* should know better too, Sage-a-roo-roo.

What got into you, you always *hated* the water!'

Sage dropped her head. Her lips trembled.

'Oh, no,' said the woman scooping her up. 'Don't start crying, now – c'mon, sweetie nibbins. C'mon, c'mon, no tears now, you're a good girl, you don't have to cry – good girls don't have to cry.'

Sage sniffed. Cried.

'Oh, please, Sagey. Mommy just doesn't want anything to happen to you. Okay? You understand?'

Sage's nose began running, and she licked away snot. Baxter said, 'Ew, boogers,' and yanked on his mother's arm.

She yanked back, raised her voice. 'Now just *set* yourself down – both of you.' Pushing both children down onto the sand. 'Good. Now just stay there – don't move or . . . no TV and no pizza or F.A.O. Schwarz or Digimon or Pokémon or nothing. Okay?'

Neither child responded.

'Good.' To me: 'You must think I'm a *horrible* mother. But he's impossible, never sits still. When he was a baby, every time I walked through a doorway carrying him he used to stick out his head and – *bump*! Banging his head on *purpose*! Raising these lumps! I used to worry everyone would think he was abused or something, you know?' A glance back at Sage. 'And now, you too!'

The little girl said, '*UUUUU!*'

The woman blew a raspberry. Smoothed her dress again, heightening the virtual nudity. 'She's usually my good one. What a day.'

I smiled. She smiled back. Stuck out her hand. 'I haven't thanked you, have I? I'm *really* horrible – thank you *sooo* much. I'm Cheryl.'

'Alex.'

'Thank you, Alex. Thank you very very much. I don't know what I would've done if you hadn't . . .' The green-blue eyes took another trip down my wet suit. 'Do you live around here?'

'No, I was just kayaking.'

'Well, thank *God* you were. If you hadn't happened to . . .' Tears filled her eyes. 'Ohmigod, it's just starting to hit me – what could've – I'm so—' She shivered, hugged herself, looked at me as if inviting a hug. But I just stood there, and she emitted several high-pitched whimpers, plucked at an eyelash.

Now her lip quaked. Both kids stared up at her. Sage seemed stunned, and for the first time Baxter looked penitent.

I squatted down beside them, sifted sand through my fingers.

'*Mama kie,*' said Sage, with wonder. Her lower lip jutted.

'Mama will be fine,' I said, drawing a small circle in the sand. Sage dotted the middle.

Baxter said, '*Mommy?*'

Cheryl stopped crying. Crouching down, she gathered both children to her artificial breasts.

'Mama fine?' said Sage.

'Yes, I am, nibby-nib. Thanks to this nice man – thanks to Alex.' She held on to the kids as her eyes locked into mine. 'Listen, I want to give you something. For what you did.'

'Not necessary,' I said.

'Please,' she said. 'it would make me feel better – to at least— You saved my babies and I want to give you something. Please.' She pointed up at the top of the cliff. 'We live here. Just come up for a second.'

'You're sure it's okay?'

'Of course I am. I'm – I'll bring the car down and we can ride up. You'd be helping me anyway. It scares me – the car. I'm always afraid they'll fall out or something. You can hold on to Baxter, you'll be doing me a favor. Okay?'

'Sure.'

Her smile was sudden, warm, rich as she leaned over and kissed my cheek. I smelled sunscreen and perfume. Baxter growled.

'Thank you *so* much,' she said. 'For letting me give *you* something.'

She walked over to the straw hat, lifted the brim, and pulled out a small, white remote-control unit. The push of a button triggered the cable car's descent, soundless but for an occasional bump where an odd rail protruded.

'Neat, huh?' she said. To the kids: 'Neat, right? Not too many people have something this cool.'

Neither child answered. I said, 'Sure beats climbing.'

Cheryl laughed, tossed her hair. 'Well, you couldn't exactly climb that unless you were a – a lizard or something, I dunno. I mean, I like to work out – we've—

390

There's a great gym up at the house, and I'm real physical, but no way could I climb that, right?'

'No way,' I agreed.

'No-ay,' said Sage.

'I could climb it,' said Baxter. 'Pizza cake.'

'Sure you could, honey.' Cheryl patted his head. 'It *is* kind of neat, being able to ride down whenever you want. He – it got put in a long time ago.'

Muffled thump as the car came to rest six inches above the sand. 'Okay, here we go, all aboard. I'll take Sage and you hold on to him, okay?'

The compartment was roofless. Glass panels in a redwood frame, redwood benches, large enough for four adults. I got in last, feeling the car sway under my weight. Cheryl sat Baxter down, but he immediately stood. 'No way, José,' she said, returning him to his bench and stretching his arm toward mine. I gripped his hand, and he growled again and glared. I felt, strangely, like a stepfather.

'Close the door, Alex. Okay? Make sure it's locked good— Okay, here we go.'

Another button push, and up we went, hugging the cliff. The transparent walls gave the ride a weightless feel – floating in air as the view expanded to infinity. A brief, dank wave of vertigo washed over me as I caught a stunning brain-full of ocean and sky and endless possibilities. Norris might be right about the millionaires and their pitiful scraps of beach, but this was something too.

The trip was less than a minute of Baxter squirming, Sage growing drowsy, and Cheryl staring at me from under half-lowered lids, as if I had something to look forward to. Her legs were long, smooth, subtly muscled, perfect, and as she flexed she allowed them to spread, offering a view of soft inner thigh, high-cut lace panties, the merest hint of post wax stubble and goose bumps peeking out beyond the seam.

Baxter was staring at me. I held on tight to his hand. When we reached the top the car paused for a second, changed course, drifted horizontally, bumped to a halt under the metal arch.

'Home sweet home,' said Cheryl. 'At least, kind of.'

twenty-eight

The funicular set us down on a concrete platform, and we walked to a waist-high redwood-and-glass fence set twenty yards behind the cable unit. The barrier stretched the width of the property – at least three hundred feet – and halfway to the northern edge: a husky man in a gray uniform stooped and sprayed glass cleaner from a blue bottle. The area between the cliff edge and the fence was a hundred thousand dollars' worth of packed brown Malibu dirt. No need to conserve space; the expanse before me was twenty acres minimum, maybe more.

Twenty calculated acres. The earth had been bunched into too-gentle slopes of a symmetry that would've amused Mother Nature, then cloaked with emerald sod. Beds of tropical vegetation had been cut into the grass, and medallions of flowers sprouted bauble-bright. Granite paths, some hooded by pink marble arbors laced with scarlet bougainvillea, others sun-whitened, sickled through perfect lawns under the selective shade of specimen trees. Maybe half a thousand trees,

grouped in copses and pruned sculpturally, as calculated for size and shape as Cheryl's breasts. The beat of
the ocean continued to work its way up. But it com-
peted now with new water music – waterfalls, at least a
dozen minicataracts, tumbling into rock pools that
seemed to sprout from nowhere. The soda spritz of
skyward-aimed fountains jetted from free-form rock
ponds, some occupied by swans and ducks and pink
flamingos. Bird cries in the distance didn't belong to
any native species, and something that might've been a
monkey shrieked.

I said, 'Sounds like someone's got a zoo.'

'All kinds of animals,' said Cheryl, smiling enigmati-
cally and moving several steps ahead of me, long, blond
hair flapping against her back. Sage was slung over her
shoulder, sleeping soundly, cheeks bunched, tiny mouth
a vermilion squiggle. Baxter held my hand without
offering resistance. His pace had slowed and his eyelids
fluttered, and when I lifted him into my arms he didn't
fight, and I felt his body go heavy against mine.

Cheryl walked faster. Lagging slightly behind allowed
me to check out the estate. No buildings in sight, just
greenery, and now the fountains' ejaculations had
drowned out the ocean. A few acres to the right the lawn
sloped to a silver mirror: an unfenced, dark-bottomed
swimming pool the size of a small lake. No birds. How
did they keep them out?

No swimmers either. But for us and the glass cleaner,
no humanity. The place had all the intimacy of a
restricted resort, and I half expected some officious sort

to dart out from the shrubbery and check my membership card.

Cheryl turned onto a path, and we passed behind beds of tall, flowering pampas grass, hedges of variegated mock orange, a grove of two-story Hollywood junipers studded with blue-gray berries. The trees obscured the rest of the property, and I caught up with Cheryl. When her hip bumped mine a couple of times and I didn't react, her jaw set and she surged ahead of me again. The junipers gave way to a planting of cattails, and I resumed sneaking peeks between the stalks.

Up ahead and to the right were high, peach-stucco walls. Black, angled court lights hinted at tennis, and a rubbery *thump-thump* said relaxed competition.

A sharp twist of the pathway revealed a building – a quarter mile up, at the terminus of a palm colonnade. More peach walls and an Italianate heap the size of the White House under a royal blue roof. The pathway forked, and Cheryl chose the route that took us away from the house, through an allée of orange trees. Several smaller buildings cropped up along the way – acres away, similarly colored, heavily plant-shrouded. Then a few people: women in navy blue uniforms sweeping the walkways. Stout, dark-haired women with bowed legs, dresses hanging below the knees. Norris and the parking lot dudes would be crushed.

We entered a dark, bamboo-lined cul-de-sac, walked five hundred feet, turned sharply east. At the end of the path stood a one-story house only twice the size of the average suburban dream. A trellis-topped front loggia was burdened by a mass of half-dead trumpet vine. More bamboo towered at the back. The same peach walls and cerulean roof. Up close, I saw that the stucco had been sponged to a mottled finish and lacquered glossy. The worn Mediterranean villa look, complete with artificial age scars at the corners, peeled back to reveal ersatz brickwork. Huge double doors of weathered walnut looked genuinely ancient but any attempt to evoke the Aegean or le Côte d'Azur was killed by the roof tiles – some kind of space-age composite, too bright, too blue, cheesy enough to top a pizza.

'Here we are,' said Cheryl over her shoulder. 'My place.'

'Nice.'

She tossed her hair. 'It's temporary. I used to have a place of my own, then . . . What's the difference?' She hurried toward the double doors, yanked the handle. Resistance pitched her forward, and Sage's head bobbled.

'Locked?' she said. 'I left it open – shit, someone must've locked it.' Patting the pockets of the dress. 'Shit, I didn't take a key. Now I feel *really* stupid.'

'Hey, it happens.'

She faced me, and the blue-green eyes narrowed. 'Are you always this nice?'

'Nope,' I said. 'You caught me on a good day.'

'I'll bet you have lots of good days,' she said, touching my pinkie with hers but making it sound like a character flaw. She licked her lips. Lovely California girl face. Fresh, healthy, unlined. Even the freckles were perfectly placed. Nature's bounty, if you discounted the aggressive mammaries.

'Okay,' she said, 'it looks like I'm going to have to go find someone to let me in. I can leave you with Baxter and take Sage – no, I guess you better come with me.'

'Sure,' I said.

She gave a soft, breathy laugh. 'You have absolutely no idea where you are, do you – no idea who owns this place?'

'Someone with a good stockbroker, I'd say.'

She laughed. 'That's funny.' Her eyelids shuttered closed, then opened slowly. 'Where exactly are you from, Alex?'

'As in the turnip truck?'

'Huh?'

'I'm from L.A., Cheryl.'

'Where, like the Valley?'

'West L.A.'

'Oh.' She thought about that. 'Because the Valley can be a far place – sometimes people don't know what's going on over the hill.'

'So you're saying this is some kind of famous place?' I shrugged. 'Sorry.'

'Well . . .' She winked conspiratorially. 'I bet you really do know – without *knowing* you know. Take a guess.'

'Okay,' I said. 'Some kind of celebrity . . . a movie star. If you're an actress, I'm sorry for not—'

'No, no.' She giggled. 'I've acted, but that's not it.'

'Someone rich and famous . . .'

'Now you're getting warm—'

She looped her pinkie around mine, and I thought of how Robin had held my index finger as she slept.

'C'mon,' she said. 'Guess.'

Then one of the double doors opened and she jumped back, as if slapped.

A couple stood in the opening.

The woman was tall, thin, slightly stooped, in her late thirties, with broad shoulders and long limbs. Square-jawed face, black, brooding eyes, mahogany hair tied back in a ponytail, too many worry lines for her age. Despite the wrinkles, a chapped slice of mouth, and the grainy vestiges of teenage acne on chin and cheeks, she was attractive in a forbidding way – some men would go nuts for the challenge.

She had on a slim-cut, burgundy pantsuit with black velvet shawl lapels and matching cuffs. Any curves she might've owned were concealed by the loose drape of the suit, but the gestalt was poised and feminine. No jewelry, lots of foundation masking the blemishes. No problem recognizing her: Anita Duke. Marc Anthony's heir apparent and the new CEO of Duke Enterprises.

Ben Dugger's younger sister. I searched for resemblance, saw nuances of shared chromosomes in the stoop and the sad eyes.

The man beside her was a few years younger – thirty-two or -three – and an inch shorter. He wore a cream linen suit, pink silk T-shirt, beige sandals without socks. A platinum watch with a face the size of a snowball flashed from under his left sleeve. Thick wrists, bristly reddish hair curling up to the knuckles. His face was a full, ruddy sphere atop a soft, seamed neck. Long, thick, coarsely wavy hair the color of dirty brass flowed over his ears and trailed past his collar. Some recession in front exposed a high, domed brow. Sooty puffiness below deep-set hazel eyes gave him a sleepy look. He had a small, straight nose, no upper lip to speak of. But the lower slab was full and moist, and when he smiled at Cheryl his teeth were snowy and perfectly aligned. Strongly built, the slightest suggestion of pot above the waistband of his linen trousers. If he took care of himself, he'd remain crudely handsome for a decade or two. If not, he'd end up a Falstaffian cartoon.

'Cheryl,' said Anita Duke, softly. Her eyes were on me.

'What are you guys doing here?' said Cheryl. 'Did you lock the door? I left it open.'

'We had no idea where you were so we locked it, Cheryl. Who's your friend?'

'Alex. He— I was down on the beach and – he ended up helping me.'

'Helping you?' Anita looked me up and down. Same once-over Cheryl had delivered down on the beach, but this scrutiny was impersonal – flat and suspicious – without the slightest flavor of flirtation. Trained eye accustomed to judging flesh?

The long-haired man had been examining Cheryl's wet dress. One of his hands began massaging a button of his suit.

'I had a little . . . trouble,' said Cheryl.

'Trouble?' said Anita.

'No big deal,' said Cheryl. 'So . . . what're you guys doing here?'

'We dropped by,' said the man. He had a high, nasal voice. Without looking at me, he said, 'Doing some diving?'

Cheryl said, 'He was boating, Kent. Baxter got a little bit in the water, and he helped me. So I thought it would be nice—'

Anita broke in: 'Are you saying Baxter could've drowned?'

'No, no. It never got to that point— It's no big deal, guys. He just got in the water before I could stop him and the waves got a little . . . I would've reached him just fine, but Alex here was passing by, and he was nice enough to jump in, that's all.'

'Alex,' said the man named Kent. 'Sounds kind of exciting—'

Anita Duke shot him a sharp look, and he shut his mouth.

'It was no really big deal, guys,' Cheryl insisted. 'You know what a good swimmer Bax is. It's just that I had Sage on my hands too, and by the time— Alex helped me and I wanted to thank him, so I asked him to come up so I could give him something.'

'A tip,' said Kent.

Anita said, 'Well, that's certainly the gracious thing to do.' To Kent: 'Why don't you show him our appreciation, honey, and then you can see him off.'

Talking softly, but no mistaking the imperiousness.

There's nothing men despise more than being ordered around by a woman in front of another man. Long-haired Kent smiled and dipped his hand into his trouser pocket, but the anger settled around his eyes and his mouth, and he threw it back at me.

A crocodile billfold appeared, and he pulled out a twenty and waved it in my face. 'Here you go, my friend.'

'A little more than that, Kent,' said Anita. 'After all.'

Kent's mouth turned down, and his eyes disappeared among fleshy folds. 'How much?'

'You be the judge.'

'Sure,' said Kent, forcing a smile. Another twenty joined the first.

'I'd say another,' offered Anita.

Kent's smile hung on for dear life. Out came the billfold again, and he thrust the sixty dollars at me. 'My wife's the generous type.'

'No, thanks,' I said. 'No tip is necessary.'

'Take it,' said Anita. 'It's the least we can do.'

'It's just as she said, no big deal.'

Cheryl said, 'Anyway, I need to get the kids inside.'

'I'll help you with them,' said Anita. 'Give me Baxter – he's always a handful for you.' Stepping forward, she placed her hands around the boy's rib cage, took him from me, kept her face close to mine. 'Let's make it an even hundred dollars and then you can go, Alex.'

'Nothing,' I said. 'I'll go anyway.'

'Oh, dear,' said Anita. Holding Baxter tight, she walked into the house.

Cheryl flashed me a look – helpless, apologetic – then followed.

Kent said, 'Let me give you some advice: When someone offers you something, you should take it. Just out of courtesy.' He waved the three twenties.

'Donate it to charity,' I said.

He smiled. 'I thought I was— Okay, you're a stubborn guy. Let's get you back to your canoe.' Placing a hand on my shoulder. Squeezing a little too forcefully, and when I resisted he dug his fingers in even harder. I freed myself from his grip, and his hands rose protectively. Boxer's instincts. But still smiling.

I turned and headed back down the pathway. He caught up, laughing, his pink T-shirt spotted with sweat. He wore a strong cologne – orange brandy and anise and some other scents I couldn't pinpoint. 'What exactly happened with Cheryl and Bax?'

'Just what Cheryl said.'

'The kid wasn't drowning? You just decided to play hero?'

'At the time it seemed the right thing to do.'

'I'm asking because sometimes she gets careless,' he said. 'Not intentionally, more like . . . she doesn't always pay attention.' Pause. 'Did she wave for you or did you just volunteer?'

'I saw the boy out in the water, couldn't tell he was a good swimmer, and went after him. That's it.'

'Oh boy,' he said, chuckling. 'I've rubbed you the wrong way. Sorry, I just wanted to know. For the sake of those kids. I'm their uncle, and more often than not the responsibility falls on my wife and me.'

I didn't answer.

He said, 'We're talking child welfare here, my friend.'

'I volunteered,' I said. 'I probably overreacted.'

'Okay,' he said. 'So now I've got a straight answer. Finally.' Grin. 'You're making me work, bro.' He wiped his forehead.

We walked to the fence in silence. When we got there he placed his hand on the gate latch. 'Look, you did a good deed, I really would like to compensate you. How about two hundred, cash, and we call it a deal? Also, I'd appreciate it if you don't tell anyone about this— You live around here?'

'Tell who?'

'Anyone.'

'Sure,' I said. 'Nothing to tell.'

He studied me. 'You don't know who she is?'

I shook my head.

He laughed, whipped out the billfold.

I shook my head. 'Forget it.'

'You really mean it, don't you?' he said. 'What are you, one of those Samaritan guys? Okay, listen, if there's anything I can do for you – like if you need some work – do you do construction stuff? Or maintenance? I've always got something in development. Did you come from Paradise?'

I nodded.

'The restaurant,' he said. 'That's one of mine – we're going to turn it into a landmark. So if you need a gig . . .' He slipped a white business card out of the fold.

Kent D. Irving
Vice President and Projects Manager
Duke Enterprises

'Duke,' I said. 'Not the magazine?'

'Yes, the magazine, bro. Among other things.'

I smiled. 'Then how about a free subscription?'

'Hey, there's an idea.' He slapped my back, drew his head back, and looked into the sun. Edging closer. Crowding me. 'Give my office a call, we'll send you a coupla years' worth.'

I said, 'I can see why you wouldn't want me talking to anyone.'

'Can you?' Harder slap. 'Well, there you go. And I know you'll show some class. Not showing class would make a lot of people very unhappy, and you don't look like the kind of guy who wants to spread unhappiness.'

'God forbid.'

'God doesn't always forbid it,' he said. 'Sometimes we have to look out for ourselves.'

He held the gate open, waited until I'd walked to the cable car and boarded, then produced a remote-control unit of his own. Big smile and a thumb flick and I was descending.

He waved bye-bye. I waved back, but I was staring over his shoulder, a hundred feet beyond, by one of the rock ponds, where a man in tennis whites stood and tossed something to the flamingos.

Thick torso, bulky shoulders, a cap of cropped black hair.

Black Suit, now in tennis whites. Drawing back his arm, he pitched to the birds. Scratched his head. Watched them eat.

Kent Irving kept his eye on me as I sank out of view.

twenty-nine

When I got back to the broken pier, Norris was sitting in the sand, legs yogi-crossed, smoking a joint. As I dragged the kayak to shore, he got up reluctantly and looked at his bare wrist. 'Hey, right on time. Any wildlife?' He offered me the j.

'No thanks. Just birds. The feathered kind.'

'Oh well,' he said, toking deeply. 'Listen, any time you wanna take a ride, let me know. Keep bringing cash and I'll keep giving you a discount.'

'I'll bear that in mind.'

'Yeah . . . good idea.'

'What is?'

'Bearing shit in your mind and not somewhere else.' Rocking on his knees, he settled, sucked hungrily on the cannabis, stared out at the darkening ocean.

I drove up from the cove to the coast highway, turned right, and parked on the beach-side shoulder, with a hundred-yard view of the entrance to the Duke estate. One more hour – what could it hurt?

I ran the tape deck as I slumped in the front seat. Old recording of Oscar Aleman riffing on a shiny silver National guitar in some thirties Buenos Aires nightclub. Aleman and the band peeling off a ha-ha rendition of 'Bésame Mucho' that would have done Spike Jones proud, but no mistaking the artistry.

Seven songs later the copper tentacles spread and a gardener's truck emerged, hooked a left, and sped by. Then nothing, as the rest of the album played out. I inserted another cassette – the L.A. Guitar Quartet – listened to one complete side, and was about to pack it in when the gates swung back again and a black Expedition shot out and barelled south on PCH.

Silver-gray trim along the bottom of the door panels, oversized tires, chrome running boards, windows tinted nearly black. Cheryl's car, as described by Norris, but no way to tell if she was behind the wheel. I followed from a safe distance. The Expedition's brake lights never flashed, not even around sharp curves, and it paid no homage to the speed limit.

The former Mrs Duke in her usual hurry? She hadn't displayed any signs of impatience down on the beach, or up at the estate. Why was she still *living* at the estate a year after the divorce? Maybe not of her own free will. The appearance of Anita Duke and Kent Irving had thrown her. The two of them letting themselves into the guesthouse without apology. Anita calling the shots. Cheryl had capitulated easily to Anita's will.

Under the thumb of the Duke family? Some sort of custody issue? Kent Irving had alluded to her poor maternal skills, and Baxter's near drowning backed that up. Perhaps the Duke clan was pressuring her to give up the kids, had negotiated her staying close.

Were the kids with her right now? The Expedition's black windows made it impossible to know.

I stayed with her past Pepperdine University, maintained the tail as the SUV turned off on Cross Creek, bypassed the fast-food joints and the newer businesses fronting the shopping center, and entered the Malibu Country Mart. The vintage stores were a series of low-rise wooden buildings arranged around U-shaped parking lots and topped by hunter green banners. Nice view of the Malibu hills and land-side homes in the distance.

Not too many vehicles at this time of day, and I waited until the Expedition found its spot – hogging two spaces opposite Dream Babies Fragrance and Candle Boutique. I parked the Seville as far as I could. Near the dumpsters – a pattern seemed to be forming.

Cheryl Duke climbed out of the SUV, slammed the door, and headed for the candle shop. Alone, no kids. She'd changed into a red silk tank top that exposed a band of flat, ivory belly, pipe-stem white jeans, and white sandals with high heels. Her hair was pinned up loosely, and big, white-framed sunglasses blocked the top half of her face. Even at this distance the bottom half seemed grim.

She threw back the Dream Babies screen door and entered, and I sat there checking out the neighboring establishments. More 'shoppes' than shops, bikinis and gym wear, nostrums to sooth the skin and the ego, souvenirs and tourist art, a couple of cafés on opposite ends of the U.

The eatery farthest from the candle shop advertised coffee and sandwiches and provided two flimsy outdoor tables. I took the long way over to avoid being spotted, bought a bagel and a cup of Kenyan roast from a sickly looking kid with a blue goatee and a Popeye tattoo on the side of his neck. Someone had left a folded *Times* on the condiments counter, and I expropriated the paper and brought it outside. Both tables were dirty, and I cleaned one off and sat down and busied myself with the daily crossword puzzle, keeping my head bent except for brief glances at the fragrance boutique.

Ten minutes later Cheryl Duke exited toting a pair of shopping bags. She hooked immediately into Brynna's Bikinis, spent another quarter hour inside, and I made my way through the acrosses before being stymied by a five-letter word for 'old fiddle.' She reemerged with an additional bag, dipped into Bolivian Shawl and Snuggle for thirteen minutes, and when she left that store she was toting three more sacks but looking no happier.

Heading my way.

I lowered my head, filled in a few more blanks, came up with 'rebec' for the fiddle, because it was the only thing that made sense. Just as I'd wrinkled my brow over a three-letter clue for 'Catullus composition' I heard her say, 'Alex?'

I looked up, feigned surprise, saw my twin reflections in her sunshades.

Smiling. Surprised. Mr Innocent.

'Hey,' I said. 'Know a six-letter word for "Indian pony"? Starts with *c* and ends with *se*?'

She laughed. 'No, I don't think so – I can't do that stuff. This is weird, seeing you again. Do you come here a lot?'

'When I'm in Malibu. How about you?'

'Sometimes.'

'We probably passed each other without knowing it.'

'Probably,' she said.

'Doing some heavy shopping?'

She placed the bags on the ground. 'No, just . . . It's just something to do – maybe it's like karma or something. Seeing you. Or like when you think about someone and then they keep turning up – you know?'

I grinned. The sunshades said I was doing okay. 'Karma sounds fine to me. Care for some coffee?'

'No, thanks—' The dark lenses moved from side to side, taking in the parking lot. Her bare arms were smooth and lightly freckled. No bra under the tank top. Those nipples again. 'Sure, why not. I'll go get some.'

'Let me.' I stood and handed her the puzzle. 'See what you can do with this in the meantime. Cream and sugar?'

'A little milk and some artificial sweetener.'

As I turned she took hold of my arm. Leaning forward and giving me a view of fat, white breast tops.

Her finger made a tiny circle on my elbow.

'Also decaf,' she said.

When I returned she was hunched over the paper,

white-knuckling the pen, tongue tip protruding between her lips. Her hair was down, and it looked freshly combed.

'I think I got a couple of them,' she said. ' "Lynx" for "wild cat," right? And "Burnett" for "comedienne Carol." But not that pony one – maybe "cochise"? Isn't that Indian or something?'

'Hmm,' I said, handing her the coffee. 'No, I don't think that's it. This connecting one's "mayfly," so there has to be a *y* in there.'

'Oh, right . . . sorry.'

I sat down, picked up my cup. She did the same.

'Mmm, good,' she said, sipping. 'People who do these things – puzzles. I always think it's amazing. I've got street smarts, but I never really cared much for school.'

'Which streets?' I said.

'Phoenix, Arizona.'

'Hot.'

'Like an oven. Sucked. I left there when I was seventeen – dropped out before graduation, fibbed about my age, and got a job in Las Vegas rollerblading in "Magic Wheels." '

'The skating show,' I guessed.

'Yeah, you know it? I used to be a great skater – skated since I could walk.'

' "Magic Wheels," ' I said. 'That went on for a while, didn't it?'

'Years. But I was only in it for six months, sprained my ankle and it healed okay but not good enough for serious skating. Then I got a place in the line at "Follies du Monde." '

Off came the sunglasses. Her eyes looked serene. Talking about herself had relaxed her. I sat back and crossed my legs, looked at the three diamond rings on her right hand, the three-carat ruby on her left.

'A showgirl,' I said.

'Well, it really wasn't all that – just your basic dancing and kicking,' she said. 'First thing they did was change my name. The producers. They said I was gonna be a headliner, needed a new name.'

'What's wrong with Cheryl?'

'Cheryl Soames,' she said. 'It's not exactly Parisian.'

'So what'd they come up with?'

'Sylvana Spring.' She stared at me, waiting. 'It was like a big meeting between me and the choreographer. We came up with it together.'

'Sylvana. Pretty.'

'I thought so – it means the woods, so like, let's take a walk in the woods. And Spring because what's the best time to walk in the woods – the *spring*. I thought it was kind of fresh and poetic. Anyway, I danced my tush off for a year but they never made me a headliner but I kept the name.'

'Another injury.'

'No.' She frowned and put the sunglasses back on. 'It's all politics. Who does what to who.'

'So how'd you end up in Malibu?'

'*That* is a long, long story.' She tapped the newspaper, looked away. 'Would you mind if I break off a tiny bit of

413

your bagel? I haven't eaten all day – watching the carbs, but I am kinda droopy.'

'Take all of it.'

'No, no, just a nibble.'

'Don't tell me you're on a diet.'

'No,' she said. 'I just watch. Because— I mean, how long do you have what you have?'

She broke off a crumb, chewed, swallowed, took a bigger bite, ended up finishing half of the bagel.

'Kids napping?' I said.

'Yup. Finally – it's hell getting them tired enough to nap. That's why we were down on the beach. What a day— So anyway, I figured why not use the time to look after little old me?'

'Makes sense,' I said. 'I want to be honest with you, Cheryl. Your brother-in-law told me who owns the property.'

'My brother-in-law?'

'Kent Irving. He said he was Baxter's and Sage's uncle, which would make him your brother-in-law, right? He gave me his card with Duke Enterprises on it. I didn't realize I was on famous ground.'

She frowned. 'He's not their uncle. He just likes to say that because it's . . . simpler to explain.'

'What do you mean?'

'His wife – Anita – she's actually their sister – Baxter's and Sage's. Their half sister. Not their aunt. That makes her *my* stepdaughter, so I guess Kent's my stepson-in-law.' She giggled. 'Pretty weird, huh?'

'It is a little complicated.'

'She's a lot older than me and I'm her mom— Don't laugh, okay? If I start laughing this coffee's gonna go right up my nose.' Tipping down the sunglasses, she flashed green-blue innocence. 'It *is* complicated. Sometimes I can't believe I'm in the middle of it.'

'Hey,' I said. 'Blended families. Happens all the time.'

'I guess.'

'So Kent's their brother-in-law,' I said. 'And he works for . . . He is your husband, right? You're married to the famous Tony Duke.'

'Not anymore.' She looked into one of the shopping bags. Pulled out a red string bikini and held it up. 'What do you think?'

'The little I can see is nice.'

'Oh, you,' she said. 'Men – they just can't visualize.'

'Okay,' I said, closing my eyes. 'I'm visualizing . . . The little I can see is terrific.'

She laughed and dropped the swimsuit back in the bag. 'Men think naked is the best, but let me tell you, a little bit of cloth's a whole lot sexier.' Her hand lowered toward her coffee cup, digressed, and brushed against my knuckles.

'So you're the *ex*–Mrs Duke.'

She slapped my wrist, lightly. 'Don't say it like that. I hate that.'

'Being an ex?'

'Being any kind of *Mrs*. I'm twenty-five years old – just think of me as Cheryl, okay? Or even Sylvana. *Mrs* is like someone *old*.' She breathed deeply, and her breasts budged reluctantly.

415

'Cheryl it is.' I finished my coffee, went in for a refill, and bought another bagel. 'Here you go – more nutrition.'

'No way,' she said, showing me a palm. 'A few bites of that and I'll bloat up and have to be rolled home.' But after another sip of coffee, she began taking tiny chipmunk nibbles, and within moments she'd gnawed off the top of the bagel.

'Look,' she said, 'I shouldn't even be talking about this – Anita, Kent, Tony. We've been divorced for a year, if you need to know. But, what the hey, no one can tell me what to do, right?'

'Right.'

'The thing about Tony is, I still feel close to him. He's really a great person, not at all what you'd think.'

'What would I think?' I said.

'You know, the whole sex thing. The dirty old man stuff. I really did – do love him. Just in a different way, now. He's—' Shaking her head. 'I really *shouldn't* be talking about this.'

I ran a finger across my lips. 'Don't mean to pry.'

'You're not prying, I'm blabbing. The thing is, it's totally my life, right? Why should I be always listening to people telling me what to do?'

'Who tells you what to do? Anita and Kent?'

She picked up the crossword puzzle, squinted at the grid, blinked. 'These letters are tiny, I probably need a new contact lens prescription . . . You know, I think that pony clue might be "cayuse." That's got a *y* and I think I remember some Indian word like that from Arizona –

Cayuse ponies, whatever. Take a look – what do you think?'

She pressed forward, bosoms resting on the table, slid the paper toward me.

'You know,' I said, 'I think you're right – excellent.'

A huge smile spread across her face as I filled in the blanks, and for a moment she looked very young.

'You must be smart, doing these. Maybe I should start doing them too,' she said. 'To keep my mind active. I get bored a lot – there's not much to do.'

'At the estate?'

'I know, I know, it's everyone's idea of Paradise, what am I bitching about? But believe me, it's boring. There's tennis, but I hate tennis 'cause of the sun, and how many laps can you swim, how many times can you ride that cable car, up and down, up and down, and stare at the ocean? Even Tony's zoo – he's got these rare goats and some monkeys and other stuff, but it smells bad and it's noisy and I don't like animals. Even the kids are bored with it. When they're up and running around, I keep pretty busy, but when they nap, like now . . . I want to put them both in preschool, but so far it hasn't worked out.'

'Why not?'

'So many details,' she said. 'Finding the right place, arranging transportation. Making sure about security.'

'Security?' I said. 'Like a bodyguard?'

'At least somewhere we can be sure they'll be safe. There are plenty of movie stars in Malibu, and they send their kids to preschool, but we want to be especially careful.'

'Could I ask a personal question?'

'I might not answer it.'

'Fair enough,' I said. 'If you've been divorced for a year, why are you still living there?'

'Well,' she said, 'that's another long story.' Her hand rested on mine. 'I still want to thank you. For being there, you know? Because Baxter can swim, but he could've been in trouble. I didn't want to make a big deal about it in front of Anita, so I have something else to thank you for – not saying anything.'

'No problem.'

'What do you do for a living?' she said.

'This and that. I have some investments.'

'Ooh,' she said. 'That sounds rich. I bet you're not as rich as Tony.'

'No argument there.'

Her hand trailed up my arm, tickled my chest, touched my lips, withdrew.

'Why am I still living there,' she said. 'Well . . . after the divorce, I had my own place. Up in Los Feliz hills, a really cool place. Tony got it for me because of the gates and the security – it was a real safe place. Or at least we thought so. Tony wanted the best for me.'

'Sounds like a friendly divorce.'

'He was sweet . . . Anyway, me and the kids were in this great old house in Los Feliz – lots of land, all these fancy details, this gigantic bathroom with a view of the hills. And close to Hollywood, so one day I took the kids to the Egyptian Theater to see *A Bug's Life* – it was cool, they had this whole sideshow next door about bugs and stuff, computer games, toys, Bax and Sage went crazy. Afterwards we went out for dinner and ice cream and it was late when we got home and Sage was already sleeping on my shoulder and Bax was pretty close to conking out. Anyway, I turn the key and we walk into the house and instead of greeting me with a big bark the way she always did, Bingles – that's our dog – was – this gorgeous standard poodle who won a ton of shows – instead of greeting us, Bingles is lying in the entry hall, not moving, with her tongue stuck all out and her eyes real dull.'

'Oh boy,' I said.

'I *freaked*, Alex. If the kids hadn'ta been with me, I would've screamed. Baxter runs over to shake Bingles, but I could tell from the way her tongue was sticking out that she was gone and I'm screaming at him not to touch her and then Sagey wakes up and starts crying and then I smell it. This horrible gas smell. I got us all out of there fast, called Anita. She sent a driver for us, brought us out here, sent some specialists to Los Feliz. Turns out there was this massive gas leak – the house was old and the pipes weren't great and somehow the main flue got clogged or something. They said it was lucky we left when we did because all the windows were closed because of it was a cold night. They said we could've died in our sleep. Or if I'da lit a match, the whole place could've gone up. They fixed the problem, but we've been here ever since. Eventually, I'll get another place – but closer to Tony because . . . he *is* their dad.'

'Scary,' I said.

'Close call. Just like today.' She rubbed my thumb with two of her fingers, and the gems in her rings glinted. 'There must be an angel looking down on me, or something.'

She finished the rest of the bagel. 'Anyway, that's how Hollywood Me became Malibu Me again.'

'You never did say how you got from Vegas to Malibu.'

'Oh, that,' she said, wiping crumbs from her lips. 'After they wouldn't make me a headliner, I got bored and decided to see what I could find in L.A., figured I'd try modeling or acting or something. I had some money saved up, got myself a neat apartment in the Marina, hit the agencies. But they didn't want full-figured girls, and I didn't want to do sleazy stuff, you know?'

I nodded.

'Nudies, hardcore— I mean the body's beautiful, but you have to keep standards . . . Anyway, I checked out a few agents for commercials, but they were all losers. I'd started thinking about taking a boring job or something. Then one day I saw this ad in the paper offering good money for being in a psychology experiment. And I said, Girl, if there's one thing you know, it's psychology. 'Cause back when I danced, it was all psychology. Fix your eyes on certain guys in the audience and play for them, pretend you know them and they know you. It set the tone – so you could be . . . realistic, you know? It made it more real, and that pleases the audience, and when the audience is happy, everyone's happy.'

'Connecting,' I said.

'Exactly.' She rolled my thumb some more. 'So I

figured, what the hey, it might be fun doing some psychology. So I checked out the ad, and the guy running it was really sweet and it turns out all he wanted me to do was be in a room with some guys – just be myself – and see what they would do.'

'That's it?'

'He – the psychologist – was measuring reactions to what he called stimuli. For commercials, ads, whatever. I guess he figured I was pretty stimulating. Another good thing, it was down in Newport Beach, so during lunch-time I got to sit on the sand and chill. I've always loved the ocean; there isn't much of that in Phoenix.'

'All you had to do was sit there and he paid you?'

'That was it,' she said. 'Like modeling, but better. 'Cause there was no photographer making me twist in weird positions. And Ben – the psychologist – was a sweet, sweet guy, never made a move on me. Which, for me, is a twist, you know?' Squeezing my thumb.

I said, 'I'll bet,' and she grinned.

'At first, I figured he was just waiting for the right time, but then I could see he just wasn't into it, so I started to think he was gay. Which was fine, I like gay guys – I mean I wasn't disappointed or anything like that. I am not *like* that.'

Suddenly her voice hardened, as if I'd accused her of something. Her nail dug into my thumb, and I lifted it gently.

I said, 'Men come on to you even though you don't encourage it.'

'Exactly. You listen, don't you? I mean *really* listen.'

'On good days.'

'He's like that, too – Ben. A good listener. Anyway, I did this experiment for a month or so, and finally he did ask me out. But not like a come-on. More like father-daughter, being friendly, wanting to know how I enjoyed the job. He took me to the Ivy at the Shore. He was a perfect gentleman, wanting to know me as a person, we had a real good time even though I didn't feel any – you know: *sparks*. And then – and this is the karma part – we're leaving to get into his car, waiting for the valets to bring it up, and this other car drives up. This gorgeous maroon Bentley Azure, and another guy gets out – older, really well-dressed, really well-groomed – but mostly I'm looking at the car, 'cause how many of those do you see – chauffeur, chrome wheels, a million coats of lacquer. But Ben is staring at the guy who gets out. He knows him. And the other guy knows him, too – the two of them start hugging and kissing and I'm thinking I was right, he *is* gay. Then Ben says, "Cheryl, this is my father, Tony," and the other guy bows and kisses my hand and says, "Enchanted, Cheryl. I'm Marc Anthony Duke" – which shocked me. Because once I heard the name, *of course* I connected it to the face, but you don't expect someone like Tony to know someone like Ben, let alone be his dad. Ben doesn't even *go* by Duke – he uses the real family name. And he's nothing like Tony – I mean *nothing*. You couldn't have two guys more different.'

She paused to catch her breath. Licked her lips, threw back her shoulders, and thrust out her chest. 'Anyway, that's how I met Tony and I must've made an impression, because the next day, he called me. Said he'd gotten Ben's permission – which was a twist, right? So cute. He asked me out, and the next thing I know, we're flying to Acapulco, and the rest, as they say, is history. Basically, he swept me off my feet.'

'Whoa,' I said.

'Whoa, Nelly,' she said. 'Now you tell me something, and be honest, okay?'

'Okay.'

'I'll bet when I told you I'd been married to Tony you figured I'd posed for him and that's how he discovered me, right? You figured I was a Treat of the Month?'

'Not really—'

'Oh, yes you did,' she insisted, slapping my wrist. '*Everyone* assumes that. And that's okay. But Tony always told me I was *his* special treat. Did you know I'm the first woman he had babies with since Ben and Anita's mom died? And I gave him beautiful babies.'

'Adorable.'

Her fingers spider-walked to my wrist. 'You're very nice— So what kind of investments do you do?'

'I own some properties.'

'Sounds profitable.'

'I get by.'

'Nice,' she said. 'Good for you. Having time to hang out. But you're intellectual, I can tell that. I have a sense for people. So what else besides boating do you do for fun?'

'Play a little guitar.'

423

'I *love* music— Tony's tone-deaf, but he pretends to like music. For parties, you know? He brings in the best live bands. Catch 159, Wizard, the last one we almost got the Stone Crew.'

'Sound like incredible parties.'

'Sometimes,' she said. 'Other times it was a thousand strangers invading and stuffing their faces, and all these tramps from the magazine shoving their tits in *Tony's* face. Sometimes it was for causes – like charity, you know – and Tony would let other people come in. Like retarded people, burn victims. Thank God I won't have to deal with that anymore.'

'Because of the divorce,' I said.

'That and Tony doesn't throw parties anymore.'

'How come?'

'Things change.' She freed my hand, ate more bagel. 'I am definitely going to bloat up.'

'I doubt that. So did Ben turn out to be gay?'

She stared at me. 'Who cares?'

'Not me, just making conversation.'

'Well, he's not,' she said. 'He's just one of those – you know – not *into* it. Like a priest.'

'Asexual.'

'There are people like that, you know.'

'Life would be pretty boring without variety,' I said.

She smiled. 'You like variety?'

'I thrive on it.'

'Me, too . . . Seeing as we both thrive on it, would you like to get together or something?'

'When?' I said, touching the side of her face.

She drew away. Smiled. 'How about right now – no, just kidding, got to get back to feed the kids before someone accuses me of neglecting them. But maybe some day you could glide by in your little *canoe* and I could just *happen* to be on the beach. Maybe wearing this.' Tapping the bag with the bikini.

'That sounds very good,' I said.

She reached into a bag, brought out a small appointment book, wrote down a number, tore out the page.

'This is my private cell phone.'

'I feel privileged,' I said, taking the slip.

She reached out, took my face in both her hands, kissed me too hard on the mouth, pressing her teeth against my lips and ending with the merest swipe of tongue. 'This has been very cool, Alex. Lately, no one seems to be appreciating me. Bye, now.'

thirty

Hypotheses confirmed:

Ben Dugger used his experiment to pick up women – young blondes. Relinquished his catch when Dad asserted a preference.

Snaring women but acting the 'perfect gentleman.' Asexual – at least in the beginning. Something off sexually – Monique Lindquist's laughing aside about his not wanting to talk about sex rang in my ears.

So did Cheryl Duke's remark about not wanting to be judged neglectful: definitely worried about losing her kids. The accidental gas leak. Living at the estate as the Duke family called the shots.

Black Suit also bunking down there. Playing tennis. More than just hired help.

Threads of suspicion – a net. But nothing that told me why Lauren and the others had died. Nothing to tell Milo.

As I drove back home I wondered how I'd recount the day to Robin.

Hey, hon, I played frogman and spent most of the

afternoon flirting with a much younger woman. Cheryl's private number was wedged in my wallet. There was no reason for her aroma to linger in my nose, but I kept catching whiffs of suntan lotion and good perfume.

I arrived just before five. Spike greeted me at the door with a dismissive snort, but no sign of Robin. He led me into the kitchen and groused until I fed him some leftover brisket, and that's where I found the note: 'Taking a nap, alarm set for six-thirty.'

I checked the answering machine. Four messages, none from Milo. Booting up the computer, I plugged in 'Anita Duke,' came across the personal website of another woman with the same name – a computer programmer in Nashville – offering the universe a peek into her private life. Why do people do that?

The Anita I was looking for merited a dozen hits, almost all of them citations I'd already pulled up – the transfer of executive power from father to daughter. But down at the bottom of the list, a two-year-old citation from *Entertainment News* caught my eye:

Duke Magazine Exec Weds: Magazine heavy Anita Duke ties the knot with boyfriend in Malibu ceremony . . .

I downloaded and printed.

In a star-studded, ocean-view ceremony this past weekend, the only daughter of magazine tycoon Marc Anthony Duke was married to her companion.

Anita Catherine Duke, 33, a graduate of Wellesley College and Columbia University Business School and newly appointed CEO of Duke Enterprises, was given away this past Saturday by her father and stepmother, Sylvana, as she tied the knot with Kent Irving, 31, former president of M'Lady's Couture, an L.A. garment manufacturer and now Projects Manager for Duke Enterprises. The nuptials took place under a veil of secrecy at the posh Shadowridge Lodge in the hills of Malibu, but sources cite the attendance of several showbiz heavies including

The rest was all famous names and catering details. No mention of a honeymoon. Or of Brother Ben's presence at the happy event.

M'Lady's Couture.

The rag trade. Lauren's turf before Kent Irving had married himself into the Duke family.

Now I did need to talk to my friend the detective.

I got hold of him at the robbery-homicide room.

'Oh, happy days,' he said. 'Despite my express instructions, Andy Salander has split. I was trying to reach him to see if he knew more than he originally told us about Lauren's schmatte connections – I've spent the bulk of the past two days downtown, dead-ending on that. No one at the Fashion Mart remembers her doing runway work, and none of the modeling agencies ever signed her up. Which probably means another lie – her real gig was hooking, and who's going to admit being involved with that? I did find a couple shirts at discount, but that's about it for productivity.'

'Funny thing you should mention the rag trade. Ben Dugger's brother-in-law used to be involved in that. Outfit called M'Lady's Couture.'

'Oh,' he said. 'Well, how about you just borrow my badge and give me a few days off in Palm Springs?'

'You hate the desert.'

'I hate this case more . . . M'Lady's Couture . . . I've got the Mart directory right here, hold on . . . Nope, no listing, let's try the phone book . . . Uh-uh – zilch.'

'No surprise,' I said. 'The story said "former president." Irving's moved on to brighter prospects.'

'How'd you find this out?'

I thought about telling him of my day at the beach. Said, 'Hurtling through cyberspace. The M'Lady connection was cited in Anita Duke's wedding story. It makes me wonder. Irving married Anita two years ago, but they probably dated for a while before that – let's say six months to a year. That's part of the time period Lauren claimed to be working the Mart. I agree, modeling was a cover, she was hooking. But the garment-biz part of it might have been true. If Irving was one of her clients – a big-time regular, throwing around big money – his marrying megamillions would make that an embarrassing bit of biography. What if Lauren tried to profit from that – told Michelle, et cetera, et cetera, and Michelle did the same. Or someone thought she was going to. As in Gretchen Stengel. Who also knew Irving from the good old days and told him. And he had the problem taken care of.'

Long silence. 'So now you've got a new bad guy.'

'Big bucks at stake – an executive type – would fit with the professional hit scenario. As well as leaving the bodies to be found. Warning off others. It would also explain the theft of Lauren's computer records. In addition to Anita's money, Irving's got a top job at Duke Enterprises, and he's part of a group that's developing Paradise Cove. Lots at stake. Any way to find out if his name comes up in Gretchen's case file?'

'And Dr Dugger? No more sexy secrets?'

'I'm not abandoning him,' I said. 'Just suggesting an alternative. And even if Dugger wasn't directly involved in the murders, he could've set everything into motion without intending to. By trying to get something going with Lauren – bringing her to the Duke estate. She and Irving came face-to-face – talk about a blast from the past – and she started leaning on Irving. *That* could explain Dugger's strong reaction when we told him about Lauren's death. He was surprised. But he's also aware of his role in it – however unintentional. Suspects Irving. He can't say a thing, because he doesn't want to expose his family. So he claims innocence, cooperates up to a point, starts sweating when you get too close to his personal life.'

'All this from cyberspace . . . And where does Shawna Yeager figure in this grand production?'

'That I don't know. Unless Irving had something going with her too.'

'This guy gets around.'

'Maybe I'm totally off base,' I said, 'but wouldn't a look at the Gretchen files be a place to start?'

'The Gretchen files,' he said, 'are a problem. The feds took over from the locals, they're the ones who prosecuted her, they orchestrated the plea bargain. Throughout the whole thing, no customers' names were ever exposed, and, believe me, the papers tried to get hold of Gretchen's files. That was the whole point of the deal. Protecting johns in high places. Gretchen kept her mouth shut in return for a short sentence. I'll call the U.S. attorney, but don't get your hopes up. First, though, I need to find Andy Salander. His rabbit really bugs me . . .'

'When did he leave?'

'Middle of the night, no notice, a month's rent due, packed all his clothes, left the furniture behind. The landlord is not pleased and neither am I. Salander was the last person to see Lauren alive. With all due respect to your creative mind, wouldn't it be a peach if this comes down to a stinking little roommate thing?'

'You really see Salander overpowering, trussing, and shooting Lauren in the head, then dumping her in the trash?' I said. 'Doing the same to Michelle and Lance and burning their bodies?'

'Alex, I've been doing this too long to be surprised by anything. For all we know Michelle and Lance were shot because of something totally unrelated to Lauren.'

'And Jane?'

'Mel Abbot shot Jane, friend. That's the way it's going down, and I have nothing to say it shouldn't. What I do have is Salander cutting out after he gave his word that he wouldn't. I was just by The Cloisters. The manager said Salander didn't show up for work yesterday or today, didn't phone, which is a switch – he's always been reliable. Something's definitely not right.'

'Maybe he's scared,' I said. 'Knows something he shouldn't. Jane Abbot's death just hit the news. Maybe Salander figured he could find himself in the same situation and panicked. Because he knows what Jane knew.'

'What – Lauren has this big valuable secret and she tells everyone?'

'Lauren was a loner. And lonely. Salander made a point of telling me what a good listener he was. And perhaps Lauren didn't tell him everything, merely hinted around, or gave him a partial story. Now that people are dying, he's worried that's enough.'

'Fine,' he said. 'Maybe. But if he knows something, that's all the more reason for me to go after him ASAP. The manager at the bar says he had an on-again, off-again boyfriend, and that's the lead I'm chasing.'

'Could be on-again,' I said. 'The first time I met Salander, he was waiting for someone to show up, implied it was a former flame, some sort of reconciliation. Who's the boyfriend?'

'Some film agent who works for one of the big outfits. Manager thinks Andy said William Morris. He dropped in at The Cloisters infrequently, drank Singapore slings, schmoozed with Andy, not too friendly with anyone else. Last time was months ago, but I've got a description –

forties, dark hair, slim, tiny little eyeglasses, Armani suits – and maybe a name. Manager thinks he heard Andy call this guy Jason or Justin. I'm heading over to Morris right now. Maybe they'll buy my screenplay.'

'Didn't know you had one.'

'Throw cash at me and I can write one in a couple of days, win an Oscar – have you seen the crap that gets on-screen?'

'What, cop against the odds?'

'Charming genius cop as sensitive soul and savior of the world.'

I laughed. 'If you dead-end in Beverly Hills, you might try Salander's parents. He had a snapshot of them in his room, taken in—'

'Yeah – Bloomington, Indiana. Called this morning. Salander's mother hasn't spoken with him in nearly a year. Seems Andy Senior has troubles with his only child's lifestyle, Junior left home a year shy of high school graduation, never returned to the Old Home-stead. He sends Mommy a Christmas card and she mails him money that she saves from the grocery stash. When I hung up she was crying – I love my job. Anyway, thanks for the Irving info. Feel free to call with additional inspiration.'

'Actually . . .'

'What?'

'Try to stay calm,' I said.

'If I could *get* calm, I could *stay* calm. *What?*'

'I've been traveling through more than cyberspace.' I told him about my day at Paradise Cove, the time with

Cheryl Duke, meeting Anita and Irving, catching sight of Black Suit in tennis garb.

'So you actually met the guy.'

'Just for a few minutes.'

Long silence.

'*Kayaking?*'

'It's good exercise.'

'Alex,' he said. Then he trailed off. More dead air. Finally: 'Mr Schmatte wears linen and the goombah plays tennis. Summer fun in the winter – maybe Joe Mafioso's another kind of pro. Brought in to improve the old guy's backhand.'

'He's built more like a power lifter.'

'Fine, fine, but lobbing balls across the net makes him even less likely to be some hoodoo hit man. If he was, they wouldn't put him up on home turf. Alex, I can't believe you actually took out a goddamn *boat* and did marine surveillance.'

'No law against enjoying the great outdoors,' I said. 'Lucky I was there. The boy might've drowned.'

An exaggerated sigh hissed through the receiver. 'Myyyy *heeeero* – so now Mommy's bonded with you. You going to date her?'

'Very funny.'

'You took her number.'

'What was my choice?'

'How about self-righteous indignation? You might've told me at the outset that you knew Irving from more than the Internet—'

'I was waiting for the right moment.'

He laughed. 'What's the use? Okay, so is there a reason, other than the garment link, that Irving twangs your antenna? What's he like in person?'

'He kowtows to his wife but likes to come across in charge. Styled hair, dresses like reruns of *Miami Vice*, tough-guy swagger – he impressed me as someone who wants to be seen as a player.'

'If bad taste and phoniness were felonies, L.A. would be one big penitentiary,' he said. 'Okay, he's got poor fashion sense, that's why he bombed in the garment game. Give me something else – something ominous that I can work with before I go chasing around town.'

'Can't,' I admitted. 'I'm just trying to connect the dots. There is one other issue that might or might not be relevant. Cheryl's pretty nervous about being judged a neglectful mother. And Irving suggested to me – a perfect stranger – that she was. I think he wants that information out there. I've done enough custody consults to develop a nose for impending conflict, and this one reeks of it. Rich families are the worst – enough funds to pay lawyers for too long, and it's never about the kids, it's about control. And money. In this case, big money. Cheryl said she and Duke split amicably, but that could be wishful thinking, or just a lie. Or taking the kids from her might not even be Duke's intent. The feeling I'm getting is that he's receded into the background. Hasn't thrown a party in nearly two years, Cheryl implied there wouldn't be any more. Duke's handing the corporate reins to Anita and, by extension, to Kent Irving. So maybe it's all part of Anita and

Irving's power grab. Those two kids are heirs, two more slices of the pie. If Anita and Kent can gain custody of Baxter and Sage, they consolidate their grip on the empire. A power grab also fits with the need to get rid of nuisances – like blackmailers who push too hard. I can see Irving hiring a hit man, maybe even being arrogant enough to put the hit man up at the estate. Because mobbing up is glamorous.'

'Forget what I said about screenplays,' he said. 'You write it, I'll sell it.'

'The other thing,' I said, 'is I was right about Dugger using his experiment to pick up women.' I told him about Cheryl being a confederate in the intimacy study. Dugger wining and dining her, only to pass her along to Tony Duke.

'The experiment,' he said. 'Applied science. Dutiful son.'

'Young blondes,' I said. 'Both father and son like young blondes. So, despite what Dugger claims, I'm not eliminating Shawna from whatever scenario turns out to be true.'

'Sex, money – take your pick, huh? Quite an amalgam.'

'I'm an equal opportunity theorizer. Lauren bought a weapon for self-protection, might've been carrying it the night she was murdered, but never used it. That would fit with her knowing the killer. Underestimating the threat. Lauren loved the money she got from hooking, but what really turned her on was the power. Domi-nance. If the killer was a john, or posing as one, she might have been deluded into thinking she was in

437

charge. The killer dispatched her, dumped her, took her gun for future use. Setting up Jane's death. Using Lauren's gun on Jane, then planting it on Mel Abbot. A family gun, an obvious accident.'

'Creative,' he said. 'Terrifyingly creative.'

'Any major flaws to the logic?'

No answer.

I said, 'It would sure be good to get a look at Jane's papers, see if she left behind anything provocative. What about Lyle Teague? He show up yet?'

'Suspect number one trillion?' he said. 'No, I called the Castaic sheriffs and they promised to look for his truck. They haven't called me yet, so I assume he's still out there, hunting. Which is what I should be doing.'

'I've still got those photos of Dugger and Black Suit.'

'Oh yeah, those. Let me see how the time shakes out. I'll have my people call your people.'

Forty minutes later he called. 'Visited the Morris agency. Andy Salander's on-again is probably a guy named Justin LeMoyne. Fits the description, and he called in sick yesterday, canceled all his appointments. And guess what: He's your neighbor – lives right on Beverly Glen, maybe half a mile down. I'm on my way there now. Want to meet me and give me those photos? If Andy's there, you can observe my masterful interrogation, psych the lad out.'

Robin would be sleeping for another half hour. I said, 'Sure.'

438

Justin LeMoyne's home was a petite, beautifully maintained white bungalow that had obviously once been the guesthouse of the Spanish colonial mansion on the neighboring property. A pair of Canary Island pines sentried the door, and wisteria vines twisted above the hand-painted tile address numerals. The front yard was planted with drought-tolerant specimens, obviously new. A single garage abutted the house. No car in the driveway.

Traffic on the Glen was a slow choke. I got there before Milo, parked and waited. No movement in or around the bungalow, but the same could be said for every house in the neighborhood. The only signs of life were the pained looks of the motorists caught in the crush, as they filed past miles of inanimate real estate. As if everyone were leaving L.A., in anticipation – or the wake – of the latest disaster.

Milo's unmarked finally appeared, spewing exhaust, bumping over the grass parkway bordering LeMoyne's driveway, and bounding over the curb. He drove up behind the Seville, exited while yanking the knot of his tie, and headed straight for the door. By the time I got there he was jabbing the bell. No answer. A hard knock elicited the same result.

'Hey,' he said, eyeing the traffic. 'Let's hear it for quality of life.' His skin was gray around the edges, and his eyes seemed to be fighting to stay open.

I offered the envelope containing the Black Suit snaps. He stuffed them in his jacket pocket. Another bell jab. Nothing. 'Let's try the neighbors.'

439

At the mansion a black-uniformed, fair-haired maid with a lumpy face answered, and Milo asked her about Justin LeMoyne.

'Oh heem,' she said in a Slavic accent. The look of disdain was unmistakable.

'Problem neighbor, ma'am?'

'He ees, you know . . .' She proffered a limp wrist. 'Flit-flit.'

'Gay.'

'Ya, homo.'

'Does that create problems, Ms . . .'

'Ovensky, Irina. You here, so dere must be problems.' Big smile, gold incisor. 'Vat did he do, awfficer? Something wit a keed?'

'Does he bring kids here?'

'Naw, but you knaw dem.'

'Did Mr LeMoyne create any specific problems for you, Ms Ovensky?'

'Yah, wit de dogs. Missus Ellis has dogs – de Pekes – and dey bark a leetle, vy not, dere dogs, no? But *eem*' – she hooked a thumb toward LeMoyne's house – 'is de beeg baby, always coplain, always wit dee-bark dem, dee-bark dem.'

Irina Ovensky drew a finger along her throat.

'He wants you to debark the dogs.'

'Ya. Crrooo-el, no?'

'Not an animal lover,' said Milo.

'A *boy* lover,' she said.

'He brings boys here?'

'Jus wan.'

'How old?'

Irina Ovensky shrugged. 'Twenny, twenny-two.'

'A young man.'

'Yah, but leetle, like a boy. Skeeny, wit de yellow hair up here' – patting her head – 'and de tattoo, here.' Her hand lowered to her shoulder.

'What does the tattoo say?' said Milo.

'I don' know, I don' get dat close.' Ovensky stuck out her tongue.

'When's the last time you saw Mr LeMoyne and this person?' said Milo.

'Las' night. Dey get in de car and go.' Flick of the hand.

'Mr LeMoyne's car.'

'Mertzedes. Red.'

'What time was this, ma'am?'

The sight of Milo's notepad set off sparks in Ovensky's brown eyes.

'Eleven, eleven-tirty,' she said. 'I hear dem tawkin, so I look tru de vindow.'

'Eleven, eleven-thirty,' echoed Milo.

'Yah. Is important?'

'Could be, ma'am. Any idea where they went?'

'Who know? Wherever dey types go.'

'Were they carrying luggage – suitcases?'

'Yah, two big suitcases. Maybe dey stay away and we don' get no dee-bark dem, dee-bark dem. De dogs have a right to sing, no?'

'Two suitcases,' said Milo, back at the unmarked. 'Not a year-long cruise, but enough for a while.'

He glanced back at the mansion. Irina Ovensky remained in the door, and she smiled and waved.

'A saint,' I said.

'The type you take home to Mom.' He waved back, smiling. His jawline knotted as he opened the car door, got in, took out the envelope. 'Okay, let's have a look at these.' Flipping through the photos quickly, he paused at a close-up of the stocky man's face. 'He does have that mechanic look . . . Still, what I said holds. If he was doing wet work for the Dukes, why would they keep him close? If I have time, I'll run this by the Organized Crime Task Force.'

'Didn't know there was one,' I said.

'Since the fifties. Not much mafia in L.A., so for years the task force guys enjoyed long lunches. Now they're tied up with Asian and Latin drug gangs, but who knows – maybe this mug'll show up in their files. The Morris office is closed now, but I'll be there first thing tomorrow morning, see if I can learn anything about Justin LeMoyne's travel habits before they kick my butt out to South Rodeo— Think I should wear a designer suit?'

'You own one?'

'Yeah, fashion by Sir Kay of the Mart. I put a call in to a guy at the DA's office who worked on Gretchen's case – let's see if Kent Irving's name shows up, for what that's worth. I also placed my third call to Leo Riley, still no answer.'

'So much for professional courtesy,' I said.

'More likely he's got nothing to tell me. We law-enforcement types don't like to dwell on our failures.

Meanwhile, I'm packing it in for the evening. Rick has informed me that we're going to eat at a genuine restaurant tonight, where we will pretend to be persons deserving of fine cuisine and impeccable service. And then, maybe a movie. He says if I bring the phone, he will dismantle it with surgical precision.'

'Frustrated.'

'I tend to do that to people.'

thirty-one

I cracked the bedroom door. Robin was curled on her side, the top sheet pulled down to her bare belly, mouth parted, breathing slowly. As I approached the bed and shut off the alarm clock, her eyes opened.

'A minute to six,' I whispered. 'Good morning.'

She yawned and stretched. 'I got tired . . . didn't see you much today – what'd you do?'

'Took a little drive up the coast.'

'Oh . . . I was thinking maybe we'd have dinner somewhere at the beach. Guess not, now that you've already—'

'The beach is one thing,' I said. 'The beach with you is another.'

Kissing her chin. What a sweet guy. But all the time thinking: Malibu's a small place. Running into someone I knew would not be pretty.

By the time we left the house it was eight P.M., and we reached the coast highway twenty minutes later. I bypassed all the trendoid-infested spots-of-the-week and tried a place we'd never been before – a gray-wood café resembling an oversized bait shack perched on a mound of dirt above PCH. On the land side, just past Big Rock, where massive mudslides are the rule and thirty-foot-wide beach properties level off at a million and a half bucks. The decor was rickety picnic tables, sawdust floors, daily printed menus with all the polish of a high school bulletin, char broilers on overdrive, beery dialogue. The room was high enough to catch a clean vista of black ocean, and if the grandmotherly old waitress who greeted us with 'Hello, dearies' had ever harbored showbiz illusions, they predated Technicolor.

Several miles before Paradise Cove.

We huddled at a tiny table in the corner, gorged on the mixed seafood grill, fresh corn, creamed spinach, decent Chablis, terrible coffee.

Having a life, and when Robin said, 'You seem a little more relaxed,' I hid my surprise and nodded innocently. Cheryl Duke's number sat in my wallet, but Robin never goes through my things.

I reached for her hand. She allowed me to hold it for a few minutes, then let go, and I wondered if I was less Olivier than I'd given myself credit for.

'Everything okay?' I said.

'Everything's fine. Just a little tired.'

'Still?'

'Guess so.'

We went to bed without making love, and I slept restlessly.

The next morning she was up way before me, and by the time I reached the kitchen she was heading out with Spike.

'Errands?' I said.

'Elvis, again. He still thinks he can sing— Stay safe.'

'You too.'

'Me?' she said. 'That's never an issue for me.'

Before I could respond, she was gone.

I didn't hear from Milo until three P.M. 'No progress on LeMoyne and Salander's travel plans, couldn't get past the front desk at Morris, and the prosecutor who handled Gretchen's case has been kicked upstairs to Washington, D.C. Her assistant has taken over, and she says Kent Irving's name doesn't ring a bell. I asked her to check anyway – suppose there's a chance she will. I asked her about garment guys, period, and she did admit that Gretchen's girls had worked the Mart – servicing buyers, that kind of thing. But the main reason I'm calling is I identified your Mr Goombah.'

'The task force knows him?'

'Didn't have to go to the task force. I had the photos spread out on my desk last night, and when Rick came in to drag me out to dinner he glommed onto them and said, "How do you know Maccaferri?" As in *Dr* Maccaferri. First name, Rene. The guy's a renowned physician, Alex. Big-time researcher headquartered in Paris, but he consults to the National Cancer Institute. Rick recognized him because he attended a seminar Maccaferri gave last year. Prostate cancer. It's his specialty.'

'Oh,' I said. 'Tony Duke's sick.'

'And Dutiful Son went to the airport to pick up his doctor.'

I laughed. 'So much for my big-time mafia theories.'

'Hey, you tried.'

'Maybe the rest of it's worthless . . . Cancer – that's why the parties have ended. Why Cheryl said there'd be no more. Tony passed the banner to Anita because he's in no shape to run things. That may also be why Cheryl and the kids moved back – the gas leak story could be a ploy to keep Tony's illness quiet.'

'Hold on,' he said. 'Maccaferri's no big bad torpedo, but Lauren and a lot of people are still dead. So let's not be too hasty. And I'm still left with little Andy Salander. Alex, the more I think about his cutting out so abruptly the less I like it. He and LeMoyne packing and leaving in the middle of the night – it's a clear rabbit. The rest of my day will be spent on the phone with the airlines. Maybe I'll luck out. Anyway, thanks for trying, have a nice day.'

Renowned physician.

So much for my big-time intuition. Milo had been gracious, but was the rest of it – including suspicions of Ben Dugger – just as off base?

Still, Dugger *was* an odd man who'd paid good money to Lauren and Cheryl and who knew how many other beautiful blondes to sit in a cold little room and entice men.

Hiring female flesh, compiling data that hadn't been

published or put to any apparent use.

Hidden cameras, grids in the floor . . . voyeurism masquerading as science. Dugger had eschewed the flash and spark of Tony Duke's lifestyle for . . . what?

I thought of how easily Dugger had relinquished Cheryl to Tony Duke the moment the old man had made his interests known. The personal trip to LAX to pick up Maccaferri – a job easily accomplished by a factotum.

Maybe Dugger was a strong adherent to the Fifth Commandment. But perhaps, now that his father was seriously ill, there was a more practical reason to be attentive.

Back to the money: millions of dollars' worth of motivation.

Tony Duke's death was more than theoretical now. One day – perhaps sooner rather than later – Duke Enterprises would be divvied up. Ben *Dugger's* lifestyle was far from lavish, but his market research seemed to generate very little income, and someone had to pay for the ocean-view high rise offices in Newport and Brentwood.

And now he was closing down Newport and shifting operations to Brentwood.

Same reason: sticking close to Dad during the final days.

Dependent upon Dad's good graces. But with his sister at the helm of Duke Enterprises, was he in danger of being cut off? Knowing how Ben and Anita got along would help answer that, and the only indication I had was the fact that there'd been no mention of Ben's attendance at Anita's wedding.

Then there was the matter of the two other sibs: Sage and Baxter. And Kent Irving, of the pink shirt and Hollywood wink.

All in all, high risk for conflict. For the type of endgame litigation that meant big winners and catastrophic losers. Big-time rage.

Cheryl aka Sylvana was no genius, but she had to be aware of the financial ramifications. That could explain her anxiety about being branded a bad mom. Yet that hadn't stopped her from dozing off on the beach. Or giving me her private number.

Poor judgment . . . pliable.

Unlike Lauren, toughened by years on the street. *Big tips.*

I thought back to Jane Abbot's first call to me. Panicked about Lauren's disappearance, even though Lauren had been on her own for years, had traveled in the past.

Because the two of them had finally started to reconnect and Lauren had confided in her. Maybe even bragged about her lucrative dodge.

Perhaps Jane had tried to talk Lauren out of the blackmail scheme – the control issue Lauren had complained about to Andrew Salander.

Lauren refusing. Signing her death warrant, and that of her onetime partner/friend Michelle. And her mother.

Milo was chasing down Salander's whereabouts, and maybe that would lead to something. But I couldn't help thinking that any solution lay crouching behind the walls of the Duke estate. High walls, electric gates, closed circuit TV, cable car that shimmied up and down the cliff side. All of it emitting a clear message:

Keep out, Stupid.

And, for the life of me, I saw no way in.

thirty-two

L A.'s first commandment. When in doubt, drive.

Years ago – ages ago – when I arrived in the city as a college freshman, the first thing that hit me was: *The streets are asphalt rivers.* In high school I'd played guitar in a wedding band and filed paper at an architect's office in order to scrape up enough cash for a puke-colored, emphysemic Chevy Nova that my father, a Ford man, despised. (Quoth Harry Delaware: 'It's crap, but at least you earned it – nothing you don't earn is worth half a crap.') That Bondoed, duct-taped chariot whisked me from Missouri to California, and, when it reached my dorm, promptly sputtered and died. For most of the first year I was left to the mercies of L.A.'s afterthought bus system – house imprisonment. The following summer a series of late-night jobs had earned me a moribund Plymouth Valiant, chronic insomnia, and the habit of stumbling out of bed before dawn, cruising dark, empty boulevards, and wondering about my future.

Now I sleep later, but the urge to escape on wheels has never died. It's a different L.A. from my college days, traffic all bunched up and angry and irrevocable, less and less open space until you get up in the Santa Monica Mountains or out on some old stretch of blacktop made redundant by the freeways, but I still love to drive for the sake of driving. It's a trait I share with a certain sub-sample of psychopaths, but so what – introspection can be a sucker game.

After Milo hung up I sat at my desk listening to the empty house. Wondering if Robin's increasing absences had to do with more than her work. Wondering how I could've been so wrong about Rene Maccaferri ('He doesn't look like a brain surgeon, Milo') and what else I'd screwed up. I got into the Seville. Tony Duke sick, maybe seriously so, amid Malibu splendor. I switched on the tape deck, listened to the Fabulous Thunderbirds being tough enough at way too high a decibel level. Tooling up the glen to Mulholland, turning east into the Hollywood Hills, playing with turns and twists, zoned out, wanting to empty my head.

Without intending to, I ended up in the heart of Hollywood and back at Sunset Boulevard. No more relaxed, still plagued with supposition. About Lauren's pathway from rebellious kid to garment center hooker to . . . whatever she'd been when the bullet had bounced around in her brain.

I remembered the paper she'd written for Gene Dalby's social psych class. 'Iconography in the Fashion Industry.'

Women as Meat.

Bitter about the trade-offs she'd made? Had that

played a part in fueling a blackmail scheme, or had she just been greedy?

It took a long time to crawl through Beverly Hills and the eastern fringe of Bel Air – two of the 'Three Bs' to which Shawna Yeager had aspired – and when I reached the glen I got caught in the jam and crawled, feeling strangely at home, like a member of some vast, inertial conspiracy.

No stress from the automotive stalemate; the chrome clog was no worse than the neural traffic in my head. I was trying to figure out what to do with the rest of the day when I realized I'd inched toward Justin LeMoyne's house. As I passed the white bungalow, a flash of movement caught my eye.

The garage door closing. Just a foot of opening at the bottom as the wooden sheet slid into place. At the first side street I managed to hang a left across both lanes, hooked a three-point turn, pulled to the corner, and waited. Seven minutes later the garage door opened and a red Mercedes convertible, its top up, nosed out with its left turn signal blinking. Whoever was at the wheel was trying to swing across and head south.

Letting the Mercedes in wouldn't have ruined anyone's day, but human kindness was at an ebb and the red car just sat there for a long time, blinking. Finally, a gardener's truck relented, and the convertible was allowed to join the go-nowhere-fast club. Ten car lengths later, so was I.

Trying not to dwell on the ludicrousness of my tail job of Ben Dugger and Dr Maccaferri, I tagged along, struggling to keep the Mercedes in view. No mean challenge, because the red car squeaked through the light at Sunset and left me in a queue of five cars. I kept my eye on its rectangular taillights. Right turn. By the time I followed suit, no sign of the red car, and I rolled along with all the other automatons, at a bracing fifteen miles per. Then brake lights flashed in series, and the congestion that anticipated the 405 freeway put the Mercedes back in my sights.

Thirty yards up, in the left-hand lane. I managed a few less-than-courteous lane changes, and when the Mercedes chose the Sepulveda alternate to the southbound freeway, I'd narrowed the gap and was able to make out the cloudy outline of a solitary driver through the convertible's plastic rear window.

He stayed on Sepulveda, crossed Wilshire and Santa Monica and Olympic, driving as quickly as traffic would permit. Past the spot where Lauren's body had been dumped. Across Pico and Venice, into Culver City, then a right turn at Washington, a quarter-mile zip, and a quick swing into the parking lot of a small hotel called the Palm Court.

North side of Washington, two-story mock colonial wedged between an ARCO station and a flower shop, auto club badge of approval tacked above the door. Clean, white clapboard façade that I couldn't help comparing to Jane and Mel Abbot's house. The parking lot was sun-grayed, one-third full. The Mercedes pulled to the far left side, well away from other vehicles, and came to a short stop.

A man got out and hurried toward the motel's glass doors. Forties, tall, slim, and sunken-chested, with long, stringy arms and kinky, graying hair. He wore a snug yellow polo shirt over pressed khakis, brown loafers, no socks, tiny eyeglasses. Carried a cardboard file case in his hands. Justin LeMoyne making a quick trip back home for paperwork? He shot a worried look over his shoulder as he shoved the doors and stepped in.

The phone booth at the ARCO station smelled of too-old burrito, but the dial tone was clear. I called Milo at the station, and before he could speak said, 'Finally, something real.'

'Yeah, they're both in there,' he said, returning to the Seville and leaning in the driver's window. 'Room two fifteen. They checked in yesterday under LeMoyne's name.'

It had taken him a quarter hour to arrive. He'd left the unmarked on the opposite side of the lot, conferred for a couple of minutes with the desk clerk, emerged nodding.

'Cooperative fellow?' I said.

'Ethiopian fellow studying for the citizenship exam, very yessir, nosir. I promised not to bring in a SWAT army if he didn't fuss or notify LeMoyne and Salander. He seemed duly impressed by the badge— Why should he know that justifying a warrant, let alone a GI Joe ground assault, is about as likely as Ghaddafi marrying Streisand.'

'Let's hear it for TV.'

'And here I was thinking it was my commanding aura.

457

He also volunteered that Salander just called down and asked where he could order a pizza. He directed them to Papa Pomodoro on Overland, told me they've got a guaranteed half hour delivery or it's a freebie. So I'm gonna knock on the door in five minutes, and just maybe they'll open it with pepperoni expectations.'

'And when the real delivery boy shows up?' I said.

'We'll have a party— Thanks for noticing LeMoyne's car, Alex.'

'Hard not to, I was right there.'

'And they say no one in L.A.'s neighborly.'

'If he checked in under his own name, LeMoyne wasn't exactly being cagey,' I said. 'Driving up to his house in broad daylight, staying this close to home? Doesn't smell like a frantic rabbit.'

'Then what're they doing here? Vacationing in Culver City?'

'Maybe taking a breather,' I said. 'Giving Andy Salander time to figure out what to do with the information he got from Lauren.'

'Or he was Lauren's partner in crime.'

'No sign she shared the wealth. She was the one with the wardrobe and the investment portfolio. Salander barely scraped by on his bartender's salary. No, I think she took him in for company – nonsexual company – just like he said, and he became her confidant. Maybe she didn't even give him details, just told him enough for him to figure things out when people started dying. Reconciling with LeMoyne couldn't have come at a better time for him – allowed him to leave the apartment,

move in with LeMoyne. He told LeMoyne of his suspicions, scared LeMoyne enough to bunk down here.'

'And he didn't call me because . . .'

'Because why should he, Milo? If he's a TV baby, how
many times has he seen the old witness protection
bungle story? Not to mention all those police corruption
scenarios. Fictional or otherwise.'

'Untrustworthy?' he said. '*Moi?*' He gazed at the hotel.
'Or maybe the two of them are trying to figure out how
to take over the blackmail scheme.' He looked at his
watch. 'Okay, time to be Simon the Pie man— Wait
here, and if it's okay for you to come up, I'll let you
know. If the delivery guy does show up, you can say the
pizza's yours and pay him.'

'Is the department going to reimburse me?'

He dipped in his trouser pocket and pulled out his
wallet.

'Put that back,' I said. 'Just kidding.'

'Sure,' he said, flashing teeth. 'I can be trusted.'

Seven minutes later a small, fine-featured black man in
his late twenties stepped out of the Palm Court, sighted
across the parking lot, spotted the Seville, and waved. I
jogged over, and he held the door open. After ushering
me into the skimpy, dim booth the hotel passed off as a
lobby, he led me to a chipped, brown-metal elevator,
cupped his hand over his mouth, and spoke so softly I
had to lean toward him.

'Detective Sturger rogers you to ascend, sir.'

'Thanks.'

'Room two fifteen. You may take the elevator. Please.'

The lift rattled dangerously, and the one-story ride took nearly a minute. The second floor was a single, low, pink-vinyl hallway crowded with gray-green doors fitted with cheap locks. The sand-colored carpeting beneath my footsteps was unpadded and grimy around the edges. Midway down the corridor, an ice machine gurgled. DO NOT DISTURB signs dangled from three knobs, and every few feet canned laughter oozed through the vinyl.

No sign on 215. I knocked and Milo's voice said, 'Enter.'

Blue room. Gold bamboo over turquoise paper, a queen-sized bed made up carelessly with a navy spread, a black-painted desk and chair, a nineteen-inch TV bolted to the wall, rental movie–video game box riding on top. No closet, just open shelves next to the bathroom door, bare but for two six-packs of Budweiser and a collection of Chinese take-out cartons. A pair of older Vuitton suitcases had been shoved into a corner, sad as impoverished nobility.

Justin LeMoyne sat on the edge of the chair twirling an unlit cigarette between the fingers of one hand. His shoes were off, and the file case I'd seen him take from the car rested near his bare feet. In his lap was a black-bound script, and on the desk was a cell phone and a ThinkPad. Up close he looked older – early fifties – neck puffing and hollowing in all the wrong places, facial skin losing its grip on the bone. The kinky hair was worn down over his collar at the back, but a feathery, precise hairline in front said transplant. Behind the tiny glasses his eyes were dark, bright, uncertain.

Andy Salander was perched near the foot of the bed, dressed similarly to LeMoyne in khakis and a polo shirt – his, white with an olive collar. On the nightstand near his elbow was an open can of Bud. The ashtray on the opposite stand overflowed with butts, and the room reeked of tobacco and restless sleep.

Milo stood behind them, up against the beige chenille drape that dirtied the light leaking through the room's single window.

Salander said, 'Hi, there, Doctor,' in a breakable voice.

LeMoyne gripped the script and pretended to study dialogue.

'Hi,' I said.

'This is Justin,' said Andy.

'Pleased to meet you, Justin.' LeMoyne sniffed, thumbed pages.

'Mr Salander and Mr LeMoyne are on "retreat," ' said Milo. 'The question is from what.'

'Last time I checked it was a free country,' said LeMoyne, without looking up.

'Justin,' said Salander.

The older man looked up. 'Yes, *Andrew*?'

'I – we . . . Forget it.'

'Excellent idea, Andrew.'

'Oh, my,' said Milo. 'Such a simple question.'

LeMoyne said, 'Nothing's simple. And you have no right to invade our privacy.' To Salander: 'You didn't have to let him in, and there's absolutely no reason we should permit him to stay.'

'I know, Justin, but . . .' To Milo: 'He's right. Maybe you should go, Detective Sturgis.'

'Now I'm hurt,' said Milo.

'Knock it off,' said LeMoyne. 'The cute stuff chafes. We've already put up with the indignity of being frisked and having our belongings pawed through. If you have something to say, say it, then let us be.'

Milo fingered the drapes, pulled them aside, turned and peered through the window. 'Gas station view.' He let the chenille drop. 'If I lived in Beverly Glen, I wouldn't retreat here, Mr LeMoyne.'

'To each his own. *You* of *all* people should *know* that.'

Salander winced.

Milo smiled. 'The thing is, Andy, this whole free country thing – people recite it like a mantra, but we're really not all that free. The law imposes restrictions. I've got handcuffs in my pocket, and I can take them out, place them around your wrists, and take you to jail and be operating in a perfectly legal manner.'

A tiny tremor scooted across Salander's lips.

LeMoyne kept turning pages. 'He's trying to intimidate you, Andy.' To Milo: 'That's rubbish. On what grounds?'

'The thing is, Andy,' said Milo, 'there's a legal status called material witness that can reduce your freedom substantially. Same for "suspect".'

Salander blanched. 'I didn't see anything, and I didn't do anything.'

'That may be so, but my job is to suspect, not to adjudicate. And after a couple of days in custody—'

'Bullshit,' said LeMoyne, starting to get up. 'Stop scaring him.'

'Please stay seated, sir.'

'Bullshit,' LeMoyne repeated, but he settled back down. 'This is obscene. Oppressive. You of all people should—'

Milo turned his back on LeMoyne. 'The thing that bothers me, Andy, is I specifically asked you to be available. Because you're the last person who saw Lauren Teague alive, and that makes you a definite material witness. From my perspective, the fact that you agreed to be available but reneged makes you an interesting person.'

Long pause.

Salander said, 'I'm sorry—'

'Oh, Christ,' said LeMoyne. 'Stop talking, Andrew. Shut up—'

'You went back on your word, Andy. That and the fact that you're hiding out in this garden spot—'

'We are *not* hiding,' said LeMoyne, picking up the phone. 'I'm calling my lawyer. Ed Geisman. Geisman and Brandner.'

'Be my guest,' said Milo. 'Of course, once that happens, I won't be able to control the ensuing publicity – agent and suspect apprehended in cheap hotel, I'm sure you can fill in the blanks.' Half turning back toward LeMoyne. 'It was my impression that agents preferred to sell stories, not create them.'

'Defame me and I'll sue you.'

'If I defamed you, I'd deserve to be sued, sir. But release of accurate facts doesn't constitute defamation.'

Salander said, 'Justin, this is crazy, why are we fighting? I didn't *do* anything. All I want is— I don't *care* about the story.'

'Quiet,' snapped LeMoyne.

Milo smiled. Edged closer to the bed. 'The story. So this is a story conference.' He laughed. 'You guys are taking a meeting.'

'It's not like that,' said Salander, wiping moist eyes.

'Stop blubbering,' ordered LeMoyne. 'It's unbecoming.'

'I'm sorry, Justin—'

'Stop *apologizing*!'

'Let me guess,' said Milo, stepping between the men. 'Insider's view of a blond beauty's murder. Are you thinking big screen or made for TV?'

'No,' said Salander. 'No, no, it's just— Justin said if we registered the idea with the Writers' Guild we could be protected – it would be like life insurance.'

'Ah,' said Milo. 'You think if someone comes gunning for you, the Writers' Guild'll ride to the rescue? Must be a new service they provide.'

Salander began crying.

'You asshole,' said LeMoyne. 'You enjoy scaring him, don't you.'

'He's already scared,' said Milo. 'Isn't that right, Andy?'

'Don't call him by his first name. It's demeaning. Call

him "mister." Treat him with respect.'

'I don't care what he calls me, Justin.' Salander sniffed. 'I just want to be safe.'

'That's the problem,' said LeMoyne.

'What is?' Panic in Salander's voice.

'You don't *care*. You always fall short in the caring department. As well as in the thinking-things-through department.'

'Stop it, Justin—'

LeMoyne slammed the script shut. 'This is bullshit. I've got appointments on hold, canceled meetings— Do what you want, Andy. It's your life, take it where you want to—'

'The thing is,' said Milo, 'I don't *care* if you register the story. Make a million bucks from Lauren's death, it's the American way. But not before you tell me what you know. Because if you hold out, that puts into play yet another restriction of your freedom: withholding evidence.'

'Oh, bullshit,' said LeMoyne. 'This is just total bull-shit. I'm out of this, Andrew.'

'I need your help, Justin.'

LeMoyne gave a sick smile. 'Oh, I don't think so, Andy. I think you do just fine by yourself.'

'I *don't*.' Salander wiped his nose with his arm. 'I really need support, Justin—'

'That's a brand-new shirt, use a *tissue*, for God's sake.'

Salander looked around the room helplessly. Milo located the Kleenex box on the floor and handed it to him.

'What should I do, Justin?'

'Do what you want.'

Silence.

'I don't know,' said Salander, throwing up his hands. He reached for the beer can.

'No more,' said LeMoyne. 'You've had enough.'

Salander's hand jerked back. He hugged himself. 'Oh!' he said. 'This is . . . so restrictive.'

LeMoyne shook his head. 'I'm leaving.' But he didn't move.

'What should I do?' Salander repeated.

Milo said, 'How about telling the truth?'

Arms still wrapped around his torso, Salander began to rock. His smooth forehead creased. Thinking hard.

LeMoyne said, 'For this I give up a lunch at Le Dome.'

thirty-three

Salander's decision came moments later, heralded by a long, breathy sigh.

'Yes, I am scared,' he said, shivering. 'First Lo, then her mother.'

No mention of Michelle and Lance. He had more to fear than he knew.

Milo said, 'Jane Abbot's death confirmed your suspicion.'

Salander nodded.

Milo leaned over him. 'I need to tell you, Andy. There may be others as well.'

'Oh my God—'

'Terror tactics,' muttered LeMoyne.

Milo stepped over to the desk and shadowed the older man. 'A little fear wouldn't be a bad idea for you either, sir.'

LeMoyne's face lost color, but he smiled. 'I've swum with the sharks, my friend.'

Milo smiled back. 'You've swum with *trout*, my friend. We're talking Great White.'

'Ah,' said LeMoyne. 'I shudder.'

'What others?' said Salander.

'Associates of Lauren,' said Milo. 'Now tell me what scares you, Andy.'

'I think I may know why Lo was murdered – I mean, I can't be sure – but right from the beginning I wondered about it.'

'Wondered about what, Andy?'

'The money. It's always about money, right?'

'More often than not.'

Salander rocked some more.

Milo said, 'Tell me about the money.'

'She – Lo— I always wondered how she supported herself. 'Cause she never worked much except for that part-time research job and that couldn't pay for Moschino and Prada and Jimmy Choo, right? Also, her attitude – she had that relaxed thing about money that you only get if you have it, know what I mean? In fact, when I first met her I thought she was a rich kid – inherited wealth. But she said she'd been on her own for years, so— I mean, I wasn't nosy, but it made me wonder. She was a full-time student. Where was it all coming from? Then – after I moved in, maybe a month after – she happened to leave some mail out on the kitchen counter. On top was investment stuff, her port-folio, from some broker up in Seattle. I'm no snoop, but she left it right out there on the table, so how could I help but see the zeros?'

'Lots of zeros.'

'Lots,' Salander agreed. 'I never asked her about it, we

never talked about it. And she was supergenerous –
when we went out for a meal together, she always
insisted on paying. When we antiqued, she'd buy me
things – cuff links, vintage shirts.'

'Must be your boyish charm,' muttered LeMoyne.

Salander's hand balled. 'Once upon a time *you*
thought so! Stop picking at me!'

LeMoyne brought the script closer to his eyeglasses.

Salander said, 'You're a grump, but I still love you,
Justin.'

LeMoyne whispered something.

'What?' said Andy.

'Love you, too.'

Salander smiled. 'Thank you.'

Low grumble. 'Welcome.'

Milo said, 'So the source of Lauren's money puzzled
you. Did she ever talk about any other jobs she'd held?
Before the research thing?'

'Modeling,' said Salander. 'She said she'd modeled – I
told you that, didn't I.'

'Anything besides modeling?'

Salander stared down at the bedspread. 'No. Like
what?'

'The girl was a *hooker*,' said LeMoyne. 'I keep telling
you that.'

'You don't *know* that, Justin!'

'Oh, Jesus, Andrew, I *met* her. She had hooker written
all *over* her.'

Milo said, 'How many times did you meet her, Mr
LeMoyne?'

'Two or three times – in passing. But that was enough to know what she was. She was high-priced – no doubt about that. But she had the moves – the look, the walk, the whole phony-class thing going on. For all I know, she was trained by Gretchen Stengel.'

'You know Gretchen Stengel?'

'I know *of* her,' said LeMoyne. 'Everyone in the industry does. We've never lunched, but I've certainly seen her around. And run into many of her little vixens. Back when Gretchen was plying her trade, you couldn't go anywhere that was anywhere without *tripping* over them.'

'Easy to spot,' said Milo.

LeMoyne rolled his eyes. 'Even for you, Sherlock. Gretchen went for a *type* – cool but remotely friendly, the ready rap, the body, the clothes. The clothes were always the tip-off. A girl who shouldn't have been able to afford five grand worth of couture but wore it well.'

LeMoyne smiled and closed the script. 'Not that it helped. If you knew the difference between real class and bullshit. Every one of those girls had a certain . . . commonness. Trailer-park trying to morph into Grace Kelly.'

He crossed his legs. 'Beleeeve me, Detective, that takes more than aerobics and a crash course on what fork to use. Still, you can fool most of the people . . .' To Salander: 'She was a *hooker*, Andy.'

Salander gazed up at Milo.

Milo said, 'She did have that in her past, Andy.'

'Oh . . .' Another labored sigh. 'I'm *très naïve*, aren't I?

I guess it was right there in front of me, but I just didn't want to know— Not that it would've mattered. I don't judge, why should I judge? And I *swear* the whole time we lived together she never did anything illegal or brought anyone home – I guess when she took those long weekends she was . . . She told me . . . I can't be blamed for believing her. Okay, fine, I'm naïve and stupid.' Staring at LeMoyne.

LeMoyne shook his head and reopened the script.

Milo said, 'What did she tell you about the long weekends, Andy?'

Salander squirmed. 'I didn't say anything when you first came around because I wasn't sure— And it looks like now maybe it *didn't* have anything to do with it. Now that you're telling me she was . . . The thing is, I didn't want to make things complicated—'

LeMoyne's laughter cut him off. 'You're babbling, Andrew. They have no clue what the hell you're talking about.'

Milo edged closer to Salander.

'What, Andy?'

'Her family,' said Salander. 'Her real family. She said she was going out to Malibu to reconnect with them. Since she'd learned who her real father was. Tony Duke. I guess she was . . . fantasizing, right? It's the world's greatest fantasy, right? Live your life one way and then find out all of a sudden that you're on a whole different level.'

Milo sat down on the bed.

So did I.

★ ★ ★

Milo's notepad was out. His tie was loose. 'When and how did she learn about this, Andrew?'

'*When* was last year,' said Salander. 'Maybe a year ago – just before we started rooming together. *How* is her mother told her. The two of them had started relating again. They hadn't talked for a long time, and then Jane started making overtures and they began trying to patch things up. Slowly – having lunch once in a while. It was at one of those lunches that Jane told her. They'd finished off a bottle of wine, gotten all girlie-chatty, and Jane just spilled it out. She said she'd met Duke while working as a flight attendant on a jet Duke had chartered – taking some models and a bunch of other people to the big island of Hawaii for a big photo spread and partying. Jane ended up serving Duke personally, and he invited her to spend the layover at some mansion he was renting. And . . . it *happened*. Jane and Lo's dad – the one she thought was her dad, the asshole – were going together but hadn't decided to get married. When Jane found out she was pregnant, she convinced him to marry her.'

'Talk about your false pretenses,' said Justin LeMoyne. 'It really does have story elements.'

'The funny thing is,' said Salander, 'finding out about Duke caused things to make sense for Lauren. Like why she couldn't stand her father – the one who raised her. She said she'd never related to her father, she'd always felt like a stranger to him – like there'd been this wall between them. Now she understood it.'

'Jane never told him about Lauren's true paternity,' I said.

'Lauren said no way, his temper was too bad for that. The marriage broke up anyway, but Jane told Lauren the whole time she was pregnant, she was paranoid he would find out, do something violent. Luckily, Lauren resembled Jane.'

'Paranoid, but she kept the baby,' I said.

'She told Lauren she'd always wanted a baby.'

Tish Teague's outburst came back to me. Recounting Lauren's cruel parting comment: 'You don't deserve a damn thing from me – you're not even my family and neither is he and neither are your rugrats.'

No blood connection between Lauren and Lyle's little girls, yet Lauren had sought them out, brought them Christmas presents, only to withdraw. Ambivalent. How lonely she must've been . . .

'So Jane told Lauren about a year ago,' said Milo. 'When did Lauren tell you?'

'Soon after I moved in – maybe a couple of months later. At first, after we started rooming together, she was real up – happy all the time. Probably 'cause she'd just found out. But then her mood changed – she slid way down. Being a natural listener, I kept trying to help her open up . . . When she did, it was after I'd cooked this big Italian dinner and we'd finished a whole bottle of Chianti – cheap wine's the great conversation starter, right?'

Milo shifted his bulk. 'What was her mood when she told you?'

'At first she was kind of giddy about it – like isn't that cool, my real dad's a zillionaire. But then she got *real* quiet. I thought maybe because she felt she'd missed out on stuff – all those years she could've been a princess. I said something to that effect, but she said, no, that wasn't it at all. She wouldn't trade her life with anyone's, but the whole thing had just thrown her off balance. And – this was the main thing – after Jane told her, she got all freaked out and started pressuring Lo to forget about it, not to try to get in touch with Duke. Lauren thought that was cruel and manipulative, and she was right, don't you think? You can't just go and dump something on someone then try to hold them back. Lo was furious at Jane.'

I said, 'That's when she complained about Jane wanting to control her.'

'Yes, exactly. She said Jane was a coward and a liar and totally full of shit to think she – Lauren – would just sit there and let someone else make up the rules. She was also mad that Jane had tried to bribe her to keep quiet – said it was sleazy.'

'Bribe her how?'

'After Jane got divorced, she was real poor for a while. So she wrote to Tony Duke and he started sending her money. For her and for Lauren. Even though Lauren wasn't in the picture – she and Jane had lost contact for years. Jane claimed she spent only her part, put Lauren's share aside. When she and Lo connected, she started giving Lo a regular allowance, but she never told Lo where it really came from.'

Milo and I exchanged glances. Both of us remembering the deposits in Lauren's portfolio. A hundred thousand payment four years ago, then fifty a year since.

'Big money?' said Milo.

'Lauren didn't specify, but it must've been, right?' said Salander. 'All those zeros. And the way she dressed. But the point was, Jane wasn't up front about it. Lied to Lauren about where Lauren's allowance was coming from.'

'What did she tell her?'

'That her second husband was giving it to her – to Jane – and that Jane was sharing with Lauren, out of the goodness of her heart.'

'Lauren believed that?'

'He's a rich TV producer, Mr Abbot. Real generous with Jane. Jane was living like a rich woman now. But then, when Jane was trying to pressure Lauren not to blow the lid off the Duke thing, she told Lauren where the money had really come from, tried to make herself a saint – like "I put myself on a limb for you, all those years you never talked to me, I still put your money aside." And then she offered to give Lauren even more money if she'd stay away from Tony Duke.'

'Why was she worried about that?'

'She told Lauren it would create a big mess, there was nothing to gain from it. Lauren suspected what she was really worried about was ticking off Tony Duke and jeopardizing her own allowance. Protecting her butt. In Lo's mind, Jane was just trying to buy her off, and she was tired of being bought.'

Salander turned silent. 'I guess I know, now, what she meant.'

'*Ding*,' said LeMoyne, miming a bell ring.

Milo said, 'So Jane wrote a letter to Duke, and he just started sending her money.'

'Jane wouldn't give Lo the details – that was part of the frustration. Jane got drunk and spilled out the whole story, then she just curled up and wouldn't tell Lauren any more.'

'Can you blame her?' said LeMoyne. 'The girl was a hooker. The mother had a golden goose farting into her hand and knew that if Duke found out he had a hooker kid, that would screw the deal. He's Mr Wholesome Tits and Ass, a daughter who earned her living on her knees would be bad PR.' Smiling at Milo: 'Right?'

'Good story line.'

'It's my job.' Chuckling, LeMoyne returned to the script.

'So Jane tried to hold Lauren back,' I said. 'But Lauren wouldn't be held back. Made contact with the Dukes and went to see them in Malibu.'

Salander said, 'She never gave me the details, but she did say thank God for her computer – she used it to research the Dukes, didn't need her mother or anyone else 'cause she had technology on her side. She even showed it to me – had this cute little family tree thingie in there – this actual little tree full of apples with people's names on them.'

Milo said, 'Did you notice any of the names?'

'No, she didn't let me get that close – just wanted me

to see the tree, and then brought it back into her room. Like she was proud of it. She said it was a genealogy program; she'd bought it and downloaded it herself.' Salander flinched. 'And then when you called and asked about the computer and I realized it was gone . . . That's when I started to worry.'

'That maybe someone wanted to get hold of the family data.'

'That and the fact someone had gotten into our place. Then, when I heard about Jane.' Salander bit his lip. 'I started thinking: Maybe Lauren had misjudged her mother. Maybe Jane didn't want Lauren to get too close not because she was worried about getting cut off but because it was dangerous. What if Jane really cared and Lauren was never able to see that?'

Milo stood, paced the space between the bed and the window. 'Did Lauren indicate that she'd ever actually made contact with Tony Duke?'

'No,' said Salander. 'All I know about is that tree thingie. But he does live in Malibu, right? That humongous place, with all the parties.'

'What else did she tell you that could help me, Andy?'

'That's it, I promise. After that one time she spilled her guts, she pulled back – just like Jane did with her. Mostly she stayed in her room, in front of that computer.'

'Did she ever talk about other family members? Besides Tony Duke?'

Salander shook his head.

'What about girls she'd worked with?'

'Not that I recall.'

'Michelle Salazar?'

'No.'

'Shawna Yeager?'

'Uh-uh. She never talked about the past. And like I told you the first time, she didn't have any friends. A real loner.'

'A girl and her computer,' said Milo.

Salander said, 'So sad.' Then: 'Now what?'

'Have you told anyone besides Mr LeMoyne about any of this?'

'No.' A glance at LeMoyne. 'And all Justin wanted was to write up a treatment and register it—' He stopped. 'That could be dangerous, huh? If someone at the Guild saw it and—'

'Oh, please,' said LeMoyne. 'No one in the Industry *reads*.'

'Still,' said Milo.

'Fine, fine,' snapped LeMoyne. '*Fine*.'

Milo turned to Salander. 'Andy, I'll be needing you to repeat everything you've told me for a formal statement.'

Salander blanched. 'Why?'

'It's the rules. We'll do it in a couple of days. Either down at the station or somewhere more private, if you're straight with me about sticking around. This time.'

'More private,' said Salander. 'Definitely more private. Do you think we can move back to Justin's place? I mean, if Lauren and Jane died because Lauren was Tony Duke's daughter and I know about it—'

'That's the point, son,' said Milo. 'No one knows you

know. If you're discreet, I don't see any imminent danger. If you're not, I can't promise you anything.'

Salander laughed hollowly.

'Something funny, Andy?'

'I was just thinking. About those times you came into The Cloisters, and I served you. It's really a great job, tending bar. You have the power to make people happy – their moods just kind of fall into your hands. Not just the booze, it's everything – the listening. I knew you were a cop, someone told me. At first it bothered me. What an ugly world you must live in— I hoped you wouldn't start talking, didn't want to soak up all those negative vibes. But you never did. You just sat there and drank – you and that handsome doctor. Neither of you talked, you just drank in silence, then left. I started feeling sorry for you – no offense. Soaking up those vibes yourself. But I also felt good about helping you – not that you had a problem, but you know what I mean. I was in charge, got those beers and shots delivered right on the money and everyone was happy. And now . . .'

Another laugh. 'I'll be discreet, all right,' said Salander. 'I'm the soul of discretion.'

Outside, I said, 'No imminent danger?'

'Not if he keeps his mouth shut.'

'No grounds for protective custody?'

'That's TV crap – LeMoyne's world. So was my line about Salander being a material witness. The truth is, he and old Justin are free to fly off to Antigua any damn time they please.' He looked back at the Palm Court, cracked his knuckles. 'I always knew it was about money, but Tony Duke's daughter . . . Talk about high-stakes blackmail.'

I watched the traffic on Washington Boulevard, thinking about things Lauren had told me – that her parents hadn't been married when she'd been conceived. That they'd 'brought me up with lies.' The wall of ice between her and Lyle. The remark to Michelle about her mother 'screwing up.'

How early had she sensed something wrong? What had the truth done to her?

Jane had called me in a panic after Lauren had disappeared. Knowing what Lauren was up to, suspecting the five-day absence was more than just another extended weekend. Trying to motivate the police but holding back facts that might've helped. Even after Lauren's death Milo had felt Jane had been less than helpful. I thought back to any hints she might have dropped, came up with only one: 'Lauren's never gotten anything from her father, and maybe that was my fault.'

Guilty – she had to have been tormented. Yet it hadn't led her to finally open up. Worrying about her own safety. Justifiable fear.

And maybe something else: Lies had been the poisonous glue that held this family together.

'The time line fits,' I said. 'Lauren was arrested for prostitution in Reno when she was nineteen, called Lyle for bail money but he turned her down. I always wondered why she phoned him and not Jane, but maybe it was because she still cared what Jane thought. Still, stuck in jail, she might've turned to Jane. And maybe Jane came through. But she didn't give Lauren any of the money she'd collected from Tony Duke because she didn't think Lauren could handle it. Instead, she tried to reconnect with Lauren. It was a slow process – Lauren had been on the streets for three years, was sitting on a lot of anger, and she continued to hook and strip. But Jane persisted, and some kind of bond must've been formed. Because two years later – when Lauren was twenty-one – Jane did give her the money, using the Mel Abbot cover story. You remember how Jane emphasized to us how well Lauren and Mel got along.'

He nodded. 'Mel being a nice guy made it easier for Lauren to believe.'

'Shortly after Lauren received the hundred thousand, she set up her investment account, went back to school, got her GED, enrolled in community college, quit working for Gretchen. Maybe all of that was part of a deal with Jane, or Lauren really wanted to get her life together. Every year after that she invested another fifty-thousand-dollar annual payment.'

Milo said, 'A deal. Give up the life, get rich.' His hand landed on my shoulder, and his eyes took on that sad, sympathetic droop – the look that comes over him when he delivers bad news.

'I know,' I said. 'Lauren continued to freelance. Cash income, most of which she never declared and used for spending money.'

Big tips. Expensive tastes. Rapprochement with her mother or not, Lauren had remained a very angry

481

young woman. About missing out on all those years as Tony Duke's daughter. About the trade-offs she'd made.

What Andy Salander had called every little girl's fantasy had become Lauren's reality – only to twist and abort.

'Maybe it wasn't blackmail,' I said. 'Just Lauren claiming her birthright – stepping forward and upsetting the family applecart.'

'What, someone tied her up and shot her because she wanted emotional validation?' Milo's hand got heavy, then it lifted. His eyes remained sad, and his voice got soft. 'I know you want to believe something good about Lauren, but cold execution and all those other people dying says she tried to use her *birthright* to hit on the old man big-time. A fifty-grand-a-year allowance is one thing, a chunk of Duke Enterprises is another.'

'Maybe I am denying it,' I said. 'But think about it: Blackmail would only have worked if Tony Duke had something to hide, Milo. He sent money to Jane – and by extension to Lauren – for years. If he wanted to eliminate nuisances, why not do it right and have them killed right at the beginning?'

'Because he was dealing with Jane and Jane was reasonable. But once Lauren knew the truth, things got nasty— O impetuous youth. Jane knew what Lauren was capable of. That's why she tried to hold her back from contacting Duke. That's why when Lauren disappeared she suspected something was off. Not that it led her to tell me the truth.'

'Jane tells her who her daddy is, then holds her back,' I said. 'It was manipulative.'

'Or just a screwup. People make mistakes. Salander's right about cheap wine. Jane had been living with the secret for over twenty years. Her inhibitions finally dropped and she ran her mouth. Then she realized what she'd done, tried to get the Furies back in the box.'

'Still,' I said. 'Dr Maccaferri's presence at the estate says Duke's seriously ill. Why would he be worried now about acknowledging Lauren's paternity? On the contrary, wouldn't he want to connect? But there *are* people who'd view Lauren as the *ultimate* threat: a giant slice cut out of the inheritance pie.'

He jammed his hands into his jacket pockets. 'Dugger and his sister.'

'Lauren carried a gun but never used it. My theory was that she knew and trusted the killer. Half sibs would fit that bill. Especially a half sib like Ben Dugger – outwardly such a nice guy. Lauren thought she had him pegged, let down her guard. She thought she was the actress and he was the audience. That delusion cost her.'

A pizza delivery truck sped into the lot, stopped, checked the address, continued toward the front door, and screeched to a halt in a No Parking zone. A kid wearing a blue baseball cap got out toting two flat, white boxes.

Milo said, 'Yo!' and waved him over. The kid stood there, and we jogged to his side. Hispanic, maybe eighteen, with hair cropped to the skin, Aztec features, puzzled black eyes.

'Here you go, friend,' said Milo, peeling off two twenties. 'Room two fifteen, just knock and leave it outside the door. And keep the change.'

'Thanks, man – sir.' The kid sprinted for the hotel, shoved at the door, vanished.

Milo said, 'The Pizza Olympics. Offer enough positive reinforcement and we'd have ourselves a winning team in track and field.' He motioned toward the unmarked, and we started walking across the lot.

I said, 'Lauren probably thought she was after the money, but she was searching for Daddy. Pathetic.'

'I wonder,' he said, 'if Lyle ever suspected Lauren wasn't his kid.'

'Why?'

'Because it's just the thing Lauren might have told him out of spite. His finding out would explain how hostile he was when we notified him. Also why he's eager to pump me about Lauren's will. Not being her blood relative, he knows he's got no legal right to anything she left behind. But with Jane gone, who's gonna argue with him, and under the law his paternity's presumed. The Duke family's sure not gonna protest if he ends up with the money in Lauren's investment account. And even if he does manage to connect Lauren to Duke, he'd keep his mouth shut about it, 'cause that would squash his claim to three hundred grand. To them, that's chump change. To Lyle, it would be the windfall of his life.'

'Lauren did make a crack to Tish Teague about her daughters not being family, so I can see her taunting Lyle. But he told us he and Jane had tried to have other kids, but all they could squeeze out was Lauren, so it was obviously Jane's problem. Still, if Lauren did take a dig at his manhood, it could've led to something else. Lyle's an angry guy who likes to drink and surrounds himself with firearms. He could've just lost it. Gone after Lauren, then Jane. Revenge for the lies. And now he hopes to profit.'

'An alternative scenario,' he muttered. Five steps later: 'Nah, I don't like it. If Jane suspected Lyle had killed Lauren, that's something she would've been happy to spill. And Lyle doesn't connect to Michelle and Lance – he'd have no way to know them. No, the way Lauren was dispatched wasn't a crime of passion. Lyle's just a circling vulture who never gave a shit about Lauren – this girl had some life.'

'Short life,' I said, and my eyes began to hurt.

We reached the car.

'Lauren sitting at her computer,' he said. 'Researching her family tree.'

'Discovering Ben Dugger. Learning about his experiment. She applied to be a paid subject – not for the money, for the connection. Got a confederate job instead, because she was beautiful and poised. Used her looks and her charms to wangle her way into Dugger's confidence. He sweated, got irate, when you pushed him about having a personal relationship with Lauren. Maybe she turned him on sexually, took advantage of that because that was her specialty. But eventually she sprang the truth on him.'

'Guess what, I'm your sister.'

485

I nodded. 'As family reunions went, it was a bust. The money, but maybe also something else. I've always thought Dugger had some kind of sexual hang-up – at the very least he's sexually unconventional. If Lauren aroused him, discovering she was his sister could have ignited some serious incestuous panic. And rage. Toss in Lauren trying to horn in on his inheritance, and she was finished. She couldn't have picked a worse time to surface.'

Big tips. Lauren deluding herself that she was the dancer, knew the steps. But her life had been choreographed for her.

He opened the car door and got in. 'Inheritance makes me wonder about something else, Alex. That story Cheryl Duke told you about the gas leak. What if that was no accident but an attempt to eliminate another couple of slices?'

My throat got tight, and my breath caught. 'Baxter and Sage. The dead dog tipped Cheryl off – she and the kids got lucky. But they also ended up back at the Duke estate. Under the control of the Duke family. It puts a whole new flavor on Kent Irving's remark about Cheryl being a neglectful mother: setting the stage so no one's shocked when the kids fall in the pool or tumble over the cliff or have a grisly mishap on that funicular or drown in the ocean.'

'Cheryl fell asleep on the beach, so she's giving them more to work with.'

'True,' I said. 'She's no genius. And why should she suspect? People without the capacity for evil can't

486

imagine the worst of intentions.'

'People who can't imagine become sweet targets.'

'Those kids.' I pictured high walls, metal gates, closed-circuit TV. Riptides.

He shook his head.

'Oh, Jesus,' I said.

'Look, Alex, these people are bad, but they're not stupid. Bumping off the kids is gonna be messy, period. Doing it so soon after Lauren's death would be foolish – on the chance that anyone ever connects them to Lauren.'

'But there might be some time pressure here. Tony Duke dying, wanting to tie up loose ends before the will's read. Isn't there some way in – just enough to scare them off?'

'What I can do right now is call Ruiz and Gallardo and ask for a look at Jane's finances. If some sort of money link between her and Duke can be verified – if she made copies of those letters she wrote him – that'll go a way toward establishing a motive and justifying another visit to Dr Dugger and hinting around. The risk, of course, is that Dugger and Anita and Brother-in-Law pull up their tents, get rid of evidence, hide behind lawyers, do whatever they have to do.'

'Money and power,' I said. 'Some things never change.'

He started up the car. 'People in their position . . . Why should I lie to you? Getting to them is not going to be easy.'

thirty-four

Robin wasn't home. That bothered me. It also made me feel relieved, and that ate at me further.

She'd left a message on the machine. 'Alex, I'm still tied up with you-know-who. Now his publicist wants me to stick around for some photographs – showing him how to hold the guitar, finger chords accurately . . . Silly stuff, but they're paying by the hour . . . After the photo session, which could be late, we may go out to dinner. A bunch of us – he's got an entourage. Maybe at Rue Faubourg, over on Hillhurst, you can try me there later. Or sooner, here at the studio – we've moved from the manse to Golden Horse Sound, here's the number . . . Be well, Alex.'

I phoned the recording studio, got voice mail, left a message. Was thinking about Baxter and Sage when Robin called back.

'Hi,' I said.

'Hi. Sorry for the long day.' She sounded tired and distant and not the least bit sorry.

'Everything okay?'

'Sure, how about with you?'

'You're not still angry?'

'Why would I be angry?'

'I don't know, maybe I've been a little absent recently.'

'Well,' she said, 'it's not like I'm not used to that.'

'You are angry.'

'No, of course not— Listen, Alex, I really can't talk right now, they're calling me—'

'Ah, stardom,' I said.

'Please,' she said. 'We'll talk later – we need to get away, together. I don't mean dinner and an orgasm. Real time – time away – a vacation, like normal people take. Okay? That fit your schedule?'

'Sure.'

'Are you? Because whatever you've been involved in – that girl – has taken you to another galaxy.'

'I always have time for you,' I said.

Silence. 'Look, I won't go to dinner with the gang. They make a big deal about it – Elvis and his hangers-on. Like summer camp, everyone does everything together. But I'm not part of it, I don't need to participate.'

'No,' I said. 'Finish up, do what you need to do.'

'And leave you all alone? I know you need solitude, but I think I've been giving you too much – that's what I'm trying to get across. Both of us have let things slip.'

'It's me,' I said. 'You've been fine.'

'Fine,' she said. 'Damning with faint praise?'

'Come on, Robin—'

'Sorry, I guess I am . . . feeling a little displaced.'

'Finish up and come home, and then we'll fake out being normal and plan a vacation. Name the place.'

'Anywhere but here, Alex. There's nothing going on that a little mellowing out won't cure, right?'

'Nothing,' I said. 'Everything will work out.'

I waited until well after Robin's phone call – until the sound of her voice, the tone, and the content had finally stopped resonating – before pulling the scrap of paper out of my wallet.

Nine-fifteen P.M. My office windows were black, and I'd been imagining a black ocean, small faces bobbing in the waves, sucked down, the circling of sharks, a mother's endless wail.

Cheryl Duke answered on the fifth ring. 'Oh. Hi.'

'Hi.'

'Wow. You called.'

'You sound surprised,' I said.

'Well . . . you never know.'

'Oh,' I said, 'I don't think you get ignored too often.'

'No,' she said, merrily. 'Not too often. So . . . ?'

'I was thinking maybe we could get together.'

'Were you? Hmm. Well, what did you have in mind?'

'It's a little late for dinner, but I could handle that if you haven't eaten. Or maybe drinks?'

'I've eaten.' Giggles. 'You've been thinking about food and drink, huh?'

'It's a start.'

I've been thinking about your babies murdered. About finding some way to warn you.

491

'Got to start somewhere,' she said. 'Where and when were you thinking?'

'I'm open.'

'Open-minded, too?'

'I like to think so.'

'Bet you do . . . Hmm, I just got the kids down . . . How about in half an hour?'

'Where?'

Another giggle. 'Just like that, huh? Johnny on the Spot Agreeable?'

'When I'm motivated.'

'I'll bet,' she said. 'Well . . . how about no drinks, just some intelligent conversation?'

'Sure. That's fine.'

'*Just* conversation. At least for now.'

'Absolutely.'

'Mr Agreeable.'

'I try,' I said.

'Try and you'll succeed . . . Um, I can't go too far – the kids.'

'How about the same place – the Country Mart?'

'No,' she said. 'Too public. Meet me up the beach from where I am, down by the old Paradise Cove pier. Down where the Sand Dollar used to be – where you got your kayak. It's quiet there, nice and private. Pretty, too. I go down there by myself, sometimes, just to look at the ocean.'

'Okay,' I said. 'But there's a gate arm down by the old guard shack.'

'Park along the side of the road and walk the rest of

the way down. That's what I do. You'll see my Expedition pulled to the side and know I'm there. If I'm not, it means something came up – one of the kids woke up, whatever. But I'll do my best.'

'Great. Looking forward to it.'

'Me too, Alex.'

At night the drive was an easy glide, and I pulled off PCH onto the Paradise Cove turnoff at 9:55. I navigated the speed bumps and drove slowly, searching for Cheryl's Expedition. No sign of the SUV as the gate arm came into view, and I pulled to the left, parked, sat for a while, tried to figure out how I'd transform what she thought was a date into the scariest conversation she'd ever had.

A date. I hoped I'd get back before Robin got home. If I didn't, I'd just say I'd been driving.

I remained in the Seville awhile longer, coming up with no easy script, wondering if Cheryl would actually show and, if not, would that be enough for me to drop the whole thing and leave town with Robin . . . be normal.

I got out of the car, descended toward the construction site on foot, using a tentative quarter moon as my compass. Reached bottom, dodged nails and planks and shingles and boards.

Chilly night, purplish black sky freckled by starlight, the water below inky, identically blemished. Off to the south the remains of the Paradise Cove pier listed like a drunk, pilings angled dangerously toward the ocean.

Someone had peeled back the chain link that blocked access, and for a moment I wondered if I was alone. But when I stopped I saw no movement other than the breeze-nudged boughs of sycamores, heard nothing but the tide.

I walked around aimlessly, no more insightful than when I'd arrived. A husky engine hum filtered down from the road. Then a car door slamming. Footsteps. Rapid footsteps.

Cheryl Duke's hourglass shape appeared seconds later, descending the slope smoothly. Making herself easy to spot in a tight, pale cardigan, white T-shirt, and white jeans. Swinging her arms, purposeful but relaxed. Lithe.

I said, 'Over here,' and headed toward her.

She looked at me, waved.

When I reached her she was smiling. The cardigan was pink cashmere, cropped above her firm waistline, straining at the chest. 'I dressed so you could see me.'

'Oh, I saw you all right.'

She laughed, threw her arms around my neck, kissed me full on the lips. Her tongue pressed its way through my teeth, licked my palate, filled my throat, retreated. She threw back her head, laughing. Wiggling the tongue – huge and pointed – curling the tip upward and tickling the bottom of her nose.

'See,' she said, 'size matters all kinds of ways.' One hand cupped the back of my head as sharp little teeth nibbled at my chin, and I thought of her son biting down on my ear. A family of carnivores. My arms were at my sides and she grabbed my hands and planted them on her rear. Her breasts asserted themselves against my chest, obstructive, unyielding. Her pelvis rotated against mine; then the palms of her hands replaced the breasts as she shoved me away.

'That's all you get, for now.' Her hair was loose, full, bleached white by the moon, and she turned tossing it into a production.

'Shucks,' I said, still feeling her tongue in my gullet.

'Aw,' she said. 'Poor baby.' Another soft shove. 'Why should I let you fuck me? We barely know each other.'

'A guy can hope.'

Laughing, she took my hand as she led me back toward the construction mess.

'Where're we off to?' I said.

She pointed to the remnants of the pier. 'I love it up there – the way it just goes off into nowhere.'

'Eternity.'

'Yeah.'

As we neared the peeled-back fence, I said, 'Is it safe?'

More laughter. 'Who knows?' She pulled me onto the broken promenade, let go of my hand, and began skipping along the warped boards. I felt the wood beneath my feet hum in response. My toe caught on a splintered shank, and I almost lost my balance. Cheryl was well ahead of me, dancing across planks separated enough for black water to shine through. I watched her pick up speed, break into a run toward the pier's shattered end, as if building momentum for a high dive.

She stopped short, inches from the edge, shoulders

thrown back, hair wild, hands set on the arc of flesh that curved above the waistline of her jeans. I caught up just as she crossed her arms and pulled off her sweater and her T-shirt, flung both garments aside. The manufactured breasts bobbled like saddlebags as laughter shook her upper body, nipples big and erect and aimed skyward like the heat-seeking weapons they were.

She edged backward, so that the heels of her running shoes tipped over the pier's terminus. Vertigo clamped around my gut as she began bouncing lightly, and I backed away.

'Aw,' she said, 'c'mon. It's a great feeling.'

'I'll take your word for it.'

'Flying's not your thing?'

'Not tonight.'

She bounced some more, spread her arms. 'Probably not any night. What if not doing it means I don't fuck you?'

'Like I said before. Aw shucks.'

Louder giggles, but shaky, tinged with hurt.

She began sidestepping along the edge. Breathing fast, she spoke again, her voice constricted. 'Pretty cool, huh? I could always balance.'

'Impressive.'

'I can swallow swords, too.'

'Spent some time with the circus?'

'Something like that.' She reached the far end, side-stepped her way back, stood on one foot, arched the other behind her, into space. I watched and didn't say a word and wondered how I'd ever get across the concept of danger. She began humming tunelessly. Closed her eyes. Walked several steps, blind.

Humming but not without fear. Starlit streams of sweat ran from her armpits and coursed the swell of her chest. She began gasping for breath but kept going.

Finally – without warning – she stepped away from the void and shouted 'Yes!' at the sky. Massaged her breasts and shouted again. Then she sat down on the misshapen planks, drew her knees to her chin, lowered her head.

'You okay?' I said.

'I'm great— C'mere.'

I stepped closer, and she pulled me down beside her. 'You're a wimp, but you're cute.' Nuzzling my neck, she leaned her head on my shoulder. 'We could do it right here. If I was into doing it.' She grabbed my hair, tugged gently, then harder. 'The picture in my mind is we're back there.' Hooking a thumb at the edge. 'You on bottom, me on top, with your head hanging over the side, and you're looking up at me, deep *inside* me, your balls knocking against my ass, so into how I'm making you feel that you wouldn't care even if you *did* fall over – how does that sound?'

'I'm open to new experiences, but—'

'You're saying no?'

'I'm saying I'd rather live a few more years.'

'Wimp,' she said, airily. 'You'd turn down something like that 'cause of a little danger?' Patting me on the head with smiling contempt, she stood, bent low, swung her breasts toward my mouth, then curved away.

'Too bad, little man. I need dedication,' she said in a

hard voice. 'Had enough of wimps and losers—'

I got up on my feet. 'Tony Duke's a wimp?'

Smiling, she came toward me. Reached out a hand and stroked my hair again. Polished nails spit back starlight. Touching the tip of my chin, she reared back and slapped me hard across the mouth. My head rocked, and my teeth buzzed as if I'd sucked current from a live wire.

'You don't know me, don't make like you do.'

My lip throbbed. When I touched it, my fingers came away wet.

'You ruined the mood,' she said.

'By not hanging over the edge.'

'Aw,' she said. 'You really are a wimp – your loss.' She patted her crotch. 'What I've got here could snap you like a turtle and drain you like a pump.'

Practiced patter. Hooker talk.

Had she freelanced, just like Lauren? Between skating and dancing, or had it been her main gig before meeting Ben Dugger and Tony Duke?

She wiggled back into her shirt and sweater, spread her legs – not enticingly, a combat stance – and shot me the finger. 'He thinks he's so smart.'

Putting me in the third person. The grammar was more than symbolic, and I knew more was wrong than my failure to meet her sexual demands.

An audience. Before I could put the threat in place, figure out what to do, a man emerged from the shadows at the other end of the pier. Approached us.

Cheryl turned her back and walked toward him. He

was barely visible because, unlike her, he'd dressed for concealment.

Black sweatsuit, black shoes. He and Cheryl met in the center of the pier. Everything rehearsed – I'd been the only one ad-libbing.

'He thinks he's smart,' said Cheryl.

Kent Irving said nothing. His brassy hair had been tied back in a ponytail, emphasizing the breadth of his round, ruddy face. Impassive face. Something silvery and reflective in his right hand.

Cheryl flashed teeth and tucked her white T-shirt tight.

'Baby,' she said.

Irving's one-lipped mouth stayed shut.

'It's good you came when you did, baby,' she told him. 'He was ready to fuck me blind, would've raped me and tossed me over the edge.'

She kissed his ear. Irving still didn't react. He stepped closer. I had nowhere to go but into eternity, but I stepped backward anyway. The automatic in his hand was level with my face.

'He thinks we're stupid, baby,' said Cheryl. 'Thinks he can just *happen* to be boating by, just *happen* to be sitting there doing his crossword puzzle like it's some big fucking coincidence and we're not gonna suspect anything. Asshole.'

I said, 'Suspicion's a two-way street. The police know I'm here.'

She said, 'Right.' Irving remained silent and still. How far was the drop? How high was the tide? Would I hit water or slam into hard-packed sand, collapsing my spine like a twig? If I could calculate the drop in the darkness, would rolling on my side help, allow me to escape with only crushed ribs, internal injuries? I hadn't consulted a tide chart, had no reason to, terrific planning—

Kent Irving walked some more, and I stood my ground. The barrel of the gun was ten feet away. Chromium lips and a tiny black mouth that said, 'Oh.'

Cheryl stayed behind Irving, yammering, showing all those teeth, tossing her goddamned hair—

'Enough,' Irving told her, in that thin, high voice.

She pouted. 'Sure, baby – you saved me, baby. He was an animal, would've rammed me without mercy, just used me and threw me away.' She placed a hand on his meaty shoulder.

'Yeah,' he said.

'Yeah, baby, so you saved me. You're gonna be happy you did.'

'You really think it's happy days?' I said. 'The police really do know I'm here. Meeting *you*, Cheryl. He can't afford that. You're expendable – just like Baxter and Sage—'

'Enough,' Irving said, softly. Same word he'd used with Cheryl. The lack of inflection said it all.

No sweat, no strain. Eyes as animated as gravel. Business as usual.

Maybe he'd hired someone to shoot Lauren and Michelle and Lance and Jane, but if he had, it had been out of convenience, not apprehension. He could pull that trigger like brushing his teeth. Eat breakfast moments later without giving it a second thought.

I said, 'You know I'm right, Kent. You can't chance her talking to the police. Sooner or later, she's got to go anyway. She's stupid and nuts and undependable. Actually thinks you'll leave Anita for her and the two of you will end up with all of Tony's money and live happily ever after, the Prince and Princess. You know better. She's no princess, you've had dozens like her. Just another stupid hooker with plastic tits—'

Cheryl charged toward me, but Irving blocked her with his free arm.

'Fuck you!' she shrieked. 'Fuck you in hell— Don't let him talk to me like that, baby. He can't dis me like that – don't fucking *let* him!'

Pushing against Irving's arm. He closed his hand on her wrist. The gun arm had never wavered. If he'd blinked I hadn't seen it. Giving him a polygraph would be academically interesting.

Cheryl said, 'Give me the gun and let *me* do him— I can do it, you know I can. I'll do it right now, just like I did her, come on.'

'Her,' I said. 'Lauren or Michelle or Jane or Shawna?'

The last name caused Irving's eyes to wander for the tiniest fragment of a second. Uncertainty. Lack of familiarity.

'Bitch Lauren,' said Cheryl, smugly. She spat on the pier. '*Cunt* Lauren. She thought she could be my friend. Thought we had *rapport*, that I was just like her—'

'She had a point,' I said. 'You both sold sex—'

'*Fuck you!*'

'Quiet,' said Irving. His hand was still clamped to her wrist. Something he did made her say, 'Ouch.'

Then: 'Baby?'

'Hurts so good?' I said. 'What a fun couple. So how'd you lure Lauren?'

'Art,' said Cheryl, making it sound like a disease. 'She thought she was so cool – we made a date to meet at the art museum and then—'

A twist of Irving's wrist shut her mouth. 'Easy,' he soothed.

'He's the boss, got you to set up Lauren, then do her,' I said. 'With a woman she'd let down her guard – two girls and pretty pictures. She'd already told you her secret— Tell me, did you watch while he hog-tied her? Did you help him toss her in the trash?'

'It was great—'

Irving rotated his hand again, and she cried out.

I said, 'You're toast, Cheryl. Maybe it won't happen tonight, but don't make any long-term investments. Even if you weren't stupid and unpredictable, you wouldn't figure into his plans, because your kids are a problem. Think about that gas leak— What's the next installment, Kent? Tossing Baxter over the cliff? Then Sage happens to toddle over to the pool? Or maybe you'll just disappear them in the ocean.'

Irving smiled. Cheryl never saw it, but his silence made her eyes go wide and scared.

'Maybe I will let you do him,' he told her.

'Creative,' I said. 'Her prints get on the gun, then a

bullet finds its way into *her* head – murder-suicide, lovers' quarrel out on the pier. You're an old hand at that kind of thing – took Lauren's gun out of her purse after Cheryl shot her and used it a week later on Jane Abbot. Setting the old man up. How'd you get Lauren alone for the kill, Cheryl?'

'Girl talk, asshole—'

'Shh,' said Irving. 'No more dialogue— Yeah, I will let you do him.'

'Lots of bodies piling up,' I said. 'At least it's not one of those senseless crime sprees. You've got a definite goal in mind. Tony'll be dead soon, and what he leaves behind is sure worth working for. You're doing Ben and Anita's dirty work, and maybe they'll even let you stick around to enjoy the windfall. But you never know – the rich can get funny with hired help.'

Irving didn't move.

Cheryl said, 'Baby?' very softly. 'You do love them, right? Bax and Sage?'

'Sure,' said Irving.

'He's capable of love like you're qualified to be a nuclear physicist,' I said. 'He'll love them as two cute little corpses. No way will they make it to first grade. *Baby.* You sure are a great mom. *Baby.*'

Cheryl raised clenched fists. *'Shut up! Gimme it, let me do him now!'*

Irving didn't budge.

'Ke-ent!' she whined.

'Okay, c'mere,' said Irving.

He removed his hand from her wrist, and as she

stepped forward lowered his arm and circled her waist. Keeping the gun trained on me. Reaching around, he squeezed her breast. Pinched her nipple.

'Umm,' she said.

He pinched her again.

'Ow, that was too hard!'

'Sorry,' said Irving. Cradling her chin, he kissed the tip of her nose. Shoved her hard.

As she staggered backward, he moved fast. Staring at me as he swung the gun around. He shot her twice in the face, stepping back to avoid the blood spray. By the time she hit the boards, the gun was back on me.

She landed on her side.

'Thanks,' he told me. 'You gave me a good idea. Yeah, I had plans for her, but this is even better.'

'Happy to oblige,' I said. 'But maybe she wasn't the only one with delusions. Think about what I said: Will Anita and Ben really be happy sharing? Spoiled rich kids aren't big on gratitude.'

He shrugged. Blood streamed from under Cheryl's head, oil black in the starlight, and he inched away from the welling pool.

'Doesn't matter, does it?' I said, not looking at the body. 'You've got plans for them too. Really think you're going to walk away with everything.'

He snorted, sighed. 'Let's get this over with.'

'I wasn't lying about the police,' I said. 'You're a prime suspect. They know about your garment biz days, meeting Lauren back when she worked the Mart. Must've been a shock when she showed up at the estate with Ben – good old Ben screwing up again, picking up another dumb blonde. He's got a thing for them, doesn't he? Uses his experiments to find them and to hit on them, but once he gets them, the poor schmuck doesn't know what to do with them. Cheryl, Lauren, Shawna Yeager – what happened to her? How did she get in the way?'

That same flicker of confusion in his dead eyes. Cheryl's blood kept spreading closer to his shoes, and he sidled away, again. Despite myself I looked at her. Life juice leaking from the mop of blond hair, dipping to a low spot between the boards, trickling through. They say sharks can smell a drop in millions of gallons. Was the shark Internet buzzing?

Irving raised the automatic.

'Another blonde,' I said. 'But Lauren wasn't dumb. Anything but. She was a double threat – knew you from the bad old days, the hooker-a-night days. Knew stuff you strongly preferred Anita didn't find out about. And on top of that, she tells you who she *is* – what she *wants*. Talk about insult and injury.'

Irving sighed again. The sweats made him look pudgy. His ponytail made him look like nothing but Mr Midlife Crisis, and as he aimed the gun at my face, a sick, sour thought flashed in my head: *So this is how it happens, a clown like this.* Then: *Sorry, Robin.*

Then a voice behind Irving shouted, 'Kent? What're you doing? What's going on?' and Irving blinked and turned as footfalls twanged the pier.

A man running toward us. Irving moving reflexively,

the gun arm wavering, realizing his error and pivoting back toward me, but I'd already thrown myself at him and was grabbing for the automatic.

Managing only to jar his elbow.

He fired up in the air.

The new voice said, 'Oh, my God!' and Irving slashed out at me and I chopped at him, keeping myself close, fighting for the weapon. A new set of hands grabbed for Irving. Irving, growling now, fired again.

The new voice said, 'Oh!' and went down, but Irving had been thrown off balance, and I brought my knee up hard into his groin and, as he doubled over, stabbed at his eyes with my fingertips.

I made contact with something soft, and he screamed and stumbled and I shoved him, kept shoving him, down to the planks, got on top, straddled him, kept hitting him. It had been a while since I'd messed with karate, and what I did to him was more blind rage than martial arts, chopping at his head and his neck over and over and over, using stiff fingers and frozen fists, bloodying my knuckles, slashing and slamming until well after he'd stopped moving.

The gun had landed several feet from his arm. I picked it up, aimed it at Irving.

He didn't move. His face was pulp.

A few feet away, Ben Dugger moaned. I went to see how he was doing.

thirty-five

'**W**rong,' I said. 'By light-years.'

Dugger smiled. 'About what?'

'About you. About lots of things.'

It was eleven A.M., three days after I'd watched Cheryl Duke die.

During that time Robin had left one message on the machine. *Sorry I missed you. I'll try to call again . . .* No home number was listed for her friend Debby and when I tried Debby's dental office, I got voice mail informing me the doctor was out for a week.

For three days my life had been stagnating, but Ben Dugger had traveled: from the ambulance I'd called, to the ER at St John's, to three and a half hours of surgery – tying together blood vessels in his thigh – to recovery, then two nights in a private room at the hospital.

Now this place, bright yellow and vast and dim, the air sweet with cinnamon and antiseptic, lots of inlaid French furniture – everything ornate and antique except the bed, which was all function and much too small for the room, the IV stand, the bank of medical gizmos.

The room was on the third floor of his father's mansion. Doting nurses hovered round the clock, but he seemed mostly to want to rest.

I'd phoned yesterday to request permission, waited half a day for the call back from a woman who identified herself as Tony Duke's personal assistant's assistant, had been allowed through the copper gates an hour ago.

I'd driven up, sat scrutinized as the closed-circuit camera rotated for several minutes, then the tentacles parted and a mountainous bouncer type in a fudge brown suit stepped out and showed me where to park. When I exited the car he was there. Escorted me through a fern grove and a pine forest to the peach-colored, blue-roofed house. Stayed with me as we entered the building, exerting the merest pressure at my elbow, propelling me across an acre of black granite iced by two tons of Baccarat chandelier hanging three stories above, the entry hall commodious enough for a presidential convention. Flemish paintings, carved, gilded baseboards and moldings, blue velvet walls, the elevator cut so seamlessly into the plush fabric that I could've walked past it.

Finally, this room, with its canary-colored damask walls. Bad color for recuperation. Dugger looked jaundiced.

He coughed.

I said, 'Need anything?'

Smiling again, he shook his head. Pillows surrounded him, a percale halo. His thin hair was plastered across his brow, and beneath the sallowness his skin tone was dirty snow. The IV taped to his arm dripped, and the instruments monitoring his vitals blinked and bleeped and graphed his mortality. The ceiling above him was a trompe l'oeil grape arbor painted in garish hues. Silly in any context, but especially so now. If not for the way I felt, I might've smiled.

'Anyway,' I said. 'I just wanted to—'

'Whatever you think you did, you made up for it.' He pointed shakily at his bandaged leg. Irving's stray bullet had passed through his thigh, nicked his femoral artery. I'd tied back the wound, stanched as much of the bleeding as I could, used the cell phone in the pocket of Irving's sweatpants to call 911.

'Not even close to a tie,' I said. 'If you hadn't shown up—'

'Hey, it's a soft science,' he said. 'Psychology. We study, we guess, sometimes we're right, other times . . .' Weak smile.

The door opened, and Dr Rene Maccaferri marched in. Those same appraising eyes. White lab coat over black turtleneck and slacks, pointy little lizardskin shoes on too-small feet. He looked like a goombah playing doctor, and I told myself I could be forgiven my theories.

Mr Wrong.

Maccaferri ignored me, checked the monitors, approached Dugger's bedside. 'They taking good care of you?'

'Too good, Rene.'

'What's too good?'

'I'm not used to it.'

'Try,' Maccaferri told him. 'I talked to the vascular surgeon. He'll be over today to look you over, monitor you for infection, make sure no thromboses. You look good to me, but better to make sure.'

'Whatever you say, Rene. How's Dad?'

Maccaferri's thick, black, fuzzy-caterpillar brows knitted, and he glanced at me.

'It's okay, Rene.'

'Daddy is about the same,' said the doctor, turning to leave.

'Okay, Rene. Thanks. As always.'

Maccaferri stopped at the door. 'There's always, and there's always.'

Dugger's eyes went moist.

When the door closed I said, 'I'm sorry to add to your burden.'

Both of us knew what I meant: Life had thrown him a double dose of grief. Anticipation of the loss to come, pining for the sister he'd never really gotten to know.

Meeting her, losing her.

He turned his head to the side and fought back tears. 'I know the road to hell's paved with good intentions, but I'm one of those people who still takes intention into account. Whatever you did, it was because you cared about Lauren— My throat's a little dry, could you please hand me that 7UP?'

I poured soda into a paper cup, held it to his lips.

He drank. 'Thanks— How long did you actually treat her? Tell me about that – tell me anything you can.'

He'd shared his story. I had no option but to

reciprocate. I recited, speaking automatically, while another lobe of my brain remembered.

The anxiety in his eyes when Milo had questioned him about Lauren. What I'd taken for guilt had been pain – a solitary ache.

Lauren and I agreed to do it the right way, not just spring it on everyone. There was Anita to think about – Dad's illness has plunged her lower than I've ever seen her, and she doesn't do well with change. And Dad, himself. I was concerned about the impact. So was Lauren, she wanted whatever happened to go smoothly or not at all. She said Dad knew about her – years ago, when Lauren's mother wrote to him, he called, wanted to meet Lauren, but her mother put it off, said Lauren had emotional problems, she wasn't ready. Dad tried a couple more times, then Dad backed off. That was just like him – make his offer, then not push. Maybe it's a character flaw – emotional laziness, I don't know. Sometimes, growing up, I felt Dad was too laid-back – as if he didn't care. But on balance it was better than his trying to dominate Anita and me . . . In Lauren's case, maybe if he would've pushed . . . How can you second-guess? By the time Lauren did build up the courage to meet me and tell me who she was, Dad was sick and weak. I was worried about the shock. Maybe I— What's the use . . . ? Right from the beginning Lauren and I got along so well – clicked, as if we'd known each other our whole lives. And – this is going to sound childish – we had fun. Imagining what things would be like once we . . . Our little experiment, we called it – figuring out a way of integrating Lauren into the family.

I said, *The phone booth.*

He nodded, winced. Moved his leg and his breath caught. *That was part of our . . . arrangement. When we built up the courage to bring Lauren to Dad's house. She'd call me at Point Dume, and if it was okay – relatively quiet at the house – I'd pick her up. I told people she was my friend – childish, I know. I think we both liked the cloak-and-dagger aspect. I would have so liked to know her better – longer . . . My little sister.*

At that point he'd broken down and sobbed, and I'd turned away, feeling low and intrusive, until his voice drew me back.

Don't worry, I've had enough therapy not to be ashamed of my feelings. I guess what I want you to know is that Lauren had value *to me – dammit, she* deserves *to be cried over. Maybe that's what bothers me the most. There's no one left to cry for her but me. That time you and Sturgis showed up at my apartment and told me what happened to her – it was as if my entire world was imploding. I'm not the most spontaneous person, but, right then, I could've just . . . gone mad. Of course, I didn't. Too controlled . . . too much at risk . . . The thing about Lauren was that she made me feel like a kid – something I rarely felt when I actually* was *a kid. The two of us were planning and scheming, laughing about what we had in common. Our differences – she'd find something we just couldn't see eye to eye on and laugh and say, 'So much for chromosomes.' That kind of thing— No one knew. Not Anita or the women at the office, no one. At least I thought so . . . Then I started seeing things. Looks passing between Kent and Cheryl, and Lauren would be going off with Cheryl talking. When I asked her about it, she just said Cheryl was nice but*

512

*not too bright. I never liked Kent, but never did I imagine –
how can you imagine things like that? . . . Poor Anita –
outwardly she's tough, but it's an act. She's always been frail,
has irritable bowel syndrome, asthma, migraines – most of her
childhood was spent in doctors' offices . . . Kent was . . .
vulgar, but how could I know? . . . I keep asking myself that
– Lauren going off with Cheryl, more and more – was there
some way to know?*

No, I'd told him. *No one knew.*

He asked for more 7UP, drank, sank back against the
pillows, closed his eyes.

A controlled man. A kind man. Delivering toys to a
church, with no ulterior motive. Donating fifteen percent
of his trust fund, every year, to charity.

No one had a bad word to say about him because
there was nothing bad to say.

I'd persisted in thinking of him as a warped killer.

Sometimes a cigar is just a cigar.

I supposed I'd saved his life, but given all that and the
bullet he'd taken for me, it seemed a feeble twist of
reciprocity.

He'd been charitable enough to grant me another false
equality: sharing Lauren. As if my stint as a failed
therapist could come close to the bond he'd shared with
her. Only to have it ripped from him.

A nice guy. In another place, another time, I wouldn't
have minded shooting the breeze with him. Talking
about psychology, learning what it had been like growing
up Tony Duke's son.

But I had nothing more to offer him, and what he'd been through – what Lauren had been through – would stay with me for a long, long time.

So would the loose ends.

Anita. Baxter and Sage.

And now I had my own problems to deal with.

As I rang for his nurse, I knew that most likely I'd never see him or anyone else in the Duke family again, and that would be just fine.

thirty-six

The nurse called for someone to see me out, and another big man showed up, a lobster pink blond with a shaved head wearing a lime green suit over a black T-shirt. I gave Dugger a small salute and walked out of the yellow room.

'Nice day, sir,' said my escort, using the same elbow steer to guide me through the black walnut hallway. Gilded niches were filled with statuary, urns brimmed with flowers, monogrammed *D*s punctuated the blue-and-gold carpeting at twenty-foot intervals.

On the way to the elevator we passed a room whose double doors had been shut when I'd arrived. Now they were spread open, and I caught a glimpse of a ballroom-sized space with zebra-striped walls.

Another hospital bed, the stoic Dr Maccaferri standing by the headboard, drawing blood through a syringe that he'd jabbed into an IV line.

Another too-small bed. A tiny, bald head barely visible above blue satin covers. Wizened, elfin. Sleeping or approximating slumber. Gaping mouth, toothless. Motionless.

The pressure on my elbow intensified. Mr Nice Day said, 'Please keep moving, sir.'

I drove home, knowing the house would be empty.

After that night on the pier, I'd spent hours at St John's Hospital. Had phoned home twice, gotten the machine. Returned just after two A.M. to find Robin wide awake, in the bedroom, packing a suitcase.

When I tried to hold her, she said, 'No.'

'Early vacation?' I said. Everything was wrong, and I was talking gibberish.

'By myself,' she said.

'Honey—'

She threw clothing into the valise. 'I got home at ten, was worried sick until you just happened to call at midnight.'

'Honey, I—'

'Alex, I just can't take this anymore. Need time to settle myself down.'

'We both do,' I said, touching her hair. 'Let's stick with the original plan and get away together. I promise—'

'Maybe in a few days,' she said, suddenly crying. 'You don't know the pictures that filled my head. You . . . again. Then Milo told me what happened – what were you *thinking*? A *date* with a *bimbo*? Another undercover adventure that nearly got you *killed*!'

'Not an adventure. Anything but. I was trying to

help . . . some kids. The last thing I thought would happen was—'

'You can help kids by doing what you were trained for. Sit and talk to them—'

'That's how this started, Robin.' Unable to keep my voice steady. 'Lauren was a patient. It just got . . .'

'Out of control? That's the point. When you've involved, things tend to . . . expand. It's like you're a magnet for ugliness. You know me, I'm a structured person – I work with wood and metal and machines, things that can be measured. I'm not saying that's ideal, or the only way. Maybe it means there's something wrong with *my* psyche. But there's something in between. Alex, the uncertainty you keep putting me through – every time you step out the door, not knowing if you'll come back.'

'I always come back.' I reached for her again, but she shook her head and said, 'Let me go.'

'I'm sorry, let's talk about it—'

She shook her head. 'I need . . . perspective. Then maybe we'll talk.'

'Where are you going?'

'San Diego – my friend Debby.'

'The dentist.'

'The dentist,' she said. 'She and I used to have fun together. I used to have *friends*. Now all I've got is you and Spike and my work. I need to expand.'

'Me too,' I said. 'I'll take up a hobby – golf.'

'Sure,' she said, smiling in spite of herself. 'That'll be the day.'

'What – impossible?'

'If there was something less likely than impossible, you and golf would be it. Alex, I'm not trying to tame you. I want you healthy – that's the point. You standing around on the links in funny shoes, all that dead time, is not a prescription for well-being. Let's not prolong this. I'll call you.'

Latching the suitcase, she headed for the door. 'Spike's in the truck. I'm sure you won't mind that.'

'Not only am I abandoned, it's for another man.'

She kissed me hard on the lips, turned the doorknob, said, 'Take care.'

'When will you call?'

'Soon. A couple of days.' Short, hard laugh.

'What?' I said.

'I was just about to say, "Be careful, baby." Like I always do when we're about to go our separate ways. Rotten habit. I shouldn't have to say that.'

thirty-seven

The first day she was gone, I was miserable, and the next one was shaping up the same way when Milo dropped by at nine A.M. and showed me Jane Abbot's correspondence with Tony Duke.

'She kept copies,' he said. 'In her safe-deposit box. On the bottom, under some stock certificates.'

Two letters. In the first Jane reminded Duke of their time in Hawaii and informed him he had a daughter. A penciled notation on the bottom was dated five days later:

TD called, 3 pm, no prob with $, wants to meet L.
I said probs, maybe later.

In the second Jane thanked Duke for his quick response, apologized for restricting him from Lauren, describing her as 'a very bright young lady, but unfortunately – through no fault of yours, dear Tony – she is currently emotionally ill and highly troubled.'

TD called 3X, says he knows doctors. Put him off.

519

*Lauren gone, again, no idea where. Next time, bail
or not?*

A final page in Jane's handwriting laid out the financial
agreement. Fifty thousand dollars a year placed in trust
for Lauren, to be supervised by Jane, with the understanding that Jane would do everything in her power to
effect a reunion and that, by the time Lauren reached
twenty-six, Duke would get to meet her.

Father and daughter had fallen short by six months.

I gave him back the papers. 'What's the status on Mel
Abbot?'

'He should be released soon, though no one's sure
where to put him. The closest relative they can find is a
cousin in New Jersey, almost as old as Mel. Meanwhile,
Irving's right down the hall from Abbot, in the jail ward
– you did good work on his face. The DA will file
multiple counts of conspiracy and first-degree homicide
with special circumstances for mass murder, cruelty, and
profit motive. Gretchen's helping them put the case
together in order to plea down her own conspiracy rap—
The feds finally came through and verified that Irving
had been one of her big-time clients. All we've got on her
is her pal Ingrid knowing I was looking for Michelle and
Gretchen entering the Duke estate the next day.'

'Gretchen works the system again,' I said.

'What the DA wants is Irving on a platter, and
Gretchen can fill in the blanks. She can also supply the
motive for Michelle – no, there wasn't any blackmail, no
one's sure Michelle even knew anything dangerous. But

Irving thought she did – to be brutally honest, my mentioning Michelle's name to Gretchen signed her death warrant – and no, I'm not blaming myself, I was doing my job. It's just the way things happen sometimes.'

He rubbed his face. 'And Gretchen's still claiming she's never heard of Shawna. I'd like to say I've been right about Shawna not being part of this, but at this point I don't know what's real and what isn't. For all I know Irving took pictures of her, boffed her, killed her.'

'Gretchen set up Michelle and Lance and she walks.'

'Maybe she'll get hers one day . . . I also found out that Irving's rag biz went under because of "financial irregularities" – he left behind an army of creditors, and that beach construction project is leveraged to the hilt. Plenty of claws being sharpened— He ain't gonna find too many character witnesses.'

'What about Anita?'

'So far, she doesn't appear to be dirty,' he said. 'When I saw her she looked worse than Dugger – some kind of intestinal problems; she actually threw up four times during a one-hour interview. She seems genuinely shocked by what her husband and Cheryl were up to – we're talking emotionally shattered. Even my jaded detective ears ain't ringing. As I was leaving the mafioso doc was putting her on tranqs . . . What else— Oh, yeah, Charming Lyle the Model Father finally showed up. Looks likes he really was hunting. Rangers picked him up for shooting a doe out of season, caught him skinning it by the side of his truck. Big-time fine, and they sent him back home, bitching all the way. Asshole actually

called me up again yesterday, wanting to know if I'd
learned anything about Lauren's will.'

'What'd you tell him?'

'Well,' he said. 'I controlled myself, didn't allow myself
free expression of pent-up emotions.'

He ambled to the fridge, stuck his head in, emerged
empty-handed, walked over to the window and played
with a houseplant.

'What I told him is Lauren died poor. Which is the
truth, right?'

thirty-eight

By the third day Robin still hadn't called, and I tried to drag myself out of inertial sludge into a walking depression.

Finding Agnes Yeager was easy.

Olivia Brickerman, LCSW, a friend and former mentor at Western Pediatrics, now a professor of social work at the gracious old school crosstown, had full command of the Medi-Cal and private insurance data banks, and it took thirty seconds for her to pull up the name.

'The age of privacy,' she said. 'Always wear clean underwear. Yeager, Agnes Mavis, DOB fifty-one years ago ... Looks like she did some time at County Gen ... From the billing codes, endocrinology, cardiology, some lung workups ... a psych consult – short-term consult, four sessions. After that she was transferred to the rehab unit at Casa de los Amigos for a month, then discharged to an aftercare facility in San Bernardino – SweetHaven. Sounds like something from a kiddie book. That's the last thing I've got. Last billing was thirteen months ago.' She read off the convalescent home's phone number. 'So how's Gorgeous Robin?'

'Terrific.'

'And you?'

'The same.'

'Yeah?'

'What, I don't sound terrific?'

'The doctor gets defensive,' she said, cheerfully. 'You're forgetting, boychik, that before I became a big-shot academic I did what you do. And right now my third ear is telling me you're not smiling.'

'Okay, now I am,' I said. Actually forcing my lips into position. 'How's that?'

'Meat but no motion, boychik – you're sure you're okay?'

'I'm terrific. How about you?'

'Changing the subject. Don't you think I deserve a more subtle form of resistance— *I'm* fantastic, Alex. Menopause is everything they claim and more. But my fine spirits should be obvious. Unlike *other* people I don't have that schleppy tone permeating my voice.'

'Lack of sleep, that's all.'

'Lack of sleep and Agnes Mavis Yeager?'

'No,' I said. 'It's complicated.'

'With you it tends to be. We should have lunch, it's been a long time. You can tell me stories and I'll pretend to be your mother.'

'It's a deal, Liv.'

'Yeah, yeah, yeah. Meanwhile, I won't eat on the chance that if you do call my mouth won't be full.'

524

A phone call to SweetHaven Convalescent Home leavened by a few lies got me the information that Agnes Yeager had moved out three months ago. Forwarding address: the Four Seasons Hotel, on Doheny. The personnel office there confirmed that Ms Yeager was cleaning rooms on the eight A.M. to three P.M. shift.

Working again, so she'd mended, physically.

Returning to L.A., so maybe she hadn't given up.

At 2:15 P.M. I drove to the Four Seasons, handed the doorman a ten, and asked him to keep the Seville up front. I'd just had the car washed and waxed, and he smiled as he nosed it between a Bentley Arnage and a Ferrari Testarossa.

The lobby teemed with grim, skinny things in all-black, and I pushed past them and used the house phone to call Housekeeping. Once I got a supervisor on the line, I talked quickly and ambiguously, said it was important that I speak to Mrs Yeager, old friend, some kind of family issue.

'Is this an emergency, sir?'

'Hard to say. I just need a few minutes.'

'Hold on.'

Several minutes later a weak, sibilant voice came on. 'Yes?'

'Mrs Yeager, my name is Alex Delaware. I'm a psychologist who works with the police and I've been looking into Shawna's case— I've just begun, nothing to report, I'm afraid. But I was wondering if we could talk.'

'A psychologist? What, some kind of research?'

'No, ma'am. I consult to the police, am trying to find

some answers – I know it's been a long time—'

'I like psychologists. One of them helped me. I was sick – they thought it was . . . Where are you, sir?'

'Down in the lobby.'

'Here? Oh. Well, I'm off in a few minutes, I'll meet you out on Burton Way, near the employee exit.'

She was there by the time I walked around the corner, a small, thin, gray-haired woman wearing a charwoman's pink uniform. Her hair was cropped and coarse, and her eyeglasses were steel-rimmed rectangles. Freshly applied scarlet lipstick screamed from chapped lips, and her cheeks had been rouged. High-waisted and flat-chested, she looked ten years older than fifty-one.

'Thank you so much for doing this, Dr – was it Delavalle?'

'Delaware. I'm afraid I can't promise you—'

'I'm past promises. I'm parked a few blocks down, do you mind walking?'

'Not at all.'

'It's a nice day anyway,' she said. 'At least weather-wise.'

We headed east on Burton, and she thanked me again for reopening Shawna's case. I tried to offer a disclaimer, but she wasn't hearing it. Went on about how it was about time, the police had never really investigated fully. 'And that detective they assigned – Riley. Didn't do a darn thing. Not that I want to speak ill of the dead.'

'He died?' I said.

'You didn't know? Just over two months ago. Retired

to the desert and spent all his time playing golf and just keeled over on the golf course. I know because I used to call him – not too often, because frankly I didn't have much faith in him. But he was . . . a link to Shawna. He wasn't a bad man, Riley. Just not . . . energetic. He did give me his home number when he retired. Last time I phoned him, his poor wife told me, and I ended up comforting her. So you see, I'm not hoping for miracles, but at least I have an open mind. 'Cause in my opinion, Riley and the rest of them never did. I'm not saying they deliberately set out not to care, but I feel, to this day, that they just thought finding Shawna was hopeless and never really tried.'

No anger. A speech she'd recited often.

'What do you think they could've done?'

'Publicize more. I tried the newspapers, but they weren't interested. You have to be rich and famous to get attention. Or get killed by someone rich and famous.'

'Sometimes it's like that in L.A.,' I said.

'Probably everywhere, but all I know is L.A., 'cause that's where my Shawna died – you see, I'm not denying that anymore. I got past that. The last time I spoke to him, Leo Riley tried to tell me not to hope for the best. It was kinda funny the way he got all nervous and stuttery, like he was telling me something I didn't know. But I'd gotten there a long time ago. No way could my Shawna be missing this long without telling me and not be . . . gone. All I want, now, is to know what happened. Know where she is, give her a decent Christian burial. The psychologist I talked to – Dr Yoshimura – she said everyone made a big deal about closure but closure was foolishness made up by people who write books – it didn't exist, how could you ever heal something like that?'

She tapped her chest. 'It leaves a big hole that can never be filled, but you try to learn what you can, and if you succeed maybe you coat it around the edges a little. She was terrific. Yoshimura. I did counseling with her 'cause one day I collapsed – everything went black and I fell down. Everyone thought I had a heart attack, they put me through every test known to modern mankind, found out I did have high cholesterol but my heart was still okay. In the end they said it was nerves. Anxiety. Dr Yoshimura taught me how to relax. I became a vegetarian, stopped smoking. I could accept relaxing from Dr Yoshimura because she wasn't telling me to get some closure the way everyone else was. That was the thing about Mr Riley. He was real relaxed except when it came to talking about *real* things. Like the fact that he hadn't learned a thing about Shawna— He'd pretend to listen, but I knew he wasn't. I called him even after he retired because I figured it was rent he should be paying. And now he's gone . . . Here, I'm parked on Swall.'

We turned up a tree-lined block full of luxury apartment condominiums, and she led me to an old Nissan Sentra, once red, now faded to dusty rose. The car's trunk was littered with leaves.

'Two-hour limit,' she said, pointing to a parking sign, 'but usually they don't check. Sometimes I park in the employee lot under the hotel, but sometimes it's full.

And I don't like those subterranean things. Spooky.'

She unlocked the car. 'Do you mind sitting in here? All my Shawna things are in here.'

I got into the front passenger seat, and she opened the trunk and closed it and came back with a foot-square box marked KITCHENWARE and tied with a yellow ribbon that she loosened.

'I know I shouldn't keep it in the car,' she said, 'but I like to have it close by. Sometimes I get a sandwich and come out here and go through it. Dr Yoshimura said that was fine.'

Looking to me for confirmation. I nodded.

She pulled a small, pink satin album from the carton and handed it to me. 'This is Shawna when she was little.'

Thirty pages of snapshots, from infancy to sixth grade. Mostly solos of a beautiful, golden-haired girl. From early on Shawna Yeager had possessed a flair for the optimal pose.

Agnes Yeager was present in a handful of shots, dark-haired, plain. A few others – early, faded photos – featured a very tall, fair-haired man with a movie-idol face marred by protuberant jug ears. In the snaps where he and Agnes were together, both parents smoked. Shawna surrounded by loving smiles and haze.

'Shawna's dad?' I said.

'My Bob. He was a long-distance trucker, worked for himself, then Vons Markets. He was killed by a drunk driver when Shawna was four. Not even driving. Walking from the men's room to his rig at a truck stop in Indio.

Shawna didn't remember him – even when he was alive he wasn't home much. But he was a loving man and a virile man. Not much for expressing his feelings, but never a cross word. And he did love Shawna – she got her looks from him, color-wise and size-wise. He was six-foot four and a half, a big basketball star in high school. Shawna ended up five-nine. I'm five-two and a quarter.'

As I studied Bob Yeager's face, something struck me. I kept it to myself, returned the album, only to receive another, larger, blue-bound.

'This is her pageant stuff,' said Agnes. 'Local newspaper stories, each time she won. I never pushed her into none of it. The first time she saw the Miss America Pageant on TV she said, "Mommy, dat what I want." She was four.'

I paged through the clippings, endured smile after smile.

Agnes Yeager said, 'I know none of this will help you, but maybe this – the stories this kid reporter for the college paper did. He was really interested in Shawna, wrote up a lot of stories—'

'Adam Green.'

'You talked to him.'

'I have.'

'Did he tell you his suspicions about Shawna?'

'Suspicions?'

'That she'd taken off her clothes and posed for dirty pictures— He didn't actually come out and say it. He thought he was being subtle, but from the questions he was asking, I could tell that's where he was leading. So of course I got mad and managed to end the conversation and didn't take any more of his calls. Later, I wondered if that had been a mistake. 'Cause that boy was the only one who seemed to have any interest in what happened to Shawna. And even though I got offended . . .'

'Do you think there's a chance Shawna might've posed?'

Her shoulders rose and fell. 'I wish I could say no way. But time passes and your head clears— The truth is Shawna loved her looks. Loved her body. One day she came home with an old mirror she'd picked up at some junk shop and hung it in her bedroom – a huge mirror. She was fourteen. I didn't argue – everyone also says choose your battles. Besides, you didn't want to go up against Shawna. She was headstrong. The truth is, if she could've hung four walls of mirrors, she would've. Probably my fault, a day didn't go by when I wasn't telling her how gorgeous she was. And if *I* wasn't, other people were.'

'Did she have any boyfriends back home?'

'The usual. Boys coming and going, she'd dump them like the trash. One of them – this stringbean named Mark, a basketball player like her dad – seemed a little more serious, and I asked her if they were boyfriend and girlfriend and she laughed and said, "*No*, Mom." You know, in that tone they get? "No, Mom. He's just my boy, comma, friend." '

'Mark was her age?' I said.

'No, he was a senior, and she was a freshman, the

older boys always went for her, and it was mutual – she liked them mature, looking old for their age. And tall, real tall. Why do you ask about Mark?'

'Just trying to get a feel for her state of mind.'

'You're thinking 'cause she lost her dad she was looking for a dad, right? Someone older and tall. Maybe some older guy asked her to pose and she did it because she was vulnerable.'

I stared at her.

She said, 'I've had plenty of time to think. So am I right?'

'That did cross my mind.'

'Crossed mine, too. And Dr Yoshimura's. She and I went all through that, her helping to analyze everything. But as far as Shawna having any much older boyfriends back home, I don't think so. Mostly she didn't have time for dating, was really concentrating on her pageants and getting into college— That's one thing about Shawna, she was always a serious student. I never had to tell her to study. And if she didn't get an A it was a world tragedy, she'd be arguing with the teacher.' Weak smile. 'And sometimes she got her way – let me show you. Those report cards are on the bottom.'

As she rummaged I said, 'Just to be thorough, where's Mark now?'

She looked up. 'Him? Oh, no. He joined the Army right out of school, got stationed in Germany, married a German girl. He was out of the country when Shawna disappeared. Wrote me the sweetest condolence card when he found out – I've got that, too. Right here.'

A hearts-and-flowers Hallmark landed in my palm. Soppy verse, and a block-printed notation:

Dear Mrs Yeager,

Please accept our sincerest condolense about Shawna. We know she's up with the angels.

Astrid and Mark Ortega, and Kaylie

Stapled to the facing page was a studio shot of a skinny, blond, young man, crew-cut and mustachioed, a chubby brunette woman, and a grinning, pie-faced baby.

'Nice boy,' said Agnes. 'But Shawna was too much for him. She needed someone to stimulate her brain. Lord knows I couldn't do it, never finished high school— Here we go, these are her report cards.'

She handed me a rubber-banded stack. Twelve grades' worth of nearly straight As. Achievement tests consistently above the ninety-fifth percentile. Teachers' comments: 'Shawna's a very bright little girl, but she does tend to visit with her neighbors.' 'A joy, wish they were all like her.' 'Has a firm grip of the material and loves to learn.' 'Strong-willed, but she always ends up doing the work.'

At the bottom of the stack was a transcript from the U.

Four courses during the quarter she'd never finished. A quartet of incompletes.

'It arrived after she was gone,' said Agnes. 'When I

opened the envelope, I just lost it. That word. "Incomplete." When you're in that state, everything's got a double meaning. You're looking for something to be angry about. I nearly ripped this into shreds. Now I'm glad I didn't. Though I did give away the clothes Shawna left behind. Waited until a few months ago, but I was able to do it.'

I stared at the transcript, placed it back on the bottom.

'Smart,' said Agnes. 'See what I mean.'

'Yes, I do, Mrs Yeager. Is there anything else?'

'Well, you might tell me what you're planning to do.'

'I'm going to review Shawna's file. I know that sounds vague and bureaucratic, but I'm just starting out. If I think of something, may I call you?'

'You'd better.' She grabbed my hand in both of hers. 'I have a feeling about you. You're a serious person. However it comes out, you're going to give it your best. Thank you very, very much.'

'Thank you,' I said. 'I hope to justify your confidence.'

'I'm not asking for my daughter back,' she said. 'All I want to do is bury her. Know where she is, so I can visit on Christmas and anniversaries. That doesn't seem like too much to ask for, does it?'

'No, ma'am. Thanks for your time.' I opened the car door.

'Can I have that back?' she said.

Pointing to the stack of report cards.

'Oh, sure. Sorry.'

'Anything you need a copy of, I can get you.'

I gave her hand a squeeze and left.

thirty-nine

Five P.M. The psych building was nearly empty.

I spotted Gene Dalby from down the hall. Standing at his office door, keys in hand, his gawky frame limned by institutional fluorescence.

'Coming or going?' I said.

'Alex – hey, there. Going, as a matter of fact.'

'Could you spare a few moments?'

'Look at this,' he said. 'I don't see the guy for years and now he's becoming a fixture.'

I didn't speak. The look on my face murdered his smile.

'Something wrong, Alex?'

'Let's go inside, Gene.'

'I really am in a hurry,' he said. 'Things to see, people to do.'

'This is worth making time for.'

'Whoa, sounds ominous.'

I didn't answer.

'Fine, fine,' he said, unlocking the door. His ring was full of keys, and the tremor in his hands made it peal like a wind chime.

He sat at his desk. I stayed on my feet.

'Let me lay it out for you,' I said. 'On the one hand, I'd never have known about Shawna if you hadn't mentioned her. So that's a point in your favor – why would you open a can of worms? On the other hand, you lied to me. Pretended not to know her. "Some kind of campus beauty queen" was the way you put it. "Shane something, or Shana . . . I don't recall her exact name." But she was in your class. I just had a look at her transcript. Psych 10, Dalby, Monday Wednesday Friday three P.M. You taught Intro in addition to Social. The heavy teaching load you told me about.'

He ran his hand through his hair, raising spikes. 'Oh, come on, you can't be serious. Do you know how many kids are in a—'

'Twenty-eight,' I said. 'I checked with the registrar. Your section was a last-minute add-on, for students who hadn't gotten into the four scheduled sections. Twenty-eight kids, Gene. You'd remember each student. Especially a student that looked like Shawna—'

His giraffe neck corded. 'This is horseshit, I don't have to sit and listen to—'

'No, you don't. But you might want to, because it's not going to go away.'

His hands clawed the desk. He removed his glasses, repeated, 'Horseshit.'

I said, 'But you're not kicking me out.'

Silence.

'So you lied, Gene, and I have to wonder why. Then, when I start adding up some things I've learned about

Shawna, it gets really interesting. Such as the fact that she had a definite attraction to older men. Older, wealthy men – she was very clear about wanting the finer things in life. Ferraris. With your dot-com income, you'd fit that bill. She also prized intelligence – what she called intellectuality. Once again, who better than you, Gene, to satisfy that criterion? Back in grad school you were tops in the class. Had a talent for thinking profound things out loud.'

'Alex—'

'Also,' I said, 'I've seen pictures of her father. He died when she was four, so she really didn't remember him. Probably idealized him. Did she ever show you his picture, Gene?'

He glared at me. Flushed. A pair of huge fists rolled along the desktop. Ripping off his glasses, he flung them at the wall. They thudded against his books and landed on the rug.

'Ineffectual,' he said. 'Can't do anything right.'

'Bob Yeager,' I said. 'Six-four plus, red-blond hair, jug ears, a basketball star in high school – weren't you a starting forward all the way through college?'

He buried his face in his hands. Muttered, 'My glory days—'

'The resemblance is damn striking, Gene. He could have been your brother—'

He sat up. 'I know damn well what he *could've* been. Yes, she showed me a goddamn picture. The first goddamn time she came in here during goddamn office hours. To talk about an exam. Allegedly. And she's wearing this little black dress, sits down and it rides up . . . I stick to the topic, she's a bright kid . . . Then she whips out this picture of her old man. Thought it was funny. I told her I wasn't a Freudian— Alex, I didn't *do* anything. Never seduced her, it's not what you think, the whole thing was just a terrible— Oh, shit. You're not going to believe me, are you?'

'Whether I do or not isn't the issue, Gene. The police know.'

'Oh, no—'

'Oh, yes.'

'But what could they know?'

I said nothing.

'Let me explain, first, Alex. *Please*. Okay?'

'No promises,' I said.

'You yourself said if I hadn't told you about her—'

'But you did, Gene. On some level you wanted me to chase it.'

'Oh,' he said. His eyes narrowed, and one fist inched closer to me. 'Now I'm on the *couch*. This is *bullshit*.'

I reached for the doorknob.

'Wait! You can't bop in here like this and expect me just to capitulate—'

'I don't expect a thing,' I said. 'And frankly, right now, your peace of mind isn't paramount to me. I just spent some time with a woman who's been living a nightmare for over a year. Knowing but *not* knowing. Just like you told me the first time: "the ultimate parent's nightmare." And guess what? She has something in common with you, Gene. You both despise the word *closure*. You think it's pop-psych crapolsky, but she has a much greater understanding of the term's inadequacy—'

'Alex, please—'

'She doesn't expect a miracle, Gene. But she would like to say good-bye, visit her daughter's grave from time to time, maybe leave some flowers.'

He bowed his head again, covered his eyes with his hands. 'Oh, Jesus— Yeah, I wanted you to chase it. I guess – I don't know what the hell came over me. I wasn't planning to say a goddamn thing, and then you started telling me about that other girl – whom I really *didn't* know, that's the truth, Alex. And synapses just started clicking – memories, it's been sitting here, all this time' – touching his belly – 'but still, what the hell was I thinking? 'Cause I remember *you* from grad school. The bulldog, they called you behind your back – jokes about your being a goddamn obsessive-compulsive. You never let go of *anything*. What the *fuck* was I *thinking*!'

Tearing at his hair. When he stopped I said, 'Maybe you weren't thinking. Guilt's a great motivator. Maybe you were just feeling.' Knowing he had something else in common with Agnes Yeager. The great void. Holes that couldn't be filled.

'Shit,' he said. 'The police already know?'

I nodded. A lie, but he didn't deserve better. And those big hands could do damage in close quarters.

'I didn't— Okay, look, just give me a chance to explain. This is what happened: An accident, a goddamn stupid accident, okay?'

I stood there.

'Fuck. You can be a *sphinx*.'

'I'm listening, Gene.'

'Right.' His Adam's apple took a joyride. His armpits had grown sodden, and pink scalp shined where he'd raised furrows in his hair. 'Yeah, I was – we were having a thing. And don't preach to me about that. She came on to me— Sure I could've resisted but I didn't. Didn't want to. Why would I resist? Jan and I never— Forget excuses, you don't want to hear them. The truth is she was the hottest thing I've ever come across. I've been married twenty-three years, and I've been basically faithful. But this girl – Shawna – she was something else. Gave off a heat— She was the girl every guy wants in high school but can't get unless he's a . . . No need to get into that. We had a thing, it was mutual, she was madly in love with me – said she was. I knew that was horseshit, this was a fling – once she figured out I wasn't going to leave Jan she'd end it. But in the meantime . . . she could do things with her . . . Also, she was smart as hell, not just a body. We could talk— Even at her age, she had things to say. Number one in my class, so there was no conflict of interest, no trading grades for—'

He choked on his own saliva, endured a paroxysm of coughing, filled his mug with cold coffee and swallowed.

'We're talking a month, five weeks tops, Alex.'

'Right from the beginning of the quarter.'

'Soon after, yeah. The second time she came in. Little *white* dress. Like a tennis outfit— She had this fresh clean smell – this perfume of youth. It happened, I can't change that. But after that I was discreet. Meeting her

540

only off-campus— We used to drive up in the hills above Bel Air. Find a spot.' He smiled. 'Parking, she'd make a production of taking off— Oh, man, Alex, it was just what you wanted high school to be like. Then it got complicated. She was also— That's the thing about her, she was also narcissistic. Seriously narcissistic, really into her looks, her brains, the whole bit. One time she told me she could have the president if she wanted.'

'Not much of a challenge there.'

'But she meant it globally, Alex. Any president. Of anything. This omnipotence she had going – eighteen years old, all that sexual confidence.' The color left his face. 'Even now, thinking about her— I can't change what happened— Try to muster some empathy, you're a shrink, not a judge.'

'Narcissistic,' I prompted. 'How did that complicate things?'

'It led her to a bad place. The wrong people, stupid decisions. She read some ad in the *Cub* – not one of those experiments I told you about. I guess I mentioned those to throw you off. Wanting you to chase it but not wanting it— I'm fucked up. All that therapy, all those years on both sides of the couch and it doesn't mean a—'

'What kind of ad?'

'For photographer's models. Some sleazeball outfit in Hollywood, I don't even remember the name, claiming to be freelancing for *Duke* and *Playboy* and *Penthouse*. She never checked it out with me, probably wouldn't have listened if I'd advised against it. She and her roommate went for it – auditioned, ended up posing. It was supposed to be bikini shots, ended up being nudie shots. Then the sleazes asked her and the roommate to do some lesbian stuff – simulation – and the roommate didn't want to and left. But Shawna stayed. *Damn* her – so fucking in *love* with herself. They brought in another model, and she – the two of them did it. Then they must've realized Shawna could be motivated easily, so they brought a guy in, and she ended up— They got snaps of her sucking off some donkey dong, okay? And she brings them to me on our next – the next time we saw each other – like she's *proud* of them. Brought a whole packet – bikini, nudies, soft-core, then, at the bottom, her little mouth doing the Hoover. Saving the best for last. Like I was supposed to *appreciate* it. Get turned *on* by it.'

He slammed a fist on the desk. Papers jumped.

'I lost it, man. Just blew, yelled at her, called her all kinds of names. Instead of crying, she yells back, gets aggressive. Tells me the photographer worked for all the top mags, promised her a gig with *Playboy* or *Penthouse* or *Duke*, this was going to be her ticket to fame and fortune. Can you believe that, Alex? Smart girl and she falls for a shit-for-brains story like that. The narcissism – I wish I could get across how much this girl *loved* herself, Alex. Half the time when we were together I felt I was nothing more than a vibrator.'

He stopped talking. Stared at the wall. Got a glazed look in his eyes.

'What happened, Gene?'

542

'It was quick. I got pissed, she got pissed back, we had a screaming fight, she jumped out of the car— We were over by Lake Hollywood. Up in the Hollywood Hills, a spot I remembered from when Jan and I were dating. She got out, started running up the road, I went after her, and she tripped and fell and hit her head on a rock and just lay there. Silent, all of a sudden the whole goddamn city got really *silent*, a big soap bubble of silence and I was trapped inside, like a cartoon. I got down beside her. No pulse, no respiration. I tried CPR, nothing. Then I got a look at her head and knew I was wasting my time. She got hit here. Brain tissue was leaking out.'

He touched the spot where the back of his neck met his skull. 'The medulla, Alex. Basic respiration. She was gone. I got some plastic tarp out of the car – I keep it there for when Jan and I buy plants at the nursery – wrapped her up and took her somewhere.'

'Where?'

He didn't answer. 'Maybe I should talk to a lawyer.'

'Sure,' I said. 'There'll be plenty of time for talk. But think about it: Any way you can garner sympathy's gonna help you. Agnes Yeager would like to say good-bye.'

He opened a desk drawer, and for one panicky moment I thought he'd secreted a weapon there. But he pulled out paper and pencil. Drew a square. Several curving lines.

'I'm diagramming you a map. Happy?'

'Ecstatic,' I said, in someone else's dead voice.

forty

Good map. Gene had always been precise.

The Hollywood Hills, not far from where Shawna had fallen.

I called Milo first, asked for permission to let Agnes Yeager know.

'Why don't you let me get a crew there first?' he said. 'Make sure the guy didn't lie. Make sure we pick him up too. Full name?'

I told him, feeling all sorts of things but pushing them aside with images of Shawna's Christian burial. No doubt Agnes would invite me. Maybe I'd attend, maybe I wouldn't.

'Okay,' said Milo. 'I'm going to call Petra because it's Hollywood territory. Meet her up there and see what we've got. How'd you do it, Alex – no, don't tell me. We'll talk later.'

'Sure,' I said, hanging up and dialing another number.

Adam Green answered, 'Hey.'

'This is Alex Delaware, Adam.'

'Al— Oh, the shrink. What, something finally go down about Shawna?'

'Maybe,' I said. 'It could hit the papers. I wanted to reach you beforehand, keep my word.'

'The papers? Hey, your word was give *me* the story. For my screenplay.'

'That's the thing, Adam. There really is no story.'

forty-one

On the evening of the third day, several hours after I'd returned from my visit to Ben Dugger's sickroom, Robin called. I'd been lying around, watching TV, had switched off the set as the tag line for the six o'clock news blared, and poured myself a triple Chivas.

Grinning anchorman. Overlays of familiar faces.

'Professor arrested in coed's death!'

I'd taken a swallow, was listening to the whiskey whisper in my throat when the phone rang.

'Hi, it's me.'

'Hi, you.'

'You all right?'

'Serene.'

'Guess where I was today?' she said.

'The zoo?'

Silence. 'How'd you know that?'

'With San Diego, my first association is always the zoo.'

'Well, that's where I was.'

'You and the dentist?'

'Me, myself. The dentist has a boyfriend, and they went down to Tijuana for the day. Invited me but . . .'

'Abandoned,' I said. 'Sorry. So how're the animals?'

'Fine— I can't believe you guessed the zoo.'

'Blind luck.'

'Or no one knows me like you do.'

'I don't know about that.'

'Come join me down here,' she said. 'I'll rent us a room at the Del Coronado.'

'When?' I said.

'The sooner the better— You don't want to do it. You're angry at me.'

'No,' I said. 'Everything you said was true. I've been trying to process.'

'It was true but, still, I walked out on you— It hit me, walking around the zoo, alone. How did I do that? Talk about abandonment. Will you come, Alex? Meet me at the hotel?'

'What about Spike?'

'Debby's got a little Peke, and she and Spike are fast friends.'

'Till he steals her food,' I said.

'Alex?'

'It'll take me a couple of hours. You're sure you want this?'

'How can we work things out if we're not together? If I react by . . . what does Milo call it – rabbiting?'

'San Diego,' I said.

'I know it's not Paris, but . . . would you rather I come

back home? I can go back to Debby's place and pack up my stuff.'

'No,' I said. 'I'll be down there soon as I can.'

'I'll arrange everything at the Del Coronado. Meet me up in the room— I love you, baby. Love you so much.'

'Even if I am crazy.'

'Even if.'

I locked up the house, was nearly at the door when I changed my mind.

Returning to my office, I booted up the computer, fooled around for a while until I found an on-line travel service. Did some comparison shopping and purchased two nonstop tickets to Paris.

Headline hopes you have enjoyed Jonathan Kellerman's *Flesh and Blood*, and invites you to sample the first chapter of *The Forgotten* by Faye Kellerman, out now in paperback.

1

The call was from the police. Not from Rina's lieutenant husband, but from the *police* police. She listened as the man spoke, and when she heard that it had nothing to do with Peter or the children, she felt a 'thank you, God' wave of instant relief. After discovering the reason behind the contact, Rina wasn't as shocked as she should have been.

The Jewish population of L.A.'s West Valley had been rocked by hate crimes in the past, culminating in that hideous ordeal a couple of years ago when a subspecies of human life had gotten off the public bus and had shot up the Jewish Community Center. The Center had been and still was a refuge for all people, offering everything from toddler day camps to dance movements to exercise classes for the elderly. Miraculously, no one had been killed – *there*. But the monster – who had later in the day committed the atrocious act of murder – had injured several children and had left the entire area with numbing fears that maybe it could happen again. Since then, many of the L.A. Jews took special precautions to safeguard their people and their institutions. Extra locks were put on the doors of the centers and synagogues. Rina's *shul*, a small rented storefront, had even gone so far as to padlock the Aron Kodesh – the Holy Ark that housed the sacred Torah scrolls.

The police had phoned Rina because her number was the one left on the *shul's* answering machine – for emergencies only. She was the synagogue's unofficial caretaker – the buck-stops-here person who called the contractors when a pipe burst or when the roof leaked. Because it was a new congregation, its members could only afford a part-time rabbi. The constituents often pitched in by delivering a Shabbos sermon or sponsoring an after-prayer *kiddush*. People were always more social when food was served. The tiny house of worship had lots of mettle, and that made the dreadful news even harder to digest.

Driving to the destination, Rina was a mass of anxiety and apprehension. Nine in the morning and her stomach was knotted and burning. The police hadn't described the damage, other than to use the word 'vandalize' over and over. From what she could gather, it sounded like more cosmetic mischief than actual constructional harm, but maybe that was wishful thinking.

She passed homes, stores, and strip malls, barely glancing at the scenery. She straightened the black tam perched atop her head, tucking in a few dangling locks of ebony hair. Even under ordinary circumstances, she rarely spent time in front of the mirror. This morning, she had rushed out as soon as she hung up the phone, wearing the most basic of clothing – a black skirt, a white long-sleeved shirt, slip-on shoes, a head covering. At least her blue eyes were clear. There had been no time for her makeup; the cops were going to see the uncensored Rina Decker. The red traffic lights seemed overly long, because she was so antsy to get there.

The *shul* meant so much to her. It had been the motivating factor behind selling Peter's old ranch and buying their new house. Because hers was a Sabbath-observant Jewish home, she had wanted a place of worship that was within walking distance – real walking distance, not something two and a half miles away as Peter's ranch had been. It wasn't that she minded the walk to her previous *shul*, Yeshivat Ohavei Torah, and the boys certainly could make the jaunt, but Hannah, at the time, had been five. The new house was perfect for Hannah, a fifteen-minute walk, plus there were plenty of little children for her to play with. Not many older children, but that didn't matter, since her older sons were nearly grown. Shmueli had packed out for Israel, and Yonkie, though only in eleventh grade, would probably spend his senior year back east, finishing yeshiva high school while simultaneously attending university. Peter's daughter, Cindy, was now a veteran cop, having survived a wholly traumatic year. Occasionally, she'd eat Shabbat dinner with them, visiting her little sister – a thrill since Cindy had grown up an only child. Rina was the mother of a genuine blended family, though sometimes it felt more like genuine chaos.

Her heartbeat quickened as she approached the storefront. The tiny house of worship was in a building that also rented space to a real estate office, a dry cleaners, a nail salon, and a take-out Thai café. Upstairs were a travel agency and an attorney who advertised on late-night cable with happy testimonials from former clients. Two black and white cruisers had parked askew, taking up most of the space in the minuscule lot, their light bars alternately blinking out red and blue beams. A small crowd had gathered in front of the synagogue, but through them, Rina could see hints of a freshly painted black swastika.

Her heart sank.

She inched her Volvo into the lot and parked adjacent to a cruiser. Before she even got out of the car, a uniform was waving her off. He was a thick block of a man in his thirties. Rina didn't recognize him, but that didn't mean anything because she didn't know most of the uniformed officers in the Devonshire station. Peter had transferred there as a detective, not a patrol cop.

The officer was saying, 'You can't park here, ma'am.'

Rina rolled down the window. 'The police called me down. I have the keys to the synagogue.'

The officer waited; she waited.

Rina said, 'I'm Rina Decker, Lieutenant Decker's wife . . .'

Instant recognition. The uniformed officer nodded by way of an apology, then muttered, 'Kids!'

'Then you know who did it?' Rina got out of the car.

The officer's cheeks took on color. 'No, not yet. But we'll find whoever did this.'

Another cop walked up to her, this one a sergeant by his uniform stripes, with *Shearing* printed on his nametag. He was stocky with wavy, dishwater-colored hair and a ruddy complexion. Older: mid to late fifties. She had a vague sense of having met him at a picnic or some social gathering. The name Mike came to mind.

He held out his hand. 'Mickey Shearing, Mrs Decker. I'm awfully sorry to bring you down like this.' He led her through the small gathering of onlookers, irritated by the interference. 'Everybody . . . a couple of steps back . . . Better yet, go home.' Shouting to his men, 'Someone rope off the area, now!'

As the lookie-loos thinned, Rina could see the exterior wall – one big swastika, a couple of baby ones on either side. Someone had spray-painted *Death to the Inferior, Gutter Races*. Angry moisture filled her eyes. 'Is the door lock broken?' she asked the sergeant.

' 'Fraid so.'

'You've been inside?'

'Unfortunately, I have. It's . . .' He shook his head. 'It's pretty strong.'

'My parents were concentration camp survivors. I know this kind of thing.'

He raised his eyebrow. 'Watch your step. We don't want to mess up anything for the detectives.'

'Who's being brought in?' Rina said. 'Who investigates Hate Crimes?' But she didn't wait for an answer. As she stepped across the threshold, she felt her muscles tighten, and her jaw clenched so hard it was a wonder that her teeth didn't crack.

All the walls had been tattooed with one vicious slogan after another, each derogatory, each advocating different ways to exterminate Jews. So many swastikas, it could have been a wallpaper pattern. Eggs and ketchup had been thrown against the plaster, leaving behind vitreous splotches. But the walls weren't the worst part, minor compared to the holy books that had been torn and shredded and strewn across the floor. And even the sacrilege of the religious tomes and prayer books wasn't as bad as the horrific photographs of concentration camp victims that lay atop the ruined Hebrew texts. She averted her eyes but had already seen too much – ghastly black and white snapshots depicting individual bodies with tortured faces and gaping mouths. Some were clothed, some nude.

Shearing was staring, too, shaking his head back and forth, while uttering 'Oh man, oh man' under his breath. He seemed to have forgotten about her. Rina cleared her throat, partially to break Mickey's trance, but also to stave back tears. 'I suppose I should look around to see if anything valuable is missing.'

Mickey looked at Rina's face. 'Uh, yeah. Sure. Did the place have anything valuable . . . ? I mean, I know the books are valuable, but like flashy valuable things. Like silver ecumenical things . . . is "ecumenical" the right word?'

'I know what you mean.'

'I'm so sorry, Mrs Decker.'

The apology was stated with such clear sincerity that it brought down the tears. 'No one died, no one got hurt. It helps to get perspective.' Rina wiped her eyes. 'Most of our silver and gold objects are locked up in that cabinet . . . the one with the grates. That's our Holy Ark.'

'Lucky that you had the grates installed.'

'We did that after the Jewish Community Center shootings.' She walked over to the Aron Kodesh.

Shearing said, 'Don't touch the lock, Mrs Decker.'

Rina stopped.

He tried out a tired smile. 'Fingerprints.'

Rina regarded the lock with her hands behind her back. 'Someone tried to break inside. There are fresh scratch marks.'

'Yeah, I noticed. Because you have the lock, they musta figured that's where you keep all your valuables.'

'They would have been right.' A pause. 'You said "they". More than one?'

'With this much damage, I'd say yeah, but I'm not a detective. I leave that up to pros like your husband.'

Abruptly, she was seized with vertigo and leaned against the grate for support. Mickey was at her side.

'Are you all right, Mrs Decker?'

Her voice came out as a whisper. 'Fine.' She straightened up, surveying the room like a contractor. 'Most of the damage seems superficial. Nothing a good bucket of soapy water and a paintbrush can't take care of. The books, of course, are another story.' Replacing them would put them back at least a thousand dollars, money that they had been saving for a part-time youth director. Like most labors of love, the *shul* operated on a shoe-string budget. A tear leaked down her cheek.

'At least no one tried to burn it down.' She bit her lip. 'We have to be positive, right?'

'Absolutely!' Mickey joined in. 'You're a real trooper.'

Again, Rina's eyes skittered across the floor. Among the photos were Xeroxed ink drawings of Jews sporting exaggerated hooked noses. They probably had been copied out of the old *Der Stuermer* or the *Protocol of the Elders of Zion*. Again, she glanced at the grainy photographs. Upon inspection, she realized that the black and whites did not look like copies. They looked like genuine snapshots taken by someone who had been there. The thought – someone visually recording dead people – sickened her. Now someone was leaving them around as a frightful reminder – or a threat.

Again, her eyes filled with furious tears. She was so angry, so desolate, that she wanted to scream at the world. Instead, she took out her cell phone and paged her husband.

Decker had many thoughts rattling through his brain, most of them having to do with how Rina was coping. Still, there was some space left over for his own feelings. Anger? No. Way beyond anger, and that wasn't good. Such blinding rage caused people to make mistakes, and Decker couldn't afford them right now. So instead of mulling over a crime he had yet to see, he looked out the window and tried to get distracted by the scenery. By the

rows of houses that had once been citrus orchards, by
the warehouses and strip malls that lined Devonshire
Boulevard. He tried not to think about his stepson in
Israel or his other stepson at a Jewish high school. Or
Hannah, who was currently in second grade – young and
trusting and as innocent as those rows of pre-schoolers
led out of the JCC a couple of years ago after that
god-awful shooting.

He realized he was sweating. Though it was the usual
overcast May in L.A. – the air cool and a bit moldy – he
turned the air conditioner on full blast. Someone had
given him the address as a formality, but even if he
hadn't known the locale, the cruisers would have been a
tip-off.

He parked his car in a red zone, got out, and told
himself to take a deep breath. He'd need to be calm, not
to deal with the crime but to deal with Rina. A quartet of
uniforms was buzzing around the space like flies. Decker
hadn't taken more than a couple of steps when Mickey
Shearing caught him.

'Where is she?' Decker's voice was a growl.

'Inside the synagogue,' Shearing answered. 'You want
the details?'

'You have details?'

'I have . . .' Mickey flipped through his book
'. . . that the first report came in at eight-thirty in the
morning from the guy who operates the dry cleaning. I
arrived about ten minutes later, found the door lock
broken. I called up the synagogue to find out if there
was a rabbi or someone in charge. I got a machine

with a phone number on it. Turned out to be your wife.'

'And you didn't think to call *me* before you called *her?*' Decker's glare was harsh.

'There was just a phone number on it, Lieutenant. I didn't realize it was your wife until afterward.'

Decker broke eye contact and rubbed his forehead. 'S'right. Maybe it's better coming from you. Anyone been interviewed?'

'We're making the rounds.'

'Nothing?'

'Nothing. Probably done in the wee hours of the morning.' Shearing slid his toe against the ground. 'Probably by kids.'

'Kids as in more than one?'

'A lot of damage. I think so.'

'Tell me about the guy in the dry cleaners.'

'Gregory Blansk. Young kid himself. Uh . . . nineteen . . .' He flipped through more pages. 'Yeah, nineteen.'

'Any chance he did it and is sticking around to see people admire his handiwork?'

'I think he's Jewish, sir.'

'You *think?*'

'Uh . . . yeah. Here we go. He is Jewish.' Shearing looked up. 'He seemed appalled and more than a little frightened. He's a Russian import himself. Two strikes against him – Jewish and a foreigner. This has to scare him.'

'Currently, Detective Wanda Bontemps from Juvenile is assigned to Hate Crimes. Make sure she interviews him when she comes out. Keep the area clear. I'll be back.'

Having worked Juvenile for a number of years, Decker was familiar with errant kids and lots of vandalism. He had worked in an area noted for biker bums, white trash, hoodlum Chicanos and teens who just couldn't get behind high school. But this? Too damn close to home. He was so distracted by the surroundings, he didn't even notice Rina until she spoke. It jolted him, and he took a step backward, bumping into her, almost knocking her down.

'I'm sorry.' He grabbed her hand, then clasped her body tightly. 'I'm so sorry. Are you okay?'

'I'm . . .' She shrugged in his arms. *Don't cry!* 'How long before we can start cleaning this up?'

'Not for a while. I'd like to take photographs and comb the area for prints—'

'I can't stand to look at this!' Rina pulled away and turned her eyes away from his. '*How long?*'

'I don't know, Rina. I've got to get the techs out here. It isn't a murder scene, so it isn't top priority.'

'Oh. I see. We have to wait until someone gets shot.'

Decker tried to keep his voice even. 'I'm as anxious as you are to clean this up, but if we want to do this right, we can't rush things. After the crews leave, I will personally come over here with mop and broom in hand and scrub away every inch of this abomination. Okay?'

Rina covered her mouth, then blinked back droplets. She whispered back, 'Okay.'

'Friends?' Decker smiled.

She smiled back with wet eyes.

Decker's smile faded as the horror hit him. 'Good Lord!' He threw his head back. 'This is . . . awful!'

'They took the *kiddush* cup, Peter.'

'What?'

'The *kiddush* cup is gone. We kept it in the cabinet. It was silver plate with turquoise stones and just the type of item that would get stolen because it was accessible and flashy.'

Decker thought a moment. 'Kids.'

'That's what they're all saying. Why not some evil hate group?'

'Sure, it could be that. One thing I will say on record is it's probably not a hype. If he wanted something to swap for instant drug money, the crime would have been clean theft.'

'Maybe the cup is hidden underneath all this wreckage.' Rina shrugged. 'All I know is the cup isn't in the cabinet.'

Decker took out his notebook. 'Anything else?'

'Fresh scratch marks on the padlock on the Aron – the Holy Ark. They tried to get into it, but weren't successful.'

'Thank goodness.' He folded his notebook and studied her face. 'Are you going to be okay?'

'I'm . . . all right. I'll feel better once this is cleaned up. I suppose I should call Mark Gruman.'

Decker sighed. 'He and I painted the walls the first time. Looks like we're going to paint them again.'

Rina whispered, 'Once word gets out, I'm sure you'll

have plenty of willing volunteers.'

'Hope so.' Decker stamped his foot. An infantile gesture but he was so damn angry. 'Man, I am pi— mad. I'd love to swear except I don't want to further desecrate the place.'

'What's the first step in this kind of investigation?'

'To check out juveniles with past records of vandalism.'

'Aren't records of juveniles sealed?'

'Of course. But that doesn't mean the arresting officers can't talk. A couple of names would be a good start.'

'How about checking out *real* hate groups?'

'Definitely, Rina. We'll work this to the max. Nothing in this geographical area comes to mind. But I remember a group in Foothills – the Ethnic Preservation Society or something like that. It's been a while. I have to check the records, and to do that properly I need to go back to the office.'

'Go on. Go back. I'll be okay.' She turned to face him. 'Who's coming down?'

'Wanda Bontemps. She's from the Hate Crimes Unit. Try not to bite her head off. She had a bad experience with Jews in the past.'

'And this is who they bring down for a Jewish hate crime?'

'She's black—'

'So she's a black, and an anti-Semite. That makes it better?'

'She's not anti-Semitic at all. She's a good woman who was honest enough to admit her issues to me early on. I'm just . . . I shouldn't have even mentioned it.' He looked around and grimaced. 'I should learn to keep my mouth shut. I'll chalk it up to being a little rattled. Wanda's new and has worked hard to get her gold. It hasn't been an easy ride for a black forty-year-old woman.'

'I'm sure that's true,' Rina answered. 'Don't worry about her, Peter. If she just does her job, we'll get along just fine.'

Jupiter's Bones

Faye Kellerman

Dr Emil Ganz was always extraordinary, in death as well as in life. A physicist whose theories of Cosmology thrilled the world, he disappeared at the peak of his fame, to emerge years later as Jupiter, leader of a community that preached a bizarre blend of mathematics and mysticism, drawing the credulous, the unhappy and the utterly unscrupulous into their enclosed ranks.

And now Ganz's apparent suicide is threatening to destabilise this potentially explosive cult. As the battle to succeed Ganz commences, Lieutenant Peter Decker, working to uncover the scientist's precise fate, begins to fear that his death may simply be the start – and that innocents, the community's children amongst them, could be the first victims, as Jupiter's followers descend into their hellish vision of death and madness . . .

Praise for Faye Kellerman

'The most gripping of recent crime fiction' *Sunday Telegraph*

'Irresistibly plotted' *Financial Times*

'Kellerman succeeds brilliantly in making the search for understanding as compelling as the search for the murderer' *Publishers Weekly*

'Plotting as sumptuously as P. D. James' *Kirkus Review*

0 7472 5922 4

headline

Now you can buy any of these other bestselling
Feature titles from your bookshop or
direct from the publisher.

FREE P&P AND UK DELIVERY
(Overseas and Ireland £3.50 per book)

Tom Clancy's Net Force: Point of Impact		£6.99
Created by Tom Clancy and Steve Pieczenik,		
written by Steve Perry		
No Higher Law	Philip Friedman	£6.99
Neverwhere	Neil Gaiman	£6.99
Stalker	Faye Kellerman	£5.99
False Memory	Dean Koontz	£6.99
Nothing But the Truth	John Lescroart	£5.99
The Attorney	Steve Martini	£5.99
Burnt Sienna	David Morrell	£6.99
Revelation	Bill Napier	£6.99
Cradle and All	James Patterson	£6.99
The Runner	Christopher Reich	£5.99

TO ORDER SIMPLY CALL THIS NUMBER

01235 400 414

or e-mail <u>orders@bookpoint.co.uk</u>

Prices and availability subject to change without notice.